# EASTER
# BASKET
# MURDER

**Published by Kensington Publishing Corp.**

# EASTER BASKET MURDER

Leslie Meier
Lee Hollis
Barbara Ross

KENSINGTON BOOKS
www.kensingtonbooks.com

KENSINGTON BOOKS are published by

Kensington Publishing Corp.
119 West 40th Street
New York, NY 10018

All Kensington titles, imprints and distributed lines are available at special quantity discounts for bulk purchases for sales promotion, premiums, fund-raising, educational or institutional use.

Special book excerpts or customized printings can also be created to fit specific needs. For details, write or phone the office of the Kensington Special Sales Manager: Kensington Publishing Corp., 119 West 40th Street, New York, NY, 10018. Attn. Special Sales Department. Phone: 1-800-221-2647.

Library of Congress Control Number: 2023944264

KENSINGTON and the KENSINGTON COZIES teapot logo Reg. US Pat. & TM Off.

ISBN: 978-1-4967-4023-6
First Kensington Hardcover Edition: February 2024

ISBN: 978-1-4967-4025-0 (ebook)

10 9 8 7 6 5 4 3 2 1

Printed in the United States of America

# Contents

# EASTER BASKET MURDER

## Leslie Meier

# Chapter One

"It's the death of a thousand cuts," moaned Corney Clark, shaking her head sadly. "There's free shipping, next-day delivery, even same-day delivery. E-commerce is killing us; Main Street is becoming a ghost town." Corney, executive director of the Tinker's Cove Chamber of Commerce, was sitting in the office of the coastal Maine town's local newspaper, *The Courier,* where she was pitching a story to part-time reporter Lucy Stone. Corney, always professionally groomed, had her frosted hair clipped in a neat cut, and was wearing a pink plaid shirt with a matching quilted vest and trim gray slacks against the chilly spring weather. Lucy was dressed rather more casually in an oversized turtleneck sweater and jeans, but both were wearing the iconic Country Cousins duck boots that were a necessity in springtime Maine.

"It's always slow this time of year," observed Phyllis, the receptionist, philosophically. Phyllis chose her outfits according to the season and now that Easter was just around the corner was wearing a bright green sweatshirt that featured a bunny liberally bedecked with sequins. Pink leggings and polka dot reading glasses completed her outfit.

"Phyllis has a point," observed Lucy. "It's officially

spring but winter doesn't want to let go. People are still hibernating."

Corney shook her head, disagreeing. "Nope. It's the internet. We've done a study and foot traffic is definitely down, people can't be bothered to go to brick-and-mortar stores when they can push a button on their computer and get delivery the next day."

"Sounds like one way to run up a big credit card bill," said Phyllis.

"You said it," agreed Lucy. "And half the time what you get isn't what you thought it would be and you've got to return it."

"Or do like my niece Elfrida and forget all about it until the clutter gets to be too much and she donates a bunch of brand-new stuff to the thrift shop."

Lucy's eyebrows rose. "Really? With five kids at home I wouldn't think Elfrida's got money to waste."

"She doesn't," snapped Phyllis.

"Well, to get back on track here," began Corney, "the Chamber's come up with a terrific idea that we believe will encourage locals to rediscover the wonderful merchants in our town." Opening the slim leather portfolio she'd brought with her, Corney displayed an Easter card featuring a colorful image of an Easter basket, with a number of the eggs drawn only in outline. "We're sending one of these Easter cards to everyone in town."

"Well, it's nice," said Lucy, somewhat underwhelmed. "But maybe you should have finished the drawing. What's with those empty egg shapes?"

"Stickers!" proclaimed Corney, producing a sheet of colorful Easter egg stickers. "Every Chamber member in town has a supply of these stickers, which they will award to customers who spend at least ten dollars."

"Do you really think folks will want to collect stickers?" asked Phyllis, in a doubtful tone. "Stickers are for kids."

"There's more," said Corney, with a sly smile. "Everyone who completes their card and fills all ten blanks can enter a drawing for this deluxe Easter basket." She handed Lucy a photo depicting an oversized basket filled to the brim with assorted goodies. "And when I say deluxe, I mean absolutely fabulous. There's candy, gift certificates, luxury products and . . ." She paused to pat Lucy's desk in a drum roll. "A mini golden egg sculpture by Karl Klaus."

"Karl Klaus, hey, his stuff goes for thousands," said Phyllis.

"Is he still working?" asked Lucy. She knew the controversial sculptor, who was known for elevating simple household items into works of art, was a recluse who lived on a remote inland farm.

"I thought he died," offered Phyllis.

"No. He's alive and well."

"Somehow I can't see him donating one of his sculptures," said Lucy, who knew Klaus was notoriously tight-fisted, to the point of neglecting his person and his property. He lived in a huge barn that also served as a studio, and had been engaged in disputes with local officials involving a failing septic system and an ever-growing mountain of junk in his yard.

"A generous benefactor has donated the egg," said Corney, "on condition of anonymity."

"I don't suppose Klaus would be willing to be interviewed," speculated Lucy, sensing an opportunity for a scoop. She was already thinking of questions she'd like to ask the artist whose latest attempt to break into the nation's collective consciousness was a gilded toilet plunger exhibited a couple of years ago at a Soho art gallery.

"That toilet plunger was terribly derivative," observed

Phyllis. "A clear reference to that gold toilet that was stolen from Blenheim Palace." She paused, adding, "That's in England, you know."

Lucy's and Corney's mouths both dropped in surprise, as Phyllis was not known for keeping up with the contemporary art scene, or any art scene for that matter.

"Since when . . ." began Lucy.

Phyllis smirked. "I was at the dentist yesterday, and you know he's got those ancient magazines in the waiting room. He was running late due to Eddie Culpepper's impacted wisdom tooth and I ended up reading an old *Time* magazine."

"Well, that is a relief," said Lucy, chuckling. "I was afraid you'd gone all artsy on me."

"No chance."

"How's Eddie?" asked Corney.

"It was pretty awful," recalled Phyllis. "Lots of groans and he looked pretty shaky when he left."

"Poor kid," murmured Corney. "But getting back to the matter at hand, I've already spoken to Ted about a center-spread ad and I know you'll do a super story, Lucy . . ."

This was the sort of thing Lucy hated but knew only too well was part and parcel of small-town journalism. Letting advertising drive news coverage always made her feel like a shill instead of a journalist. Business news was still news, she reminded herself, especially in a town where most of the businesses were still small family affairs. Pushing her resentments to the back of her mind, she turned her attention to Corney, who was saying, ". . . and we're launching the promo tomorrow at the Seamen's Bank. I know you'll want to be there because Karl Klaus himself has agreed to a photo op."

Lucy doubted she'd heard correctly. "What did you say?" she asked.

"Karl Klaus will be at the Seamen's Bank tomorrow, eleven o'clock, for the kick-off."

"Talk about burying the lead," complained Lucy. "Why didn't you say that sooner?"

"Because I didn't want you to get too excited and start thinking about all sorts of questions. He said absolutely no interview and you know his reputation. Frankly, I'm not entirely convinced he's going to show up."

"Well, you can count on me," promised Lucy. "I'll be there."

"Thanks, Lucy," said Corney, sounding relieved. "There's a lot riding on this, a lot of our businesses are on the edge. This promo's got to work or we'll have even more empty stores on Main Street."

Next morning found Lucy at the Seamen's Bank, where a small delegation of business folk had gathered, awaiting the sculptor's arrival. Bert Cogswell, the bank president, was there, of course, along with Franny Small, representing the Board of Selectmen, and Tony Marzetti, who owned the IGA. These notables, as well as a handful of customers, were gathered around the coffee bar, a new addition to the bank, which had recently undergone a major renovation. For her part, Lucy missed the marble floor and the massive vault that had formerly held pride of place behind the barred teller's cages. She always had the feeling that her money was safe whether she was sliding a five dollar birthday check from Aunt Helen beneath the teller's cage or making a mortgage payment. Nowadays, the marble was covered with thick carpet, the vault was discreetly hidden behind a newly constructed wall, and the *associates* seemed to hang out rather casually behind an island.

Customers who needed to confer with a banker were invited to wait in a seating area with a curvaceous sofa and a coffee table on which to set their free cups of coffee. The clubby atmosphere didn't inspire confidence, thought Lucy, who carefully balanced her checking account every month.

"Ah, Lucy, are you here to cover the big event?" asked Bert Cogswell. While the bank employees were now encouraged to dress in business casual, Bert clung to his lifetime habit of navy suit, tie, and starched white shirt. His thinning hair was combed over his bald spot.

"Wouldn't miss it for the world," said Lucy as Corney arrived, toting the enormous Easter basket. She paused, looking around for somewhere to put it.

"Uh, I guess the coffee table," suggested Bert, stepping forward to relieve her of her burden.

"Super, everyone can see it there," agreed Corney. "Careful, it's heavy."

The Easter basket was set down on the table and everyone gathered around, admiring it.

"It was quite a job, fitting everything in," said Corney. "I left a little spot for the Klaus egg."

It was just then that a rather dishevelled older man entered, stumbling on the doorsill. Harold Fincham, the bank guard, stepped forward, catching him by the arm and preventing his fall, while giving him the once over. Apparently homeless, the fellow was unshaven, had thick eyeglasses held together with tape, and the sole on one shoe had come loose.

"Ah, Karl, you're here!" trilled Corney, all smiles. "Welcome!"

"Uh," offered the famous sculptor, by way of greeting. "Uh, let's get on with it."

"Right. Right," stammered Corney. "Well, everyone, this is Karl Klaus, our noted sculptor, who is on his way to New Hampshire where he will be feted and receive the prestigious St. Gaudens Sculpture Prize."

Everyone clapped and smiled, except for Karl and

Lucy. Karl never smiled, at least not in recent memory, and Lucy was fuming over the fact that Corney had failed to share this important bit of information about the prize with her.

"I've got to get going," muttered Karl, digging in the pocket of his tattered Army jacket. "Here it is." He produced a gleaming golden egg, which he was in danger of dropping until Corney snatched it.

"It's just beautiful," she enthused, displaying it for all to see.

The gathered crowd oohed and aahed, watching as Corney placed the gleaming mini-sculpture in the center front of the basket.

"Can I get a photo?" asked Lucy, as Klaus was turning to go. Corney quickly grabbed him by his arm and led him to the sofa. "Let's sit here," she invited him. "Behind the basket."

"I could take a load off," admitted Karl, in agreement. He plunked himself down, Corney slid in beside him. "Bert, we need you, too," insisted Corney, and the bank president took his place behind them. Lucy snapped the photo, making sure to get the basket front and center.

Then Corney made a little speech, congratulating the sculptor on his upcoming award, which was warmly received by the gathered notables.

"It's just a medal, no money," grumbled Klaus, in response to the group's applause. He had been studying the Easter basket with great intensity and finally reached in and snagged a box of Fern's Famous Fudge. "Something for the road," he said, standing up.

"Is there anything you're planning to say at the award ceremony?" asked Lucy, hoping for a juicy quote, or possibly even jump-starting an interview.

"Better left unsaid," muttered the sculptor, heading directly for the door, the flapping sole of his shoe requiring a sort of kick-step. Harold leaped to open the door for him and they all watched as he departed, making his way to an aged pickup truck which was double-parked in front of the bank. Moments later a roar was heard as the truck took off, slowly but noisily.

"Needs a muffler," observed Tony.

"Do you think he'll make it to New Hampshire?" asked Corney.

"Quite a character," observed Bert. "Quite a character."

Lucy decided to snap a few more photos of the Easter basket, and paused to check them on her phone. The photos didn't really do the fabulous egg sculpture justice, she decided. It looked an awful lot like the plastic eggs that used to contain a popular brand of pantyhose.

The Easter basket promotion was in full swing later that week when Lucy joined her friends at their usual Thursday morning breakfast. The group, which included Sue Finch, Rachel Goodman, and Pam Stillings, began the weekly gathering when their nests emptied and they could no longer count on casual encounters at their kids' school and sports events. The group had grown closer through the years, offering advice and support as they faced life's challenges.

Pam, who was married to Lucy's boss at the paper, Ted, had been a cheerleader in high school and retained her pony tail and her rah-rah enthusiasm. She was quite excited about supporting the promo, but admitted she'd only earned one sticker, and that was at the pharmacy when she picked up a prescription. "It's just so convenient to shop online," she said, digging into her yogurt-granola parfait. "I've arranged regular shipments of earth-friendly cleaning products, Stitch-in-Time sends me clothes on approval every six weeks or so, I get a box of Nearly Perfect groceries every two weeks, cat food and litter, even toilet paper all come right to the house. I hardly ever have to go to the store."

"But don't you miss shopping?" asked Sue, the group's fashionista, who frequented the discount mall on Route 1 looking for designer mark downs. "I love finding a good bargain; I got some beautiful Ralph Lauren towels last week on close-out. Sooo thick and soft, top quality and much cheaper than anything here in town." She paused to tuck a stray lock of hair behind her ear with a beautifully manicured hand and took a sip of coffee. "Of course, I'll do my part. I'm sure I can collect my ten stickers, too. Sid needs some new work boots and I've had my eye on a jacket at the Trading Company—I don't exactly need another jacket but it's so cute and it would be for a good cause."

Rachel was shaking her head in disapproval. "As it is, we're wallowing in stuff. We've all got too much stuff, things we don't need. We're constantly told that this new product will make us happy, it will satisfy our need for comfort and reassurance. Advertisers tear us down, telling us we have bad breath, or our hair isn't shiny enough, or we're too fat and the solution to all these problems is to buy their products. Even peace of mind is for sale, thanks to insurance companies." She picked a chunk off her Sunshine muffin. "Material things can't fill emotional needs." She glanced at Sue. "New towels can't provide human connection."

"Well, actually," began Sue, smiling wickedly, "Sid was quite interested in helping me try out the new towels after my bath last night."

"My point exactly," insisted Rachel. "You and Sid have a healthy relationship, with or without new towels."

"Well, I've barely got time to shop online or in person,"

complained Lucy, poking a toast triangle into an egg yolk. "Or the money. Gas gets more expensive every fill-up, groceries keep going up, I am struggling to stick with my budget and I don't think I'm alone. I think a lot of folks in Tinker's Cove are struggling to make ends meet."

"Well said," offered Norine, the waitress, approaching with a fresh pot of coffee. "More coffee, anyone?"

When Lucy went out that afternoon to conduct some man-on-the-street interviews about the Easter Basket promotion, she found that merchants and townsfolk alike were enthusiastic. "We all need stuff this time of year anyway," said Dottie Halmstead, exiting the hardware store with a bag of seed-starter mix and several packets of tomato seeds.

"It's nice to get a little reward," said Lydia Volpe, a retired kindergarten teacher Lucy met coming out of the bookstore. "I don't think we ever outgrow stickers."

Stopping by at Country Cousins, the general store that had pioneered catalog shopping and had now morphed into an e-commerce giant, Lucy found shoppers were stocking up on Easter treats and eagerly collecting the stickers. "We're in danger of running out," confessed Barb Conners. "We've had to order more. Everybody wants the stickers."

Stepping out of the store and onto the porch, where one bench was labeled "Republicans" and the other "Democrats," Lucy paused to watch the town's two police cars race down Main Street, sirens blaring and lights flashing. Probably an accident out on Route 1, she thought, but soon realized she was wrong. The two cruisers didn't continue on out of town, but screeched to a halt at the bank. Hoisting her bag on her shoulder, she hurried down the street, eager to find out what was happening. A bank robbery? In Tinker's Cove?

# Chapter Two

Lucy hadn't expected to be allowed inside the bank, figuring it was a crime scene, but nobody, least of all the guard, Harold Fincham, was blocking the door. Harold, Police Chief Jim Kirwan, Officer Barney Culpepper, bank president Bert Cogswell, and a couple of tellers were all gathered around the coffee table where the Easter Basket was on display.

"So when exactly did you notice it was missing?" asked the chief.

It was then that Lucy noticed the empty place where Karl Klaus's golden egg had been nestled, among the other prizes. Now, there was only a tell-tale hollow in the bright green plastic grass.

"It was one of the customers who asked what had happened to the egg," reported Bert, glancing at the tellers.

"That's right," said Jen Holden, the bank's newest hire. She was a senior at Winchester College, working part time; she was wearing a cozy velour tunic over a pair of black leggings and had long, wavy hair and a worried expression. "It was Mrs. Maloney and I noticed it was almost nine thirty, I was keeping an eye on the time because I have a poli sci test at noon."

"But it could have gone missing earlier," speculated Barney. "I mean, was anybody keeping an eye on it? It was right out here in the open, anybody could've grabbed it."

"Would've been smarter to substitute one of those plastic eggs and put the real one in the vault," said Jared Wood, the bank's senior teller, exhibiting twenty-twenty hindsight.

"Now hold on," declared Harold, in a defensive tone. "I've been here and keeping a sharp eye on that basket. That egg was here when I got in . . ."

"The bank opens at eight," said the chief. "That leaves a ninety-minute window."

"Not that long," insisted Harold. "Like I said, I kept glancing over and I didn't notice anything missing . . ."

"Until Mrs. Maloney sounded the alarm," countered Jared.

"Well, I think it was taken just before then," said Harold. "Nine thirty or so. Any sooner, I would've noticed."

"You were talking with customers, you took a coffee break, a couple of bathroom breaks . . ." reported Jared, who seemed to have a bit of a chip on his shoulder. "Anybody could have grabbed that egg at pretty much anytime this morning."

"Did you notice anything?" Lucy directed her question to Jen, thinking she was most likely the brightest bulb in this dim group.

"Not really," admitted Jen. "There was the usual rush at opening, merchants making deposits, getting change, that sort of thing. And there's always old folks checking on automatic deposits from Social Security."

"So it was busier than usual?" asked Barney.

"The bank was crowded, we both had lines of customers," remembered Jen.

The chief glanced around the space, making calculations. "So your view of the basket was blocked for much of the morning?"

Jen nodded. "That's right."

"Well," he began, with a sigh, speaking to Bert. "I'll write up a report and soon as it's ready you can come by the station and sign it."

"That's it?" asked Bert. "No fingerprints? No CSI team?"

Chief Kirwan shrugged. "I suppose you've got CCTV? We could take a look at that."

"Absolutely!" Bert jumped at the possibility. "The camera's right up there."

"So it is," said Barney. "Covers the tellers."

"But not the seating area," added the chief, shaking his head.

"Well, the tellers would be the most likely to be involved in a robbery," said Bert, rather defensively.

"Right, right," admitted Kirwan. "We'll take a look at the video, but I don't expect it to be very helpful."

"I suppose you had insurance," suggested Barney, by way of consolation.

"Yes, yes. I'll have to check on our coverage," said Bert, not sounding terribly confident.

Lucy snapped a few photos of the basket, focusing on the void left by the purloined egg, then followed the officers out of the bank. "Any chance of recovering the egg?" she asked, catching up to them by their cruisers.

"Off the record, not a chance in hell," said the chief.

"But the department will make this case a top priority," asserted Barney, who was the department's community outreach officer. "We are very confident we will identify this brazen and callous thief and return the sculpture to its rightful place." He smoothed his brush cut and settled his cap on his head. "This perpetrator will soon discover that crime doesn't pay in Tinker's Cove."

"Can I quote you on that?" teased Lucy.

Barney didn't get the joke. "Absolutely," he declared, with a nod that jiggled his jowls.

Ted wasn't impressed when Lucy called to fill him in on the breaking story. "It's probably just a prank, Lucy." He paused for a moment, then offered some advice. "What you need to do is cover the story behind the story. It's no secret there's been a lot of friction at the Chamber. I wouldn't put it past one of the discontented members to pull a stunt like this."

Lucy wasn't convinced, she thought there was a big difference between grumbling and committing grand larceny, but when she followed up by interviewing Corney she discovered that Ted was on to something. "This isn't simple theft, it's sabotage!" she declared. "It's a blot on the Chamber. Whoever did this doesn't want the Chamber to succeed."

"Are you sure about that?" pressed Lucy, who had stopped by at Corney's office in the little tourist info center on Main Street. "Why would anyone want the Chamber to fail?" She imagined the Chamber's membership as a congenial group of local businesspeople with similar interests who gathered monthly over cocktails.

"There's a lot of dissension in the ranks," confessed Corney. "Not everyone was on board with the Easter Basket promo."

"Why not?" asked Lucy, genuinely puzzled.

"It seems everybody is so fired up these days. The members are like everybody else, divided into two camps. Two warring camps."

"But they all have small businesses here in town, doesn't everyone benefit from the Chamber's activities?" asked Lucy, becoming aware that Corney was actually deeply troubled. "You've been president forever, it's like you are the Chamber," she continued. "Everyone knows what a super job you do."

"Not everyone," admitted Corney, her mouth a grim line.

"Listen, Corney, anything you share with me is off the record. Think of me as a friend, not a reporter." She paused, noticing Corney's skeptical expression. "I really mean it. We girls have to stick together."

Corney's expression softened, and Lucy pressed on. "You're not in danger of getting, um, replaced, are you?"

"Not yet, but there's a faction who are very unhappy, they say the Chamber is not supporting them. That the old way of doing business isn't working for them."

"So who are these crazy radicals?" asked Lucy, attempting to inject some humor into the conversation. "Not Bert at the bank, or Tony at the IGA."

"No, they're part of the old guard. Established businesses that are part of the town's fabric. You can add Randy Lewis at Reliable Insurance, Nate at Macdonald's Farm Store, and Dave Forrest at Cove Jewelry. I can always count on those guys to support the Chamber, they're front and center whenever we need, well, anything. Not just cash but they'll volunteer time, too. They're the first to sign up whether it's delivering canned goods to the food pantry or collecting trash at the Coastal Cleanup."

"So what's the problem?"

"It's the newcomers, the new kids on the block. They bring a lot of energy and enthusiasm, a fresh outlook that I truly value, but they want things the Chamber really can't deliver."

"Like what?"

"Well, Des Jasper is a good example. He runs a property management company, you know, takes care of second homes. He provides maintenance, he'll arrange seasonal rentals, provide cleaning and trash services, all the stuff absentee owners need."

"Wish I'd thought of that, I bet it's really profitable."

"Not according to Des. He's having a hard time finding workers. He used to be able to get folks from overseas on temporary work visas but the government is limiting the number of visas, I guess they think the program takes jobs away from Americans. He wants the Chamber to go to bat for him, but this is a national problem, not something we can do much about. I have written letters to our congressional reps, and they're sympathetic, but they say the votes just aren't there to grant more visas."

"He's got a point, I've never seen so many 'help wanted' signs."

"I know. We definitely need more workers, especially in summer. And then there's Mallory Monaco, she's got that really cute lingerie shop, Sweet Nothings. She wants to see more online advertising and shoulder season ads."

"You've always had a pretty robust shoulder season ad program," said Lucy, thinking of ads she'd seen in the *Boston Globe* and *New York Times*.

"Mallory says we need to redirect away from paper media, which she says is dying, to social media, but before I go throwing money around I need to get a handle on these outfits. Twitter? Instagram? TikTok? Which ones should I use? I would really need to hire a consultant to figure this out and we don't have the budget, not now."

"That's only two dissenters," observed Lucy. "You ought to be able to handle them."

"I saved the best, or rather the worst, for last. You've noticed the vape shop?"

Lucy definitely had noticed and didn't like what she saw. "Oh, of course. It's awful. Everybody hates that gadget he's got out front that puffs smoke."

"We've gotten a lot of complaints, but Zach Starr, he's the owner . . ."

"The guy with the motorcycle?" asked Lucy, who objected to the ear-splitting roar of Zach's engine, not to mention the loud heavy metal music that often accompanied his sorties around town.

"The very same."

"What's his beef?" asked Lucy, thinking that people who behaved in uncivil ways really couldn't criticize others.

"Pretty much everything. As far as I can tell, he likes playing devil's advocate." Corney lowered her voice. "I don't know if you've noticed, but he often wears a Yankees T-shirt."

"He's a Yankees fan?" Lucy knew this was something most, if not all, New Englanders considered to be absolutely unacceptable. While they tolerated Pirates or Orioles fans, they drew the line at Yankees fans.

"You simply can't talk to the man," declared Corney. "He's like a little kid who covers his ears and goes blah-blah-blah when you try to discuss anything with him. He's not serious, he doesn't care what other people think."

"So you think he might have taken the egg? To make mischief?" asked Lucy.

"Not so much to make mischief as to make a point. To make the Chamber look foolish and ineffectual."

"You might be right," said Lucy. "I know the little egg is valuable, but it's hard to see how anyone could cash it in. It's instantly recognizable and even if you had a passion for the thing you couldn't display it, you'd have to admire it in secret."

"So how are you going to approach the story?" asked Corney, furrowing her brow.

"Straight news. Who, what, why, when, and where. But right now, all I've got is what, when, and where. Who and why remain to be discovered." Lucy paused. "Do you want to make a statement?"

"Oh, right." Corney took a minute to gather her thoughts. "Here goes: While we at the Chamber are disappointed at this turn of events, we are confident that the Tinker's Cove Police Department will soon bring whoever perpetrated this crime to justice."

"You're a pro, Corney," said Lucy, with an approving nod, closing her notebook and getting to her feet. Leaving Corney's info booth office, Lucy admired the daffodils that were blooming in the window boxes. In window boxes and planters all over town, in fact, as a result of a recent drive by the Chamber to brighten up the town's business district. Realizing she was right in front of Reliable Insurance, Lucy decided to pop in and check with Randy Lewis about the insurance policy covering the stolen egg.

When she entered, Randy looked up from the computer screen he was studying to greet her. "Hi, Lucy, what can I do for you?"

Lucy looked around the office, which was furnished in typical New England style. The walls were paneled, there were several pictures of sailboats, a practical gray-tweed carpet covered the floor, and a number of sturdy captain's chairs were provided for clients. Randy's desk sat in the middle of the room, flanked by file cabinets. A smaller desk, now vacant, sat to one side and was occupied on a part-time basis by his wife, who helped out when needed.

"I guess you've heard about the theft," began Lucy, sitting down in one of the captain's chairs.

"Bert called me with the news," he said, shaking his head. "Terrible, absolutely terrible." Randy was a middle-aged man carrying a few extra pounds, his cheeks were red, his hair was white, and he favored button-down shirts and pullover sweaters that zipped at the neck.

"I suppose Bert was checking on the egg's insurance policy," said Lucy, pulling her notebook out of her bag. "Is the theft covered?"

"Not with me," he said. "And as I'm on the Chamber's board of directors, I'm not aware of any policy covering the egg."

"Wouldn't the bank's insurance policy cover it? They must have substantial coverage, no?"

"Bank insurance is provided by the government, but that's for deposits. I'm sure they have some liability coverage for things like slip and fall accidents, probably provided by some banking industry organization." He gave her a smile. "We're much too small to handle anything on that scale. Reliable offers home, auto, and personal umbrella policies. Also life insurance." He smiled, spotting an opportunity. "I would be happy to provide a no-cost assessment of your and Bill's coverage, make sure your insurance has kept up with rising costs."

"I think we're all set," said Lucy. "But thanks for the offer. About that egg, are you telling me it's a total loss? That there was no insurance?"

Randy shook his head and clucked his tongue. "Afraid so. It's really too bad that neither the bank, nor the Chamber, thought to provide a basic level of security for such a valuable artwork. I certainly could have arranged for a short-term policy to cover it, at minimal cost."

"I guess it never occurred to them that anyone would steal it," said Lucy, sensing some sour grapes in Randy's attitude.

"As a matter of fact, I did propose insuring the valuable artifact, but was turned down." He gave Lucy a knowing nod. "People are entirely too trusting. Do you know that most people in this town don't even lock their doors? And I've seen cars with the windows open and the keys in the ignition. Can you imagine?"

Actually, Lucy could; she only locked her house when she and Bill took a rare vacation, and as for the car, well, on a frigid winter day it was smarter to leave the engine running if she was only dashing into the Quik-Stop for a bottle of milk. But maybe she, and a lot of people in Tinker's Cove, were living in a fool's paradise.

Reaching the office, Lucy greeted Phyllis and went straight to her desk; she needed to get Karl Klaus's reaction to complete her story but wasn't at all optimistic about reaching him. She had a cell phone number, but doubted Klaus bothered to keep it charged. Nevertheless, she had to try so she punched in the numbers and listened to the ringtones, waiting for the recording inviting her to leave a message after the beep.

"Yeah." It was actually Karl Klaus, himself.

"Uh, hi. This is Lucy Stone at *The Courier* in Tinker's Cove."

"Whaddya want?"

"Oh, I don't know if you've heard. You're probably busy with your award. Congratulations, by the way. The reason I'm calling, however, is because your egg sculpture was stolen."

"Hmm."

"Do you want to make a statement?"

"Nah."

Lucy was grabbing at straws. "Any reaction at all?"

"Nope."

"Are you surprised?"

He snorted. "Pretty typical. Everybody's out for themselves."

"Is there any chance you have another egg sculpture? A replacement?"

"That was the last one."

"Could you make another?"

"No. I'm into bones these days."

"Oh." Lucy found herself speechless. "Bones. That's nice."

"Gotta go," said Klaus.

"Sure thing," said Lucy, belatedly realizing the sculptor had indeed gone.

Lucy put her phone down on her desk and powered up her PC. "Bones?" asked Phyllis, from her desk across the room.

"He's done with eggs, now he's doing bones."

"And people call it art," said Phyllis. "Personally, I like pictures with cows, or babies. And I do enjoy my Audubon calendar with a different bird every month."

"Me, too," said Lucy, hitting the keyboard.

# Chapter Three

On Friday morning Lucy followed up with a call to the police department and learned there was no progress on solving the theft of the golden egg. It didn't take long to update the theft for *The Courier*'s online edition, there really wasn't much to say. Lucy padded it with all the quotes she'd gathered, but even so it was a pretty disappointing effort that left plenty of questions that would need further investigation. She hit send, then got busy on the events listings. That took longer than usual and when she finally finished it was almost lunch time. "I didn't have breakfast, I've gotta get something to eat. Do you want anything?" she asked Phyllis.

"Actually, I'd love a big old burger with a side of fries but I brought some homemade bean soup. I'm trying to lose my winter weight."

"I'll start dieting tomorrow," vowed Lucy, grabbing her bag and heading out the door. She stopped on the sidewalk, trying to decide where to go. Choices were limited this time of year, and she was thinking of heading home, which would save some money and use up some leftovers, when she remembered that Cali Kitchen had been advertising affordable lunch specials in an effort to lure locals into the upscale eatery. Why not treat herself, while at the same time contributing some cash to the local economy? She might even, she thought, be able to claim the cost of lunch as a business expense if she interviewed manager Matt Rodriguez.

Spring had sprung, according to the calendar, and the sun was shining but a brisk breeze was blowing in off the harbor. She buttoned up her coat and jammed her hands in her pockets for the short walk to the restaurant, which was located next to the harbor parking lot and had an enviable water view. She was hit with a freezing blast of wind when she turned the corner onto Sea Street and began her descent to the harbor and was beginning to rethink her plan when she noticed a figure darting rather furtively behind the restaurant.

She picked up her pace and followed, walking alongside the restaurant wall. When she reached the end of the building, she stopped and peeked around the corner, where she saw someone lifting the cover off the restaurant's dumpster. "You don't have to do that," she said, stepping forward. "You can go to the food pantry at the Community Church."

The person, who appeared to be male, dressed in shabby clothes, turned to look at her. "Mind your own business," growled the noted sculptor, Karl Klaus.

Lucy took a second look, not quite believing her own eyes, and confirmed that the dumpster diver was indeed the famed sculptor, winner of the St. Gaudens Prize. The very man she'd spoken to yesterday on the phone, picturing him surrounded by admirers and eager journalists. All of that had been her imagining, she realized, considering the little she really knew about the sculptor. He certainly didn't have any patience for social niceties, he'd probably grabbed the prize and headed directly for home. But what had he been doing since the ceremony, four days ago? And what was he doing in the dumpster? What could he be looking for?

Her question was answered when he came up with a discarded take-out container and opened it, sniffing at the contents. Oh, no, she thought. "Don't eat that," she said. "I'll buy you lunch."

Somewhat reluctantly he dropped the container. "You sure?"

"Absolutely," said Lucy, thinking this encounter deserved further investigation. It might even be a story. "This restaurant is pretty good."

Klaus let the lid on the dumpster drop, which it did with a clang. "Okay," he said, "as long as you're paying."

"Definitely," said Lucy, taking in the sculptor's appearance, which hadn't changed since she last saw him. He was still wearing the bedraggled olive-green jacket and filthy black pants and was still kicking out one foot as he walked, due to that loose sole on one of his paint-spattered shoes. He had a tattered watch cap pulled down over his long gray hair, his beard could use a trim, and his eyeglasses were askew on his nose. He was also giving off a rather pungent fragrance which made Lucy regret her offer to give him lunch in the restaurant.

Cali Kitchen wasn't crowded, however, and Matt seated them in a rear corner, away from the handful of diners scattered throughout the restaurant. When their server presented them with menus Lucy pointed out the specials to Klaus, but while she chose the featured soup-and-sandwich option he ordered steak with fries and a bottle of Cabernet.

"Want some?" he asked, somewhat magnanimously offering to share the wine she was paying for, when the server arrived with the bottle and two glasses.

"None for me," said Lucy, hoping but not quite believing she'd be able to convince Ted that the lunch was a business expense. "So, how'd the medal presentation go?" she asked, taking a sip of water.

"Okay. Dinner was pretty decent but they wanted me to give a speech."

"What did you say?"

"I said that I let my work speak for me."

"A very short speech, then."

"Yeah." He smiled slyly, revealing many missing teeth. "Didn't wanna bore 'em."

"So you're headed home now?"

Klaus wiped his mouth with his hand. "Uh, no. I can't. Fella told me I don't own my place anymore."

The server arrived with their orders, and Klaus immediately carved off a hunk of steak and shoved it in his mouth, causing Lucy some anxiety considering the state of his teeth. Nonetheless, he seemed to manage all right with his few remaining choppers and was halfway through his meal before Lucy had managed a bite or two of grilled cheese sandwich and a few spoonfuls of tomato soup. Truth was, Klaus's odor was rather taking away her appetite.

"Did you sell your place?" inquired Lucy.

"Don't think so."

"Did the bank foreclose?"

Klaus paused to stuff a fistful of fries into his mouth, then spoke. "No mortgage."

"Well, who's the fella?"

"Mike. Used to help me, but now he says I can't come back."

"My goodness. What are you going to do?"

"I still got the truck, and people throw stuff out so I'll be fine."

"You're homeless?" asked Lucy, appalled.

"I guess." He emptied the bottle into his glass. "Sure you don't want some? We could get another bottle."

"No, thanks," said Lucy. "I think when you're ready we'll go see my lawyer friend Bob Goodman."

But as fate would have it, Bob Goodman wasn't in but Lucy was able to make a Saturday morning appointment, insisting it was a legal emergency. Their next stop was the police station, where they attempted, but were unable, to file a complaint due to Klaus's failure to provide complete information. Lucy inquired about social services for the sculptor, but was told what she already knew, that the only assistance available in Tinker's Cove was the food pantry. The nearest homeless shelter was miles away; housing and financial aid were delivered through a complicated bureaucratic process.

"Sorry, Lucy," said Officer Sally Kirwan, "but it looks like the best thing would be for you to take him home with you."

Lucy was literally speechless. Sure, she thought guiltily, she did have a big old house with three empty bedrooms now that the kids were gone, but she definitely did not want to operate a homeless shelter. "Really?" she asked.

"Just temporarily, until he gets this thing sorted out."

"Okay," agreed Lucy, wondering how she was going to break the news to Bill. She also knew she ought to check in with Ted, something she wasn't eager to do. For one thing, she was afraid Ted would want to put the sculptor's dumpster diving on the front page, while she felt somewhat more protective of the confused old fellow's privacy. Examining her motives further she acknowledged that she wanted to let the story develop further. A report on the sculptor's strange behavior would certainly interest readers, but an expose of a plot to impoverish one of the nation's premier artists would be a huge scoop. Her phone beeped, and a glance revealed Ted was calling, no doubt his Spidey-sense was telling him something was up. She made a snap decision, hit *Do not reply*, and invited Klaus to spend the night at her house. He was quick to accept, and she decided to take him there immediately. She certainly didn't want to leave him wandering about town dipping into dumpsters, she wanted to get him cleaned up and housed, and she wanted to get the story about his sudden homelessness. That was the plan when she got a text in capital letters from Ted: *UPDATE ON CHAMBER? ASAP*.

Realizing she had to deliver on the update in order to keep Ted off her scent on the Klaus story, she reluctantly responded, telling him she was working on it. That got her another text, listing the interviews he wanted, along with another *ASAP*. Mentally cursing Ted, and unwilling to lose Klaus, she walked the sculptor back to the parking lot, gave him directions to her house, and, crossing her fingers, saw him off in his rattletrap truck. Then she checked out Ted's list, headed by Mallory Monaco's name, and headed back to Main Street, where a colorful flag was flapping in the breeze outside the Sweet Nothings lingerie shop.

Opening the door, she immediately noticed a lovely, fresh fragrance and the thick carpet under her feet made her feel as if she was sinking into something a lot more luxurious than she was used to. Actually rather impressed, she paused and looked around, noticing the soft lilac walls, the bank of fitting rooms in the rear which had louvred doors that promised privacy rather than skimpy curtains, and the handful of exquisite lacy underthings that were tastefully displayed in framed niches. She took a moment to adjust to these posh surroundings, becoming aware that soft music was playing, and that the shop's proprietor, Mallory, was perched on a stool in a rear corner, staring glumly into a silver laptop propped on a display case.

"Um, hi," said Lucy.

"Oh, welcome," said Mallory, slipping off the stool and smiling broadly. She was older than Lucy expected, but radiated a youthful air, dressed in slim black pants, ballerina flats, and a cozy gray angora sweater. "I didn't see you. How can I help you?"

"Um, I'm Lucy Stone, from *The Courier*. I wonder if you have a minute for a chat?"

Mallory chuckled. "More than a minute, believe me. I'm more than happy to take a break from Quickbooks."

"Your shop is absolutely lovely," said Lucy. "I can't imagine you have any trouble attracting customers."

"Well, you'd be wrong," said Mallory, with a rueful smile. "I should have closed for the winter. Now I need to restock for the tourist season and I don't have any cash. I'm going to have to apply for a loan."

"Well, maybe my story will help bring some customers," suggested Lucy. "But the reason I came was to get your reaction to the theft of the Klaus egg."

"Well, when I saw how they had that basket out in the open in the bank, I did think it might be awfully tempting to someone."

"Like a magpie?" laughed Lucy. "Maybe. But there's some talk that it was taken to embarrass the Chamber."

"I bet Corney's taking it hard." She sighed. "Don't get me wrong, I love Corney. She's a hard worker and devoted to the Chamber, but sometimes I think the Chamber is too identified with her. She doesn't listen to anybody, she's convinced she knows best. She really pushed this Easter Basket promotion hard and, well, it seems to me we need to attract customers from outside Tinker's Cove. Face it, what's the winter population? A couple thousand folks? But there are plenty of people floating around who want lovely things and are willing to pay the price for top quality, but they have to know where to find them. I think the Chamber has been letting us, me, down in that regard. Corney's focus is much too local."

"I know there are others who agree with you," conceded Lucy. "What would you like the Chamber to do?"

"Well, for one thing, we need more of a presence on social media." She sighed. "But I've got to admit, I was naïve. I really had no idea what operating a small business really entails. I can't blame my problems on anybody else."

"Why did you decide to open a lingerie store?" asked Lucy, realizing this interview was going to take longer than she'd hoped and growing uneasy about sending Karl Klaus on alone to her house, unchaperoned.

"It was a dream," began Mallory, slightly embarrassed. "It really was. I was working as a buyer for a giant retail chain, and I'd go to all these lingerie shows and I'd see such lovely things. Some imported, others made by small producers, folks who were true masters of the craft. But I had to focus on the mass producers, price was everything for our customers, and I couldn't touch the superb high-quality stuff, which I really regretted. So when I came into a small inheritance I decided to quit my job and open a boutique that would offer unique and lovely lingerie."

"Would you give me a little tour of the shop?" asked Lucy. "It doesn't seem like you have a lot of merchandise."

"Not out on racks," said Mallory. "It's all about the personal service I provide. Customers tell me what they need, and I choose a selection for them to try on. As you can see," she said, leading the way through the shop to the dressing rooms and opening one door, revealing a generous carpeted and mirrored space complete with a curvy upholstered stool, "these fitting rooms are very spacious and private. Mirrors on three sides so they can see their backs. When a woman leaves here she can be confident that whatever she's chosen—swimsuit, bra, panties, nighties—is a perfect fit that will flatter her for years to come."

"So, say, I was shopping for a bra, what would you show me?"

"Step right up," invited Mallory, indicating a piece of furniture that looked like a painted dresser. What appeared to be drawers, however, were a false front and she took her place behind it, producing a couple of lacy bras that she displayed on the top. "Now this is a bit of a push-up, which is very flattering, but not for every day. This, on the other hand, provides more coverage, but both offer plenty of support."

"They are lovely," admitted Lucy, who was quite taken with the push-up version, which she knew Bill would love. "How much is this one?"

"Ninety-five dollars, and the other is less, at sixty-five."

"Oh," said Lucy, trying not to show how shocked she was. Truth be told, she usually bought her bras at the big box store outside Portland, often from the sale rack. "And what's the range for the nightgowns?" she asked, noticing an armoire with doors open, displaying an intriguing array.

"They start at eighty or so, and go up from there. Believe me, the skimpier they are, the more expensive they get."

Lucy suddenly understood why business was not booming at Sweet Nothings. "So tell me," she began, trying to be tactful, "who do you see as your typical customer?"

"Well, I admit I may have misjudged the market. I was hoping for women who enjoy, who insist on, the finer things in life, including personal service. What I have been getting, however, are mostly vacationers who want to treat themselves, or excite their partners." She smiled naughtily. "Perk up their relationship, you know, with a sexy little camisole or negligee. And that's my beef really with the Chamber. I'd like to see advertising to attract shoulder-season tourism, preferably in glossy, upscale travel magazines and in social media. I have a lovely website that costs me quite a bit but I need help letting people know about it."

Lucy realized she hadn't been listening closely, she'd been imagining how Bill might react if she wore one of the lacy little camisoles to bed. It might be just the thing she needed, she thought, to distract him from their unexpected guest. And one of the camis, in particular, had caught her eye. "How much is this little thing?" she asked.

Mallory fingered the tag, then made a quick decision. "To tell the truth, it's about time I marked it down. Let's say forty dollars."

"Deal," said Lucy, producing her credit card.

"My husband is going to love this," she said, momentarily forgetting her houseguest and thinking of the romantic evening ahead. "But Maine tends to be chilly, even on summer nights, and really very cold come winter. All this lace is lovely but . . ."

"I realized that," said Mallory, passing her the charge slip for her signature, "so when women came in looking for flannel pjs and nighties I brought some in. Over there," she said, pointing to a rack in the rear that Lucy hadn't noticed. Mallory sighed. "But even they haven't sold and I've put them on sale." She smiled. "I can promise you cozy nights, whether you're wearing lace or flannel," said Mallory, returning her credit card. "And, where's your Easter card? I've got a sticker for you!"

"Right," said Lucy, rummaging in her bag and producing the slightly crumpled Easter card. "My first sticker."

"I hope it's not the last," said Mallory, who was wrapping the cami in tissue paper, before sliding it into a lovely pink-and-white striped bag. She added the sales slip as well as the Easter card, now adorned with a pretty Easter egg sticker. "Have a nice day."

"Thanks," said Lucy, pleased as punch with her purchase. "You, too."

"I'll try," muttered Mallory, returning to her laptop and flipping it open.

Lucy felt rather pleased with herself as she walked down Main Street, heading for her car, carrying the ritzy shopping bag. It occurred to her as she walked along that this was something she rarely did. Most of her shopping was at the big box store, which entailed parking in a giant lot and usually involved pushing a wheeled shopping cart. She thought of scenes in movies where the heroine returned to her fancy hotel room carrying a number of bags boasting famous designer logos and chuckled at herself. One little striped bag containing a marked-down cami hardly made her a movie star or a one-percenter, but she had to admit it did give her self-esteem a little boost. She was thinking along those lines when she reached her car, climbed in, and called Sue. She felt the need to share this somewhat exciting development and who better to share it with than Sue, who lived to shop.

"Guess what?" she began, when Sue answered. "I went to Sweet Nothings and bought myself a new nightie!"

"Congratulations," laughed Sue. "Something sexy? For Bill?"

"Kind of," she admitted, feeling her face grow warm. "Do you shop there a lot?" asked Lucy, encouraged by Sue's approving tone.

"I pop in from time to time, but you know me. I'm a bargain hunter. Her stuff's lovely, but it's so expensive. I do a lot better at the outlet mall."

"She says her prices are justified by the personal service . . ."

"That's the theory," admitted Sue, "but I wonder if most women really want to bare all to a stranger for a bra fitting. It's a little too clinical, if you know what I mean."

"I do. Mammograms are bad enough."

Sue laughed. "And let's face it, most of the women around here simply aren't used to being pampered."

"I think I could get used to it," confessed Lucy, starting her car. "It's nice to treat yourself once in a while."

"Did you get your sticker?" asked Sue.

"You betcha!" crowed Lucy.

She was pocketing her phone, planning to tackle the next name on her list, when it rang and she saw that Bill was calling. Somewhat warily she answered the call.

"Lucy, there's some old guy in my chair, wearing my bathrobe, saying you sent him here. What is going on?"

This was bad, very bad. "It's temporary. Only temporary. He's the sculptor, Karl Klaus, and he needs a place to stay for the night."

"What? There's no hotels?" Bill sounded angry.

"Bill, I found him dumpster diving."

Bill was incredulous. "So you brought him home?"

"Like I said, just for the night. I don't see the problem. We have three empty bedrooms."

"You don't see the problem? There's dirty clothes all over the floor, the bathroom's flooded, and he drank all my beer. There's definitely a problem, Lucy."

Lucy's visions of a romantic evening were disappearing fast. "I admit, he's not quite civilized. I guess it's part of the artistic temperament."

"No. The guy's filthy and rude and I want him out."

"Soon, Bill. Soon. Just for one night." She swallowed hard. "It's for a story I'm working on."

"So this is a story? I shoulda known. This time, Lucy, you've gone too far. You've done some crazy stuff but you've never brought your work home. Not like this!"

"Calm down, Bill," she said, pleading. "I'll take care of this. I promise."

"You better. Because this is too much!"

"I'm on my way," she said, scuttling the rest of Ted's list. This was an emergency. "Just one quick stop and I'll be home."

"Bring beer," snapped Bill.

That was two stops, she thought, agreeing. First stop was Sweet Nothings, where she was going to exchange the cami for one of the comfy granny gowns. She did not see a romantic evening in her future any time soon.

# Chapter Four

Lucy wasn't surprised when she turned in to her drive-way on Red Top Road and saw that Bill's truck was missing. In fact, Karl Klaus's beat-up old truck was actu-ally in Bill's usual spot. She figured her husband had sim-ply decided to decamp in order to avoid an unpleasant evening. There were any number of places he could be, she thought, as she got out of the car. He could drown his sor-rows in the roadhouse on Route 1, he could hang out with one of his buddies and watch a hockey game on TV, he could treat himself to a diner dinner and catch the latest action movie. The one thing she was pretty sure he wouldn't do was book a motel room for the night. They'd had other fights throughout their long marriage, he'd occasionally taken off in a fit of anger, but he'd always come home to sleep.

And when she stepped inside the house she had to admit she didn't blame him for leaving. Karl Klaus had indeed trashed the place. He'd helped himself to food from the fridge, apparently sampling leftovers and leaving the open containers of the ones he didn't like on the counter and the round golden oak table. A half-empty plastic container was lying in a puddle of milk on the floor, and a trail of discarded beer cans led into the family room, where the TV was on at top volume. Following the noise, she discovered Klaus himself snoring away on the sofa, wearing Bill's terry cloth robe, which had fallen open, revealing what Lucy definitely did not want to see, although she was relieved he had apparently showered. She turned away and grabbed the remote, clicking off, and the sculptor stirred. She took a deep breath and faced him, noticing that he was now sitting up and had gathered the robe in his hand, covering himself.

"You're here for one night, and one night only," she said, starting to gather up the damp towels and various items of clothing that were strewn about on the floor.

"Didn't ask to come, did I?" he grumbled.

"Perhaps I misunderstood when you said you were homeless!" declared Lucy, waving a towel at him. "I guess I made a big mistake thinking you might need some help."

Klaus looked down at his bare feet, studying his horny toenails. "I was wondering what's for dinner," he admitted, with a shrug.

It was kind of funny, thought Lucy. The guy was absolutely incorrigible. But she was no pushover, either. "I'll give you dinner on one condition: You've got to get dressed."

"No problem," he said. "I noticed there's closets full of clothes upstairs. Somethin's bound to fit."

All in all, thought Lucy, hours later after Klaus had retired for the night, the evening had gone better than she expected. The old fellow actually almost complimented her on the chicken dinner she gave him and took himself off to bed early, insisting he'd rather sleep on the sofa in the family room, where he could watch TV, than in one of the bedrooms upstairs. Lucy had gotten the house back in order and was tucked up in bed in her new nightgown when Bill came home around eleven o'clock.

"That's new," he said, observing her granny gown.

"It's cozy," said Lucy, smiling at him. "Super comfy."

"I may have overreacted," he admitted, sitting on the side of the bed and pulling off his work boots.

"No. You were right. He's awful, and I should've checked with you first. But he had no place else to go."

"Where's he now?"

"Family room. He didn't want to dirty up my sheets."

"Considerate of him," chuckled Bill, heading for the bathroom.

Next morning, Lucy woke up, smiled, stretched, and picked the nightie up off the floor where it had fallen while she and Bill had enjoyed some lively make-up sex. Shivering, she pulled it over her head, and climbed out of bed. Bill had already gone downstairs; she could smell the coffee. She made a quick visit to the bathroom, then found her slippers and robe and headed downstairs. She found Bill in the kitchen, seated at the round golden oak table, digging into a bowl of cereal. "Good morning," she said, pouring herself a mug of coffee. "Where's you-know-who?"

"Still sleeping."

She sighed in relief, sat down, and took a sip of the hot coffee. "The first sip is the best."

"Yeah," he agreed, smiling at her.

"You seemed to like the new nightie," observed Lucy, teasing him.

He glanced at her. "I think it's the little blue flowers that do it for me." He picked up his mug and swallowed. "No, it's that lacy stuff around the neck. The schoolmarmish vibe."

"So that's what turns you on?"

He laughed. "You turn me on, Lucy. You could wear a burka and I'd find you madly alluring."

Lucy put down her mug. "Well, that's not happening."

Bill polished off his cereal and got up to put the empty bowl in the dishwasher. Then he stepped behind her and bent down, nibbling on her ear. "You've got flowers on your nightie, but we don't have any in the house."

Lucy wasn't sure if this was a complaint or not. "Well, mister, feel free to bring me a bouquet anytime you want."

"My bad," he admitted, laughing. "What I meant is that you used to get those flowers that smell so good, you know, in pots. They're a spring thing." He headed for the door, where he stopped to put on his jacket. "You used to put a bowl of them on the table every spring."

"Hyacinths."

"How come you haven't got them?"

"I bought them for Easter and Easter's not much fun without the kids, you know. It's not like we're going to have a visit from the Easter Bunny and a big ham dinner."

Bill didn't like the sound of this. "We can still have jelly beans and a ham." He stuck his hat on his head. "I'm off to the hardware store."

Lucy realized that Bill wasn't the only one who missed celebrating Easter and the arrival of spring, she did, too. "Okay. Ham dinner and hyacinths. I'll buy some today."

"Good. We can invite some people over, make it a party."

"Sounds like a plan," she said, reaching for a pad and pencil to make a shopping list.

After Bill left, she went into the family room to rouse Karl Klaus. They were scheduled to meet with Bob Goodman first thing in the morning and she figured it would take some time to get him up and out. Hopefully out for good, she thought, staring at his unconscious body, sprawled on her sectional in Bill's borrowed pajamas. Now that she had him, how was she going to get rid of him?

They were running late for the appointment with Bob Goodman since it had taken Lucy quite a while to get Klaus up and dressed and fed. Bob, however, had put the time to good use, following up on the information Lucy had left with his receptionist, and greeted them with good news.

"It's a simple fraud," he said, turning his monitor around and showing them the title transfer form that Klaus's assistant, one Michael Green, had filed in the county Registry of Deeds. "I can get this cleared up in no time."

"How soon would that be?" asked Lucy, grateful that Bob had agreed to see them on the weekend. He was dressed in jeans, which made him look youthful despite his now receding hairline.

"Well, normally it would have to go through the court and that would take a while. However, I happen to be on excellent terms with the Registrar, and if Klaus here doesn't want to press charges, I think we might be able to simply clear up the paperwork. Then the sheriff would evict Mr. Green and Karl could move back in. That could happen in a couple of days, a week at most, depending on the sheriff's schedule."

"What do you think, Karl? Do you want to press charges?" asked Lucy, sending up a silent prayer.

The sculptor shrugged and rubbed his nose. "I don't want to make trouble. I just want my place back."

Great, thought Lucy. But where was Klaus going to stay in the meantime? She knew a week was lightning speed in the legal system, but much too long to keep Klaus as a houseguest. "I'm afraid Karl needs a place to stay in the meantime," said Lucy.

"Hotel?" suggested Bob.

"Card doesn't work," said Klaus, shaking his head.

"Really?" Bob was sensing further trouble.

"Couldn't get gas."

"Let me see your card," he asked, and Karl pulled a worn leather wallet out of his pants pocket and handed over a handful of plastic. "I tried a bunch," he said. "None of 'em was any good."

Bob picked one up and dialed the number on the back, punched in the account number, got the last four numbers of Klaus's social security number and punched them in, and listened keenly to the recorded voice. "You've reached your limit," he told Klaus.

"No way."

"Do you think your friend Mr. Green has had something to do with this?"

Klaus chewed his lip thoughtfully, then nodded. "Could be."

Bob sighed. "Well, this definitely complicates things and will take more time," he said. "I'll do some more digging but I suspect we'll have to refer this to the DA for a full-blown investigation." He turned to Lucy. "Is there a reason Karl can't stay with you?"

Lucy chuckled. "The reason would be Bill."

Bob nodded and Lucy could practically hear the wheels turning in his head. "I have an idea," he said. "You know Rachel's been working with Rosie Capshaw, who's doing the man-eating plant for *Little Shop of Horrors*." Lucy did know that Rachel was directing this year's Little Theatre production, and also that Rosie was an acclaimed puppeteer who constructed giant figures for parades and other events. "Well," continued Bob, "she's got that big barn studio on the Van Vorst estate, she's even got a couple of apprentices living out there."

"Do you think she could use another?" asked Lucy, her heart leaping at the prospect.

"Let's call her and see," suggested Bob, reaching for his phone. Amazingly enough, Rosie declared she'd be delighted, thrilled actually, to add the noted sculptor to her little art colony.

"Anything else I can do for you?" asked Bob, writing out a receipt for Klaus's credit and debit cards. "Just sign here and I'll get started on this right away."

"You doing this for free?" asked the sculptor, narrowing his eyes.

"No. No way," said Bob. "But I will get you your house and your money back."

Karl shifted uneasily in his chair and made grumbling noises.

Lucy decided some encouragement was needed. "You'll like Rosie," she said, producing her phone and flipping through the photos. "Ah, here she is." She showed Klaus a picture of the puppeteer, taken at last year's July Fourth parade. Her long hair was blowing in the wind, she was smiling broadly, and her tiny T-shirt was dampened with sweat and clinging to her curves. She hadn't been able to use the photo, she remembered, because Rosie was braless and Ted insisted it wasn't suitable for a family newspaper.

"Okay," grumbled Klaus, taking the pen and signing his name. "Let's go," he said, slamming his hands down on the desk and pushing himself upright.

Klaus had to retrieve his truck, which was back at the house on Red Top Road, and Lucy had him follow her out to Pine Point, the late Virginia Van Vorst's estate on Shore Road. Rosie greeted him warmly, proclaiming him a master sculptor in residence. She assigned one of the apprentices to show him around and when he'd gone, turned to Lucy. "Thanks, Lucy, this is a fabulous opportunity for my crew."

"Well, you're really helping me out, too. I found him dumpster diving, you know, and brought him home but, well, he's not quite house trained."

Rosie smiled, revealing a mouthful of perfect white teeth, and tossed her enviable hair back over her shoulder. "You know Auntie collected his work," she said, referring to Virginia Van Vorst, her great-aunt, who had left the shorefront estate to Rosie's cousin, the supermodel Juliette Duff. "Juliette, too. She's bought a lot of his work, but mostly donates it to good causes. She said one or two pieces made a statement, but after that it got to be too much."

Aha, thought Lucy, suspecting that Juliette was the mysterious anonymous donor of the purloined egg.

"Well, his new interest is bones."

"Perfect!" exclaimed Rosie. "We're working on skeletons for a Halloween event next fall!"

"Serendipity, I guess," said Lucy, smiling. "Bob Goodman is working on the legal stuff, so I guess everything is working out."

"It usually does," said Rosie, waving goodbye.

Lucy felt a huge sense of relief as she left the estate, but a glance at her phone revealed a number of texts from Ted, reminding her that he needed the Chamber story.

"Never heard of the weekend, Ted?" she muttered to herself as she started her car. She had a big list of errands, but instead of stocking up on groceries she had a different list, a list of interview subjects. Glancing at it, she decided to talk to Nate Macdonald first, at his farm stand. That way she could also get the hyacinths that Bill wanted.

Nate was a fourth-generation farmer who had seized opportunity and turned the family's pick-your-own apple orchard into a seasonal bazaar that became a must-do for folks enjoying a weekend in the country. Fall was huge as leaf-peepers crowded in to buy cider and donuts, come

Christmas they returned for festive greens and hiked out to the woods to choose and cut the perfect tree, in spring the greenhouse overflowed with colorful blooming bulbs, and in summer no cookout was considered complete without a platter of Macdonald's fresh corn on the cob.

It was true, Lucy reminded herself, that she could buy hyacinths for less money at the IGA, but she knew the quality was better at Macdonald's and since Bill had requested them, she felt justified in the extra expense. Nate himself was manning the register when she chose two pots of hyacinths, one featuring pink and white, another all blue, which she planned to display in her favorite blue-and-white bowl.

"It's not spring without hyacinths," said Nate, carefully tucking the pots into paper cones. "These are Van Zandts, imported from Holland."

"They're lovely and I'm glad you've still got some. Somehow it skipped my mind until Bill reminded me."

"Are you collecting the stickers?" he asked, as she handed over twenty dollars.

"Oh, yes." She produced the card and he added her second sticker.

"This promo's been pretty good," he said. "Everybody wants the stickers, if their total isn't quite ten dollars they'll add a candy bar or something just to get one."

"So you're not one of the Chamber's critics?" she said, seizing the opening he'd given her. "I'm actually doing a story about dissension at the Chamber."

"Me? No way. I think Corney's doing a great job, and you can quote me. She knows Tinker's Cove and folks here don't like change, and neither do the tourists. They like the image of this sweet, old-fashioned town with the American flags flying and the white-steepled churches. The harbor and the lobster boats, that's what they come for. We ham it up a bit, Country Cousins is a lot more than that quaint old-fashioned country store on Main Street, their IT and logistics are cutting edge, but families from Brooklyn can still find penny candy for the kids and get a wedge of cheddar from the big wheel on the counter."

"And that candy costs a lot more than a penny," said Lucy.

Nate shrugged. "They don't mind. They're paying for the experience of choosing Mary Janes and Fireballs from those big old glass jars."

"So true." She picked up her potted flowers, then paused. "So the fact that the Klaus egg was stolen hasn't dampened enthusiasm for the stickers?"

"Not at all. It's kind of childish but they seem to get a lot of satisfaction from filling in those blanks. Who knew?"

"Corney, I guess," said Lucy, laughing. "Any idea who might've taken the egg?"

Nate lowered his voice. "Don't quote me on this, but I wouldn't be surprised if it was Zach Starr."

Lucy pictured Zach, who she'd often seen riding around town on his Harley, blasting out hard rock music, and shook her head. "What would he want with a gold egg? He's super macho, no? I bet he's never even been in an art museum or even a gallery."

"He doesn't care about the artistic value. Zach's a rebel who likes to be outrageous. Taking the egg is exactly the sort of thing he'd do, just to make trouble and embarrass all the uptight old Maine Yankees. Once the fuss dies down, I bet the egg will magically reappear."

"Sooner would be better than later," said Lucy, leaving with a pot of flowers in each arm, and a second sticker on her Easter card.

Zach was also on her list, so she decided to interview him next, following up on Nate's accusation. So she drove on into town, where she found a free parking space right in front of Sea Smoke and marched herself in under the billowing cloud of smoke, feeling a bit as if she was entering the dragon's cave. If Zach was indeed a dragon, he was a very tame one indeed as she found him hunkered down at the store's counter over a steaming bowl of oatmeal. He looked up as she entered and put his spoon down. "Don't mind me. I'm just having some breakfast. Are you looking for anything in particular?"

"No, not really," said Lucy, taking in Zach's bald head and bushy beard, the tattoos on his beringed fingers, not to mention the rings in his ears and one dangling from his nose. He was wearing a fringed black leather vest over a long-sleeved T-shirt with a picture of a pit bull on the front. She was about to introduce herself when he pointed the spoon toward a display of CBD oil.

"Just got a shipment," he said, scooping up a load of oatmeal. "Great stuff for those aches and pains of aging."

Lucy found this to be a bit of a blow, she wasn't old and she didn't suffer from aches and pains. Well, sometimes, but just normal stuff, like after working in the garden. She straightened her shoulders and stepped up to the counter, facing him. "I'm not here for CBD oil," she said, all business. "I'm Lucy Stone from *The Courier* and I'm here to get your reaction as a member of the Chamber of Commerce to the theft of the Klaus Easter egg."

"Nice to meet you, Lucy." He put down the spoon and extended his hand to Lucy. Shrugging off her sense of umbrage, she took it and found it pleasantly firm and warm. "Hope you don't mind the oatmeal—actually, where's my manners? Would you like some? I cook it in a slow cooker overnight and it's really good, I put in nuts and stuff for protein. I'm vegan, you see. Gotta take care of the corpus, right?"

This was surprising news, thought Lucy. "No, thanks, I ate at home."

He cocked his head, looking at her suspiciously. "The slow cooker is just between you and me," he told her. "For all I know it's against one of this GD town's stupid regulations. No this, no that. They're after me about the smoke machine, y'know, but I'll take them to court. I've got rights."

"Completely off the record. I am also a fan of the slow cooker," said Lucy, aiming for some common ground. "But I'm covering the egg theft and I'd love to get a quote from you for my article." She paused. "A bit of free publicity for your store."

Zach scooped up the last of his oatmeal and shoved the bowl aside. "Personally, and you can quote me on this, I think this whole Easter basket promo sucks! Who wants a dumb egg anyway?"

"A lot of people, apparently. Karl Klaus is famous and his sculptures, even the little ones, go for thousands of dollars."

"Well, I wouldn't take it if you gave it to me," declared Zach, picking up his bowl and carrying it into the store's back room. "If you ask me," he continued, returning, "it looked like those eggs that ladies' stockings used to come in."

Lucy found herself chuckling. "That's what I thought, too."

Zach grinned, revealing a couple of gold teeth.

Oh, my, thought Lucy. "Some people are saying the egg was taken to embarrass the Chamber, to make the whole promo look foolish."

"The promo was stupid before the egg was stolen, nobody had to risk going to jail for grand larceny to show how dumb it is. I mean, stickers? Who collects stickers? Apart from little kids, you know, in kindergarten. Good for you, kid, you colored within the lines, you get a pretty little sticker."

"It's kind of fun," said Lucy, who had quite enjoyed collecting a few stickers and was hoping to complete her card. "A little reward. A sort of thank you plus the chance of winning the basket. Even without the egg, it's a very nice prize."

Zach cocked his head, amused. "I got some, do you want one?"

"Well, I'm not planning on buying anything," confessed Lucy.

"So what? Trust me, most of my clientele don't want 'em. They're going to waste." He pulled out the sheet, which was only missing a couple of stickers. "Here. Take two." He peeled them off and held them out to her, stuck on his fingers.

"Okay, thanks," said Lucy, producing her card and applying the stickers. "So what sort of promos would you prefer? What do you think would bring customers to town, and to your store?"

"Okay, this is what I told them at the last meeting. I'd like to see a rock music festival, we could set up a tent in the harbor parking lot, get a bunch of bands. It'd be great. Bring in some food trucks, and beer, wouldn't it be nice? Listening to the music and lookin' out over the water, the lighthouse blinking in the distance? Now that would really attract a lot of folks."

"But where would they park?" asked Lucy.

"That's what Corney said, and the bank guy. It's not an insurmountable problem, we could figure it out. There are other parking lots in town. At Marzetti's grocery, for one. And the schools. The schools are out in summer, right. And the churches, if the festival isn't on Sunday, those lots are empty. We could use the school busses for shuttles, it could work." He shook his head. "Small minds, that's the problem. And unwillingness to try something new."

"You've definitely got a point," said Lucy, who had produced her reporter's notebook and was writing it all down.

"You could just record me on your phone," advised Zach.

"I'm used to doing it this way," confessed Lucy.

"Whatever floats your boat," he said, with a grin.

"Any other ideas for promos?"

"Well, this would never fly, but I've been to some motorcycle rallies, and those things are dope. Parking not so much of a problem, for one thing, and there's great comradery. Gathering of the clans, so to speak, town humming, practically vibrating from all the motors. It's incredible."

"You're right," said Lucy. "It would never fly."

"That's the problem, this town needs shaking up!" he declared, pounding a very large fist onto the counter and making the display of breath mints jump. "You know, they won't even let me sell pot, even though it's legal. The state puts you through a lot of hoops, but it's worth it in the end 'cause you can make a lot of money. But it does require local permission and the minute I proposed my business plan to that board of selectmen they passed a law banning the sale of recreational marijuana. Can you believe it?"

"Actually, I can," said Lucy.

He shook his head mournfully. "You woulda thought I was pushing heroin, the way they reacted. That lady in charge, the boss of the board, she actually clutched her pearls." He threw his head back and roared in laughter. "It was a scene."

Lucy pictured Franny Small, now retired from a successful career in which she built a million-dollar jewelry company from the bottom up, reacting to Zach's proposal. She was tiny, always perfectly coiffed and dressed, usually sporting a lovely scarf and a gleaming strand of pearls. Lucy had never seen her clutch those pearls, but she figured Zach was telling the truth in this instance.

"Okay, so any ideas who might've taken the golden egg?" asked Lucy.

"Like I said, I don't know why anybody would want it, but there is one guy in town who likes shiny things."

Lucy ran through the town's roster in her mind and came up empty. "Likes shiny things?"

Zach's shoulders shook. "I shouldn't name names, but Dave Forrest dominates the town's gold market."

"The jeweler?"

Zach nodded. "The very man."

"I'm not going to put that in my story," said Lucy.

Zach nodded in agreement. "Better not."

Leaving the shop, Lucy headed for the empty office, where she wrote up the story for Ted's weekend update. She hadn't got everybody on his list, but she'd interviewed a good selection. And it wasn't as if she was going to get any overtime pay, she rationalized, hitting send and heading off to the IGA, determined to salvage what remained of her weekend.

# Chapter Five

**B**ill and Lucy spent most of Sunday cleaning up their yard: picking up fallen sticks and saving them for kindling, raking up old dead leaves, and spreading mulch on the flowerbeds around the house. When she left for work on Monday morning, Lucy surveyed their property with approval, noticing that the crocuses were in bloom, the daffs were budding, and the tulips were already poking green shoots through the mulch. She made a mental note to clip some daffs for an arrangement and checked her watch, reassured that it wasn't quite eight. Ted had a habit of showing up early on Monday mornings and she didn't want to be late.

But when she got to the office, Ted glanced at the antique Willard clock on the wall above his roll-top desk and greeted her with a disapproving glare. "About time you showed up," he growled.

"Well, you know, I did work most of Saturday."

"Yeah, I got your story. Not quite up to your usual standard. I'd almost think you're up to something. One of your investigations."

Lucy didn't think it wise to respond. She glanced at Phyllis, expecting an eye roll, but instead got a sympathetic smile as she pointed to the Willard clock on the wall. That clock, which had kept perfect time for over a hundred and fifty years, indicated it was a quarter past nine o'clock.

Shocked, Lucy checked her watch again and noticed its hands were showing it still not quite eight. Uh-oh. "I am sorry, Ted," she said, dropping her bag on her desk and shrugging out of her barn coat, "my watch stopped." She stuck her arm out for him to see. "It says it isn't even eight yet." She sat down at her desk and powered up her PC. "Did I miss anything important? Did they recover the egg?"

"Well, no," he admitted, somewhat reluctantly. "But that's not the point. You're supposed to be here at eight, ready to cover whatever comes up. What if there was a big fire, or a car crash?"

"Well, I guess you could've called me on my cell and I would've hurried to the scene," said Lucy, watching the blue circle go round and round. "Come to think of it, Zach Starr said something kind of funny the other day. I asked him what he thought about the theft and he threw out Dave Forrest's name, suggesting he might've taken the egg."

"Dave?" Ted didn't sound convinced. He furrowed his brow. "Are you investigating the theft, Lucy? You're supposed to be covering the Chamber."

"Well, people are interested and it does come up in conversation. Oddly enough, everyone I've talked to has a different suspect."

"That's ridiculous," said Phyllis.

"I agree," said Lucy. "Zach's a contrarian and he probably picked the least likely person just for the heck of it."

"To make trouble," said Phyllis.

"Absolutely," agreed Lucy. "But if you think about it, the weird thing about the egg theft is that even though it's valuable it's very identifiable, which would make it very hard to cash in. Unless, of course, you were someone like Dave who has a lot of industry contacts who handle valuable things like jewelry and objets d'art."

"That's right," said Phyllis, thoughtfully. "He's got all kinds of stuff in that shop, those Lladró figurines go for big bucks and so does the Waterford crystal."

"What's the egg made of?" asked Ted. "Is it actually gold?"

"I have no idea," admitted Lucy. "I think the finish is gold leaf, but I don't know what's under it." The blue circle had stopped spinning and Lucy clicked on the Google icon, typed *Karl Klaus egg sculpture* in the search box and hit enter. "According to Wikipedia, his sculptures have a bronze base and various finishes." She read further. "Oh ho, the eggs aren't gold leaf at all, they're actually covered with a base coat of silver and then gold. Real gold."

"So a skilled artisan could conceivably recover the gold and silver?" asked Ted.

"I don't know," admitted Lucy, "but I bet Dave Forrest would know and I do need a new watch battery."

"I think you should head over there and get that battery," advised Ted.

"Yeah," added Phyllis, "you wouldn't want to be late again."

"Perish the thought," said Lucy, already grabbing her barn coat from the hook.

As she walked down Main Street, Lucy reviewed what she knew about Dave Forrest and Cove Jewelry. The shop was a local institution that people turned to for jewelry or other gifts to commemorate big life events like engagements, weddings, anniversaries, and graduations. Many a high school or college grad had received a watch or a string of pearls from Cove Jewelry, engagements were sealed with diamond solitaires and wedding vows confirmed with rings personally engraved by Dave Forrest. While Dave was the person most identified with the shop these days, Lucy knew it had been established years earlier by his wife's parents, Ronald and Mary Lenk. They were now happily retired in Florida, confident that their daughter, Sandy, was keeping a sharp eye on Dave and the business.

Stepping inside the shop, there was no sign of Dave but his assistant, Alison Souther, was manning the store. "Hi, Lucy, what brings you here? Any engagements or weddings coming up?"

Lucy chuckled, thinking of her two unmarried daughters, Sara and Zoe, busily pursuing careers. Elizabeth, her oldest daughter, was in a serious relationship, but also focused on her career. "No, unfortunately. It's my watch, it needs a new battery."

"Dave's in the back, making repairs. He can pop that battery in for you right away." Lucy handed over the watch and Alison carried it into the back room where Dave had his workshop. He was a skilled craftsman who not only repaired jewelry but worked with customers to create one-of-a-kind original designs. His ads encouraged customers to bring in old, outdated pieces to be recycled into newer, more current pieces.

"It won't be long," said Alison, returning. "Why don't you look around? If you see something you like I can make a note and when your birthday rolls around give Bill a call."

"If only," said Lucy, peering into the glass display case. "Presents in our family tend to run in the fifty-dollar range. A new sweater, maybe. A pair of gloves. That sort of thing."

"It's worth a try," encouraged Alison. "Maybe we can

get him to spend a bit more, we have some lovely pearl earrings for under a hundred."

"They're quite popular," added Dave, emerging from the back room. "Here's the watch, up and running again."

"How much do I owe you?"

"Ten dollars, and you get a sticker, too," said Dave. "Which reminds me, any news about the egg?"

"Not a peep, pardon the pun," said Lucy, opening her wallet and discovering she only had a single twenty. "Have you heard anything?"

He shook his head, taking Lucy's money and giving her a ten in change while Alison applied a fifth sticker to Lucy's Easter card. "It's a valuable artwork worth quite a lot, I don't imagine we'll see it again."

That statement caught Lucy's attention. "Did you know it's actually made of bronze coated with silver and gold?"

"I did not," said Dave, raising an eyebrow, "but it answers something that was bothering me. I thought it was most likely gold leaf but I couldn't figure out how he got that perfectly smooth, glossy finish." He continued, thoughtfully. "That wouldn't have been easy to do, he would've had to work with molten silver and gold. I guess I underestimated Klaus, he really is an artist."

"Could a skilled metalworker recover the silver and gold?" asked Lucy.

"Oh, yeah, for sure. Different metals, different melting temps. You'd need special equipment, I don't have anything like that here. I work on a much smaller scale." He paused. "I'd like to see how Klaus actually did that and what his studio is like. It would be fascinating."

"Like glassblowing," suggested Alison.

"But much harder," said Dave, "and in the end, the egg is worth more as a Karl Klaus sculpture than it would be as raw material. For sure."

"But very hard to sell," suggested Lucy.

"Not if you've got the right contacts. Take Des Jasper, for instance. He has international contacts who could sell the egg for him."

"What contacts?" asked Lucy.

"Well, you know Des relies heavily on that visa program to get seasonal workers to clean and maintain the properties he manages. There's a lot of red tape, and through the years he's put together a network of folks both here and abroad who help him. He was telling me all about it, how he's got to the top of the list for visas, due largely to the fact that he's got what he calls 'friends in high places.'" Dave sighed. "But even he admits he's having trouble, because they've really scaled back that program and are limiting work visas."

"Do you really think he'd do such a thing? Steal the egg?"

Dave looked off in the distance, then turned to Lucy with a smile. "I doubt it, but you know, when you've put your heart and soul into something it's very hard to see it fail. With an influx of cash he could keep his creditors happy at the same time he reorganizes."

As Lucy buckled her watch strap, she wondered if Dave was talking about Des Jasper's business troubles, or his own. "Don't forget your card," said Alison, sliding it across the counter.

"Thanks," said Lucy, happily noting how the empty egg outlines were filling up before she tucked the card into her bag. "Have a nice day," she said, taking her leave. Aware that she only had ten dollars in her wallet, she decided she might as well head to the bank down the street to replenish her cash at the ATM. As she walked along the sidewalk, which was free of the crowds of tourists that arrived in summer, she thought about her conversations with the various members of the Chamber. Corney was absolutely right about it being deeply divided; she chuckled to herself thinking how each member she'd spoken with had quickly named another member as the egg thief. With friends like that, who needed enemies? She wondered if the Chamber, and the town itself, could ever come together.

Nearing the bank, which was on the opposite side of the street, Lucy looked both ways. The road was clear, not a good sign for local businesses, she thought as she crossed. The ATM was located to the side of the brick bank building, in a little glassy cube that also allowed access to the bank lobby. As she entered from the street, Des Jasper was coming through from the lobby. "After you," he said, holding the door for her.

"Thanks, but I'm here for the ATM." Lucy gave him a big smile. "Since I've got you, would you mind giving me your reaction to the theft of the Klaus egg? It's for a *Courier* story I'm working on. In particular, do you think the promo was a good idea?"

"Not at all," he said, sounding eager to vent his frustration with the Chamber. "That whole promo is dumb, if you ask me. Who wants stickers and a big fat stupid egg?"

"Well, someone did," laughed Lucy, pulling her notebook out of her bag and flipping it open. "Let's leave that off the record and start over, shall we?"

"Mom said never to speak before you think," he said, shaking his head and brushing back a floppy lock of hair with his hand. Unlike most of the male population in Tinker's Cove, who favored sweaters and jeans, Des was a sharp dresser and usually wore a sport coat over a turtleneck, along with tailored slacks and polished ankle boots. He didn't patronize Cal, the town's barber, who gave everybody the same cut, but was reputed to get his hair styled in a unisex salon in Portland. "What I meant to say is that it's unfortunate, especially since the money spent on the promo, now lost, could have been used to better effect."

"How so?" asked Lucy.

"We live in a global economy, we need to look at the big picture. I'd like to see the Chamber exert pressure on our congressmen, invest in supporting candidates that are pro-business. The Chamber's got terminal myopia."

"You've got a point," admitted Lucy. "I can't remember the last time any of our state or national officeholders paid a visit to Tinker's Cove."

"They only respond to money. Donations. That's how you get influence, and believe me, we need it."

"True enough," said Lucy, thinking there was absolutely no chance whatsoever that the Chamber's membership would agree to meddling in politics. Strictly non-partisan, that was a founding tenet of the organization. "So, off the record, any ideas who might've taken the egg?"

Des shrugged and reached for the door. "It must've been someone with a motive, right? As well as somebody no one would suspect."

"Are you thinking of anyone in particular?"

"Well, Randy Lewis was sure miffed when they voted down his insurance." He laughed and pushed the door open. "Could've been an *I told you so* kind of thing."

Lucy laughed, too. "You're right about one thing, he's the last person anyone would suspect."

"Those are the ones to watch," he said, with a little nod, as he headed on outside.

Lucy stepped up to the cash machine and slid in her card, hit the quick pick for a hundred dollars and waited as the machine went through its paces, eventually producing her cash. She took her card and left, pausing on the outside steps to tuck her wallet in her bag. Hearing raised voices, she glanced in the direction of the parking lot.

There she saw Des standing on the driver's side of his Corvette, glaring at his wife, who had her hand on the passenger side door handle. "What were you doing?" yelled Cathy, angrily. "Thanks to you we're going to be late!"

"It's always me, is it? Where were you?"

"For your information, I was in the back of the hardware store, trying to keep warm while I waited for you!"

"Well, get in," he snapped.

"I would if you'd unlock the door!" Lucy heard the click of the lock and Cathy yanked the door open. "If I'd had a key . . ." she snarled, lowering herself into the car and slamming the door. No sooner had the door shut than Des floored the accelerator, causing the sports car to fishtail as it zoomed out of the parking lot. Lucy could just imagine Cathy's reaction to Des's driving as they sped off into the distance.

Not a happy marriage, she thought, heading back to the office. It did seem weird that Des didn't allow Cathy to have a key to his car, but then again, some couples liked to keep things separate. She and Bill had joint accounts, joint ownership of their house and vehicles, they'd never thought to do it any other way. She knew they were probably hopelessly old-fashioned and couldn't imagine her daughters happily depositing their paychecks into joint accounts. She remembered hearing of some socialite married to a millionaire who had famously declared, "His money is our money and my money is mine." Crossing the street, she concluded that Des saw it somewhat differently, his car was his car. What about their money? Was that all his, too?

# Chapter Six

Interesting, thought Lucy, continuing on her way to the office. She knew from her own experience that stress at work, especially financial pressure, could seep into the most solid marriages and cause all sorts of friction. Was that what was going on with the Jaspers? If Des was anxious about his business could he be taking that frustration out on Cathy? Or was Cathy resentful because he wasn't turning out to be the breadwinner she expected? Or was it a bit of both?

She remembered lean years when the economy was in recession and demand for Bill's restoration carpentry skills dropped off. Sharply. The high flyers weren't flying high, those huge bonuses weren't coming, and they had to postpone their dreams of fabulous second homes on the coast. Bill hated being idle so he offered his services for free, helping folks insulate and repair their homes, but while that would allow him to build up treasure in heaven it had made paying the bills rather difficult. Lucy became a coupon-clipper and a bargain-hunter, but with the payments due outstripping their diminished income, the mood at home became rather tense. Lucy remembered suggesting to Bill that he ask his father for a loan, "just to tide us over," and his angry reaction when she told him it was either that or applying for food stamps. He was deeply hurt and the worst of it was when he admitted defeat and made the call to his father.

They were in a much better position now, she thought with relief, as she crossed the street. Real estate was booming and those newly purchased houses needed to be updated so demand for Bill's services was higher than ever. The kids were grown and flown, they were empty nesters, and there was much less pressure on the family purse. For the first time in her married life Lucy was discovering she occasionally had money left over at the end of the month.

Yanking the door open and hearing the familiar jingle of the little bell, Lucy saw that Ted's desk was now empty; after checking in at the Tinker's Cove office he usually went on to the Gilead office for most of the week. Breathing a sigh of relief, she gave Phyllis a big smile. "Guess what? I've already got five stickers!"

"I'm way ahead of you," boasted Phyllis. "I've got seven."

"You have? What've you been doing?" asked Lucy, teasing. "Spending like a drunken sailor?"

"No. Just an average weekend," began Phyllis, ticking off her errands on a hand boasting a fabulous manicure featuring five different Easter egg colors, a rainbow on each hand. "Bought paint at the hardware store, picked up Wilf's cholesterol medicine at the drug store, got a birthday present for one of Elfrida's kids at the Toy Chest, got seeds and starter mix at the hardware store, splurged on some breakfast sausage for Wilf at the Smokehouse, collected the dry cleaning, and, oh yeah, bought a birthday cake at the bakery. Arthur insisted he didn't want homemade, he wanted a Darth Vader cake."

"Whew!" exclaimed Lucy, impressed, as she shrugged off her jacket and hung it up. "You must be made of money."

"No, Lucy. I work here."

"Right," said Lucy, sitting at her desk and powering up her computer. She was scrolling through a long list of emails when the bell jangled once again and Randy Lewis entered. He was a bit out of breath, Lucy noticed, thinking perhaps it was because he was a bit overdressed for the weather in a puffy down parka and was lugging a bulky Staples bag.

"Good morning, ladies," he said, unzipping and looking from Lucy to Phyllis. "I've got a press release for you."

"Great, give it here," said Phyllis, stepping up to the reception counter. He withdrew a folded sheet of paper from his parka's inside pocket and handed it to Phyllis, who looked it over. "Closest to the pin, eh? Lucy, maybe you want to do a little feature. It's a fundraiser for the library."

"Sure," said Lucy, who was always happy to promote the Broadbrooks Free Library. Her dear friend, Miss Julia Ward Howe Tilley, who was Miss Tilley to everyone but her closest and oldest friends, had once reigned supreme as the head and only librarian, but was now retired. She had befriended Lucy, who'd visited the library regularly as a young mother with a lively brood in tow, and the relationship had endured despite a huge difference in age. Miss Tilley was now the town's oldest resident and had recently confided in Lucy, "Like my namesake, I 'begin to have fears that I may not be, after all, the greatest woman alive.'" Lucy had, of course, reassured her that her fears on that score were entirely unfounded, but Miss Tilley's increasing age weighed on Lucy. For how much longer would she have Miss T's advice and encouragement?

For Lucy, the library was Miss T's legacy to the town and was therefore something she wanted to support and strengthen. "Sit on down and tell me all about it," she invited Randy, indicating the chair she kept for visitors. "Can

I take your jacket?" asked Lucy, noticing his face was red and a bit sweaty.

"Thanks," he said, sounding grateful as he dropped the bag with a thunk and shrugged out of the bulky parka. "My wife thought it was going to be much colder today than it turned out to be."

Lucy added his parka to the jackets on the coat stand, then joined him at her desk. "Closest to the pin? I'm not familiar with that."

"Never done it but we've heard they can be very successful. I'm on the board of directors at the library, you know, and we asked the town golf course if they'd let us do it on opening day, which is this coming weekend."

"So how does it work?"

"We'll set up at the putting green. A ten-dollar donation to the library gives a golfer a chance to compete by getting his ball closest to the pin, or even better, a hole in one. The prize is a gift certificate for dinner at the Cali Kitchen."

"Not bad. A ten-dollar night out for the lucky winner," said Phyllis.

"Yeah. And the guys who've run them before say a lot of golfers tend to toss in an extra bill or two. I did a bit of research and the pro over at Gray Owl said they had one last year that raised over a thousand dollars."

"That's a lot of books," said Lucy, who had been typing it all into her PC. "What if it rains?"

"We've got that covered, we have a rain date," he said, naming it. "I'm in insurance, Lucy, I believe in risk assessment. No sense taking chances, especially this time of year. Spring is notoriously fickle in Maine."

"So true," said Lucy, hitting the period key and turning to him. "Speaking of risk, any progress on recovering that Klaus egg?"

He shook his head. "Not yet." He paused. "As you

know, I strongly urged the Chamber to insure the egg, but I got voted down. They all scoffed at the notion that anyone in Tinker's Cove would steal it. Couldn't imagine such a thing, but I guess now, with 20-20 hindsight, they think differently. It wasn't expensive, the insurance I mean, and a relatively small investment could've saved the Chamber a lot of grief."

"So true," said Lucy, somewhat amused at Randy's self-serving insistence that he was right when everybody else was wrong. She imagined it was a theme he was only too happy to expand upon with everyone he met. "Any idea who might've done the evil deed?"

"Could be anyone, really. Another thing that the Chamber didn't take into account is the fact that crime rates are up. Not just here but nationwide. Old-fashioned values are disappearing, folks don't seem to know right from wrong."

"Are you sure about that?" asked Lucy. "I mean I've heard it on the news, about the nationwide increase, but I haven't noticed a crime wave here in Tinker's Cove."

"What do you mean?" scoffed Randy. "Somebody took that egg. Stole it. That's grand larceny, for your information."

"If you ask me, my homeowner's insurance rate is grand larceny," offered Phyllis. "Not to mention the auto insurance."

"Well, talk to your neighbors," advised Randy, sounding a bit testy. "Rates only go up because there's more claims. Like I said, more theft, more crashes, up go the rates."

"And, of course, there's climate change. Storms are worse."

"I don't know about that," he snapped. "If you ask me,

we're seeing a moral decline, and we all have to foot the bill for a few bad apples."

Lucy was beginning to feel uncomfortable and wanted to return the conversation to less controversial subjects. "Well, there's a lot of good folks like you, working hard to support our town's treasures, like the library."

"It's just part of being a good citizen," he said, shrugging off the compliment.

"Well, I'll do my best to get the preview a good spot in the paper. Thanks for stopping by."

"No problem," he said, getting to his feet and grabbing his parka off the stand and pulling it on. He picked up the bag and sighed loudly. "No rest for the wicked, I'm afraid. I've got to distribute these flyers, convince folks to let me put 'em up."

"We'll take one," offered Phyllis. "I'll tape it right to the front of the reception counter."

"Okay," he said, handing one over. He paused at the door, said "Good day," and pushed it open, letting it jangle shut behind him.

"Lucy, did you notice that he didn't say thank you? Not even when I took one of his flyers."

"I did. I also noticed that nothing ever seems to be his fault, not even his choice of outerwear."

"On the other hand, he refused to name anyone for the theft. Proof of a clear conscience."

"On the contrary," insisted Lucy. "It's proof that he's the one who did it. He took that egg because the Chamber refused to buy his insurance."

"You've been hanging around Miss Tilley for too long," suggested Phyllis. "You always think the worst of everyone."

"Not everyone," claimed Lucy, who was typing up the notes she'd taken while talking with Randy, turning them into sentences. "Besides, she's usually right."

Lucy was considering giving Miss Tilley a call, just to learn what she thought about the theft of the egg, but Corney Clark's arrival in the office interrupted her train of thought. "Hi, Corney," she said, greeting her with a smile. "Any news on the egg?"

"Unfortunately not," said Corney, plopping down in Lucy's visitor's chair. It was clear that the situation was wearing her down, thought Lucy, observing her somewhat disheveled appearance. Disheveled for Corney, who had skipped her usual lipstick and mascara, had crammed a snug little hat over her hair instead of styling it, and had thrown on a roomy fleece over her leggings. "Honestly, who would think you could walk into a bank and steal a valuable artwork and nobody would notice?"

"There was that bank robbery on Martha's Vineyard," piped up Phyllis, from her corner by the door. "I saw it on the news. Three guys burst into the bank first thing in the morning, tied up the tellers, grabbed the cash, and disappeared. It's an island, you wouldn't think it would be that hard to catch them, but no such luck."

Corney scowled. "It's not luck, it's called police work, and I hate to say it but the Tinker's Cove cops are great at keeping order for the Fourth of July parade, but that's about it."

"The chief would be only too happy to explain how he needs a bigger budget and more manpower," said Lucy, who had heard him expound on this subject numerous times. "It's his favorite subject."

"I've heard all about it," agreed Corney, glumly. "That's why I'm here. To ask you to run an appeal to the public for information about the theft. You know how they say 'If you see something, say something'? Well, I'm begging anyone who even thinks they saw something to give the TCPD a call. It's all we've got."

"No problem," promised Lucy. "I'm on it. I'll get it on-line ASAP."

"You have to think somebody would've caught something on their cell phone," suggested Phyllis. "Everybody's always snapping selfies and recording their kids and cats."

"Maybe that's the problem," began Corney, attempting a small smile, "maybe I should've had some kids and cats at the presentation." She continued, "Bert's a nice guy, but that remodeling was crazy. I really don't know what they were thinking, it doesn't give the tellers any security, and as for the CCTV, it's turned out to be absolutely worthless."

"How come the Chamber didn't insure the egg?" asked Lucy. "I'm not pointing fingers, I'm just wondering. I hear Randy Lewis going on about it all the time."

"I was all for it, but the board voted against it," declared Corney. "You get a fabulous donation, an artwork valued at thousands of dollars, and you don't insure it? Penny-wise and pound-foolish, but that seems to describe a lot of folks around here. Especially Chamber members. Investing a couple hundred dollars in a short-term policy could've prevented this whole mess."

"Well, Phyllis is on to something, I think. I bet somebody's got some video, they just haven't realized it yet," said Lucy, trying to offer some consolation to Corney.

"Hope against hope," replied Corney, standing up and heading for the door. "This is a disaster! Who's going to collect stickers if the big prize is gone?"

"Are you kidding?" Phyllis was incredulous, displaying her Easter card with its seven stickers to Corney. "I'm in it for the chocolate!"

"Me, too," added Lucy, noticing that Corney was actually smiling as she left.

# Chapter Seven

Opening day at the Tinker's Cove Golf Club was always a highly anticipated event, and the fact that it varied from year to year depending on the amount of snow remaining on the greens only added to the golfers' growing sense of impatience. This year the snow actually melted earlier than usual, but no date was early enough for the devoted players who couldn't wait to get out on the greens. Lucy wasn't surprised, therefore, when she arrived at the course and found the parking lot nearly full, with Officer Barney Culpepper directing traffic. Continuing on past the clubhouse, she noticed quite a crowd waiting at the shed to rent carts, and went straight to the putting green where the Closest to the Pin event was taking place.

The contest, it turned out, was a rather low-key affair consisting of Randy Lewis and Bert Cogswell sitting on lawn chairs at a folding table, behind a couple of hand-lettered signs announcing the event as a library fundraiser and listing the prizes. Those prizes included the dinner for two at Cali Kitchen, a fifty-dollar Country Cousins gift certificate, a twenty-five-dollar Macdonald's Farm gift certificate, and a handful of ten-dollar credits at the library's used book store. A couple of Mylar balloons in the shape of golf balls were tied to their chairs and bobbed in the chilly spring breeze. Spotting Lucy, Bert and Randy both waved at her and called to her.

"C'mon down, Lucy, and show us your swing," invited Bert, who was dressed for a long day outdoors in a parka, gloves, and a red-and-white Tinker's Cove Golf Club knitted wool hat topped with a pompon.

"Only ten dollars and you could win a Cali Kitchen dinner for you and Bill," added Randy, also dressed for the weather in his parka, plus earmuffs and deerskin gloves.

"It's a generous prize," said Bert, with a twinkle in his eye. "Enough for a couple of entrees and a bottle of wine, too."

"Okay," agreed Lucy, knowing full well she'd never live it down if she didn't give it the old college try. Problem was, she'd never actually held a golf club, much less tried to hit a little white ball with one. It didn't seem all that hard, she decided, watching Tony Marzetti deliver a smooth swing that sent the ball rolling toward the hole marked by a fluttering flag, and right on by, finally stopping about a yard away.

"Too bad, Tony," called Bert.

"I hit it too hard," admitted Tony, with a shrug and a smile. "But the money goes for a good cause."

"Want to try again?" offered Randy.

Tony cast his eye toward the deck behind the clubhouse, where he spotted the other members of his foursome, waving at him. "Looks like they're ready to tee off," he said. "I gotta go."

"Bring 'em all 'round when you're done," suggested Bert. "We'll still be here."

"Will do," promised Tony, shoving his club into his bag. He hoisted the bag on his shoulder and gave a little salute before heading up the hill to join the others.

By now a little crowd of onlookers had gathered, and a small queue of players had lined up behind her at the table, waiting their turns. Lucy handed over her ten dollars and was given a golf ball and a club, which Bert informed her was a putter. Telling herself not to think about the crowd of people watching, and picturing Tony's swing in her mind, she stepped up to the tee and placed the ball. She stretched out her arms, wrapped her hands around the club, and was about to whack the ball when Randy stopped her.

"No, no, Lucy," he said, taking the club from her and demonstrating. "You put your hands like this."

"Oh, okay," said Lucy, doing as he'd showed her and beginning to swing.

"Not so fast!" he warned, stopping her. "Your feet aren't right. Spread 'em a bit apart, like this."

Lucy observed Randy's stance, and copied it. "Now?" she asked. "Should I swing?"

He stepped back, advised her to adjust one foot, and told her to keep her eye on the ball and give it her best shot. Lucy raised the club as she'd seen Randy do, whipped it around, and sent the ball flying over the pin with its fluttering pennant and on across the green into the rough grass.

The people in the crowd groaned, a few chuckled, and Randy patted her shoulder. "Good try," he said. "Want another?"

"Uh, no," said Lucy. "It seems I'm not cut out for golf. But I'll stick around for a bit, in case you get a winner."

Randy leaned forward, and whispered into her ear, "If I were a betting man, I'd put my money on Franny."

"Really?"

He nodded, indicating the line at the table, where Franny

was up next. Somewhat surprised, Lucy noticed she was wearing golf shoes and a windbreaker with the TCGC logo, and was toting a wheelie cart loaded with a bag full of various clubs, some topped with colorful little socks. Franny, it seemed, was a keen golfer, something which Lucy had not been aware of. She was thinking of a possible feature story for *The Courier* as she joined the growing crowd of onlookers.

They all watched, chatting among themselves, as Franny handed over her money and was provided with a ball. As she proceeded to the tee Lucy noted she walked easily, as if she did this sort of thing every day. Maybe she did, thought Lucy, watching as Franny plucked a club from her bag, placed her ball, and squared up. She held the club in outstretched arms and shifted her weight from foot to foot, swinging her hips, then eyed the distance between her ball and the pin. Satisfied, she lowered her head, swung the club, and sent the ball rolling neatly across the green to the pin, where it stopped a mere inch from the hole.

"Brava!!" exclaimed Bert, as the crowd applauded. "I think we might have a winner."

"I'm not counting my chickens just yet," said Franny, with a smile. "Somebody could get a hole-in-one."

"Mebbe," added Randy, "but right now you're definitely in the lead."

"Fingers crossed," said Franny, replacing her club in her bag and pulling it along to the sidelines, where she greeted Lucy. "Great day for the fundraiser," she said, with a nod at the growing line of contestants waiting their turns at the tee. "I think they'll raise a lot of money for the library."

"You're the favorite so far," said Lucy. "I didn't even know you play golf."

Franny shrugged. "I picked it up after I retired when I

was invited to join a group of women who play every week. The guys complain we're too slow but that's ridiculous. We play hard and we're actually quite competitive. We won the Mid-Coast Ladies Championship last year."

"Good for you! I think this deserves a feature story."

Franny wasn't averse to the idea, but was quick to give credit where credit was due. "The other three are much better than I am, especially Sandy Lenk, Dave Forrest's wife. She played in college and almost went pro, but got sidelined when she married Dave. He, you know, was a top player in college and did go pro for a few years before settling down at the Lenks' jewelry store."

"Speak of the devil, there they are," said Lucy, observing Dave and Sandy, who had just arrived.

"Dave has a good chance of getting a hole-in-one, but I wonder if Sandy's going to enter the contest, too," mused Franny. "She hasn't been playing much this year, which is a real loss for our team since we have to keep recruiting a fourth."

"Health problems?" asked Lucy, thinking that even though Sandy and Dave were walking together toward the putting green, they weren't chatting with each other and seemed somewhat distant, out of sync.

"Hardly," said Franny, with a little smirk. "Rumor has it that she has a new interest."

"I assume you're not talking about stamp collecting," said Lucy, noticing that Sandy had brightened up her hair color and was unusually tanned for spring in Tinker's Cove. Spray on?

Franny chuckled. "Definitely not stamp collecting."

The couple joined the line at the table together, but when it was their turn to register only Dave signed up. Sandy stepped aside, joining the folks who were watching the contest. There was a definite buzz among the crowd when Dave stepped up to the tee; his prowess was well known among the town's golfers.

"He got a bunch of holes-in-one last summer," Lucy heard someone say.

"What's his handicap?" asked another.

"I dunno. Must be pretty good," responded the first, only to be hushed by a couple of others as Dave pulled a club from his bag.

He was well aware of his reputation and started to ham it up a bit, beginning with some stretches and then taking a few practice swings. The swings grew broader as the crowd began responding, cheering him on. Dave was clearly enjoying himself, putting on quite a show until, suddenly, he gave an extra wide swing and his club hit his bag, which was propped by his side on two extendable supports. It fell over with a clunking sound, a couple of irons slid out, followed ever so slowly by a rolling object. Not a golf ball, it was the missing Karl Klaus egg.

# Chapter Eight

Unfortunately for Dave, it just happened that Barney Culpepper was taking a break from parking lot duty and was passing by the contest on his way to the clubhouse, where he planned to use the restroom and get a coffee. Hearing the sudden silence as everyone reacted to the unexpected and shocking sight, he paused to investigate. That's when he noticed the stolen egg, nestled in a tuft of bright green spring grass, gleaming in the sunshine.

"What have we got here?" he demanded, marching right up to the egg and pointing at it. By now everybody was talking, murmuring among themselves. As for Lucy, she knew news when she saw it and had immediately pulled out her phone and was snapping photos of the egg and the encounter between Dave and Barney.

"I don't know," sputtered Dave, who seemed shocked and was quick to defend himself. "It just rolled out of my bag. I don't know how it got there. I didn't, I wouldn't steal it. I'd never do such a thing. Somebody must've put it in my bag. Hiding it. That's the only explanation."

"Well, mebbe that's true and mebbe it isn't," said Barney. "I'm afraid you're gonna have to come down to the station with me. First I gotta secure the scene," he added, calling for backup on his radio.

Dave wisely decided that the less he said, the better, so he simply stood with Barney, waiting for reinforcements to arrive. His wife, Sandy, was beside him, supposedly offering support but with a resentful expression. The contest was halted but most of the bystanders remained, curious to see what happened next. They didn't have long to wait before Officer Todd Kirwan arrived, along with his cousin Officer Sally Kirwan. They ordered everyone to move back and began laying yellow crime scene tape around the golf bag and the egg. When they finished they suggested everyone move along, insisting there was "nothing more to see here, folks."

Meanwhile, Barney led Dave away quietly while everyone was watching the other officers secure the scene with tape. Lucy noticed he hadn't handcuffed Dave, who was cooperating, but he did keep a firm hand on his upper arm. Dave clearly had a lot of explaining to do.

The crowd was beginning to disperse when Dave's wife, Sandy, suddenly burst loudly into tears. "He's innocent! How can they do this? It's police brutality, that's what it is."

Lucy somewhat cynically decided to take advantage of the moment, hoping to get some insight into this shocking development. Remembering that Franny had played on the same foursome with Sandy, she grabbed her by the hand and pulled her along to console Sandy. Stepping beside the weeping woman, Lucy patted her on the back. "Don't worry," she said. "I'm sure it will all be straightened out at the station."

"That's right," cooed Franny, handing her a tissue. "He'll be back home in time for lunch."

"I hope so," sobbed Sandy, using the tissue to dab at her eyes. "I can't imagine our home without him. He could go to prison for years!"

"There, there," offered Lucy, shocked that Sandy had already tried and convicted her husband.

"What am I going to tell my folks?" she asked, shoulders shaking. "That my husband is a thief?"

"Of course not," said Lucy. "He's not a thief. There's some innocent explanation."

"But I just don't know what it could be," admitted Sandy, swallowing thickly and shaking her head. "And I've noticed things lately. He's not quite himself, and he struggles to remember things. Misses appointments, you know, and misplaces things. I found his dirty socks in the freezer!"

"Early onset dementia?" asked Lucy.

"I'm so afraid," whispered Sandy. "What's going to happen to us?"

"Now, now," clucked Franny. "It may just be a vitamin deficiency. No need to panic."

"And there are new treatments all the time," added Lucy.

"I'm so confused," admitted Sandy. "I don't know what to do. Should I go to the station?"

"Probably not," advised Lucy. "If they're questioning him they won't let you see him."

"If I were you," suggested Franny, "I'd call a lawyer."

Sandy's eyes widened. "A lawyer! Won't that make things worse? It's like admitting guilt, isn't it?"

"Just to be on the safe side," said Franny, patting her hand.

"To protect his rights," added Lucy, dropping her phone in her bag and shouldering it. She had breaking news and needed to get back to the office. "I've got to go," she said, checking with Franny.

"Of course," agreed Franny. "I'll stay with Sandy."

Lucy couldn't quite figure out what was going on with

Sandy, who was definitely sending mixed messages claiming Dave was innocent at the same time she was offering theories about why he took the egg. She took a moment to look back as she headed to the parking lot and saw that Franny seemed to have the situation well in hand. She was taking Sandy into the clubhouse, most likely for a restorative cup of tea. Or maybe something stronger.

Driving back to the office, she continued to wonder about Sandy's reaction. She'd seen Dave just the other day in his shop, when she got that new battery for her watch. He seemed very much himself that day and wasn't the least bit confused. He'd greeted her by name, he knew who she was, and he knew what battery her watch required. What sort of game was Sandy playing? And what about Franny's claim that Sandy had found a new interest? Did she want to get rid of Dave? And if so, was she simply milking the situation or had she actually stolen and planted the egg herself?

Lucy slowed the car when she reached Main Street and thought to herself that maybe she ought to slow her runaway thoughts, too. It was one thing to speculate about behavior and motives, but she was a responsible journalist and needed to stick to the facts. Those facts, so far, were limited to the theft of the egg, and its discovery in Dave Forrest's golf bag. Dave had insisted he knew nothing about it, but there was no way for her to know if that was the truth. As for Sandy's reaction, people often reacted oddly to stressful situations. Furthermore, Franny's innuendo that Sandy was involved in an affair was nothing but rumor.

She continued on slowly, looking for a parking space and not having much luck since the town was busy on Saturday mornings as folks ticked off the errands on their lists. She'd almost resigned herself to circling back and parking in the scrappy little area behind the office when a giant SUV pulled out right in front of her and drove off at high speed, vacating a spot in front of Cove Jewelry. She swung right in, turned off the ignition, and climbed out, deciding that since she was there she might as well go in and tell Alison what happened at the golf course.

There were no customers in the store when Lucy entered and Alison was on her knees, busily spraying glass cleaner on the showcases and wiping them down with paper towels. She looked up and greeted Lucy with a smile, gave the case a final wipe, and got to her feet. "Just taking advantage of a quiet moment," she said, brushing the knees of her slacks. An attractive woman in her late thirties, she was dressed in coastal casual clothes, wearing a turtleneck sweater and loafers; she had pearl studs in her ears and a gold watch on her wrist. "What can I do for you?"

"I've got some bad news, I'm afraid," began Lucy.

"Oh, Lucy, I'm so sorry. Is it one of your kids? Bill?"

"No, no. It's Dave."

"Dave!" exclaimed Alison. "What's happened?"

"The oddest thing. He was competing at the Closest to the Pin fundraiser at the golf course and when he swung his club he knocked over his golf bag and the egg, the Karl Klaus egg, rolled out."

Alison could not have looked more surprised. "What?" she finally said, furrowing her brow and shaking her head. "That doesn't make any sense at all."

"He claims someone planted it," offered Lucy.

"Well, that must be it, then," insisted Alison. "Dave is scrupulously honest. I've seen him run down the street after a customer who got the wrong change."

"His wife was there, she suggested he's been having some senior moments . . ."

Alison cut her off. "That's ridiculous. I'm probably with him more than Sandy, if you think about it. We've even joked about it, how we're together more hours of the day than we are with our families. I know Dave pretty well and I can say he never misplaces tools or items, he knows everybody in town and remembers their names and their kids' names, and their spouses' names. He remembers who they went to school with, what sport they played, believe me, you don't need Google, you can just ask Dave and he'll reel off all the information about just about anyone in town. And if he's promised to repair your watch by a certain date, or fix that broken chain, he'll get it done, probably ahead of time. A Dave Forrest promise is a promise kept."

Lucy was somewhat stunned by Alison's defense of her employer, but also impressed. He must really be one of the good guys to inspire such loyalty. "So you're absolutely certain he wouldn't have stolen the egg?" asked Lucy.

"Absolutely. The only way that egg could be in Dave's bag is if somebody else put it there. I mean, if he'd discovered it, he would have taken it straight to the police station himself."

Lucy thought this over. The golf course had been closed until today so Dave would have had no reason to use his golf bag. "Do you happen to know where he keeps his golf bag?"

"Oh, sure. In the back of his car. It's a Honda CRV."

"Even in the off season?"

"Yeah," she said, chuckling. "He says the weight is good on icy roads, but I think he simply can't bear to be parted from the thing. And once the course is open he likes to pop over for a quick hole or two at lunch time."

Lucy knew that few people in Tinker's Cove bothered to

lock their cars, but thought it was a question worth asking. "Does he lock his car?"

Alison scoffed at the thought. "No. Not Dave. He's trusting, too trusting, if you ask me. I have to make sure the alarm is set here in the store and lock up when we leave for the night. Dave would just walk out and leave the door unlocked."

"So anyone could have put the egg in his bag," concluded Lucy.

"Absolutely."

"Thanks, Alison. You've confirmed what I thought."

"No problem, Lucy. So where is Dave? Did they arrest him?"

"I'm not sure. The police are taking it seriously. Barney took him to the station, for questioning. They're investigating the golf bag and the egg, they've set up a crime scene around it at the course."

"Golly, what a mess." Alison shook her head. "I hope Dave is cleared soon."

"Time will tell," said Lucy, wondering if Dave was the victim of a prank. She remembered Zach Starr suggesting that Dave was the thief; maybe Zach stole the egg and planted it as a joke. The more she thought about it, the likelier it seemed.

"Well, sorry to be the bearer of bad news but I thought you should know."

"Thanks for stopping by, Lucy."

Lucy walked over to the door and paused. "Keep the faith," she said, by way of parting.

Alison managed a little smile and a goodbye wave, then reached for the bottle of glass cleaner.

# Chapter Nine

Next stop was just a few doors down Main Street, at Zach Starr's Sea Smoke vape shop. If Zach had indeed set up Dave as a prank, it was high time he learned what had happened and revealed the truth. It was fortunate that Lucy didn't have far to go to the shop because her anger grew with each step. What a mean thing to do, she fumed, right foot. Imagine setting up an innocent man, left foot. How would he like it if someone did that to him, right foot. She marched along like that until she found herself under the billowing smoke and yanked the door open.

"Hi, Lucy," said Zach, completely unperturbed. He presented a somewhat forbidding appearance, dressed as he was in bike leathers and sporting a bristly beard, but he appeared to be a surprisingly adept salesman as he showed a variety of vape pens to a young woman whose hair was dyed bright pink. "I'll be with you in a minute," he told Lucy, with an easy smile.

His estimate turned out to be wildly optimistic as Little Miss Pink, as Lucy thought of her, simply couldn't make up her mind. And once she'd settled on a pen, which might be the right one but then again, might not, there was the large number of flavor options to consider. Lucy found herself drumming her fingers rather impatiently on the counter, which eventually prompted Zach to advise the girl to take all the time she needed to make her choice and turned to Lucy. "What's up, Lucy? I didn't know you vaped."

"I don't," she snapped, then caught herself and moderated her tone. She wasn't going to get much information from Zach if she was confrontational. "Sorry. It's been a crazy day so far. Police are questioning Dave Forrest about the egg; it rolled out of his golf bag at the Closest to the Pin contest this morning."

Zach was a pretty cool customer, but the news did seem to take him by surprise. "Really?" he asked, furrowing his brow in puzzlement.

"Yeah, so it seems you were right all along when you said he was the likely culprit."

Zach held up his hands in protest. "I was just playing devil's advocate, joshing, 'cause he absolutely seemed the least likely person." He shook his head. "Dave Forrest? Wow."

His puzzlement seemed entirely genuine, which caused Lucy to reconsider her suspicious thoughts. "You know," she began, "I wondered if maybe you'd planted it on him as a sort of joke."

Zach wasn't offended, he wasn't the least bit defensive. "That woulda been kind of funny, I guess, but it never occurred to me. Do you think that's what happened? A joke?"

Lucy thought of Dave, who was likely sitting in an interview room, trying to convince a team of seasoned and jaded investigators of his innocence. He was no doubt terrified, wondering if life in prison was as awful as he'd heard and hoping against hope that he wouldn't find out.

"Um, I think I'm going to go with Frulicious," said Little Miss Pink, sounding as if she was declaring something momentous. A cure for cancer, maybe, or an end to hunger.

"Great choice!" boomed Zach, turning back to her.

"But I'm not sure about the pen . . ." she said, letting her hand, which was tattooed with a blooming rose at the base of her thumb, flutter over the display. "This one is kinda cool but that one there looks more me, maybe?"

"I'll be on my way," said Lucy.

"Thanks for stopping by," said Zach, before launching into his spiel. "All of these pens are top quality but . . ."

Lucy didn't hear the rest, she was dodging the cloud of smoke outside the shop, telling herself that it must be harmless, right? You couldn't just pour cancer-causing chemicals into the atmosphere, could you?

Lucy went straight to the empty *Courier* office, where she wrote up an account of the egg's surprise appearance at the Closest to the Pin contest, as well as Dave Forrest's possible connection to the theft. She was careful not to identify him as the thief, he was presumed innocent after all, and she included quotes from Alison and Zach that she'd gathered. That job done, she resolved to forget about work for the rest of her weekend as she pulled the door shut and made sure it was locked behind her. The little bell was jangling faintly as she made her way to the car, intent on enjoying the remainder of her weekend.

Lucy kept to her resolve, ignoring the occasional pings from her cell phone that announced texts, and didn't find time to check her emails, either. Sara had come home for the weekend and she enjoyed catching up with her daughter and putting together a box of Easter treats to send to her grandson Patrick, who lived in Alaska.

Monday morning came all too soon, along with a text message from DA Phil Aucoin announcing that Dave Forrest would be arraigned later that morning in District Court. No formal press conference was announced, but she knew that Aucoin would certainly make himself available to answer questions after the arraignment. Curious as to what prompted this development, she called the police department and spoke to Officer Sally Kirwan, who occasionally gave her inside info.

"I know they wanted to press Dave hard and get a confession," said Sally, "but he got Bob Goodman in right away and he availed himself of his right to remain silent."

"Did they keep him in the lockup?"

"No. Bob got them to agree to let him go, pending arraignment."

"Do they really think they've got a case?" asked Lucy.

"Well, you know what they say about possession . . ."

"It's nine-tenths of the law," admitted Lucy, thanking Sally before ending the call. She took her time getting over to the courthouse in Gilead; court didn't go into session until ten and Monday mornings always began with a number of folks who'd gotten themselves in trouble over the weekend.

The morning arraignments were well under way when Lucy slipped into the courtroom, where she noticed Dave Forrest sitting quietly beside Bob Goodman in the general seating area. An assistant DA was standing before the judge, enumerating the charges against the various hungover OUI offenders and the scruffy, unshaven domestic abusers who'd spent the night in jail. Dave Forrest was called last, charged with grand larceny, and the assistant DA requested bail, suggesting five thousand dollars.

Bob immediately objected, pointing out that Dave Forrest did not have a record, was a respected local businessman and family man, and presented no flight risk whatsoever. His client, he claimed, was eager to prove his innocence.

The judge agreed, and Dave was released on his own recognizance. Free to go, he dodged the reporters and TV crews, leaving through a side door. DA Phil Aucoin and police chief Jim Kirwan had arranged for an impromptu presser in the lobby, and were standing behind some mics when Lucy exited the courtroom. They were already embarked on the usual litany at such events, praising interdepartmental cooperation and lauding the quick resolution of this difficult and challenging case, so when Lucy spotted Bob Goodman sitting on a nearby bench she went to join him. Bob was intent on arranging some papers in his briefcase, but looked up when she sat beside him.

"Good work in there," she said. "What are Dave's chances in the trial?"

"Pretty good, I think," said Bob. "It's pretty obvious he was set up. He's a smart guy, and if he had actually stolen the egg, why wouldn't he do a better job of hiding it? It's not that big, it would be easy enough to stash it someplace, right? Nobody in their right mind would keep it in their golf bag, especially if they were planning on playing golf."

"Good point," said Lucy, chuckling. "But Aucoin seems to be quite convinced . . ."

"It's all about votes, Lucy. There's always another election coming up and he's grabbing every opportunity to get attention."

"But what if he loses the case?"

"I guess then he won't be holding a press conference," said Bob.

Lucy laughed. "What's going on with Karl Klaus? Any progress?"

"Well, Rachel tells me that Rosie's over the moon. She can't say enough good stuff about him. The apprentices all adore him, and he's happy as a clam sculpting bones for the puppets and enjoying all the attention."

"Who'd guess?" mused Lucy. "What about that Mike guy?"

"Well, he kind of just moved in on Karl about six months ago, offering to help him with heavy lifting and stuff like that. He gradually began taking over more and more, becoming a sort of amanuensis. He did all sorts of errands, he shopped, cooked meals, handled shipments and ordering, until Karl really came to depend on him. And you know Karl, he's not exactly reality-based, so he just went along with everything. If Mike asked him to sign something, he did. That's how Mike gradually got control of all his assets and when Karl went off to New Hampshire to collect his St. Gaudens Prize Mike changed the locks."

"Are you going to be able to make a case, press charges?"

"Oh, yeah." Bob pressed his lips together, as if holding in a big secret, then broke into a big smile. "In fact, Lucy, the sheriff is going to raid the place tomorrow and arrest Mike Green."

Lucy knew this would be a big scoop. "When?"

"He didn't give me a time, but they usually do raids like that first thing in the morning. Before sunrise even, to catch 'em by surprise."

"Oh, Lord," sighed Lucy. "Are you going to be there?"

"Me? No way. I'll be in deep REM."

"I'll be thinking of you all warm and cozy when I'm out there in the dark, shivering."

"Admit it. You love this stuff, Lucy."

Lucy stood up and swung her bag over her shoulder. "Thanks for the tip," she said, smiling.

\* \* \*

Next morning, when the alarm went off at four a.m., Lucy quickly silenced it before Bill even stirred. She hopped out of bed in a spurt of unusual energy, excited about covering an actual police raid. This wasn't the sort of thing that happened every day in Tinker's Cove or even in the county, it was the sort of thing that was a mainstay of TV cop dramas but had occurred only rarely in her years as a reporter. Planning ahead, she'd laid her clothes out in the guest room and it was there that she dressed, pulling on several warm layers. She then tiptoed downstairs in her socks, switched on the coffeepot, and ate a yogurt while it dripped. When the coffee was ready she filled a thermos, pulled on her boots and added her warmest jacket, and quietly left the house.

There was no traffic on the winding country roads that led to Karl Klaus's studio and Lucy was soon there, parked discreetly along a stone wall, underneath a huge pine tree. There was a full moon so she had a good view of the barn Klaus had converted to a studio; a single glowing window seemed to indicate a night light had been left on inside. As she waited, she recalled the one time she'd been inside the studio. It was years ago when she'd been doing a series of features about local artists, and she had been struck at the time with the minimal adaptations Klaus had made in the aged structure. He hadn't really renovated the space at all but had simply knocked out the things he didn't need and added those he did. A tack room served as a sort of bedroom; he'd added a hot plate and refrigerator to one stall creating a minimal kitchen and had knocked down several other stalls in order to create a large work space. Tools of all sorts hung from nails pounded into the walls and electrical wires were strung from the beams. She'd wondered at the time that the whole thing hadn't burned down, but the fates had been on Karl's side and the wonky old barn had survived.

Lucy had finished her coffee and was debating peeing in the woods, always an awkward affair and especially so given the number of layers she was wearing, when the sheriff's cruiser appeared and rolled silently into the barn's driveway. It was followed by a second cruiser, marked K-9, and a van which was angled across the drive, essentially blocking the exit. There was a delay as final arrangements were put in place, then all the lights on the various vehicles were flipped on and the sheriff's voice was heard over a bullhorn. "Police, come out with your hands up."

Wow, thought Lucy, just like a movie. She had climbed out of her car and was standing behind the stone wall, from which vantage point she had a clear view of the events as they unfolded. She also had a camera which she could use to capture photos at night.

There was no response from the barn, so the sheriff repeated his demand. Seconds later the dog barked and strained against the leash; Green had apparently gone out a back door and was hightailing it through the woods. The chase was on, led by the barking dog, a single shot was heard, and the officers returned with Green in tow, handcuffed.

After snapping a few photos, Lucy approached the sheriff.

"What are you doing here?" he demanded.

"I had a tip," she said. "Do you have a moment?"

The sheriff satisfied himself that Green had been confined to the back of a cruiser, then turned to her. "Okay."

"I heard a shot," began Lucy.

"Warning shot, we'd caught up to him. He was tangled up in some briars."

"It seemed like a very smooth operation," suggested Lucy.

"Yup. Went pretty much according to plan. He did try to run for it, but Captain, that's our K-9 officer, was right on him."

"I assume Green's going to be charged with defrauding the sculptor Karl Klaus . . ."

"Aucoin will have all the details," said the sheriff, clearly ready to be done with the interview. "Meanwhile, we're going to search the premises, seize any evidence, the usual thing."

"Well, congratulations on a well-executed arrest," said Lucy.

The sheriff smiled. "Nobody got hurt," he said, adding with a chuckle, "apart from our suspect, who's pretty scratched up. Those briars can be real nasty."

Back in her car, with the heater on high, Lucy reviewed her photos. The little screen on her digital camera revealed she'd gotten the entire episode, including some terrific snaps of K-9 Officer Captain in action. She decided she didn't need to stay any longer, she remembered passing a gas station a short way down the road and she needed a restroom.

That mission completed, she purchased an energy bar and headed back to Tinker's Cove, chomping on the nut and grain bar as she drove. She was pretty pleased with her scoop and was thinking about the rest of her day, which she planned to quit early, after covering the drawing for the prize Easter basket, now complete with its golden egg. She had just stopped at the town's single traffic light, on Main Street, when the fire department ambulance suddenly emerged from the station with its siren blaring and lights flashing.

Lucy waited impatiently for the light to turn green and the second it did, she was off after the ambulance, which had pulled to a stop at Cove Jewelry. The EMTs were already out and racing up the outside staircase that led to the apartment occupied by Dave and his wife, Sandy Lenk; they were soon joined by police officers Sally Kirwan and Barney Culpepper. Moments later Sally came down the stairs and went into the shop.

Figuring this was her best chance to find out what was going on, Lucy got out of the car and entered the shop, where she found Alison sitting on a chair, with Officer Sally standing beside her holding a box of tissues. "I couldn't believe it, all that blood, and poor Dave," she heard Alison say before she completely broke down in sobs, shoulders heaving. Sally was pulling out tissues when she spotted Lucy.

"Sorry, Lucy, but you'll have to leave."

"No problem," said Lucy, turning to go. "Is Dave going to be all right?"

Hearing this, Alison began to wail and Sally shook her head. Taking this for a no, Lucy stepped outside, encountering Barney.

"What's up?" she asked. "Did Dave have an accident?"

"Nope," said Barney, shaking his head, jowls quivering. "Looks like he did it on purpose. Blew his brains out."

Lucy felt her knees go all wobbly and Barney grabbed her. "Steady on," he said.

"Sorry," said Lucy, taking a deep breath. "Wasn't expecting that."

"Yeah," agreed Barney. "He's the last guy you'd think would do a thing like that."

Yeah, thought Lucy, heading back to her car. Dave was sure full of surprises.

# Chapter Ten

Completely shaken by Dave's death, Lucy made her way down the street to the *Courier* office. Phyllis was at her desk, the coffeepot was dripping, the air was overheated. "Smells like a coffee shop," observed Lucy, plunking herself down at her desk, where she pulled off her hat and began unwrapping her muffler.

"Were you planning on a trip to the Arctic?" inquired Phyllis, who had gotten up and was adjusting the old-fashioned wooden window blinds to let in some daylight; not sunlight since it was a cloudy, lowering sort of day.

"No. I was up early," said Lucy. It took her a moment or two to clear her mind and recall exactly why she'd needed to dress so warmly. "I covered a predawn police raid. At Karl Klaus's studio. The sheriff arrested the guy who scammed him."

"Was there trouble?" asked Phyllis. "You don't seem quite yourself."

"The raid went off like clockwork, but when I came back I saw the ambulance racing down the street. It stopped at Cove Jewelry. I drove down and," here Lucy's voice broke and she took a deep breath before continuing, "they said Dave Forrest is dead. He shot himself."

Phyllis's eyes widened and she ran to the door, pushed it

open, and stepped outside. The little bell was still jangling when she stepped back in and shut it. "I can't believe it. Dave?" She collapsed in her desk chair. "The ambulance is still there," she said, shaking her head. "I heard it go by when I was opening up and making the coffee." She paused. "That's really awful." Another pause, as the wheels turned round. "Do you think it was because of the egg? Being accused of stealing it and all?"

Lucy was staring at her blank computer screen, her mind awhirl with competing thoughts. "I don't think so. Bob Goodman told me that case was an obvious set up. He said it was ridiculous to think someone as smart as Dave would hide the egg in his golf bag if he had actually stolen it."

"Must've been something else, then," speculated Phyllis, as the door opened and Cathy Jasper, Des's wife, came in. Her roots were showing, her lips were chapped, and she was burdened with a couple of tote bags that made her look like a woman who had a long to-do list.

"What's all the fuss down the street?" she asked, as she began digging in one of the totes.

"Dave Forrest. He shot himself," offered Phyllis.

"Dave?" Cathy's jaw dropped. "Is he going to be okay?"

"He's dead," said Lucy.

"Oh, my," said Cathy, forgetting her errand. "That's a shocker." She shook her head. "Nice guy, thriving business, good health . . . 'course there was that business with the egg. Poor Sandy . . ." she sighed. "I guess you never really know what's going on in somebody's head, not even your husband's." She resumed digging in her tote bag. "Not that I thought he actually stole it. Probably just a prank."

"Well, if that's true, this one sure backfired," observed Lucy, who had finally gotten around to booting up her PC.

"He might've been depressed about his marriage," said Phyllis. "In fact, people are saying that Sandy's having an affair."

"I've heard rumors, too," said Lucy, remembering Sandy's fake tan and frosted hair. If Dave had discovered that she was unfaithful that might have been the proverbial straw that broke the camel's back.

"Where did you hear that?" snapped Cathy.

Lucy turned to Phyllis, all ears.

"At that new lingerie shop," said Phyllis. "Elfrida dragged me there, she said I needed a better bra."

Lucy smiled, wanly. "I thought you looked uplifted lately."

"I am." Phyllis patted her bosom. "Turns out I was wearing the wrong sort of bra, the wrong size, wrong style, wrong everything. Girls like me with generous curves need extra support."

"But what about Sandy, and this affair?" asked Cathy, in a rather sharp tone of voice.

"Oh, well, while I was in the changing room . . . really nice, by the way, very fancy. And while I was trying on the bras that Mallory suggested, I heard her and Elfie talking. Elfie was saying how sexy some of the stuff was and she wished she had an excuse to buy something and Mallory was saying that you didn't need an excuse, that Sandy Lenk, for example, came in almost every week just to treat herself."

"Really? It must be nice to be able to afford expensive treats just for yourself," scoffed Cathy.

"There's more," said Phyllis, raising her eyebrows. "Elfie asked about that, like really just for herself? And Mallory said Sandy slipped one day and said something like 'He'll love this' and Mallory asked if it was for her husband and she didn't answer but gave a sort of suggestive smile."

"A smile? Could mean anything," said Cathy, finally producing a rather crumpled sheet of paper. "Here it is. It's a help wanted ad."

"Join the crowd," said Phyllis, settling back at her desk. "Everybody wants to hire, but nobody wants to work."

"It's just a formality. Des says he's got to show a good faith effort to hire locally before the government will approve visas for foreign workers." She glanced at the clock. "Gosh. I've got a car full of donuts to take over to the bank."

"Are you working at the bank now?" asked Lucy, puzzled. As far as she knew, Cathy was the working partner in the property management business while Des was supposedly the brains.

"No. It's for the Chamber. Des volunteered donuts for the Easter Basket drawing. And when Des volunteers . . ."

Lucy laughed. "It's Cathy who does the volunteering."

"You got that right," sighed Cathy. "I better get over there, the drawing's in half an hour and I have to get the refreshments set up."

"I'll see you there," promised Lucy.

"Uh, there's the matter of the payment for the ad . . ." said Phyllis.

Cathy didn't pause on her way to the door. "Just put it on our account," she said, making her escape.

Word of Dave's suicide had gotten around fast and it was a rather subdued group that gathered later that morning at the Seamen's Bank. People were huddled in small groups, murmuring and shaking their heads at this tragic development.

"Why on earth?" wondered Bert Cogswell. "Why would he do something like that?"

"Embarrassment?" wondered Nate Macdonald.

"Personally, I wish we'd never started this promotion, with that damn egg," said Tony Marzetti. "More trouble than it was worth, if you ask me."

Eddie Culpepper was helping himself to a second donut, and getting a reproving glance from his mother, Marge, when Lucy approached him. "How's the tooth?" she asked.

"Working just fine, as you can see," said Marge, in a disapproving tone.

"Boys have big appetites," said Lucy.

"Takes after his father," observed Marge, referring to Barney. She lowered her voice. "Awful about Dave. I feel so bad for Sandy. You can only imagine what she's feeling." She paused, shaking her head as Eddie reached for a third donut. "It's the ones left behind who suffer the most."

Lucy was about to respond when Corney Clark clapped her hands, announcing the drawing was about to begin. Everyone gathered around the table holding the Easter basket, which was now accompanied by a large stoneware crock containing all the completed entries.

"First of all, I want to say that our town has suffered a terrible loss this morning . . ."

There was a collective murmur of assent.

"Our thoughts and prayers are with Dave's family, especially his wife, Sandy."

Another murmur.

"Dave was a terrific guy, a friend to all and a strong supporter of our town and the Chamber, in particular, and he will be missed by many."

Nods and sighs all round.

"But now we have important business to conduct, the drawing for our fabulous Easter basket, with the Karl Klaus egg." She waved her hand gracefully, indicating the

Easter basket. "And I'm happy to report that our Easter Egg promotion was a stunning success, that crock contains over two hundred entries representing shoppers who spent at least a total of one hundred dollars collecting stickers."

Lucy sighed, aware that she was not one of them. Her card had gone missing, somewhere, before she completed it.

Corney continued, crowing about the successful promotion, declaring, "If you do the math, that adds up to twenty thousand dollars going into our local economy from this promotion!"

This announcement was greeted with applause.

Corney held up her hand, for silence. "And that is just from the completed cards; we know a lot of people started collecting stickers but didn't complete their cards." There was a murmur of agreement from a number of people in the crowd, including Lucy. Corney expressed her sympathy for the losers with a smile, then continued. "I, for one, am very grateful to all the folks who participated and now, I need a volunteer to pick the winning card."

There was a shuffling of feet and a lot of glancing, and then Jen Holden, the teller, raised her hand. "I'll do it."

"Great! Come on down, Jen."

Jen tossed back her long blond hair and made her way through the crowd, a serious expression on her face. Reaching the table, she paused and looked to Corney for direction.

"Give it a stir," urged Corney, leading a countdown, which everyone joined. "Ten, nine, eight . . ." As each number was called Jen enthusiastically stirred the entries.

"This is harder than it looks," confessed Jen, with a laugh, as they got down to the final numbers. "Two, one and here's the winner," she exclaimed, holding up a card and handing it to Corney.

"Franny Small! Franny Small is the winner. Is Franny here?"

"Oh, my goodness!" exclaimed Franny, flustered. "I never expected to win!"

"This is two times, isn't it?" inquired Bert. "You won the Closest to the Pin, didn't you?"

Franny's face turned quite red, but she quickly recovered. "I guess I'm just lucky," she said. "I never expected to win, I just wanted to support the promotion. And in that spirit, I plan to sell the Karl Klaus egg and use the money to establish a girls' golf program at the town course."

Her announcement was met with general approval and applause. Then Zach Starr cleared his throat and asked, "What about the chocolate? You going to share that, too?"

Franny's answer was quick. "No. No way," she said, which got a big laugh.

Some people began to leave, others tucked into the donuts and coffee, and Lucy approached Franny for a quick interview.

"Congratulations," she said, by way of beginning. "What made you decide to sell the egg and donate the money?"

"Well, it's something I've been thinking about for a long time. I didn't discover golf until I retired but I absolutely love it. I feel I missed out, I might've been playing my whole life, but it just never seemed like something I could do. Golf was for the menfolk, at least when I was a girl. So I thought it would be great to get a program going that would encourage girls to give it a try. I've already spoken to the pro, Billy Esterhaus, and he's all for it. Now, thanks to this egg, I think we can get it up and running very soon."

"Okay," said Lucy. "That sounds great."

Franny turned, taking a step toward Corney, when Lucy

gently took her elbow. "One more thing, Franny. Just between you and me, last time we spoke you mentioned that you thought Sandy Lenk was having an affair . . . why did you think that?"

"You think Dave knew and that's why . . ."

"Maybe," admitted Lucy. "He had that trial coming up and, well, if he'd been expecting Sandy's support, learning she'd been unfaithful certainly wouldn't have helped."

Franny nodded in agreement. "Well, I don't know for sure, but I began to wonder what was going on when she stopped playing golf, right in the middle of the tourney. She was so good, it didn't make sense, unless there was some new interest."

"That's all?" asked Lucy, thinking that was rather thin evidence.

"Uh, no," began Franny, lowering her voice to a whisper. "One day last winter I was coming back from Christmas shopping, thinking about my list and not paying much attention really to my driving, which I know isn't good but sometimes you sort of go on a mental automatic pilot, you know, and I ended up on Lakeside Drive. So there I was, on a dead-end road where I didn't want to be."

Lucy nodded, she knew the road.

"It's all seasonal cottages down there and I was looking for a place to turn around when I spotted a couple of cars parked outside one of the A-frames, which kind of caught my interest. I mean, everything was shut up down there, so it seemed odd, and then I recognized the cars. One was Des Jasper's Corvette and the other was Sandy Lenk's Audi. You can't miss that car of hers, with the ROLEX license plate." She shrugged. "Of course, they could've been talking business, it could've been a real estate deal." Her cheeks reddened. "Forget what I said, Lucy, I really shouldn't have said anything. Especially now that Dave's, um, gone, and poor Sandy has a lot to cope with. I'm really ashamed of myself, I mean, whatever was going on was absolutely none of my business."

Oh, Franny, thought Lucy, watching her make her way through the crowd. Couldn't resist the temptation to share a salacious bit of gossip, even though she knew better. And what about you, Lucy? she asked herself. You're no better, and you do it in print.

Dave's funeral was the day before Easter and just about everyone attended, including all the Chamber members. Sandy was every bit the stoic widow, dressed in black and supported by her aging parents, the Lenks. The snowbirds had returned earlier than usual from their senior residence in Florida in order to attend the funeral and be with "poor dear Sandy," something they repeated to anyone who'd listen when they all gathered in the church hall for the reception following the very brief service.

Dave, the person whose life was being celebrated, was hardly mentioned. Lucy thought this might be because his death was officially a suicide, but she learned that this wasn't necessarily the case. She was putting a couple of mini sandwiches on her plate when Officer Sally joined her. "They're opening an investigation," she told Lucy, speaking in a low tone. "There was a gun at the scene, like you'd expect at a suicide, but it looks like the crime lab may have screwed up the ballistics test."

Lucy almost dropped her plate. "What?"

"Seems like there's a big scandal at the state crime lab." Sally looked over her shoulder and spotted her cousin, police chief Jim Kirwan. "I can't say more," she whispered, and hurried away to offer her condolences to the Lenks.

"So sorry," Lucy heard her say, barely getting the words

out before Sandy's father began his tale of woe. "Had to leave sunny Florida a month early . . ."

Lucy was thinking about Sally's tip, and how she really ought to follow up, but decided there was no rush. She had a dinner party to organize and there'd be plenty of time to tackle the story on Monday.

Lucy was up bright and early on Monday morning, but instead of rushing into the office to investigate the state crime lab, she was taking out the trash. Bill's requested Easter dinner party had been a big success, she thought, at least if you went by the overflowing garbage can and the number of empty wine bottles in the recycling bin. As she tied up the liner bag she thought about the prior evening, when the Goodmans, Finches, and Stillingses had all been gathered around her table, sharing good food, lively conversation, and plenty of wine. Bob was pleased with the way the case was developing against Mike Green, who would be tried in a couple of months. Rachel reported that Rosie was continuing the artist-in-residence program with Karl Klaus, who no longer lived at the estate but was commuting a couple of days a week from his barn studio.

There was quite a bit of discussion about Dave's death, too, and whether or not it was actually suicide. "It's pretty bad when you can't trust the state crime lab," complained Bob. "Did you see the story in the Portland Sunday paper this morning? Front page."

Lucy hadn't. She'd been busy deciding what tablecloth to use.

"I did," grumbled Ted. "Wish we'd broken it."

Lucy bit her lip, unwilling to admit she'd actually had a tip about the story from Sally.

"First it was DNA, now it's ballistics," Bob was saying.

"It seems they've just been giving prosecutors the evidence they want in order to get a conviction. They've got to do a major housecleaning over there."

"Were there a lot of wrongful convictions?" asked Bill.

"They're investigating," said Bob. "But it could be dozens, even hundreds."

"And don't forget the crimes that were missed," said Rachel. "What if Dave's suicide wasn't a suicide? What if it was really a murder?"

"Doesn't really matter how he died. Nothing's going to bring him back," insisted Sue, changing the subject. "We're old friends and we're here together, let's drink to that."

And they did, remembered Lucy, dropping the trash bag on top of the recycling bin and hoisting it all up and carrying it outside. But when she reached the cans out behind the house she discovered they were all full.

No problem, she told herself, she certainly didn't need to rush to the office this morning. The story she'd intended to break had already broken. She had plenty of time to stop at the town dump, now designated a transfer center because the actual dump had been sealed and covered with an array of solar energy collectors. The recyclables were sent to specialized facilities and the actual garbage was hauled to a central processing center where it was incinerated. The transfer center was only a short drive away, which she decided was a good thing as she loaded her car with the malodorous garbage cans. Once in the driver's seat she turned on the engine and immediately cracked the windows, to get some fresh air. Then she was off, heading toward Bumps River Road, eager to rid herself of several weeks' worth of smelly trash.

She had almost reached her destination, and had stopped at the intersection, waiting for another car to clear the intersection. That car, which was coming too fast, was actually the Jasper Property Management van with Cathy at the wheel, and after it zoomed past she noticed it was trailing a black cloud of exhaust. Not good, she thought, fearing the engine might well overheat and burst into flame. Someone ought to let Cathy know the danger, she thought, realizing that nobody else was around and she was that person. Somewhat reluctantly, she turned in the opposite direction from her destination and followed the van along windy Bumps River Road. Driving along, she couldn't help but notice the thick, cloying scent of burning oil and decided to call 911, obeying the rule forbidding the use of handheld devices while driving and using the connection in her car. Better safe than sorry, she thought, as she reported the van's location. "Better hurry," she told the dispatcher, "the smoke's so bad that I'm afraid it could burst into flame at any minute."

"They're on the way," replied the dispatcher, as Lucy ended the call and stepped on the gas, honking her horn and hoping to catch up to the van. They were some distance from town and she knew that it would take at least ten, maybe even fifteen minutes for the fire truck to arrive. The safest thing would be for Cathy to pull over and get out of the van while she waited for help to arrive.

The smoke was quite thick, so thick it was hard to imagine that Cathy wasn't aware of it, but she was showing no signs of stopping. Instead, she was roaring down the road and Lucy was easily able to follow the van's trail of oily smoke. That trail eventually led Lucy off Bumps River Road and onto Lakeside Drive, where she was just in time to see the van career into the driveway of an A-frame house. The van wasn't the only vehicle in the drive, there was also a Corvette and Sandy's distinctive Audi. She quickly pulled to the side of the road and braked, watching Cathy Jasper leap out of the van and run into the house.

Lucy quickly lowered her window. "Your van's on fire," she yelled, but Cathy didn't respond. Maybe she didn't hear, thought Lucy, getting out of her car and following her up the short driveway, keeping a wary eye on the smoking van. "Cathy! Cathy!" she called, but her cries were ignored. The stench from the van was growing stronger, at the very least the other cars should be moved, and that's what she intended to tell the people inside the cottage. Now she could see heat waves radiating from the van's engine, indicating it was dangerously hot, and she feared the whole neighborhood would be in danger if it burst into flame.

She had reached the little porch and was about to bang on the door when she heard Cathy's voice, raised in anger. "You cheat!" she screamed. Lucy hesitated for a moment and glanced through the glass window in the door. What she saw stopped her in her tracks. Sandy Lenk, dressed only in a scanty camisole, was cowering behind Des Jasper, who appeared to be pleading with his wife. Whatever he said, it was the wrong thing. Cathy was having none of it. She let out a shriek and lunged at her husband, attacking him with her fists.

Things were definitely getting out of hand, thought Lucy, pulling her cell phone out of her pocket and calling 911 again. "There's a domestic here," she told the dispatcher. Remembering the van, she turned her head to check on it and discovered flames licking out from beneath the hood. "Oh, my God. That van, it's burning! We need everything you've got out here."

"Hold tight, Lucy. Fire's almost there and I'm sending police."

"They've gotta get here quick," said Lucy, turning back

to the door. She was about to start pounding on the door to warn everyone about the fire when she peered through the glass and saw Sandy, who was now standing at the kitchen table. She had grabbed her purse and was pawing through it, Lucy saw, finally pulling out a handgun. "That's enough! Stop it!" she snarled, pointing the gun at Cathy, who was still flailing wildly at her husband, pounding his head and shoulders. Des wasn't fighting back but had curled into a fetal position as he tried to defend himself.

"No, you stop it, you bitch!" screamed Cathy, suddenly turning and lunging at Sandy. The gun went off and Lucy watched in horror as Cathy fell to the floor, clutching her shoulder. Des raised his head and gaped at his bleeding wife until Sandy grabbed him by the hand and dragged him away. He resisted for a moment, then grabbed the gun from Sandy and ran with her to the door. Lucy stepped away, the door flew open, and she raised her phone, catching video of Dave and Sandy running hand-in-hand toward the driveway. Seeing the flaming van, they stopped. "What the . . . ?" said Des, frantically looking all around and spotting Lucy.

"She saw everything!" he screamed, pointing at Lucy.

"So get rid of her!" ordered Sandy.

Des hesitated and she wrestled the gun from him. Lucy started to duck into the house for cover, but paused when she heard the blare of the siren announcing the arrival of the fire truck. Praise be, she sighed, noticing it was closely followed by a police cruiser.

Sandy and Des stood motionless on one of the paving stones that dotted the scrappy lawn. Officer Todd Kirwan was already out of his cruiser, gun drawn, and ordered Des to drop the gun. Des complied, getting a nasty look from Sandy. "Arms up!" he yelled, and Des raised his. Sandy, shivering in her silky lilac cami, merely unfolded her arms, which were across her chest, and displayed her empty hands. Lucy, heart pounding, leaned back against the shingled wall of the A-frame, capturing the scene on her phone as Officer Todd Kirwan took the pair into custody, with the flaming van in the background.

Officer Sally had joined Lucy on the porch and Lucy, suddenly remembering Cath, immediately told her that a woman had been shot inside the cottage. Sally called for an ambulance, then grabbed one of the firefighters who was an EMT and sent him inside to tend to Cathy while the others put out the fire.

Lucy's heart was still pounding, and she was shivering from shock when she climbed into her car; her hands shook as she started the engine and fumbled with the knobs to turn the heat up as high as it would go. She sat there, watching as the firefighters spread foam on the van, the cruiser left with Sandy and Des, and the ambulance arrived. She was relieved to see Cathy alive and sitting up as she was wheeled out on a gurney to be transported to the hospital. Hearing a tap on her window, Lucy jumped, then realized it was Sally. "Are you all right?" she asked.

"Yeah," said Lucy.

"Want to tell me what you were doing here?"

"It was the van. It was burning oil, a big black cloud of it. I was just trying to catch Cathy and warn her." Lucy put her hands on the wheel. "Is she going to be okay?"

"I think so. Bullet hit her arm."

"Good," said Lucy, trying to muster up enough energy to shift into drive. She let out a long sigh. "I guess I better go," said Lucy. "I've got a helluva story to write."

"Drive safely," advised Sally. She paused. "Good work, by the way," then hit the roof of the car, sending Lucy on her way.

Ted was over the moon when Lucy reported on the

morning's events, especially when she sent him the video. He immediately posted it on *The Courier*'s online edition and assigned Lucy to write up the story. She found it harder than she expected, as various thoughts and images kept flooding her mind: the burning van, the screaming and shouting, the sound of the shot. It was late afternoon before she managed to create a coherent narrative and she was exhausted when she finally hit send. Her phone rang as she was packing up to leave and she was tempted to ignore it but the screen indicated the caller was Bob Goodman, and she decided to take it.

"I know you've had quite a day," said Bob, "but I've got an update for you."

"Just what I need," said Lucy, sighing. "I was almost out the door."

"Well, this is off the record, but I thought you'd want to know."

"Fine with me. Right now all I can think about is that cold bottle of chardonnay in my fridge," said Lucy, sitting down and preparing to listen.

"No surprise, Des and Sandy have both been arrested, there'll be a press conference tomorrow after their arraignments on a bunch of charges, including the murder of Dave Forrest and attempted murder of Cathy Jasper."

"How do you know all this?" asked Lucy.

"I'm defending Des."

"Not Sandy?"

"She's hired Gerald Fogarty," he said, naming a high-profile lawyer.

"I guess her folks are footing the bill," speculated Lucy. "They must be worried that she's going to be facing some serious charges."

"The DA hasn't said, not yet anyway. I've heard he's got video of her in the bank the morning the egg disappeared, so she could have taken it and planted it on her husband. Des is hoping for a plea deal, it's all I can do to get him from confessing everything. Of course, he's putting all the blame on Sandy. He said Sandy hatched the plan to steal the egg, believing that Dave would be locked up and out of the way, which would allow her to grab all their considerable assets so they could run away together. Of course, Dave wasn't locked up, so Sandy started working on him, telling Dave how useless he was, hoping he'd be so embarrassed he'd kill himself, but that didn't happen either. That's when, according to Des, Sandy finally decided she'd do it for him. Sandy's gun appears to be the murder weapon, it's the right caliber and all. The gun found by his body was Dave's own, a different caliber. Aucoin's got other evidence, including plane tickets, but I haven't seen it yet. Of course, these are just charges, they're both presumed innocent."

"Wow, Aucoin's been busy," observed Lucy. "First the Mike Green case and now this."

"I'm sure you'll hear all about it at the press conference tomorrow."

"And if he holds back, I'll know what questions to ask." A lightbulb lit up in her head. "Actually, I've got one for you," she said, thinking of Cathy's questions the day she dropped off the help wanted ad. "I know Cathy had her suspicions about Des but what made her so sure he was having an affair that she went hightailing it over to the A-frame?"

He laughed. "She found a Rolex watch hidden in his sock drawer."

"Okay, so that indicated Sandy was the woman, but how did she know to go to the A-frame?"

"She handled all the Jasper accounts and when she got the cabin's electric bill she realized somebody was using it."

"Des certainly didn't cover his tracks very well," observed Lucy.

"It's always the sock drawer, or the laundry," said Bob, in a world-weary tone. "Charge account bills, too. Men are idiots."

"Let's leave it there," said Lucy, smiling to herself. "Thanks for the info, Bob," she said, ending the call.

Finally out of the office and in her car, about to start the engine and head home to the longed-for chardonnay, Lucy got another call, this time from Mallory. "Just want to thank you, Lucy," she said.

"For what?"

"The video of Sandy in that cami. It's already gone viral and the orders have been pouring in. Everybody wants that cami."

Lucy found herself laughing. "Thanks," she said. "It's good to know something good has come out of this mess."

She drove slowly, aware that the days were getting longer and the buds on the trees were swelling, preparing to leaf out. Nature struggled on, following her own schedule, while humans seemed to behave more and more foolishly. This entire episode was a good example, thought Lucy, turning onto Red Top Road and climbing the hill to home. It all could have been avoided if Sandy had just stuck to golf, and Des had stuck with Cathy. She pulled into the driveway, looking up at the big old antique house she and Bill had bought so many years ago and thought of the life they'd lived there together. So many memories, she thought, stopping to get the mail from the box by the road. It was mostly junk, but along with the electric bill she found a rather grubby, heavily taped, recycled manila envelope addressed to herself. There was no return address and she couldn't imagine what it contained. Curious, she ripped open the flap and withdrew a neatly folded tissue paper packet. Opening it, she found a silver wishbone, engraved with the initials KK.

No note, just the wishbone. A thank-you bone from Karl Klaus. She smiled and shook her head. He hadn't been joking, she thought. He really was into bones.

# DEATH BY EASTER EGG

Lee Hollis

# Chapter One

Hayley bit down hard on her tongue. It was going to take every last bit of restraint not to say anything as she watched her two-year-old grandson, Eli, with his impish grin and mop of curly blond hair and gripping a large metal soup spoon, bang the utensil against the glass top of her brand-new round coffee table in the living room of her home.

Eli was supposed to be eating cereal, but at the moment he was just yelling gobbledygook as milk spilled out of his mouth and he wielded that spoon like Dave Grohl pounding his drumstick in the middle of a solo during a Foo Fighters concert.

Hayley feared the boy would make an irreparable crack in the glass after each violent strike, but held out the faint hope that his parents might finally intervene so she would not have to play the bad guy. After all, her primary job as grandmother was to spoil the boy, not discipline him.

But his parents just sat nearby on the couch, ignoring Eli as they breathlessly recounted their harrowing flight from Los Angeles to Boston with hours of nonstop turbulence, which caused the whole plane to dip and shake the entire trip. According to Dustin, Hayley's son and proud papa of Eli, his girlfriend, MacKenzie, literally broke down in tears fearing they were going to crash. Eli could sense her panic and spent the whole time wailing and screaming at the top of his lungs.

Hayley could only imagine how loud Eli had probably been on the plane judging from the guttural sounds bursting out from his tiny lungs at this very moment. It was a constant shriek his parents had somehow miraculously managed to tune out with practice.

Hayley started making a move to seize the spoon from Eli's possession when Bruce, who was sitting in the recliner next to her, squeezed her hand tightly, signaling that maybe she should not risk offending Dustin and MacKenzie by taking over as the responsible parent in the room.

"MacKenzie literally dropped to her knees when we got to baggage claim, and thanked God for sparing us!" Dustin crowed.

"I never went to church as a kid, my mom wasn't very religious, but I sure am a big believer now. There had to have been a higher power watching over us! I thought for sure we were all goners!" MacKenzie cried.

Eli slammed the spoon forcefully down again on the glass, so loud this time that Dustin finally turned half-heartedly in his direction and said softly, "Eli . . ."

Eli.

Just his name.

And barely audible at that.

Nothing about maybe it might be a good idea to stop destroying Gramma's expensive new coffee table that had only been delivered to the house a week ago.

Predictably, Eli was making too much noise to hear his father addressing him and continued screeching and banging.

"Anyway, we may have to rent a car and drive back to LA," Dustin said, chuckling. "I'm not sure I will ever be able to get MacKenzie back on a plane."

Bruce stood up and shouted over the screaming. "Anyone like a drink before dinner?"

"I'll take a beer, thanks, Bruce," Dustin replied softly.

"Nothing for me. Maybe just some water. I'm not drinking alcohol," MacKenzie said, turning and smiling at her little boy, as if she found the whole frenzied chaotic scene cute and charming.

Hayley had to admit that despite his tornado-like behavior at the moment, Eli was absolutely adorable. She had been thrilled when Dustin and MacKenzie had decided to fly back east and spend a week with her and Bruce over the Easter holiday. And with Gemma and her boyfriend, Conner, currently in Italy working on a show for the Food Network, it was going to be nice to have at least her son and his young family here for Easter Sunday. She was also excited about taking Eli, now a toddler, to the annual Easter egg hunt at the Emerson Conners Middle School just as she had done with her own kids when they were growing up. She just did not expect him to be such a handful despite knowing he was smack in the middle of the terrible twos.

Eli suddenly dropped the spoon and it clattered on the hardwood floor as his focus zeroed in on something else. Leroy, Hayley's aging Shih Tzu, had wandered into the room, capturing the three-and-a-half-foot-tall wrecking ball's attention. He pointed with his tiny index finger. "Dog! Dog!"

Leroy's ears shot up as the boy stamped across the room toward him, reaching out with his tiny hands to grab ahold of him by his collar.

Leroy slowly backed away, then turned and hightailed it into the dining room, finding temporary cover underneath the large oak table. Eli dropped down to the floor onto his belly and tried crawling underneath the table with arms outstretched desperately trying to get at the terrified Shih Tzu.

Hayley could see the pleading look in her dog's eyes, silently begging her to do something before he was mauled by this marauding creature that was spitting out bits and pieces of breakfast cereal as he tried snatching handfuls of Leroy's fur.

Hayley popped to her feet. "Okay, that's enough, Eli. Leroy is a little too long in the tooth to be roughhousing. He just doesn't have the energy anymore."

She tried to be as kind and casual as possible as she reached down and scooped up Eli into her arms and delivered him back to his parents. She glanced over in MacKenzie's direction and could see the wounded look on her face. Hayley knew that MacKenzie was extremely sensitive, and the last thing she wanted to do was hurt her future daughter-in-law's feelings, but somebody had to intervene. Otherwise poor Leroy might have had a heart attack from the wild child's relentless assault.

Dustin's expression remained neutral as MacKenzie jumped up and rolled Eli over, smothering his face with kisses. "Mama loves you so much!" She picked up the spoon and handed it to him. "Here, you can play with this."

Eli eagerly gripped the spoon in his fist, and with a wide smile, started banging on the coffee table again as Bruce returned from the kitchen, handing Dustin a bottle of beer and MacKenzie a bottled water. He turned to Hayley. "Can I get you something before dinner, babe?"

Hayley gave him a tight smile. "I'll have a Jack and Coke."

Bang.

Bang.

Bang.

Hayley swallowed hard. "Make it a double."

Bruce eagerly made his escape again.

Dustin took a swig of beer and again said, almost in an inaudible whisper and a lackadaisical casual tone, "Eli . . ."

Still no instruction of any kind.

Just his name.

Hayley could not take it anymore. She bent over and snatched the spoon out of Eli's hand. "Let's find something for you to play with that's a little quieter, what do you say?"

Eli answered her with a bloodcurdling, horrific scream.

He was not happy about losing his beloved spoon.

Hayley spotted a small stuffed bear sticking out of MacKenzie's large bag of toys and plucked it out. It was soft and squishy and could do very little harm to her furniture. She handed it to Eli, who promptly hurled it across the room, unimpressed. He kept one eye glued to the soup spoon in Hayley's hand and the other on the cowering dog quivering underneath the dining room table.

"We find it very important that Eli is able to express himself in whatever way he chooses," MacKenzie said curtly. "We don't want to stifle his creativity."

Hayley took a slight pause before responding. "I totally get that. But perhaps he can enjoy his freedom of expression without butchering my new coffee table."

There.

She said it.

As hard as she had tried, in the end, she just could not help herself.

Bruce ambled in with her cocktail just in time to hear her cutting remark. And now Hayley suspected he was searching his brain for some excuse to leave the room before the fireworks began.

MacKenzie's eyes pooled with tears. "I'm sorry, I'm doing my best to be a good parent."

Hayley suddenly felt awful. "No, Mac, I wasn't implying anything like that . . ."

Dustin sighed. "Mom, just forget it." He hauled himself up from the couch and scooped up Eli in his arms. "I'm going to take this little rug rat upstairs and get him washed up before dinner. Come on, slugger." Eli squirmed in his father's arms but stopped squealing as they headed up the staircase.

MacKenzie stared at her bottle of water and began picking at the paper label glued to the plastic. "I know my parenting style can seem overly permissive sometimes, but I had such a hard childhood, my mother was so strict, and I just want to be totally different with Eli. I guess I'm still trying to find the right balance."

"He's a wonderful boy. You're doing just fine," Hayley reassured her. "And as his loving grandmother, I say he can express himself any way he sees fit."

And he did.

By throwing a fistful of mashed potatoes and gravy in Bruce's face at dinner. By violently smashing two dinner plates like he was some kind of drunken Greek waiter. And by running out the front door with no pants on and screaming down the street before Dustin and Bruce could catch up to him. And all of that happened before his eight o'clock bedtime. Which on this particular night ended up stretching until well after ten.

Yes, it was going to be a long week.

# Chapter Two

Hayley's Kitchen was buzzing two weeks before Easter Sunday, especially since Hayley was offering a month-long prix fixe Easter Dinner special featuring a cocktail or champagne to start, Hayley's famous honey baked ham, scalloped potatoes, grilled asparagus with garlic and olive oil, green bean casserole served with freshly baked dinner rolls, and for dessert a homemade banana pudding pie, all for $29.95.

Needless to say, the restaurant had been straight out busy all week with locals pouring in for the good holiday deal. Hayley also profited from being one of the few businesses in town to stay open year round. It was mid-April and most of the seasonal restaurants would be keeping their doors closed until at least after Memorial Day Weekend.

As Hayley made the rounds greeting her guests and offering free extra flutes of champagne, her manager, Betty, who manned the front door and was in charge of reservations, slid in behind her as she was strolling across the dining room waving at a few recognizable faces.

Betty whispered in her ear, "I just got word from Kelton in the kitchen that we're running dangerously low on ham."

Hayley glanced at her watch. "Kitchen closes in ten minutes. Hopefully, we can make it just under the wire. But if not, I thawed out some lamb chops we can offer if we run out of ham. There is also some mint jelly in the fridge. Kelton can do his magic if he has to."

"I'll go let him know," Betty said, veering off and heading in the direction of the kitchen.

As Hayley passed by a table near the fireplace, a hand shot out and gently took hold of her wrist. She turned around to see Bill Duffy, a handsome man in his late fifties, silver haired, slim build, dining alone. He held up a forkful of potatoes.

"Hayley, what's the secret ingredient in these scalloped potatoes? You have to tell me."

"If I did that, Bill, then you could make them at home and not have to come here anymore and I don't want to lose your business."

Bill laughed. "Don't worry. I'm hopeless in the kitchen. Cindy did all the cooking."

He paused, then stared down at his plate, looking slightly beaten up.

Cindy was Bill's ex-wife. They had recently divorced, and Hayley had heard through the grapevine that negotiations to dissolve the marriage had gotten pretty nasty between the two parties. Bill was the president at Bar Harbor All Citizens Bank and so he had built up quite a nest egg in the years he and Cindy had been married. The much younger Cindy was his second wife. Bill had left his first wife, his high school sweetheart, Joanie, after meeting Cindy on the beach at their all-inclusive resort in Cancun where he was vacationing with his wife and kids in the early aughts! It was an awkward time for the whole family, not to mention their mutual friends, who were forced to choose sides. But now, after over twenty years with Cindy, he was single and ready to mingle once again.

"I'm afraid you'll be seeing my face around here quite a lot in the next few months. For someone who can't boil water, there aren't a lot of choices when it comes to dining out this time of year."

"I'm going to try and take that as a compliment, Bill," Hayley said, laughing.

Bill, realizing his faux pas, broke into a wide smile. "That didn't come out right. Trust me, I love your food, Hayley!" Then he guzzled what was left in his champagne glass.

"I will have Betty bring you another sparkling wine on the house. You enjoy your meal, Bill."

"Thank you, love," he said with a playful wink.

If you identified as a female, then Bill Duffy was going to flirt with you regardless of your relationship status.

Hayley circled back around to the hostess station near the front door, where Betty had returned from the kitchen and was turning away a couple who had just barreled in hoping to get seated for dinner at the last minute.

"I'm so sorry, the kitchen's closing. I do have an opening for tomorrow evening at eight thirty?"

The couple conferred with each other and then snapped up the reservation, deciding to return the next day. As they headed out the door into the chilly night, Betty turned to Hayley. "Kelton thinks we're going to be okay. We can save the lamb for a second special this weekend."

"Good. When you have a moment, could you swing by Bill Duffy's table with another sparkling wine?"

Betty eyed him curiously. He was scraping the last of the scalloped potatoes off his plate with his fork, and then shoved it into his mouth. "He looks sad."

"He should. I heard Cindy took him to the cleaners," Hayley remarked before noticing a slight twinkle in Betty's eyes as she stared at the handsome, now single again bank executive. "You know, Betty, why don't you go over there and talk to him?"

Betty cocked an eyebrow, surprised. "What? Me? Why?"

Hayley shrugged. "He's still very good-looking, and he's always been exceedingly charming. Now that he's back on the market, and you're single and open to some companionship, I don't know, maybe you two could be a match."

"Are you *serious?*" Betty scoffed.

"You'll never know unless you try."

"You're forgetting one very important fact, Hayley. Bill tends to ignore a large segment of the female population, a group I currently belong to."

"And what's that?"

"Anyone over thirty."

"Oh, come on, Bill and Joanie were the same age when they first got together."

"And look what happened. He ditched her for a twenty-two-year-old he picked up on the beach in Cancun. She was eighteen years his junior! As a woman approaching my forties, I'm far too over the hill for Bill Duffy to even consider as a *girlfriend.*"

"Okay, I admit Cindy was slightly younger than him—"

"Almost two decades!"

"But that doesn't mean he can't be attracted to a more mature, seasoned, smart, vibrant, beautiful woman like you, Betty—"

"You can stop with the flattery, Hayley, there is no way I am going to put myself out there and ask him out on a date. The risk to my self-esteem is far too great."

"Fine. Forget I asked."

Suddenly a commotion erupted. A woman was standing up and yelling at her dining companion at a table in the corner. He appeared to be laughing and mocking her tantrum, so she scooped up her glass of Chardonnay and tossed it in his face. He reared back, his face wet, eyes blazing, nostrils flaring. Then he jumped to his feet and gripped the ends of the table with his big hammy hands as if he was about to overturn it in a fit of rage.

Hayley immediately recognized the feuding couple. The woman was Janet Cook, a young teller at Bill's bank, All Citizens, and her boyfriend was Whiskey Shields, muscle-bound, thickheaded, and a local plumber. Both were in their mid-twenties. They had been dating for about a year, and from what Hayley could gather from gossip around town, the relationship had been volatile from the start.

"I hate you! You're a despicable human being!" Janet cried, pointing at him with a long fingernail splodged with a glittery varnish. She turned to leave.

"Where are you going?" Whiskey bellowed.

"I am not going to stay here and continue to allow you to demean me and insult my friends and my family. I'm sick of you judging me all the time. I'm going home and you better not show up later. The door will be locked and I have no intention of letting you in!"

"Where am I supposed to sleep tonight?"

"I'm sure that pretty cashier at the Big Apple you're always flirting with will let you crash at her pad!"

"This is the problem! You always get so damn jealous! I don't even know that girl's name!"

"You never know the names of the girls you try to get in the sack! And that says just about everything there is to know about you! We're done, Whiskey! It's over! I never want to see you again!"

He reached out to grab her arm but she eluded his grasp. "You can't just walk out on me, Janet!"

At this point, Bill Duffy was up out of his chair and marching over to the feuding couple. He positioned himself in the middle of them, facing Janet.

"Janet, maybe it would be a good idea if you and your boyfriend took this outside?"

Janet sniffed, mortified. "Mr. Duffy, I-I didn't know you were here. I'm so, so sorry."

"You apologize to your boss at the drop of a hat, but you can't seem to find it in your heart to ever apologize to *me*!" Whiskey griped.

"Why should I? Every fight we've ever had has always been *your* fault!" Janet spit out.

"I'm warning you, Janet, you don't want to make me angry!"

"Why? Are you going to suddenly turn green and grow ten feet tall like the Incredible Hulk? I don't think so because you're not some superhero like in your feeble brain. Not even close! You're just a petty, small-minded little man who masks his insecurities by popping steroids and putting on muscle!"

This cut deep.

Red-faced and furious, Whiskey grabbed the table again and turned it over, sending plates and cutlery smashing to the floor.

The other diners jumped, some gasping.

Bill planted a firm hand on Whiskey's shoulder. "Buddy, you need to calm down!"

"Get your hands off of me!" Whiskey raged, shoving Bill away from him. Bill stumbled back, about to fall, but Janet scooted forward to catch him so he could regain his balance.

Hayley shot forward, and without hesitation, got right up close in Whiskey's face. "If you do not leave my restaurant this minute, Whiskey, I will call the police and you will be arrested for public disturbance and destruction of property."

Whiskey studied the room, noticing the entire restaurant had fallen into an uneasy silence with everyone staring at him. Janet sobbed quietly as her boss, Bill, put an arm around her shaking shoulders to comfort her. Whiskey glanced once more at Hayley, quickly surmised that she was not bluffing, and then stormed out of the restaurant, embarrassed and humiliated, slamming the door shut behind him so hard Hayley thought the glass window might shatter.

Janet, sniffing, tears streaming down her cheeks, reached out to Hayley. "Please, forgive me, I never meant to cause such a scene. I will pay for any damage—"

Hayley cut her off. "Don't worry, Janet. It's all good."

Bill escorted her to the door. "Come on, dear, I'll give you a lift." He turned to Hayley with a look of concern. "I just want to make sure she gets home safely."

"Of course," Hayley said before turning around to see all her remaining diners still staring in stunned silence.

It was time to do a little damage control.

"Free banana cream pie for everyone!" Hayley declared.

And the silence gave way to raucous cheers and applause.

# Chapter Three

When Hayley breezed into the Bar Harbor All Citizens Bank a few days later with her bagful of restaurant receipts and cash from the previous evening, she instantly sensed a palpable tension in the air. There were only two customers at the teller windows. The employees kept their heads down as they silently counted money and cashed checks. No one seemed to be socializing. Hayley was struck by the strained silence. She turned to the bank's security guard, Raymond Dobbs, who was in his late sixties, average height, barrel-chested, handsome with a graying goatee. Raymond had been working at the bank since the mid-nineties, when Hayley had briefly been employed as a teller during the summer following her high school graduation. Raymond usually greeted her when she came into the bank with a bright smile and a friendly hello, most of the time ready to hit her with one of his corny jokes, but today he remained stone-faced as she passed by him.

She did a quick turnaround to face him. "Hey, Ray, why did the bank teller get fired on her first day?"

He stared glumly at her and shrugged. "I don't know, Hayley."

"Oh, come on, you're not even going to take a guess?"

"Sorry. Not today."

"But I've been saving this joke for you all week. You really don't want to know why the teller got fired on her first day?"

He sighed, resigned. "Okay, why?"

"Because a customer asked her to check his balance, and she pushed him over."

Hayley managed to get a slight crack of a smile from Raymond, who simply could not resist a dumb joke, as he mumbled, "Good one."

"I expected a much bigger reaction from you, Ray. Maybe I should work on my delivery," Hayley said, winking.

Raymond cleared his throat.

He obviously wanted her to just continue with her business and leave him alone.

Hayley was at a loss.

Raymond was usually so much more gregarious and playful.

Something was definitely bothering him.

She decided he probably would not appreciate her prying into his personal business so she decided to move on, waiting in the front of the line for one of the tellers to finish with a customer. After a few minutes, a man grabbed a fistful of cash and ambled off as Hayley took his place at the teller window where Janet Cook stood, looking miserable.

"Good morning, Hayley," Janet muttered.

"Hi, Janet," Hayley said brightly. "I'd like to make a deposit, please."

She pushed the bag of money and receipts toward Janet, who emptied the contents onto her desk and began counting through the bills as Hayley patiently waited.

Like Ray the security guard, Janet was also not her usual

perky self today. But Hayley chalked it up to her having just broken up with her boyfriend a few nights earlier at her restaurant.

Hayley glanced around at the quiet, morose atmosphere. "What's going on, Janet? It's like a morgue around here today."

Janet leaned in closer to Hayley and whispered, "Bill's in a really foul mood. We're all just trying to keep our heads down and avoid his wrath."

"Bill? But he seemed fine the other night at the restaurant."

"He's under a lot of pressure today. He's got a very wealthy client coming in at any moment from Northeast Harbor. She's very high maintenance and always manages to find something to complain about."

"Natalie Van Dyke?"

Janet's eyes widened in surprise. "Yes! How on earth did you know?"

"I know Mrs. Van Dyke well. She's dined at my restaurant a few times. That woman is demanding wherever she goes. She sent her entree back three times."

Bill Duffy came barreling out of his office and up to Janet's window, ignoring Hayley. "Is she here yet?"

Janet shook her head. "No. Not yet. I'll buzz you when I see her arrive so you can come out to greet her."

"Fine," Bill said, frowning. "Is he almost done? I want him gone by the time Mrs. Van Dyke arrives."

"Last I heard, he was going to have to snake the drain to clear out whatever's clogging up the toilet."

Bill sighed loudly. "It's always *something*!"

Then he stomped back inside his office.

Before Hayley could ask, Janet spoke softly to her as she began sifting through the pile of receipts. "On top of everything else, Raymond went to use the bathroom right before we opened the bank this morning and when he flushed it, water started overflowing, and we had to call a plumber. Well, there was only one that was available to come over here to diagnose the problem and fix it before noon."

Hayley had a sinking feeling. "Oh, dear, don't tell me."

"Yup. Whiskey."

Janet's boyfriend.

Or ex-boyfriend as of three nights ago.

No wonder she was so sour this morning.

"Believe me, I called around all over town. I even tried a couple of plumbers up in Ellsworth, but Whiskey was the only one who got back to me right away. Of course I was the first person he spotted when he came in."

Hayley's eyes narrowed. "He didn't bother you, did he?"

"Oh no. He didn't acknowledge me at all. He just looked away the second we made eye contact. He's obviously still very angry at me for breaking up with him. But to his credit, he did manage a half-hearted apology to Bill for his meltdown the other night at your restaurant when Bill came out of his office to escort him to the bathroom. Whiskey said he just had too many martinis at dinner. That's classic Whiskey. Always ready with an excuse for his boorish behavior."

As Janet continued working on Hayley's deposit, the glass door to the bank flew open and Natalie Van Dyke swept in, clutching a dog leash attached to a pink diamond-studded collar around the neck of a black toy poodle who trotted a few steps ahead of her. Natalie was in a matching pink LaCoste pullover and a blue jean skirt.

Janet dropped Hayley's receipts and grabbed her phone. "Excuse me for a moment, Hayley." She nervously gripped the receiver, waiting, then whispered urgently, "She's here."

Bill Duffy bounded out of his office, hand outstretched

to greet Natalie Van Dyke. "Mrs. Van Dyke, welcome. We've been expecting you."

Her eyes fell upon his outstretched hand and she scrunched up her nose. "I do not shake hands. I have a very delicate immune system and I will not haphazardly risk someone passing along a deadly respiratory illness."

"I understand completely," Bill said, quickly withdrawing his hand and wiping it on his pants as if he was attempting to remove any lingering germs. "Can I get you some coffee? A Danish, perhaps?"

"No. I do not have a lot of time. I'm a very busy woman. As I explained on the phone when I called earlier this morning, I just need something from my safety deposit box."

"Yes, of course. Follow me," Bill said, guiding her across the room. "By the way, you will be pleased to know we are updating our security system."

"Why? What's wrong with the old one?" Natalie asked, her voice dripping with disdain.

Bill gasped. "Nothing! Nothing at all! We just decided it was time to modernize our technology. In fact, we're switching over to a keyless system allowing access just by scanning a fingerprint."

Natalie stared at him, unimpressed. "What's wrong with the old-fashioned way? It's worked up until now," she loudly proclaimed. "I prefer the two-key system with me unlocking my own box in tandem with you. It's much simpler and hacker-proof, wouldn't you agree?"

"I understand, but I can assure you that this new way will be absolutely safe and secure, even more so than the old two-key system. Trust me."

"I don't trust bankers. Never have."

Hayley could see sweat beads begin to form on Bill's brow.

"Of course. Would you follow me, please, Mrs. Van Dyke?" Bill asked as he escorted her to the vault in the back.

"Come along, Gigi," Natalie cooed, tugging on the leash to coax her toy poodle along, who had stopped to sniff Raymond's pant leg, much to the security guard's annoyance.

Janet finished tallying Hayley's deposit and printed her a receipt. "There you go. Have a nice day, Hayley."

Only a few seconds had gone by when suddenly the bank employees and handful of customers were startled by a bloodcurdling scream, which came from inside the vault.

Bill, ashen-faced and in a state of shock, stumbled out. "Janet, call the police!"

Janet reached for her phone. "What happened?"

Bill gulped. "Someone has cleaned out all the jewelry and valuables from Natalie Van Dyke's safety deposit box!"

# Chapter Four

The annual Easter egg hunt at the Emerson Conners Middle School the week before Easter was packed with excited children racing around the classrooms and hallways with their baskets in search of as many painted eggs and candied eggs as they could find. There were seventy-five kids and their parents in attendance this year, which Hayley guessed might set a new record.

Eli was jumping up and down, screaming at the top of his lungs. Judging from the brown smears staining his face, Hayley figured he was on a dizzying sugar high from devouring too many chocolate eggs. Eli raced forward and slammed into one girl, knocking her to the ground. But luckily the girl was a trouper and did not cry. She just hauled herself back up to her feet and continued her frantic search for more eggs.

Hayley glanced around and spotted MacKenzie noshing on her own basket of edible eggs and not paying any attention to Eli, who was still running around yelling and generally causing a ruckus.

Finally, when one of Eli's high-pitched screeches caused everyone to stop what they were doing and turn to see who was causing such a commotion, MacKenzie's eyes slowly drifted over toward her boy, and she half-heartedly

called out, "Eli, behave." Then she went back to languor-
ously unwrapping another egg, which she then popped in
her mouth.

Hayley had seen enough. She hoofed it over to retrieve
Eli and deposit him back at his mother's side. However,
when she reached out to take hold of his arm, he giggled
and shot out of her reach. "Eli, come here . . ."

She made a move toward him.

He jumped back, again avoiding her grasp.

He was under the impression they were playing a game.

Suddenly he dashed off, disappearing into the crowd,
laughing and clapping his hands excitedly.

Hayley let out an exhausted sigh.

As adorable as Eli was, she was reaching the end of her
rope. She made her way through the throngs of parents
proudly watching their children focused on the Easter egg
hunt, emerging to see Bruce strolling out of the bathroom
just in time to spot Eli barreling toward him.

Before Eli could zip past him, Bruce scooped the little
hellion up in his arms and carried him back to Hayley.
"Looking for this one?"

"Yes, thank you. I think he needs a time-out. Why don't
we take him back to his father so he can watch him for a
while?" Hayley suggested.

Hayley followed Bruce as he carried Eli back to the
gymnasium and delivered him to MacKenzie and Dustin,
who were sitting on the bleachers now staring into each
other's eyes, smiling, oblivious to the world around them.

*Ah, young love*, Hayley thought to herself.

When Bruce plopped down a squirming Eli next to
them, their googly-eyed romantic moment was finally broken. Dustin turned and knelt down to inspect Eli's baby
blue Easter basket. It was nearly empty.

"What's the matter, Eli? Are the other kids finding all the eggs before you?" Dustin asked.

"No, he's doing quite well, he's just not bothering to put them in his basket. He's eating them all the second he finds them," Hayley said, chuckling.

MacKenzie tossed another tiny chocolate egg in her mouth and said with a dose of irony, "He's got such a sweet tooth. I have no idea where he gets that from."

A harried-looking man in his late forties tried hurrying past them. It was Ed Fennow, the school principal. Bruce intercepted him before he could pass.

"Ed, I just came from the bathroom. Your toilet is overflowing."

"I know. One of the parents just told me."

"We should find Mucca."

Mucca Smith was the school custodian.

"I already did. He says it's above his pay grade so I've called a plumber to come take a look at it. Excuse me. I've got about a dozen other fires to put out. Apparently, Alberta Cochran, our history teacher, left her desk drawer unlocked and Ricky Sanborn, a fourth grader, found a stack of love notes that the phys ed teacher, Tom Simmons, wrote to her, and now Ricky is reading them aloud to some of the parents! This day is turning out to be quite the nightmare!"

He then pushed past Bruce and scurried off.

There was another ear-splitting screech out of Eli's mouth as he frantically pointed across the gym at the giant white Easter Bunny who had just sauntered into the gymnasium waving at all the kids who suddenly surged toward him. Eli broke free from his father's grip and raced over to greet him with the other kids.

Hayley knew who was underneath that big bunny head. It was Raymond Dobbs, the Bar Harbor All Citizens Bank security guard. Hayley could tell from the way he was bending over and hugging all the kids that Raymond was in a much better mood today than he had been a few days earlier at the bank, the day Natalie Van Dyke had discovered her safety deposit box empty.

Bill Duffy had immediately called the police, and Chief Sergio arrived within minutes. However, with Bill and Natalie the only two people with keys to open the box, and with no sign of forced entry, there was a disturbing dearth of clues. Sergio had tried assuring Mrs. Van Dyke that his department would stop at nothing to retrieve her valuables and bring the thief to justice. But Mrs. Van Dyke had much less faith in the Bar Harbor Police Department than its cheerleading, fully capable chief. She was also furious with the bank for allowing such a flagrant crime to happen under their noses in broad daylight, and was now threatening a major lawsuit. So Hayley was keenly aware that the overall mood at Bar Harbor All Citizens Bank had probably soured even more during the past few days.

Dustin and MacKenzie watched with glee as the Easter Bunny picked up Eli and spun him around before setting him back down and handing him some yellow Peeps, a marshmallow confection shaped like little birds. Eli began packing them all in his mouth as the Easter Bunny grabbed his tummy with his big white furry hands, laughing at Eli's stuffed cheeks loaded with Peeps.

Hayley dreaded another sugar high on the horizon.

Raymond Dobbs had been playing the Easter Bunny every year since the mid-1990s when Hayley was working at the bank with him. Raymond had to take over for his grandfather Ebb, who had played the role since the 1960s, but who had sadly died during the winter before Raymond was recruited to fill in for Ebb the Easter after his passing.

Hayley noticed the lovebirds Dustin and MacKenzie

holding hands in a corner staring longingly at each other. She returned her gaze back over to the Easter Bunny so she could keep an eye on Eli since his parents were preoccupied again. He was among a gaggle of children that were circling Raymond like vultures with their eyes fixed on his stash of candy in his giant yellow Easter basket. Raymond, who as everyone knew had an incurable sweet tooth, had a habit of inhaling more of the candy than he doled out to the children. But today he appeared to be on his best behavior as he tossed Easter eggs at his fawning prepubescent admirers.

Bruce nudged Hayley. "Well, well, well, look who appears to be an item." He nodded in the direction of the bleachers in the back of the gym. Hayley turned to see Bill Duffy and Janet Cook standing together exchanging lovey-dovey looks that were even more saccharine than the ones going on between Dustin and MacKenzie.

Bill beamed as Janet giggled at something he said and she briefly rested her head on his shoulder. As much as everyone in the gym wanted to pretend they were not watching, every person present was obviously interested in this scandalous new development.

"They must be here with Bill's granddaughter Lauren. I saw her running around earlier," Hayley noted.

"I thought Janet was dating Whiskey Shields," Bruce said.

"She was. But they had a very public breakup last week at my restaurant. Bill basically came to her rescue."

"Looks like she fell head over heels for her knight in shining armor," Bruce remarked.

Given all that was going on at the bank and the enormous pressure he was facing in the wake of the recent brazen theft, Bill appeared as if he did not have a care in the world.

Lauren, an adorable ginger-haired moppet, bounced over to Bill and Janet. She grabbed Janet's hand, urging her to come with her to help her hunt for more candy. Janet, who seemed touched by the girl's sweet affection for her, nodded and trotted off with her, leaving Bill behind to watch them with a euphoric look on his face.

"How old is Lauren now?" Bruce asked.

"Six, I think. She belongs to Bill's daughter Caitlin."

"And how old is Caitlin?"

Hayley paused. "Older than Janet, that's for sure."

"Bill certainly likes them young, doesn't he?"

Hayley nodded before noticing Raymond take off his bunny head, surprising a few adoring children who were still hanging around him, and march over to Bill Duffy. Bill was taken aback by Raymond in the giant furry rabbit costume confronting him and poking his big furry bunny paw in his chest.

Bruce arched an eyebrow. "What do you think they're arguing about?"

"I have no idea." Hayley shrugged. "But it looks serious."

Bill tried calming down Raymond, to no avail. He put a hand on Raymond's shoulder, but Raymond violently shook it off and skulked away, nearly plowing down a few children trying to surround him.

Bill glanced around nervously, hoping no one had noticed the uncomfortable altercation.

Hayley had the urge to follow Raymond and try to find out what had upset him so much, when suddenly MacKenzie rushed up to her, anguished and distressed.

"I can't find Eli!" she wailed.

"What?"

"He was there one minute and then he was gone the next. I've looked everywhere in the gym. There is no sign of him. Dustin is now searching the hallways and class-rooms."

"He couldn't have gone far. Come on, let's fan out and find him," Hayley said, heading for the door.

Hayley had a sickening feeling in the pit of her stomach. She had seen Eli bolt out the front door of her house when left unattended for a split second. She worried that if he did it again, here at the school, he might flee out of one of the exit doors where cars on Eagle Lake Road were zipping past at high speed.

The boy could be in serious danger.

She had to locate him.

And fast.

# Chapter Five

Hayley, in search of Eli, waded through the wild pack of hyperactive children running up and down the halls. She spotted a curly-haired blond boy in a blue sweatshirt that she thought was Eli, but when she took him by his tiny shoulders and spun him around, she realized it was not him at all. Just a kid who resembled him from behind.

Suddenly she heard a familiar voice bellowing nearby.

"I'm warning you, do *not* eat that!"

Hayley whipped around to see her BFF Mona pointing a finger at a chubby, precocious, adorable little boy around five years old, who was holding a candied egg close to his mouth, ready to gobble it up.

Mona took a deliberate step toward him. "I said no, Cameron. You have had more than enough candy. Don't you dare disobey me and put that in your mouth!"

The boy gave her a sly grin and then defiantly raised it right up to where it was touching his bottom lip.

Mona shot her hand out. "Give it to me right now, Cameron. I'm not fooling around."

He opened his mouth wide, giggling.

"Don't even think about it!" Mona warned him again.

And then, the egg disappeared, sucked between the boy's

lips. He was chewing with his mouth open and laughing hysterically.

Mona's head dropped. "When did children just stop listening to their elders? I thought my own kids were bad enough, but these grandkids, they're in a league of their own!"

"How many of your grandkids are here with you today?" Hayley asked.

Mona shot her a withering look. "How the hell should I know? Hayley, I got nine kids and half of them have been popping out offspring faster than I can count. I lost track after seven, no eight, wait, no seven. I got seven grandkids and counting. Four of 'em can walk, but one's got a cold today, so I am guessing there are two more around here somewhere wreaking havoc besides this little hellion Cameron, who doesn't listen to a damn word I say!"

Cameron swallowed the candy with a devilish grin.

Mona mustered up her most menacing stare, pointing a finger at him again. "You are going to pay severely for that, mister man!"

The boy studied her for a moment, and then burst out laughing, not the least bit intimidated.

Mona threw her hands up. "See? I used to be someone kids were so scared of they'd walk around on eggshells fearing I might blow like Mount Vesuvius. But these grandkids, they don't see me as a threat, just their sweet ole grandma Mona, all talk and no action."

"Because that's kind of what you are these days, Mona," Hayley gently reminded her. "And besides that, you spoil them rotten."

"Like you don't indulge Dustin's little terror tyke."

"Have you seen him? His parents lost track of him and we can't find him anywhere."

"I did see a little blond demon with chocolate all over

his face running past me a few minutes ago. It might have been him, but I couldn't swear to it. I haven't seen Eli since he was a baby."

"Which direction was he headed?"

Mona pointed down the hall. "That way. Toward the art room."

Hayley groaned. "The art room? With all those crayons and cans of paint? I smell a disaster in the making."

"You better hurry," Mona said, turning her attention back to Cameron, who was already hoarding candy eggs from a six-year-old girl's Easter basket as she stared at him, horrified.

"Cameron, those aren't yours! Put them back!" Mona cried, chasing after him.

Hayley darted off in the opposite direction, down the hall to the art room, poking her head in and heaving a big sigh of relief. On the floor clutching a bright yellow Easter basket was Eli happily gorging on chocolate eggs as fast as his tiny fingers could unwrap them from the Technicolor foil.

Hayley nervously glanced at the supply shelf in the back of the room and was satisfied that the potential weapons of mass destruction were untouched, the paint sealed up in cans and the crayons safely tucked inside their boxes.

She walked over and knelt down beside Eli. "Where did you get that pretty yellow Easter basket, Eli?"

His mouth full of chocolate, Eli simply mumbled gibberish.

Hayley picked up the basket and inspected it. It looked just like the one Raymond Dobbs had been carrying while parading around the kids in his Easter Bunny costume.

She dipped her hand in the basket and rummaged through all the candy and empty wrappers and at the bottom she felt something solid and pulled it out.

It was an EpiPen. An auto injector for the emergency treatment of severe allergic reactions.

This confirmed it.

The basket definitely belonged to Raymond Dobbs.

Since working with him at the bank all those years ago, Hayley knew Raymond had a lifelong peanut allergy and carried around an EpiPen with him at all times in case he consumed any nuts by mistake. Eli must have snatched the basket from Raymond when he was not looking. She knew she had to return this EpiPen to him right away.

Dropping the device back inside the basket and grabbing Eli by the hand, Hayley hustled back to the school gymnasium, which was now crowded with parents and children milling about with their baskets of candy wondering what happened to the Easter Bunny, who was supposed to be there entertaining them.

Hayley, with Eli in tow, made a beeline for Mona, who was trying to corral her grandkids. "Mona, I'm looking for Raymond Dobbs."

"You and everybody else around here. A lot of the parents have been complaining about the Easter Bunny doing a disappearing act."

Hayley suddenly felt a sense of dread.

She handed Eli over to Mona. "Here, can you watch him for a few minutes while I try to locate Raymond?"

"Sure, what's one more rug rat? It's not like I'm already going insane babysitting my own grandkids. Come on, Little Lord Fauntleroy, play with Cameron and the other two, Grace and . . ." She stared at a towheaded boy with an impish smile. "You, what's your name again?"

"Theo!" he proclaimed proudly.

"Right, Theo. Someday I'll get all your names straight. Go play with Grace and Theo," Mona ordered, shoving Eli in their general direction.

Hayley scanned the gym, and seeing no sign of Raymond, exited to the adjacent administration offices. After turning up nothing there, she continued down the hall, stopping in each classroom. She was almost back to the art room where she had found Eli when something caught her eye as she passed the geography classroom adorned with world maps and a giant globe next to the teacher's desk. Poking out from the side of the desk was what looked like a giant bunny ear.

Hayley's heart leapt into her throat.

She cautiously entered the classroom to get a closer look.

As she approached, she could clearly make out white fur and pink felt that made up the ear. As she slowly circled around the desk, she could plainly see the giant Easter Bunny head with its big eyes and rabbit teeth and long whiskers lying upended on the floor. She bent down to inspect it.

Why had Raymond abandoned part of his costume?

She picked up the head and set it down on the desk as her eyes fell on something in the back of the classroom. More white fur and bunny feet lying prone on the floor. Hayley suppressed a gasp and raced over, stopping suddenly at the sight of Raymond Dobbs in the rest of his bunny costume, sprawled out on his back, an upended yellow basket next to him and a sea of foil-wrapped Easter eggs scattered around him. It was suddenly obvious why he had pulled off his bunny head. He had been in a panic, suddenly suffering from an allergic reaction, because his face was puffy and covered in hives, his tongue swollen and sticking out of his mouth, his eyes wide open in shock.

Raymond Dobbs was also very much dead.

# Island Food & Spirits
## by
## Hayley Powell

I simply cannot believe Easter has come around again when it seems like just yesterday we were celebrating Christmas and shoveling out from yet another winter snowstorm. But here we are knee-deep into April's mud season, and I am running around shopping for Easter treats for my grandson, who is already two years old, not to mention quite a handful, I must admit!

His curiosity at the ripe old age of two rivals his aunt Gemma's when she was that age, and I am already seeing signs that there will be lots of mischief and trouble ahead for Eli's young, doting, well-meaning parents.

I remember years back when Gemma was in the first grade, the holidays suddenly became even more exciting to her since they were also celebrated at school with Halloween costume parades downtown, Thanksgiving lunches with all the fixings, Christmas parties, gift exchanges, Valentine's Day cards; the list went on and on.

So by the time Easter rolled around, my daughter was downright over-the-moon excited for the arrival of the magical Easter Bunny after weaving her own Easter baskets, painting eggs, and planting seedlings to bring home over the Easter break.

I, on the other hand, was consumed with worry about money as my now ex-husband Danny had been out of work since right around Christmastime. He had proclaimed that he needed to find himself because the corporate world was too constricting, which was preventing him from exploring his artistic side. I never considered our small town of Bar Harbor even had "a corporate world."

Against my wishes, Danny decided to leave his steady "part-time" gig as a cashier at the Big Apple convenience store and he went to work at a Christmas tree farm in Ellsworth Falls for a whole two weeks until Christmas Eve, when he was handed a check and told, "Merry Christmas! See you next year!"

Apparently, my genius husband had not given much thought to the fact that people don't really have a big need for Christmas trees *after* Christmas! So he was jobless again.

Next, he moved on to shoveling walkways for people who were not physically able to clear the snow on their own, mostly the elderly, which would have been nice except for the fact that it was the first winter in twenty years where it mostly rained, and we had a historic snowfall of only twenty-four inches in four months, which averaged a mere six inches per month.

In Maine, we like to call that a dusting.

A light dusting.

You can see where I'm going with this. As you can imagine, my job answering phones at the *Island Times* was just not enough to support an entire household (dreamer included), and I feared we might soon be living on credit cards and coupons while Danny was exploring his artistic side stretched out on the couch watching TV.

By April I had suffered enough. The bills were piling up, and so were Danny's excuses.

So when I saw an ad in our local paper that the Walmart in Ellsworth needed someone to play the Easter Bunny every day up until Easter Sunday, I knew exactly who was going to fill the role!

I immediately informed Danny that for the money they were going to pay for the next three weeks to have someone slip into a bunny suit and take pictures with kids all day, I did not care how he did it, but I wanted to see him in that costume when I got home from work that day! And if I didn't, then he needed to pack up his things and hop on down the bunny trail and find another place to live.

That evening when I arrived home from work and went upstairs to change, there stood Danny dressed as the Easter Bunny in the middle of our bedroom floor with his arms outstretched holding a bouquet of flowers from the Shop 'n Save. I exhaled a huge sigh of relief, secure in the knowledge that at least this year we would have enough money to be able to do something for the kids for Easter and pay a few bills to boot.

My relief was short-lived, however, after only his first day. Danny came home grumpy, tired, and already complaining how awful it was playing this particular role. When he pulled his bunny suit out of his gym bag I could smell the stench from across the room.

Apparently, Jimmy Higgins's mother was so anxious for him to have his picture taken with the Easter Bunny at Walmart, she ignored little Jimmy's protest about not feeling well. The poor kid cried the whole time his mother pushed him in front of Danny, and then little Jimmy, who by now had worked himself into a tizzy, opened his mouth to protest again, but instead he spewed his entire lunch all down the front of Danny's bunny suit.

As Danny whined on and on about how much he hated this new gig, I grabbed his costume and threw it in the washing machine. I told him in no uncertain terms that he had to just suck it up. It was only for three weeks! I stared daggers at him, not budging, until finally I saw Danny pouting and nodding and mumbling, "Okay." Knowing I was not going to change my mind, he walked away sulking, and I knew I had gotten my point across, at least for now.

For the rest of the week Danny headed off in the morning and returned home that evening in a much better mood, and I was happy to see that he was finally showing some responsibility.

When the Saturday before Easter rolled around and it was Danny's last day working at Walmart, I decided to dress up the kids in their best Easter outfits that my mom had sent, and drive up to Ellsworth so they could have their photo taken with Danny dressed as the Easter Bunny. I thought it would be a fun memory for them to have a picture with their dad the year he helped out playing the Easter Bunny so the real Easter Bunny could get ready to deliver Easter eggs to all the children around the world.

The kids were excited standing in line waiting for their turn, and they kept waving to their dad, who amazingly stayed in character. I was very impressed at what a great job he was doing, and there was not one crying kid in sight. I imagined Danny was quite relieved.

Finally, it was our turn and the kids ran to hop up on their dad's lap. I was paying the photographer who was in charge of taking the pictures, and said to her, "The Easter Bunny is actually my husband and the kids are so excited to see their father, but don't worry, they won't tell anyone who he really is!"

The photographer, who was probably in her forties, gaped at me for a moment, then she threw my change at me and started screaming, "That's it, Harold! I told you if you ever cheated on me again, we were through!" She spun back in my direction, yelling in my face, "You can have him! I am so done with that clown!"

And then she stormed away.

You could have heard a pin drop in the Walmart and everyone was staring at me. I was horrified and turned to Danny, who shot up to his feet so fast that both the kids slid off his lap and fell to the floor, crying.

Then he yanked his bunny head off and hurled it on the floor. I simply stared in shock because the Easter Bunny was definitely *not* Danny!

Obviously, this was the aforementioned Harold.

I was mortified.

Where in the world was Danny?

Poor Harold just stood there calling after his wife, "Vivian, they're not my kids! I swear they're not my kids!"

I grabbed Gemma and Dustin by their hands and sheepishly asked Harold, "Do you by any chance know where Danny is?"

But he just wagged his head and chased after his wife.

I was furious and told myself that when I got my hands on Danny, he would be lucky if he lived to see Easter Sunday.

By the time we got home from Ellsworth, someone from the island who had witnessed what had happened at the store had already called Danny to warn him, so he had plenty of time to think and was already full of excuses and apologies.

I did not speak to Danny for the entire rest of the month, but he did eventually manage to get his job back at the Big Apple and the kids did end up having a nice Easter. So I finally forgave him because, as infuriating as he could be, I still did love the big lug.

Unfortunately, I knew in my heart that it was only a matter of time before his next big idea popped into his head so I had better prepare myself.

These recipes are two of my favorite Easter treats and I am sure they will become favorites of yours as well once you give them a try!

# Lemon Vodka

*Ingredients:*

2 ounces vodka
1½ ounces lemon juice
1 ounce simple syrup
Club soda
Lemon slices (optional)
Ice

Fill a cocktail glass with ice and add the first three in-gredients, stir, and add a splash of club soda. Garnish with lemon slices if using.

## Scalloped Potatoes

*Ingredients:*

¼ cup butter
1 large onion, diced
2 cloves garlic, minced
¼ cup flour
2 cups milk
1 cup chicken broth
2 cups shredded cheddar cheese (optional)
3 pounds Yukon yellow potatoes, thinly sliced
Salt and pepper to taste

Preheat oven to 350 degrees.

For your cream sauce, melt butter in medium saucepan, add onion and garlic, and heat over low heat until onion is softened, about five minutes. Add flour and whisk to combine until smooth.

Combine your milk and broth and add to saucepan a little at a time, whisking to thicken. Keep adding the liquid while still whisking until all combined and thick and creamy. Add salt and pepper to taste. Turn off heat. Add shredded cheese, stirring to combine (if using).

Grease a 9x13 baking pan and place ⅓ of the thinly sliced potatoes in the bottom of the pan and pour ⅓ of the cream sauce over potatoes.

Repeat layers ending with the cream sauce. Cover with foil, bake for 50 minutes or until tender. Broil for a few minutes to brown top.

Rest for 15 to 20 minutes before serving. Enjoy!

# Chapter Six

The paramedics, who had arrived on the scene minutes before Police Chief Sergio Alvares and his phalanx of officers, sadly declared poor Raymond Dobbs deceased just as Hayley had feared. Before moving the body, Hayley's brother-in-law Sergio conducted a preliminary investigation to determine exactly what happened.

His right-hand man, Lieutenant Donnie, always eager to prove himself to the big boss, approached Hayley with a stern look on his face. "I'm sorry, Hayley, but you're going to have to leave. I know it was you who discovered the body, big surprise there, but this is police business now so I suggest you wait out in the hall with everybody else."

Hayley ignored him, scanning the classroom. She quickly zeroed in on a tiny wadded-up purple Technicolor foil next to the body. She bent over and plucked a still wrapped chocolate Easter egg off the floor nearby.

"Hayley, what are you doing? You can't be touching anything! This is a potential crime scene," Lieutenant Donnie snapped, scowling.

Still tuning him out, Hayley unwrapped the egg and took a bite out of it. The outer coating was pure milk chocolate but inside the filling was peanut butter.

Sergio, having completed his initial sweep of the classroom, ambled up to Hayley and Donnie, who at the moment was on the verge of a major meltdown.

"Hayley, are you even listening to me? You need to leave right now!" Donnie wailed.

"Relax, Donnie, she can stay," Sergio said.

Donnie glared at Hayley, put off by the obvious nepotism at play since Hayley was related to Sergio by marriage. Anyone else would have been promptly ejected from the room.

"This is not a crime scene, in my opinion," Sergio said. "This is just a tragic accident. I believe Mr. Dobbs accidentally ingested some kind of nut, which he was allergic to, and died from anaconda shock."

He said it with a straight face.

English was native Brazilian Sergio's second language and on occasion he had a tendency to mix up some of his words.

His lieutenant did not dare to correct him.

Hayley was much braver. "Anaphylactic shock."

"That's what I said," Sergio declared, annoyed.

"Yeah, that's what he said!" Donnie lied, hoping to score a few points with the boss.

"You said anaconda, that's a really big snake. Anaphylactic shock is what happens when you have a severe allergic reaction," Hayley calmly explained.

Sergio muttered something under his breath that Hayley could not hear, which might have been a good thing.

She bent back down, grabbed another chocolate egg, unwrapped it, and then popped it in her mouth. As she chewed, she scooped up another, and then another, and another, speedily unwrapping them all and tossing them in her mouth one right after the other.

"Am I the only one bothered by the fact that she is eating candy off the floor?" Donnie asked no one in particular.

Sergio folded his arms, curious. "Hayley, do you mind telling me exactly what you're doing?"

She stood upright, talking with her mouth full. "They all have peanut butter filling, not cream filling. *All* of them! Why would Raymond carry around a whole Easter basket filled with peanut butter eggs if he was deathly allergic to them?"

"There is a simple explanation for that, Hayley," Donnie said with a condescending smirk. "He was pretending to be the Easter Bunny. His job was to give out candy to the kids, not hoard it all for himself. If he didn't eat the peanut butter eggs, they couldn't hurt him."

"But he *was* eating them right out in the open. In all the years I knew Raymond he has always craved sweets. I saw him inhaling some from the basket earlier and he was fine. They had to have been the ones with cream filling."

Sergio stared at her blankly. "So what are you trying to say?"

"I'm saying the yellow Easter basket Raymond was carrying around with him earlier was not the same yellow Easter basket that was found next to the body."

Donnie's forehead scrunched up. "I'm confused."

Hayley shot him a withering look. "Yes, Donnie. I know." Then she returned her attention back to Sergio. "If Raymond had accidentally ingested peanuts, then he would have just injected himself with his EpiPen, which he always had on him in case of an emergency. But he didn't have it on him. It was in an identical yellow Easter basket that I found with my grand . . ."

She always had trouble saying it.

She tried again.

"My grand . . ."

Still could not quite get it off the tongue.

Sergio sighed, losing patience. "Your grandson!"

"Yes. Eli."

"What was he doing with Raymond Dobbs's EpiPen?" Donnie asked, trying to insert himself back into the conversation.

Hayley shrugged. "I have no idea. But the chocolate eggs that Eli was eating from that basket were definitely cream-filled. There can only be one explanation."

Donnie scratched his head. "I'm still not getting it."

"Somebody switched the baskets!" Sergio snapped.

A sliver of light finally seemed to dawn inside Donnie's brain. "Ah, that makes total sense to me now!"

Hayley was on a roll as she considered the possible scenario. "They deliberately swapped out Raymond's yellow basket with another one filled with peanut butter eggs, knowing he wouldn't be able to resist squirreling a few for himself. When Raymond realized he had ingested peanuts he went for his EpiPen only to discover it wasn't there."

Donnie leaned forward, intrigued. "Where was it?"

"In the other basket, you moron!" Sergio roared. "Keep up!"

Donnie shrunk back. "Just so you know, name-calling can be very hurtful and lead to low morale, Chief."

Sergio balked. "You millennials need to toughen up!"

"Just to sum up, Donnie, there's a killer on the loose around here somewhere," Hayley announced, trying to hide her impatience.

Donnie's eyes widened in astonishment.

Sergio held up a hand. "Now let's just hold on a second. I will admit, it's a plausible theory, but we should not jump straight to homicide just yet, okay?"

Hayley gave him an incredulous look. "Why not?"

"Yeah, why not?" Donnie piped in, still stung by Sergio's insensitive words a few moments earlier.

"Because it's very early on in the investigation," Sergio cautioned.

"But you were ready to declare Mr. Dobbs's death as a tragic accident not five minutes ago," Donnie reminded him.

"Shut up, Donnie!" Sergio yelled before exhaling a heavy sigh. "I just need a little more time investigating before I make any final decision. Is that all right with you two?"

Hayley and Donnie, now finding themselves unexpected allies, exchanged quick looks and both nodded.

"Thank you," Sergio said.

But Hayley did not need any more time.

She was one hundred percent convinced at this point that someone had intentionally caused poor Raymond Dobbs's death.

And she was determined to find out who.

# Chapter Seven

Eli squealed with delight as he pushed his John Deere Monster Treads Lightning Wheels Tractor across Hayley's kitchen floor, scuffing it up with a trail of black marks as Hayley listlessly gave up trying to keep him relegated to the carpeting where he could do far less damage. Bruce sat at the table scarfing down yellow marshmallow Peeps left over from the ill-fated Easter egg hunt at the Emerson Conners Middle School the day before. Dustin and MacKenzie were curled up on the couch in the living room watching the glorious Technicolor classic *Easter Parade* starring Judy Garland and Fred Astaire on TCM and chowing down buttered popcorn and hot cider. Hayley had offered to keep an eye on Eli while his parents kicked back and enjoyed a little break.

"Hey, buddy, want a Peep?" Bruce offered, holding out a little marshmallow yellow birdie in the palm of his hand.

Eli's eyes widened and he broke out into a gleeful smile as he abandoned his tractor and bounded over to Bruce and snatched the treat out of his hand, jamming it into his mouth.

"Bruce, he just came down from one sugar high, you want to wind him up all over again?" Hayley sighed.

Bruce shrugged. "We're his grandparents, babe. We're supposed to spoil him. It comes with the job."

Eli chewed and chewed before finally swallowing the Peep and returned to pushing his tractor all over the kitchen again. Hayley's Shih Tzu, Leroy, was hiding under the table, eyes flicking back and forth, nervously keeping a close watch for Eli's next move, fearing he might find himself once again in the crosshairs.

Bruce noticed Hayley grimacing. "Come on, out with it. What's on your mind?"

"The yellow Easter basket and the EpiPen I found with Eli. How did he get it? Where did he find it? Did someone give it to him?"

"Why don't you just ask him?"

"He's barely two years old and not even speaking in full sentences yet, Bruce."

"Wouldn't hurt to try."

Hayley thought about it for a moment.

Bruce was right.

Why not see if the boy could recall something important?

She needed to know because she feared that Eli may have come across Raymond Dobbs's basket, grabbed it while he was not looking, and just run off with it, leaving poor Raymond high and dry when he most needed his EpiPen to ward off a severe allergic reaction.

Which would mean Eli could be directly responsible for Raymond's sudden, untimely death.

Eli banged the tractor into the refrigerator door. Hayley took the wheel from Eli. "Let's park this for a second so we can have a quick chat, okay, sweetheart?"

Hayley knelt down in front of her grandson.

He impulsively threw his arms out and hugged her around her waist, holding tight.

She had to admit the kid was absolutely adorable.

"Eli, do you remember where you got the yellow Easter basket from? Did you find it? Did someone give it to you?"

Eli nodded vigorously, giggling.

"Which is it? Did you find it?"

Eli continued nodding and cooed, "Found it! Mine!"

Okay, this was a working theory.

The basket itself was not an original design. They were sold by the dozens at the local Walgreens drugstore. If Eli made off with Raymond's basket, then it was entirely possible that Raymond spotted a similar-looking yellow basket nearby and just assumed it belonged to him.

But there were still some lingering questions bothering Hayley. How likely was it that an identical-looking Easter basket nearby would be filled with nothing but peanut butter eggs? And what was the mysterious issue between Raymond and Bill Duffy? What had they been arguing about?

Bruce stood up from the kitchen table. "I know what's going through your mind, Hayley, but we can't know for sure that Eli was responsible."

"Responsible for what?" a voice asked meekly.

Hayley closed her eyes, dreading the conversation she was about to have now with her future daughter-in-law. She pivoted to see MacKenzie hovering apprehensively in the kitchen doorway.

"Did Eli do something wrong?" MacKenzie asked shakily.

"No! I mean, we don't know yet."

Hayley took a deep breath and quickly explained how she had found Raymond's EpiPen in the Easter basket Eli was carrying around.

The blood slowly drained from MacKenzie's face. "Are you suggesting . . . ?"

Dustin ambled down the hall from the living room, immediately sensing the tension. "What's going on?"

"Your mother thinks Eli killed the Easter Bunny!" MacKenzie cried.

Dustin's mouth dropped open. "*What?*"

"I said no such thing! We don't really know anything yet. Like Bruce said, Eli could've wound up with that EpiPen a number of ways. We can't assume he just ran off with it," Hayley tried assuring his panicked parents.

But she was not doing a very good job of it.

"But what if he did? Then, it's totally Eli's fault. How will he be able to live with himself when he gets older and finally understands what happened? This is a nightmare!" Dustin whispered.

"Now hold on, please don't go jumping to conclusions. Let me do a little more digging, find some answers before we assume the worst."

"Your mother's right," Bruce joined in. "This could have gone down a number of different ways."

"Please, Hayley, I don't know what I will do if it turns out that Eli . . ." MacKenzie could not finish the sentence. The idea was just too disturbing for her to comprehend at this point.

Hayley touched her arm and gave her an encouraging smile. "Don't worry, MacKenzie, I'm on it."

She then squeezed MacKenzie's hand, which was trembling.

Hayley knew what she had to do.

She had to prove that the death of Raymond Dobbs had not been caused by her hyperactive grandson, because the alternative would most likely tear this beautiful young happy family apart.

# Chapter Eight

When Hayley breezed into the Bar Harbor All Citizens Bank the following morning with a cardboard box full of her freshly made lemon cupcakes with lavender frosting, her heart ached over the memory of longtime security guard Raymond Dobbs, who for decades was always found standing at attention by the front door ready to greet everyone who came in with a welcoming smile. His obvious absence cast a pall over the entire bank and the tellers and customers were quietly conducting their transactions in a reflective silence. Hayley knew her Easter-themed cupcakes would do little to improve the somber mood. She could see Bill Duffy in his office. The door was open and he was chatting with Ed O'Brien, a retired fireman who she had heard was looking for part-time security work. Bill was wasting no time interviewing potential replacements for Raymond. She did not want to interrupt him so she stood in line until she got to Janet Cook's window.

"Good morning, Janet," Hayley whispered.

Janet forced a smile. "Hi, Hayley."

She set the box down in front of Janet. "I brought cupcakes for the staff hoping to cheer everybody up. I know it's a very sad day around here."

"That's a lovely gesture, thank you. I'll pass them out on my break." She took the box and set it aside, then she began fiddling with the pearl necklace around her neck. "Bill has been on edge all morning trying to find a replacement for Raymond."

Bill Duffy escorted Ed O'Brien out of his office, clapping him on the back. "Thanks for coming in, Ed. I'll be in touch soon."

Ed looked slightly disappointed he had not been offered the job on the spot, but nodded with a half smile and shook Bill's hand before sauntering out the door. Bill noticed Hayley hovering by Janet's teller window. He frowned as she quickly crossed over to him.

"Bill, I was hoping we could have a quick chat," Hayley said, eyeing his office and hoping he would invite her inside, but he made no such effort.

"As you can plainly see, Hayley, now is not a good time," he said curtly.

"When might you be available?"

He glared at her before answering evenly, "I will call you when I have some free time to talk."

"It's just that I saw you and Raymond arguing at the Easter egg hunt and I was wondering—"

He cut her off. "In my office, now."

Bill grasped Hayley by the arm and steered her inside his office, shutting the door behind her. "What do you think you're doing?"

"I just want to know—"

He cut her off again. "I understand, but do you have to interrogate me in front of all my employees, like I'm some sort of suspect? That was bad form, Hayley, really bad form."

It had also been entirely intentional. She was trying to gauge his reaction when he learned that she had witnessed his heated argument with Raymond.

"I'm sorry, it's just that Raymond has always been so friendly and easygoing, it's difficult to imagine what he could have done to raise your ire like that."

"Isn't it obvious?" Bill scoffed. "Somebody robbed the bank right under our noses! Raymond was our first line of defense. He failed in his job and now it's going to cost us all big-time."

Or more to the point, it was going to cost Bill Duffy. Big-time.

"So you fired him?" Hayley asked.

"I had no choice! He's the security guard!" Bill studied Hayley's expression. "Don't give me that look!"

"What look?"

He pointed at her face. "There! That look! Like you're judging me! I didn't want to fire poor Raymond. He had been with the bank for nearly thirty years! But somebody had to take the fall for this disaster, and it sure as hell was not going to be me!"

And there it was.

Bill's blatant admission of using Raymond Dobbs as a scapegoat to cover up his own culpability with the powers that be.

Bill stared outside the large picture window separating his office from the rest of the bank. His head drooped. "Oh no. Just when I thought this day could not get any worse."

Hayley spun around to see Natalie Van Dyke marching into the bank, dragging her toy poodle, Gigi, by the leash. She was accompanied by a short, skinny young man with a mop of red curly hair and freckles all over his face. He was wearing an expensive-looking suit jacket that needed to be tailored because he was practically drowning in it.

"I better go deal with this," Bill muttered, careening out the door with Hayley following behind him.

She was not going to miss this confrontation.

Natalie's nostrils flared as she spoke. "May I ask why there is not a security guard posted at the door?"

"G-G-Good morning, Natalie," Bill stuttered.

"You may call me Mrs. Van Dyke," she seethed.

"Yes, sorry, Mrs. Van Dyke. As you may have heard, our longtime security guard, Raymond Dobbs, tragically passed away recently."

"Of course I heard! It's all anyone on the island is talking about. But at the risk of sounding slightly callous, the man died the day before yesterday! What have you been doing? Haven't you had enough time to find a suitable replacement?"

She sounded more than *slightly* callous.

"I have been busy interviewing potential candidates and checking references and I am sure I will hire someone by the end of the day."

"And what about in the meantime? Are you just going to allow more thieves to waltz in here and make off with more money and valuables belonging to your customers?"

"No, of course not. We have been on high alert ever since the incident with your safety deposit box. And once we install the new hand scan system, the bank will be more secure than ever."

"Well, what good does that do me? *My* valuables have already been stolen!" Natalie sniped.

"We will retrieve everything that was taken. I can promise you that, Nat . . . I mean Mrs. Van Dyke," Bill croaked.

Out of the corner of her eye, Natalie spotted Janet Cook munching on one of Hayley's lemon cupcakes with lavender frosting. "Am I interrupting some kind of Easter party?"

Bill audibly groaned as he watched Janet self-consciously wipe some frosting off her cheek with her finger. "No, Mrs. Van Dyke. I have no idea where those came from."

"Hayley brought them in. They're delicious," Janet offered helpfully. "Would you like to try one?"

Natalie Van Dyke was not amused. "No, thank you. I am not here to attend your little office soiree. I am here on official business."

Bill nodded, relieved. "How may I help you today?"

Natalie turned to the young man hiding behind her. "This is my grandson Elroy."

Bill shot out a hand. "Nice to meet you, Elroy."

The boy limply took his hand.

He looked as if he wanted to be anywhere else.

"Elroy just graduated top of his class from Suffolk University Law School," Natalie said, finally managing a smile. It was a crooked, unattractive smile, which would probably explain why she rarely bothered using it.

"Congratulations!" Bill crowed.

Elroy, stone-faced, nodded impassively.

He obviously took after his filthy-rich sourpuss grandmother.

"Tell Mr. Duffy who is your very first client," she prodded.

"Granny," Elroy muttered.

Natalie took him by the chin. "That's right. And Granny is so, so proud of you." She slowly turned back around, her demeanor returning to its natural wretched state. "I have hired him as my attorney in my lawsuit against you."

Bill's face twitched. "Y-You're suing the bank?"

"Not just the bank, I am suing you personally!" She pointed at him with a crooked finger. "You were the only one besides me who had a key to my safety deposit box. You need to pay out of your own pocket for your reckless disregard for proper security measures."

"Please, Mrs. Van Dyke, is going to court absolutely necessary? Can't we find another way to somehow work this out?"

She ignored his desperate plea. "I suggest you find yourself a damn good lawyer because my brilliant grandson here is going to bleed you dry, Duffy! Come along, Gigi!"

She tugged on the leash as Hayley noticed Mrs. Van Dyke's poodle squatting in the middle of the floor of the bank.

"Oh, look, everyone, Gigi just made a deposit," Natalie said with a raucous laugh.

Sure enough, Gigi had done a number two on the floor and did not even look embarrassed about it.

Natalie, nose in the air, glared down at Bill. "You better clean that up before someone steps in it." Then she swept out of the bank with Elroy and Gigi on her heels before Bill could say another word as everyone in the bank, customers included, watched in stunned silence.

Why Janet thought now might be a good time to hand out Hayley's cupcakes was anybody's guess. She probably just felt the burning desire to do something besides watch her boss and boyfriend, Bill Duffy, melt into a puddle in front of all his employees.

As Bill rushed off to find a broom and dustpan and the other tellers tried to make small talk with Hayley, complimenting the tasty treats she always dropped off to them every Easter, Hayley was reminded of the time, many years ago, when she had worked at the same window as Janet Cook, when Janet was not even born yet, that first Easter when Raymond Dobbs took on the role of the beloved Easter Bunny of Bar Harbor.

# Chapter Nine

*Good Friday, 1996*

It was only Hayley's first week working as a teller at Bar Harbor All Citizens Bank and she was already going to be late. She had stayed up late baking peanut butter oatmeal Easter cookies for her co-workers and fell asleep on the couch in the small one-bedroom apartment she shared with her new husband, Danny. The apartment was located above the Rexall drugstore on Main Street. They had only been married a few months right out of high school and were facing the responsibilities of adulthood without financial help from their parents.

Danny, who had begged his parents to pay for his bartending school tuition and promised a quick return on their investment, had surprised everyone by actually finishing the course and receiving a bona fide certificate. Even Hayley, his devoted young wife, thought he would get bored and drop out but he had stuck with it. And with his engaging personality, Danny even managed to land a job tending bar in the afternoon at the popular local watering hole the Thirsty Whale (years before Hayley's brother Randy bought it and rechristened it Drinks Like a Fish).

But unfortunately, true to form, Danny had been promptly fired by the boss during his second shift for sneaking free cocktails, with top-shelf booze no less, to all his regular drinking buddies. So now, like it or not, at the ripe old age of eighteen, Hayley was the sole breadwinner of the family.

Hayley had never been particularly good at math so working in a bank was hardly a natural fit, but she had managed to make it through the training period with little difficulty, and was now muddling through with check cashing, deposits, withdrawals, transfers, loan payments, cashier's checks, and opening and closing of accounts. She kept telling herself that this was simply a temporary situation until she could figure out what she really wanted to do with her life.

Danny had been so distressed by his sudden termination, he had commiserated with too many beers the night before, passing out early. Hayley slept on the couch to avoid being kept awake all night with Danny's deafening snoring, which was a side effect when he drank too much alcohol. Unfortunately, the couch was out of earshot of her alarm in the bedroom. When Hootie & the Blowfish began playing on her clock radio indicating it was time to rise and shine, a bleary-eyed, hungover Danny had testily reached out from underneath the covers and pressed the snooze button before drifting back to sleep. When the morning sun began shining through the living room blinds, finally waking Hayley up, she suddenly realized it was twenty minutes past eight and she had to be at the bank by eight thirty. She skipped her shower and makeup routine in order to quickly iron a wrinkled blouse and box up the cookies she had baked the previous evening before dashing out the door, annoyed that Danny had blissfully been able to sleep through the pandemonium of her running around frantically trying to get ready for work.

When Hayley sailed through the door of the bank just a few doors down from her apartment and across the street, she was somewhat relieved to see that she was only four minutes late. No one seemed to mind either, especially when she began handing out delicious-looking cookies to everyone. There was a new security guard in his early to mid-thirties and quite handsome posted at the door. He filled out his uniform rather nicely.

"Good morning," Hayley said brightly. "I'm Hayley."

"Raymond Dobbs," he replied with a slight military salute.

Hayley had heard there was going to be a new security guard starting at the bank today but had not been told who it was. She knew the name Dobbs but had never met this fine specimen of a man. "Would you like an Easter cookie?"

Raymond studied the cookies. "What kind are they?"

"Peanut butter oatmeal."

He crinkled his nose. "Uh, no, thank you."

Hayley tried not to feel insulted but he had recoiled at the sight of her cookies in such an obvious manner that she could not help but feel just a little hurt.

"Welcome to All Citizens Bank," she said before moving on to the mortgage loan officer, Bill Duffy, who was young but quickly making a name for himself. Bill soothed her wounded pride by snatching not one, not two, but three of her cookies and stuffing them into his mouth and crowing about how tasty they were.

As Hayley took her place behind her teller window, she overheard Bill talking to Raymond.

"Sorry to hear about your grandfather, Raymond."

"Thanks. But he'd been ill for a while. I hate to say it, but his passing was almost a blessing at this point."

"Well, I know a lot of people in town who are sure going to miss him, especially all the little kids at the Emerson Conners Easter egg hunt when he dresses up as the Easter Bunny. Any idea who they're going to get to replace him?"

"You're looking at him," Raymond said. "I volunteered to fill in this year, just this once, in order to give the town council more time to find somebody permanent to take over."

"That's awfully nice of you, Ray," Bill said, patting him on the back. "I'm sure the town appreciates your service."

At nine o'clock sharp the doors officially opened and Hayley's BFF, Liddy, who was home from college on a break, was her first customer. Luckily, Liddy did not have anything too complicated for Hayley to do. She was just cashing a three-hundred-dollar check from her mother. Hayley began counting out the amount in tens and twenties.

"I told Mom the money was for textbooks," Liddy confided to Hayley. "But I'm actually using it to buy tickets to the Garth Brooks concert in Boston next weekend! I'm taking my roommates!"

"Your secret is safe with me," Hayley said, knowing three hundred dollars was basically a rounding error in her mother Celeste's checkbook.

Liddy leaned forward and whispered, "By the way, who's the hot guy at twelve o'clock?"

Hayley sighed. "I'm not good with the time thing. I never know where to start looking on the clock. Which way is twelve?"

"By the front door. The sexy man in uniform."

"Oh! That's Raymond, the new security guard. He just started today. Cute, isn't he?"

"He's gorgeous!"

"I thought so too until he made a rude face when I offered him one of my homemade Easter cookies."

"Well, I'm certainly ready to forgive him," Liddy cooed, scooping up her wad of cash after signing the back of her mother's check. "By the way, I know you're probably going to Danny's parents for Easter dinner on Sunday, but tomorrow you have to help me with Mona duty. I can't face her alone."

Hayley's other BFF Mona, like Hayley, had also married right after graduation. Her high school sweetheart, Dennis, was about as ambitious as her own husband, Danny, except without the charm or personality. Dennis's biggest talent seemed to be procreation because Mona was already knocked up with their first child (the first of many to come). Unfortunately, poor Mona was suffering through a difficult pregnancy, and since Dennis was essentially useless, Mona's mother, Jane, along with Hayley, were picking up the slack taking care of all her needs. And now that Liddy was home visiting, she had been roped into helping as well.

"I'll swing by your mother's house around eight tomorrow morning and pick you up," Hayley offered.

Liddy breathed a sigh of relief. "Thank you. Mona's hard enough to deal with under ordinary circumstances but her being six months pregnant takes it to a whole new level!"

Liddy blew a kiss to Hayley, pocketed her money, and then sashayed toward the door where Raymond politely opened it for her. She stopped to chat and introduce herself, flirting shamelessly on her way out.

The following morning Hayley left Danny at their kitchen table pretending to pore over the local job listings while drinking his coffee, but she knew it was all for show.

The second she was out the door he would be on the couch, channel surfing.

When Hayley arrived at the Crawford house, Liddy was not even dressed yet. Her mother, Celeste, had left the day before for a weekend shopping trip in Portland, so Liddy had the whole house to herself. Hayley tried nudging Liddy along because she knew Mona was probably already yelling at the top of her lungs from her bed wondering why her two nursemaids were running so late.

Liddy stood in front of her mirror trying on a bulky green sweater. "Does this make me look fat?"

"You look fine. Come on, just pick something. We need to go," Hayley said.

"No, I look like an avocado. I have a beige cashmere in the closet. Could you get it for me?"

Hayley knew there was no point in arguing. Liddy would not budge until she was absolutely satisfied with her appearance.

When Hayley opened the closet door, she stopped dead in her tracks. Hanging on the rack was a giant Easter Bunny costume. The head was on the shelf staring down at Hayley. She let out a surprised gasp.

Hayley took a moment to collect herself. "Um, Liddy?"

"Did you find it?"

"I found something. Would you mind explaining this?"

Liddy turned around and suddenly looked ill, her face turning almost as green as her sweater. "Oh . . . I forgot that was there. He had to run out early this morning to run an errand and said he'd swing by later to pick it up on his way to the Easter egg hunt."

She could only be talking about one person.

"Raymond Dobbs?"

Liddy nodded.

"Raymond Dobbs was here?"

"All night," Liddy said almost proudly.

"Liddy, you're a college freshman. He's like twenty years older than you."

"Fifteen, maybe seventeen. Age is just a number, Hayley. We have a very special connection. I honestly believe he could be the one."

Hayley had no time to question this latest revelation.

Liddy had on countless occasions declared that she had met "*the one.*"

In fact, there had been so many "ones" they had now surpassed double digits. But if Hayley knew one thing about her best friend Liddy, when it came to men, she just would not listen to anyone's advice. And she knew a relationship with Raymond Dobbs probably would not last.

And it did not.

The whirlwind romance came to an unceremonious end a week later at the end of spring break when Liddy received a phone call from the boy she had broken up with the weekend before she came home, begging her to take him back. He had a Mustang convertible and offered to drive her and her roommates to the Garth Brooks concert in Boston so the romance was instantly back on, leaving poor Raymond Dobbs high and dry.

Although Raymond never spoke of Liddy to anyone, especially his co-workers at the bank, Hayley could see his heart was broken. She decided to cheer him up with some leftover dessert she had made for Sunday dinner at Danny's parents' house, no-bake peanut butter bars, which were Danny's favorites.

Upon presenting the plate to Raymond, he once again turned his nose up in disgust and declined. Hayley kept a stiff upper lip and made a beeline to her teller window.

Bill Duffy, who had been approving a large withdrawal at another window, casually sauntered over to Hayley.

"Don't take it personally. He's allergic to peanuts. Just a whiff could send him straight to the hospital, or worse, kill him." Bill plucked one of the bars out of the box and took a big bite. "Luckily, I'm not!"

"Oh, that's so nice to hear!" Hayley cried. "I mean not the dying part, but the fact it has nothing to do with me or my baking skills." She stole a glance at Raymond, who stood at his post, staring forlornly at the floor, not the friendly greeter he had been since his first day. She resolved to return the next day with some Thin Mint whoopie pies or pink lemonade rolls, something one hundred percent nut free.

Everyone at the bank was soon acutely aware of Raymond's nut allergy. It became an unwritten rule to never bring any food into the bank that was laced with nuts of any kind. Long after Hayley left the bank to go work at the *Island Times* newspaper as office manager and eventually food columnist, she would continue delivering treats during the various holidays to her former co-workers at All Citizens, always carefully avoiding nuts as an ingredient. Everyone, from longtime employees like Bill Duffy, now the president, to the more recent hires like Bill's pretty, new, much younger girlfriend, Janet Cook, all knew about Raymond's lethal nut allergy.

Anyone could have used that key information to their advantage.

And as Hayley recalled those early years at All Citizens, it was impossible to ignore the obvious common denominator Bill Duffy and Raymond Dobbs shared—an intense attraction to much younger women. And she could not help but wonder if that might have had something to do with Raymond's hasty and unexpected demise.

# Chapter Ten

As Hayley descended the stone steps leading from the parking lot to Sand Beach with her dog, Leroy, in tow, she knew her hunch had paid off. She had heard from a few locals that Natalie Van Dyke always drove her dogs over from Northeast Harbor every weekday morning at six to let them run along the unique stretch of sand and shell fragments, with few people around to bother them.

Sand Beach in Acadia National Park was one of the most popular destinations on the island during the summer months, a small 290-yard inlet nestled between the granite mountains and rocky shores of Mount Desert Island. And there, strolling back from the opposite end of the beach on this frightfully chilly April morning, was Natalie Van Dyke, her toy poodle Gigi snug in the crook of her arm as her two larger dogs, German shepherds, raced each other as they sidestepped the crashing waves rushing up the beach.

When Hayley reached the bottom of the steps, she unhooked Leroy from his leash and he bolted toward the dogs four times his size, not the least bit intimidated. The German shepherds paused, staring at the tiny missile heading straight for them. When Leroy was upon them, they began the ritual of sniffing the little one's backside.

Hayley could see Gigi squirming in Natalie's arms, desperate to greet this new addition to the sandy dog park, and so Natalie finally set her down so she could go join in on the fun. The sun was just cresting over Cadillac Mountain, shining brightly enough that Natalie had to raise a hand over her eyes to see who was approaching. She offered a wan smile when she recognized Hayley.

"Good morning!" Hayley chirped, acting surprised to see anyone else on the beach this early in the morning, although she had carefully arranged this "chance" meeting.

"Is he friendly?" Natalie asked, scrunching up her nose, gesturing toward Leroy.

"Oh, yes! Very!"

Hayley could not for the life of her imagine Leroy nipping at the pair of German shepherds, who could so easily tear him apart at a moment's notice. As for Gigi, she was keeping a safe distance until she was certain Leroy was a friend and not a foe.

Natalie stared at Hayley suspiciously. "I haven't seen you out here before."

"That's because Saturdays are usually the only day I can sleep in. But my little guy has been cooped up in the house all week, so I thought I'd get him out for some fresh air."

Natalie glanced over at the dogs to see Leroy and Gigi, fast friends now touching each other's noses as the German shepherds continued running alongside each other down to the far end of the beach.

"Your husband called yesterday wanting to ask me questions for his column. I thought you might have shown up here to try and convince me to do an interview about my stolen valuables."

Bruce worked as a columnist at the *Island Times* covering local crimes.

"He doesn't really discuss the stories he's working on

with me," Hayley assured her, hoping the little white lie was not so obvious to Natalie.

"Well, you can tell him when I'm ready to talk, it's going to be for a much more consequential paper like the *Boston Globe* or the *New York Times*."

Hayley had to suppress a laugh. Would the paper of record, the *New York Times*, ever be interested in a story about some jewelry and documents pilfered from a small-town bank's safety deposit box? It seemed Natalie Van Dyke had a much higher opinion of herself than Hayley initially assumed.

"There is a conspiracy going on at that bank and I believe Bill Duffy is at the heart of it, especially given his past history!" Natalie said sharply.

It was true. Bill Duffy did have a checkered past at All Citizens. Back in the early aughts, there was a federal investigation involving some approved fraudulent loans just after Bill was promoted to vice president. The rumor was that Bill was almost indicted by the feds, but in the end he was offered immunity from prosecution in exchange for his testimony pointing the finger at his replacement, a recent transplant from Worcester, Massachusetts, who was toiling in the mortgage loans department. Everyone assumed Bill would be fired, but with no charges brought against him, and the fact that he had helped put away the main culprit, Bill managed to wriggle his way out of the depths of the scandal, get a slap on the wrist, and miraculously remain employed at the bank.

The air of suspicion around him eventually cleared up and he was appointed president in 2014 even though the fall guy for the crime claimed Bill had been in on the illegal scam the whole time. Now, after so many years had gone by, most people in town considered Bill an honest, stand-up guy, and he worked very hard to maintain his restored reputation.

However, Natalie Van Dyke was buying none of it. "Once a crook, always a crook!"

"I just think Bill is way too smart to try something as brazen as steal from one of the wealthiest people on the island."

"I'm not wealthy, I'm comfortable," Natalie insisted.

Something most rich people say.

"And have you heard the latest rumor? He's now dating a young woman who could be his daughter, maybe even his granddaughter! I find that highly objectionable. It speaks to his character. At least in my case . . ." She quickly allowed her words to trail off.

There was an uncomfortable silence.

Hayley could not resist. "At least in your case what?"

"Never mind," Natalie snapped.

Hayley detected a slight curl in the corners of Natalie's mouth as if she was about to break into a smile.

Hayley leaned in closer. "Are you dating someone, Natalie?"

Natalie's husband of forty-two years had died three summers ago following complications from a stroke. According to local gossip, Natalie had shown little to no interest in entering any kind of new relationship after his passing. She was perfectly content to focus her attention and vast amounts of money on her three dogs.

"I'd rather not talk about it," Natalie said, unable to subdue the sly smile now creeping across her face. She was actually blushing. Her eyes even twinkled a bit.

"Does he live on the island?"

Natalie sniffed, reclaiming her typically dour demeanor. "You're nosier than that reporter husband of yours! I said

I do *not* wish to discuss it." She clapped her hands. "Duke! Rocky! Gigi! Time to go!"

The two German shepherds snapped to attention and trotted back toward her while Gigi remained rolling in the sand playing with Leroy. "Goodbye, Hayley." She started off but then stopped and twirled back around. "Mark my words. If it's the last thing I do, I am going to make sure that sticky-fingered lying cheat Bill Duffy goes straight to prison!"

Hayley desperately wanted to keep the conversation going and find out the identity of Natalie Van Dyke's mystery suitor. She also concluded that if Natalie was comparing her new beau to Bill Duffy's recent girlfriend, Janet Cook, then it could be safe to assume that the man who had so obviously captured Natalie's heart was much younger as well.

Hayley was now on a mission. Because a new man in Natalie Van Dyke's life could potentially hold the key to this whole baffling case.

# Island Food & Spirits
## by
## Hayley Powell

My mother has always gotten a kick out of surprising us with very short-notice visits over the years, secretly flying up from Florida to Maine and just blithely marching through the front door with warm hugs and kisses. I might be going out on a limb here, but ten times out of ten these impromptu visits have never worked out the way she had imagined them in her head: her bursting through the front door, arms outstretched, announcing, "Surprise! Nanny's here!" Us jumping up from a beautifully set dinner table and tossing our linen napkins down on the table next to our healthy green salads, and rushing into her arms in our perfectly pressed clothes, enveloping dear, sweet Mother in a gigantic family bear hug.

Nope.

It had never happened that way.

Not even close.

Usually her unexpected arrival involved her walking in at the exact moment my daughter, Gemma, and I were screaming at the top of our lungs at each other for some unknown reason, Dustin playing his video games full blast. And don't let me get started on the state of disaster that the house was usually in with dirty dishes and soda spills on the coffee table as she stood there in the doorway with a look of utter horror on her face, taking in the chaotic scene, before yelling over the sounds of a gun battle on TV, "Maybe I should stay at a hotel?"

That was more in line with the reality of her surprise visits that began when her two grandchildren were born. So I really should have been more prepared for the phone call announcing her imminent arrival the Easter when Gemma was eight years old and Dustin was five. With less than a day's notice, I began running around the house like a chicken with its head cut off wildly throwing everything that was on the floor and furniture into a laundry basket and then dumping it all out into a closet.

My BFF Mona had happened to stroll in that morning to witness the frenzied commotion. She guffawed and said, "I'm just going to take a wild guess. Is Mama Sheila showing up today?"

I threw her an exasperated look and sarcastically asked her what made her think that as I pulled out snack wrappers stuffed between the couch cushions.

"Because you have copies of *Better Homes and Gardens* and *House Beautiful* magazines on your coffee table instead of soda cans and pizza crust."

The two magazines she mentioned were subscriptions my mother had bought me for Christmas after her last visit, hoping I might learn something. But the joke was on her. I loved the recipes so I was not terribly offended by the gesture.

Mona sat on the couch and patted the seat beside her. I sighed and plopped down next to her, already exhausted.

She told me to stop making myself crazy because in a few days it would all be over and forgotten until the next visit.

But this time was different. I told Mona not only had my mother requested that the kids and I attend church with her Easter morning as well as the church egg hunt, but she had also asked if I would fill and donate two dozen or more plastic candy-filled eggs since she would not have time to do it herself when she arrived. She planned on having lunch with her two dearest friends: Jane, Mona's mom; and Celeste, my other BFF Liddy's mom.

I agreed and barely made it to the Shop 'n Save in time before they closed to buy candy. Luckily, I had leftover plastic eggs from the ones I had already filled for Jane's yearly Easter party and seafood buffet that she threw for close friends and family. She even had an adult-only Easter egg hunt which everyone loved.

Mona announced that she was just stopping by to pick up the eggs for her mom's party so they could hide them after church, and if I wanted, she would take my eggs for the church with her as well since she was also dropping some off from her mother.

Mona shook her head, laughing, and said after all those years of trying to get out of going to church, it seemed like she was in that house of worship more now than ever. Resigned, I went to the hall to pick up the eggs and handed them over to Mona.

The next few hours flew by, and before I knew it, Nanny was practically catapulting through the door with stuffed Easter bunnies and wet sloppy kisses, but not before I caught her glancing around the house for a quick inspection while I prayed she would not look in the closets.

The following morning, as we were getting ready for the church service and egg hunt, Mom mentioned for about the sixth time that she could not understand why my then-husband Danny would work on a holiday. I told her it was a busy day, being the only store open in town for gas or quick items, knowing full well he had requested the shift two days ago when he found out my mother was coming for a visit.

Danny had always sworn that my mother cried so loudly during our wedding ceremony on purpose just to drown out our vows. A claim she denies to this day. But honestly, I think everyone in attendance would agree with Danny on that one.

After the Easter service, we all filed out of the church to the side yard and watched as all the excited children raced around collecting the hidden Easter eggs and stuffing them in their baskets.

I had to admit it was shaping up to be an incredible day. Mom was happily catching up with old friends, and with her besties at her side, along with me and my own besties, Mona and Liddy, we were all looking forward to Jane's raucous seafood buffet and adult Easter egg hunt later in the afternoon.

Finally, all the eggs had been found and the excited kids plopped down on the grass to inspect their spoils, dumping them out and eagerly cracking them open to see all the goodies inside.

Mom sauntered over, gave me a big hug, and told me what a wonderful time she was having. And seeing her adorable grandchildren hunt for eggs on Easter was an added bonus.

Just then, Dustin stood up and started yelling at the top of his lungs, "Mom! Mom! Look what I got! A bottle of wine just like you drink!" I thought, what in the world is that boy talking about? Turning to Dustin, I suddenly saw him standing there holding a tiny minibar-sized bottle of Cabernet in the air, waving it around, grinning from ear to ear. I darted over to him and snatched the bottle out of his hand.

Oh no! No!

This could not be happening.

Horrified, I watched as all the kids began waving small airplane bottles of different liquors (rum, vodka, whiskey, you name it!) in the air as if they had won the grand prize, and me standing in the middle of this gaggle of little people, unable to retrieve them all because there were just too many!

Parents frantically ran toward their children, scooping up all the liquor bottles out of their kids' hands as they shot confused and angry looks in my direction. I just wanted the ground to open up and swallow me whole.

But instead, I tried to calm everyone down and explain that it was all a huge mistake, and that the liquor bottles were meant for Jane's adult Easter egg hunt and the bags must have somehow gotten mixed up! But no one seemed to listen as they began furiously dragging their children away. I did catch Mr. Stevens grab a tiny bottle of Jim Beam away from his daughter Katy, unscrew the top, and swig it down when he thought no one was looking.

Just when I thought things could not get any worse, I suddenly heard my mother's bellowing voice over the commotion. "Hayley Lee Powell!"

I took a deep breath and slowly turned toward the voice of doom. I knew I would not hear the end of this anytime soon. Mom would be dining out on this unfortunate mishap for months, if not years!

In the end, however, it all worked out. Surprisingly, the voice of reason turned out to be Reverend Booth, who quickly calmed everyone down and even laughed about it, telling all the parents that mistakes happen, and we should all go home and enjoy the rest of Easter day with our loving families.

Which, thankfully, everyone did without further drama.

As I walked to the car with my mom and kids, I heard Reverend Booth call my name. I turned, and he said with a wink, "I'll see you in church next Sunday, Hayley!" I must have hesitated because I felt my mother's elbow jab my side and I found myself smiling and waving. "See you next Sunday, Reverend!"

I hope everyone is ready for Easter, which is right around the corner. But if you need some more mouthwatering recipes for side dishes, I have a delicious potato recipe. One can never, ever have too many potato recipes, I always say.

But first, it's always best to enjoy a lovely cranberry cocktail before getting started in the kitchen.

I always say that, too!

## Cranberry Cocktail

*Ingredients:*

1 ounce cranberry juice
1 lime wedge
Sparkling wine or favorite champagne
Frozen cranberries

In a chilled champagne glass add the cranberry juice and a squeeze of fresh lime. Top your glass with the champagne and add a few frozen cranberries and enjoy.

# French Onion Potato Casserole

## *Ingredients:*

3 pounds potatoes
1 cup sour cream
1 cup half and half
1 whole package Lipton French Onion Soup mix
2 cups shredded cheddar cheese (or cheese of your choice)

Preheat your oven to 400 degrees. Slice your potatoes into ¼-inch slices (I use a food processor). You want them all to be pretty much the same size.

In a large bowl, whisk the sour cream, half and half, and soup mix. Add the sliced potatoes and one cup of the cheddar cheese and mix until well combined.

Pour into a three-quart casserole dish or 13x9 pan and spread to fit pan.

Cover with aluminum foil and bake for 50 to 55 minutes.

Remove from oven and check to see if potatoes are soft. If not, cover and place back in oven until soft.

When done, remove from oven and add the rest of the shredded cheese and place back in the oven for 10 to 15 more minutes until cheese is melted and just beginning to brown.

Remove from oven, then let sit for 15 minutes.

Serve and enjoy!

# Chapter Eleven

"Hayley, thank you so much for babysitting Eli while Dustin and I have a date night," MacKenzie said as she and Dustin threw on their coats.

They were heading to Reel Pizza, a local cinema/pizza joint that was having a revival of classic superhero film series. Tonight's screening was a double feature of the first two Tim Burton–directed Batman movies starring Michael Keaton. Dustin had been obsessed with watching them on DVD as a kid and was not going to miss the chance of seeing both of these films, which had had such a profound impact on his childhood, on the big screen. Hayley was more than happy to look after her grandson for the evening.

"If he starts acting up, just put on a CoComelon video and he'll calm right down," MacKenzie advised.

"Oh, I'm sure I won't have to do that. He's been an angel all afternoon," Hayley assured her, even though at the moment Eli was in his high chair throwing Cheerios and milk at Bruce, who appeared as if he was about to be sick because he was so grossed out.

Hayley also refrained from offering her opinion about all the videos they allowed Eli to watch. CoComelon was a huge hit among the toddler set, but there was controversy among parents who claimed the videos were triggering tantrums and delaying speech. MacKenzie was aware of these accusations, but thought that like most things, small doses could not do any harm. Hayley held her tongue but she did not agree. Although the videos touched upon typical preschool themes, Hayley strongly felt they were hyperstimulating, acting as a drug, a stimulant. So for tonight, at least, she was not going to allow Eli to watch anything CoComelon-related.

Once Hayley saw Dustin and MacKenzie off, she headed to the kitchen, where Bruce was attempting to mop up the mess Eli had made with his milk and Cheerios.

"Why did you feed him cereal for dinner?"

"Because I thought I would literally vomit if I had to watch him squeeze mashed potatoes through his fingers again!"

"Now that we've fed him, I thought we might take him on a nice car ride," Hayley suggested.

Bruce stared at her blankly. "Why?"

"Because he's been cooped up in the house all day."

"So why can't we just take him out into the backyard for a few minutes to get some fresh air?"

"Because it's a nice evening and I'm in the mood for a drive around the island," Hayley said more forcefully.

Bruce was suddenly suspicious. "But why fuss with a car seat? And you know I just got my Mazda detailed and we have a lot of accumulated evidence that Eli can be quite destructive when he wants to be."

"We could take mine, but your Mazda has a much bigger back seat for Eli's car seat. It just makes more practical sense."

"Okay, but what doesn't make sense is this scenic drive you want to go on that a rambunctious two-year-old will hardly appreciate. He's more impressed with popping bubble wrap. What's really going on here?"

"Bruce, don't make a whole court case out of it, okay? I just thought we'd all enjoy a relaxing drive!"

Bruce folded his arms, still not convinced. "Okay, where did you have in mind?"

Hayley breathed a heavy sigh. She sometimes hated how well her husband knew her. "Nowhere in particular. Maybe we could head over toward Northeast Harbor."

He smiled knowingly. "Northeast Harbor? Why not Southwest Harbor?"

Hayley picked up a dry cloth off the kitchen counter and began wiping Eli's mouth and hands clean. "There is that cute little ice cream parlor that might still be open, and we could get Eli a small cone and park somewhere and people watch."

Bruce nodded. "Any people in particular?"

Hayley shrugged. "I don't know. Whoever is out and about."

"Like Natalie Van Dyke?" Bruce had her dead to rights and he was enjoying every minute of it. "Maybe park outside her estate and get a glimpse of this new mystery boyfriend she almost spilled the beans to you about?"

"You're talking like I want to go on some kind of a stakeout!" Hayley replied haughtily.

Hayley finished wiping the milk and Cheerios off of Eli and Bruce lifted him out of the high chair.

"Come on, Eli, let's get your coat on so you, me, and Grandma can go spy on people!" Bruce chuckled.

"You make it sound so crass!" Hayley cried.

"Because it is!" Bruce countered. "But I never said I'm not game. You forget I'm a crime reporter. I'm interested in uncovering the facts just as much as you are! So let's go!"

They bundled Eli up and loaded him into the car seat in the back of Bruce's Mazda CX-5, and then drove over to

Northeast Harbor, a quiet enclave for the rich and famous on Mount Desert Island. The ice cream parlor had closed only minutes prior to them arriving and Eli was already getting antsy. He was kicking the newly detailed back seat, leaving scuff marks, so Hayley dashed into a mini-mart at the nearest gas station and bought him some chocolate candy, which he used to smear the upholstery.

Bruce, to his credit, did not make a scene or even whisper a disparaging comment out of the side of his mouth. He knew it would be up to Hayley to scrub everything down the next morning since this family outing had been her bright idea.

They parked across the road outside the large, imposing wrought-iron gate that led into Natalie Van Dyke's massive sixty-three-acre estate. Eli was now hyped up on candy and trying to free himself from his car seat prison, kicking and screaming, his tiny hands wrapped around the strap, desperately trying to pull it off him.

Hayley tried a game of peekaboo, which did nothing to calm him down. Then she tried entertaining him with a coloring book and crayons, but he just hurled the book at her before using a red crayon to draw on the leather seat headrest in front of him.

"Please, Hayley, do something!" Bruce begged.

She knew there was only one solution, although she loathed the idea of implementing it. But if they were going to be able to remain on this stakeout for more than five minutes, she was going to have to relent.

After all, desperate situations required desperate measures.

She pulled out her phone, tapped the YouTube app, and did a quick search. Within seconds she was playing a Co-Comelon video. She handed her phone to Eli.

Suddenly he fell silent, enthralled with the video.

No longer would she ever be able to judge anyone else's parenting skills.

Now with Eli happily occupied, Hayley and Bruce could keep their eyes fixed on the Van Dyke estate, waiting to see if anyone would come in or out. Hayley's whole premise for this stakeout was based on the probability that Natalie Van Dyke's new boyfriend might show up after work to see her, if he was not already a man of leisure who did not have to bother holding down a paying job. Hayley's plan was for them to hang out for a few hours and see if her hunch would pay off.

They did not have to wait long.

Within ten minutes, a truck pulled up to the front gate. The window rolled down and a man reached out to press the call button on the security pad. Seconds later, the creaky gate began to swing open.

There was a logo on the side of the truck that Hayley knew well. It was for Shields Heating & Plumbing. Either Natalie Van Dyke was having plumbing issues or the young, handsome, volcanic Whiskey Shields was her brand-spanking-new secret lover.

# Chapter Twelve

"Come on, Hayley," Bruce scoffed on the other end of the phone from his office at the *Island Times*. "You honestly expect me to believe you right now?"

Hayley, standing in her kitchen, was indignant. "Yes, Bruce. As my husband I absolutely expect you to believe me when I tell you something!"

She could not blame him for his skepticism because she could hardly believe what she had said herself.

Earlier that morning Hayley had been drinking her third cup of coffee and noshing on a poppy-seed bagel when MacKenzie decided to give Eli a much needed bath. She filled up the tub and unpacked his favorite bath toys, especially his sing and swim blue baby shark that paddled around the water playing a mind-numbing repetitive song. Hayley could hear Eli splashing and giggling as the song played over and over.

*Baby Shark Do Do Do Do Do Do Do . . .*
*Baby Shark Do Do Do Do Do Do Do . . .*

Again and again.

Over and over.

It was slowly driving her to insanity.

Dustin had been spared this torture because he was out on a run around Eagle Lake.

Hayley had to do something quick so she grabbed Leroy's leash off a hook in the laundry room, attached it to his collar, and took him out for a nice long walk while silently praying that bath time would be over when they finally returned home, and that annoying song would no longer be echoing through her brain.

She had brought her iPhone and earbuds and played Lizzo, Billie Eilish, Taylor Swift, Ed Sheeran, anyone to help her get that annoying, repetitive kiddie tune out of her head.

Nothing seemed to work.

After forty minutes, Leroy had tuckered out and defiantly tried steering Hayley back home, but she slowed their pace down, hoping to buy a little more time.

Finally, when they had arrived back at the house and barreled through the back door, Leroy scampering straight for his water bowl, Hayley stopped to listen.

The song was mercifully no longer playing.

But then she had noticed water dripping from the ceiling in the corner in the kitchen just underneath where the bathroom was located and heard a commotion upstairs.

Hayley bounded up the steps to see Eli running around naked as MacKenzie gripped a plunger, desperately trying to unclog the toilet that was overflowing onto the tile floor and pouring out into the hallway.

"MacKenzie, what happened?" Hayley cried.

"We were done with bath time and I was drying Eli off with a towel, and I turned my back for one second, and the next thing I knew the toilet was overflowing. I think Eli tried to set his baby shark free by flushing it down the toilet and now it's stuck in the pipes!"

Hayley could see that MacKenzie was unraveling fast, so she snatched the plunger from her grasp and began working to unclog the toilet herself, but with no luck. If one of Eli's toys was down there, it was well out of her reach. She had to call a plumber.

To be fair, she did try contacting her regular plumber, Nan Kelly, but her partner informed her that Nan was out on a call and was not expected back until later in the afternoon. This just could not wait. So despite the fact that there were three other professional plumbers in her contacts that she normally would have tried first, she found herself calling Whiskey Shields, who was, much to her relief, available to come over immediately.

As they waited for him to show up, Hayley had called Bruce to fill him in on the situation and immediately got accused of staging the whole drama as an excuse to get Whiskey over to the house so she could pump him for information.

Hayley took umbrage with Bruce so quickly pointing the finger at her. But again, given her checkered history with poking her nose where it did not belong, she could understand why he was so suspicious. She could talk until she was blue in the face and no one, not even her loving and trusting husband, would believe that this sudden plumbing emergency had not been a calculated strategy.

Still, she could not help herself.

She had to keep trying.

"Just so you know, Bruce, I wasn't even home when it happened! I was out walking Leroy! Ask MacKenzie!"

"Did you try calling Nan Kelly?"

"Of course I did but she was unavailable! And I know what you're thinking! There are three other plumbers I could've called before Whiskey Shields but I was so frazzled, and there's water leaking from the ceiling in the kitchen right now, and his name just popped into my head because, let's face it, we saw him just last night, and so I called him and luckily he was free to come over and help us!"

Although not fully buying her thought process, Bruce decided to drop it for the sake of maintaining the peace on the home front. "All right, keep me posted."

"I will," Hayley promised as she dropped her phone on the counter and placed a plastic bucket on the kitchen floor to catch the water dripping from the ceiling.

She heard a truck pulling up out front and ran to the door to see Whiskey Shields getting out of the driver's side and heading up the stone walk to the porch.

Hayley threw open the door to greet him.

"Good morning, Whiskey, thanks for coming on such short notice," Hayley said in as friendly a tone as she could muster.

"No problem," he grunted, eyes downcast. He stopped short of entering the house and finally lifted his gaze to make eye contact with her. "I've been meaning to stop by your restaurant the past few days."

Hayley gave him a curious look. "Oh?"

"Yeah," he mumbled. "I wanted to apologize . . . for my behavior last week. I'm very ashamed of the way I acted, causing such a scene. It was way out of line."

"You really scared Janet," Hayley reminded him, not quite ready to let him completely off the hook.

He nodded. "I know. There's no excuse for it. But I talked to Janet, told her I was sorry, and we're in a much better place now that we've gone our separate ways and gotten some distance. Some people just don't belong together, I guess. But I'm hoping we can get to the point where we can be friends again."

"Me too," Hayley said with an encouraging smile, studying his face, trying to gauge his sincerity.

"So what can I help you with today?"

Hayley had almost forgotten.

Her toilet was still overflowing.

She pointed upstairs. "Toilet emergency! Follow me!"

They pounded up the stairs to where MacKenzie was trying to corral a still-naked Eli, who was running around screaming and laughing.

Whiskey stopped in his tracks, giving MacKenzie a quick once-over, which Hayley noticed.

Even though he was apparently romantically involved with a much older lady, he certainly still had an eye for women of all ages, Hayley concluded.

"This is my daughter-in-law, MacKenzie. Well, not technically my daughter-in-law, but we're hoping one day soon!" Hayley chirped.

MacKenzie broke out into a wide smile.

She liked hearing that.

Whiskey gave her a nod. "Nice to meet you."

"You too," MacKenzie said shyly as she finally got ahold of Eli's arm. "And this is my son, Eli. He's the root cause of our problem. I think one of his toys is lodged in the pipes."

"Let me take a look," Whiskey said, trudging into the flooded bathroom, shedding his coat and throwing it on the sink basin, snapping on some rubber gloves, and reaching his arm deep down into the toilet.

MacKenzie pulled Eli toward Dustin's bedroom. "Let's get you dressed, Eli. This isn't a nudist colony."

He resisted, but his mother showed her strength by hauling him inside and shutting the door behind them.

Hayley returned her attention to Whiskey, who was still on his knees twisting a valve to turn off the water to the toilet in order to stop the overflow.

As she watched him work, Hayley suddenly realized

that Whiskey Shields had been present at both crime scenes. He was at All Citizens Bank dealing with a plumbing problem when Natalie Van Dyke discovered her safety deposit box had been robbed and he was also at Emerson Conners fixing a toilet on the day of the Easter egg hunt when Hayley discovered Raymond Dobbs's body.

It was too much of a coincidence.

If Raymond's death was indeed a homicide, then Whiskey Shields was Hayley's current number-one suspect.

Whiskey was suddenly back up on his feet and sauntering out of the bathroom. "Plunger's not going to do the trick. That sucker is lodged way down deep in the pipes. I'm gonna need a snake from my truck. Be right back."

He hustled down the steps and out the front door.

Hayley had a minute or two before he came back.

She scurried into the bathroom, almost slipping and falling on the wet floor, and snagged Whiskey's coat off the basin. She began searching his pockets and found his phone. She pressed the home button. There was no way she was going to figure out his passcode to gain access in such a short amount of time, but she was able to see all the recent texts that had come through in the last hour or so appear on the screen, including her own. But the one from 9:38 a.m. was the one that interested her the most.

It was a text from Janet.

There was only one Janet she could think of who knew Whiskey.

Janet Cook.

And it was hardly just an innocuous check-in to see how he was doing.

No, this text was much more than that.

**Baby, I can't stop thinking of you. When this is all over, I never want to spend this much time apart ever again.**

That was followed by a string of kissing emojis.

This was not the typical text one would expect from an ex-girlfriend, someone you claim you're trying to move on from.

No, what was happening here was obvious.

Despite what Whiskey and Janet were telling everyone in town, including their new relationships Natalie Van Dyke and Bill Duffy, they were still very much an item.

But why keep it a secret?

This startling revelation just opened the floodgates to a whole host of new questions.

Questions Hayley was finally prepared to answer.

"What are you doing?"

The hairs stood up on the back of Hayley's neck.

She had not heard Whiskey come back into the house.

She slowly turned around to face him.

Whiskey stood menacingly in the doorway to the bathroom, gripping his metal drain snake like a whip, staring at his phone, which was plainly visible in the palm of Hayley's hand.

# Chapter Thirteen

Hayley's mind raced.

She had to come up with something fast.

"I was going to wash my hands so I moved your jacket from the sink and was folding it up and the phone fell out of the pocket. I was just about to put it back."

Whiskey eyed her suspiciously.

He obviously did not believe her.

He slowly stepped into the bathroom, his hand held out. "May I have it, please?"

"Of course," Hayley said, hesitating a moment before handing him his phone.

He glanced down at the screen and grimaced.

Hayley could tell he was worried she had seen the text from Janet. He quickly stuffed the phone in the back pocket of his jeans, where it would be safe from any more prying eyes.

Then he glared at Hayley. "I don't like people looking at my phone."

"I told you, I just picked it up off the floor to put it back in your coat pocket. I didn't see anything," she fibbed.

He raised the drain snake as if he might strike her with it.

Hayley shrunk back, preparing for the worst.

"Gramma!" Eli screeched, running into the bathroom,

pushing past Whiskey's left leg to hug his grandmother. MacKenzie had finally gotten him dressed in a red pullover and jean overalls. He flung his little arms around Hayley's waist.

"Eli!" MacKenzie called. "Let the man find your toy!"

Whiskey's bloodshot eyes darted back and forth.

He was vastly outnumbered and so he mumbled something under his breath, and then began working on retrieving the baby shark toy from the toilet drain. Hayley seized the opportunity to scoop Eli up in her arms and carry him out of the bathroom, handing him over to MacKenzie, suggesting they play a game downstairs in the living room until Whiskey finished. Then she went to the bedroom, closing the door behind her, and called Sergio at the police station.

Officer Earl answered. "Bar Harbor Police Department."

"Earl, I need to speak with Sergio right away," Hayley said in an urgent whisper.

"He's busy now, can I take a message?"

"It's an emergency!"

"Then hang up and call 911," Earl suggested in a bored voice.

"Earl, I am not fooling around. This is Hayley Powell and there is a man here in my house who I suspect is a criminal."

"Are you in any immediate danger?"

"Well, no, but—"

"Then the chief will have to call you back."

Exasperated, Hayley shook her head. It was no mystery why Earl had never been promoted like his best bud, Lieutenant Donnie.

"Earl, I'm warning you. Don't hang up on me. I will tell the chief about the time you drove your squad car into a mailbox, and it was not because you were chasing a suspect. It was because you were playing online poker while driving!"

"That's just a nasty rumor some disgruntled person started! You can't prove it!"

"No, but I'm sure your body cam footage can. You have to turn that in to the department every week, right?"

There was a long pause.

"Hold, please, for the chief."

Earl finally put her through.

Sergio picked up on the second ring.

"This is Chief Alvares."

"Sergio, I need you to come over to my house ASAP."

"Hayley, what's wrong?"

"I can't explain right now. Please, it's very important."

"On my way."

She ended the call, crossed the room, opened the door, and stepped out into the hallway where Whiskey was waiting for her. In one hand, he still gripped the drain snake; in his other, he had the baby shark toy.

"All done," he said flatly.

He tossed her the bath toy, which she managed to catch. "Thank you, Whiskey. I appreciate you coming over here so promptly and taking care of this."

"Uh-huh. Anything else you need?" he asked testily.

"No, that does it. I'm sure you have other customers to attend to so I don't want to keep you."

She gestured toward the staircase behind them.

He did not budge.

He just glared at her.

A menacing look in his eye.

Hayley felt a twist of panic, bracing herself for what he might do next.

The tension was finally broken by Eli downstairs erupting in laughter and screaming at the top of his lungs.

Whiskey suddenly snapped out of whatever dark thoughts were running through his head, did an about-face, and stomped down the steps and out the front door.

Hayley followed to make sure he actually left the house. She saw him outside, tossing the drain snake in the back of his truck, and then lighting up a cigarette. She watched through the window as he stared back at the house, tugging on his cigarette, blowing out a cloud of smoke, contemplating his next move.

He could see her through the gauzy white curtain staring at him and he could tell she was frightened by him. He flicked the cigarette to the pavement, snuffing it out with the heel of his boot, and made a move to come back to the house.

Hayley was about to order MacKenzie to take Eli upstairs to Dustin's room and lock the door when Sergio suddenly pulled up behind Whiskey's truck in his squad car. Whiskey gave up any plan he may have had brewing in his mind as they exchanged a few words before Whiskey hopped in his truck and peeled away.

Sergio hurried up the steps to the front porch, where Hayley was waiting for him.

"Okay, Hayley, what's going on?"

"I know who robbed Natalie Van Dyke's safety deposit box at the bank."

Sergio nodded, intrigued. "I'm listening."

"There were no signs of forced entry, which is why Natalie is so convinced that Bill Duffy was somehow involved. In order to gain access, you need to use two keys simultaneously: the owner's key and the bank's key. Natalie had one in her possession and Bill Duffy had the other. Bill had no motive whatsoever to steal from one of his most important customers. But a young couple in love wanting to get out of town and start their lives together without having to worry about money? Well now, that's a workable motive."

Sergio arched an eyebrow. "Are you talking about Whiskey and Janet? I thought they broke up. At your restaurant."

"They did. Very publicly, in fact. The whole town's been buzzing about it ever since it happened. But what if the whole scene was staged?"

"I'm not following you."

"Janet knew her boss, Bill, had a huge crush on her and she fell well within the typical age range of women to whom he was usually attracted."

"Women under twenty-five?"

"Exactly. She was probably keenly aware of the looks he would steal at the bank, the double takes, the flirtatious banter. I saw it for myself whenever I showed up with my restaurant receipts. So she knew that if she were to break up with Whiskey, Bill would be there to help pick up the pieces. It was no accident they broke up at my restaurant on a night Bill was dining there as well. They planned it that way. Bill played his part to perfection. He tried to intervene, and then after Whiskey stormed off, he offered to drive Janet home. I don't believe twenty-four hours went by before they were dating. Simultaneously, a now single man-about-town Whiskey set his sights on the wealthy widow Natalie Van Dyke. Natalie had been a widow for some time and without a lot of family around to offer her ample warning, she basked in the much desired attention of a handsome young suitor. Of course, this gave both Janet and Whiskey quick access to the keys, which they could somehow get copied."

Sergio scratched the stubble on his cheek as he took in Hayley's theory. "So on the day of the robbery, Janet intentionally clogged the toilet at the bank and Whiskey just happened to be free to come fix it right away."

"Placing them both at the bank at the same time with the two keys that could access Natalie Van Dyke's safety deposit box when no one was looking, and no one would be the wiser until Natalie showed up and discovered the contents missing."

Sergio pulled out his phone.

"Who are you calling?"

"The bank. I want to make sure Janet is working today before I head over there to have a little one-on-one chat with her." He paused. "Yes, this is Chief Alvares. Is Janet Cook there?"

Hayley strained to listen but could not hear to whom Sergio was speaking.

Sergio's face darkened. "When was that?" He nodded again. "I see. Thank you." He ended the call and glanced at Hayley. "She left just a few minutes ago. Apparently, she got a call from someone, then moments later told her supervisor she wasn't feeling well and went home."

"Whiskey! He must have been calling to warn her we're on to them!"

Sergio made another call and put the phone to his ear. After just a few seconds, he ended it. "I tried Shields Plumbing but he's not answering. It went straight to voicemail."

Sergio bounded for his squad car and slid into the driver's seat. He scooped up his radio and pressed the talk button. "This is Chief Alvares. I need you to put an APB out on two possible suspects, Whiskey Shields and Janet Cook. Also alert Lieutenant Donnie that I need a roadblock at the Trenton Bridge." He let up on the radio talk button and turned to Hayley. "If they have any ideas about leaving the island, I want to make sure that window is closed."

The search was on.

# Chapter Fourteen

When Hayley arrived at her restaurant to conduct her daily inventory check to make sure they had enough food to get them through the evening rush, she instantly sensed something was wrong. There was a draft billowing into the dining room from the kitchen and when she went to investigate, she discovered the back door wide open and the lock busted.

Someone had broken in.

She closed the door and immediately raced to the office to make sure the safe was still locked.

She tugged on the handle.

Fortunately, it was still secure with no signs of tampering. She checked the drawers of her desk. All her paperwork appeared to be organized and untouched. She walked out into the kitchen, inspecting the utensils and cookware, the dishes, silverware, and wineglasses.

Everything seemed to be in order.

She opened the walk-in freezer.

Nothing touched since last evening.

Her last stop was the pantry.

As she circled around, glancing in the pantry and surveying the shelving units stacked with canned goods, bags of flour and sugar, and rows of spices lined up like soldiers on a battlefield, she suddenly heard a muffled cough.

Hayley froze in her tracks, her eyes darting to what appeared to be two shadowy figures hiding behind one of the ceiling-high shelving units.

"W-Who's there?" Hayley sputtered, her voice cracking, as she slowly reached for her phone in her back pocket.

Whiskey Shields, wielding a metal pipe he must have dug out of the utility closet, stepped into the light. His girlfriend, Janet Cook, followed, hovering over his right shoulder, a distraught look on her face.

Hayley bravely stood her ground. "What's going on? What are you two doing here?"

A smile inched up Whiskey's face. "Come on, Hayley, you know exactly what's happening. You figured it all out at your house when I was there fixing your toilet. I knew Janet and I had to blow town before you called the cops so I called her at the bank and she faked feeling ill so we could meet up and make a run for it. But you were too fast for us. By the time we got in the car, I heard on my police scanner that there was a roadblock waiting for us up at the Trenton Bridge. We were trapped. We didn't know where else to go."

"So you came *here*?" Hayley asked incredulously, keeping an eye on the pipe Whiskey gripped in his hand, trying not to buckle under the fear of him using it on her.

Whiskey noticed her staring at the pipe so he began to slap it menacingly in the palm of his free hand, trying to intimidate her. "Yeah, you're going to help us get off the island."

"Why on earth would I do that?"

Whiskey jabbed the pipe toward her, forcing her to take a step back. "Because you don't want to make me *angry*, Hayley!"

Hayley's eyes flicked toward Janet, who was on the verge of tears, probably wondering when their perfect plan to get rich went so spectacularly off the rails. "Janet,

I've known you since you were a toddler. This isn't you, you've just gotten mixed up in something that's gotten way out of hand. It's not too late to—"

Whiskey cut her off. "Don't talk to her!"

Hayley ignored him, keeping her focus on Janet. "I know all about the theft, Janet. The two of you using Bill Duffy and Natalie Van Dyke to get your hands on the manual keys to the safety deposit box so you could make copies before the system was updated. I am in no position to make promises, but if you just return the stolen items—"

Janet, trembling, shook her head. "It's too late, Hayley. It's way too late. There's no turning back now."

It suddenly dawned on Hayley what Janet was trying to say.

Raymond Dobbs.

They could not turn back because they were not just responsible for a bank theft, their crimes involved a murder, too. Hayley could almost see the guilt washing over Janet Cook's body.

Whiskey, on the other hand, appeared unmoved.

"Janet, no . . ." Hayley whispered.

Janet broke down in sobs, covering her face with her hands. "I feel awful. Raymond was always so sweet to me . . ."

"Buck up, Janet!" Whiskey ordered. "Don't let her make you feel bad. We did what we *had* to do!"

Hayley's eyes flicked between Whiskey and Janet as she laid out her theory. "Janet had to know about Raymond's peanut allergy. Everybody at the bank knew, going all the way back to when I was working there on his first day in the nineteen nineties. What happened? Why did he become a target? Did he catch you in the act? Did he walk in on you two cleaning out Natalie Van Dyke's safe deposit box?"

Whiskey's eyes narrowed, his mouth firmly shut.

But Janet, her whole body fluttering with nerves behind him, was unconsciously nodding, confirming everything she was saying.

"So why didn't he just turn you in right then and there?" Hayley wondered aloud.

"Because he wanted a cut!" Whiskey spit out.

Hayley recoiled, horrified.

"That's right. Sorry to burst your little bubble, Hayley, but good ole sweet and kind Easter Bunny Ray wasn't as morally upstanding as everyone in town believed. He was just as greedy as the rest of us!"

"I don't believe you," Hayley said.

"It's true!" Janet piped in, tears streaming down her cheeks. "He told us if we gave him half the share of the entire haul, he would keep his mouth shut and just go along! It wouldn't matter if Bill fired him after the theft because he would have plenty of money to retire on."

The rest of the pieces of the puzzle began falling into place for Hayley. "So you two agreed to the deal, but never planned on going through with it, right? You decided to play along until you could get rid of him before you had to turn over any of your spoils?"

She could tell from Janet's pained expression that she was definitely on the right track.

"Why not take advantage of his nut allergy, common knowledge at the bank, in order to get him out of the way? At the Easter egg hunt, you were both there. Raymond is nothing if not predictable. Every year he keeps his EpiPen in his basket in case of an emergency. He also has an incurable sweet tooth and was always stealing a few eggs for himself while parading around in front of the kids. So one of you swapped out his Easter basket for an identical-looking one when his back was turned. Poor Raymond had no idea he was about to munch on chocolate eggs filled with peanut butter and that his EpiPen would be out of his reach when he began having a severe allergic reaction. What a cruel way for him to die."

"He shouldn't have been so greedy!" Whiskey snapped.

"You hid Raymond's basket in a classroom where you thought no one would find it, but you don't know my grandson. When it comes to hunting for candy, he's like a shark tracking its prey. I found him with Raymond's basket. I thought he might've taken it and that he was responsible for Raymond dying."

"Well, now you can sleep easy knowing the truth," Whiskey scoffed. "Okay, here's what's going to happen, Hayley. We're going to all get in your car, Janet and I can hide in the back, and you're going to drive us up to the Trenton Bridge. The cops won't search your car. You're the police chief's sister-in-law. Once we clear the roadblock, we'll head on to Ellsworth. We'll drop you off in the Walmart parking lot and be on our way. You'll never have to see us again."

"And my car?"

"You can buy another one with the insurance money."

"I am not helping you escape," Hayley growled.

Whiskey raised the pipe in the air, swinging it around in a threatening manner. "Don't make this harder on yourself, Hayley. I really don't want to have to use this."

They suddenly heard the bell on the front door jingle.

"Good morning!"

It was her restaurant manager, Betty.

Hayley had been expecting her later in the afternoon.

But she had shown up early.

Seizing the distraction, Hayley, with a roundhouse kick, knocked the pipe out of Whiskey's hand. It clattered to the floor. Hayley and Whiskey both dove for it, Hayley reaching it first, managing to wrap a finger around the one end, but Whiskey grabbed at it with both hands as they rolled across the floor, wrestling for possession. A petrified Janet stood frozen in place.

Alerted by the commotion, Betty sprinted into the kitchen, gasping at the sight of Hayley and Whiskey grappling over a thick metal pipe. Just as Whiskey wrested it from Hayley's hand, raising it in the air, Betty scooped up a frying pan off the stove and whacked Whiskey in the head with it, stunning him. He toppled over backward, landing hard on his back. The pipe skittered underneath the oven.

Betty helped Hayley to her feet and they bolted past Janet, still frozen like a statue, out of the pantry, into the dining room, and out the front door where they jumped into Betty's car and squealed away to safety. They drove straight to the police station and Sergio radioed the state police to be on the lookout for a couple in a stolen vehicle, but Whiskey Shields and Janet Cook never made it off the island.

Knowing they would never slip past the roadblock at the Trenton Bridge, they headed in the opposite direction, toward Tremont on the backside of the island to hide out until things quieted down, but a young eagle-eyed rookie with the Southwest Harbor Police Department, who had just received the alert and spotted Hayley's license number, flipped on his siren in hot pursuit. The car chase lasted less than two minutes before a porcupine in the middle of the road caused Whiskey to swerve to avoid mowing it down. He lost control of the wheel and smashed into a tree as the young officer called for backup. Banged up a bit but otherwise fine, Whiskey and Janet were placed under arrest. Hayley's car, however, was totaled. Although she pretended to be upset, secretly Hayley was thrilled. She had been angling for a new car, and now she could put a nice down payment on a new one with the insurance money.

In the words of Shakespeare, all's well that ends well.

# Chapter Fifteen

Hayley's Kitchen was open on Sunday afternoon for her delectable prix fixe Easter dinner from noon until three and was fully booked. Her menu of Roast Lamb with Mint Jelly, Lemon and Rosemary Potatoes, Asparagus with Bread Crumbs and Parmesan, Cauliflower with Golden Raisins and Almonds, and a Grand Raspberry Trifle for dessert drew raves from all her guests, and her entire staff worked their butts off to make sure everyone left the restaurant full and satisfied.

By the time she locked up the restaurant just before five for the day so she could go home and have Easter dinner with her own family, she was sweaty and exhausted, her feet throbbing from running around all afternoon tending to her customers and keeping the kitchen on track with all the orders pouring in nonstop.

Kelton had boxed up the leftover food for the staff to take with them, and Hayley was relieved she did not have to race home to start cooking. She had enough meat and side dishes to serve her entire brood and then some. All she needed was an oven and microwave to heat everything up. She hitched a ride home with Kelton since she would not have a car to drive until the insurance company paid her claim.

When Hayley barreled through the front door carrying her big box of food, she could hear Eli stomping around upstairs, giggling hysterically.

She could also hear Dustin leading him around. "Hey, little buddy, I think I see something over there!"

Bruce was sitting in the living room, a bottle of beer in hand, watching an old Jason Statham action movie on TV. "The kids decided to do their own little Easter egg hunt for Eli since the last one didn't work out so well. They spent the entire time Eli was down for his nap hiding candy eggs around the house."

There was an ear-splitting screech that caused Bruce to wince. "Guess he found another one."

Finished searching upstairs, Eli pounded down the steps carrying an Easter basket with about a half dozen eggs in it. Both his parents followed closely behind him. Eli flew into the living room and began scanning around for any sign of candy, checking behind a lamp, stuffing his hands down in between the couch cushions, dropping to his knees and peering underneath the recliner Bruce was stretched out in. Leroy hid under the coffee table, desperately trying to stay out of the path of Hurricane Eli.

Then, Eli's eyes locked onto a Peter Rabbit figurine Hayley had set out for the occasion on top of the TV. Right in front of it was a tiny blue candy egg. Eli squealed with delight, clapping his hands, and then bounded over, scooped it up, and popped it into his mouth.

"Hey, save a few for later. We're having dinner soon," Dustin said, tousling his son's mop of curly blond hair as MacKenzie snapped photos of him on the hunt.

Hayley noticed the table had been set for four for dinner with a high chair off to the side for Eli. She turned to MacKenzie. "Thank you for setting the table, MacKenzie, but we're going to need two more table settings. I invited somebody from work to join us and she asked if she could bring a friend."

"Of course. There's plenty of room. I'll take care of it right now," MacKenzie said, turning to Dustin and handing him the camera. "Would you take over the photos for a few minutes? I'm documenting Eli's Easter egg hunt for Instagram."

"Sure," Dustin replied, sweetly bussing her cheek before chasing after his son, who was now in the laundry room tossing dirty sheets and pillowcases out of a large wicker basket in search of more candy eggs.

Bruce's ears had pricked up at the mention of extra guests for Easter dinner. "Who did you take pity on now?"

Hayley sighed. "I didn't take pity on anyone. I just thought, Betty lives alone, and I didn't want her being all by herself on Easter so I asked her to join us for dinner. She was thrilled over the invitation. Are you okay with that?"

Bruce nodded his head. "Sure. I like Betty. So who's the friend tagging along with her?"

Hayley shrugged. "She didn't say. I never expected her to ask if she could bring a date. But we have plenty of food, so why not?"

"Are you certain it's a date?"

"No, not at all."

The doorbell rang.

"But I suppose we are about to find out," Hayley concluded.

Bruce, curious, hauled himself up out of his recliner and joined Hayley as she walked out to the front door and opened it.

Betty stood on the steps, beaming, holding hands with the man next to her.

It was Bill Duffy.

Hayley and Bruce exchanged a quick glance.

"Happy Easter!" Hayley proclaimed.

"Thank you for inviting us at the last minute," Bill said. "I'm not much of a cook and Betty was busy working all day at the restaurant so we were looking at grilled cheese sandwiches and potato chips for Easter dinner."

"We're happy to have you," Hayley said. "Come in, come in."

"I'm so excited! Just staring at all that lamb and those potatoes and the trifle all afternoon was just too much! I'm starving!" Betty exclaimed.

Betty and Bill shed their coats, handing them to Bruce, who went to hang them on the rack.

"Have a seat in the living room. We'll be eating soon. What would you like to have to drink?"

"Gin and tonic," Bill said, settling down on the couch next to Betty and squeezing her hand. "Pinot Grigio?"

"That's right," Betty said, resting her head on his shoulder. "You're learning fast."

"Coming right up," Bruce said, hustling toward the kitchen with Hayley hot on his heels.

As he unscrewed the top off the gin and began pouring some into a glass, he whispered to Hayley, "Looks like Bill has tossed out his rule about only dating women half his age."

"I knew they would make a perfect match! I just hope Betty isn't some kind of a placeholder until he can find a much younger woman. I should get him alone and make sure—"

Bruce put a finger to her lips. "Honey, this is coming from love, but maybe you should just stay out of it this time."

Hayley thought about this. "You're probably right. It's none of my business."

Bruce spilled some gin on the counter. "Look what you made me do. I was shaken by the shock of hearing you admit I'm right for once."

"I said you're *probably* right! Don't get too cocky!"

She left him to finish making Bill's drink and wandered into the dining room, where MacKenzie was placing silverware on one of the Easter Bunny placemats.

"MacKenzie . . ."

She jumped, having not heard Hayley come into the dining room behind her. Clutching a fork and spoon still to be placed, she put her hand to her heart. "I'm sorry, I didn't see you there."

Hayley took a deep breath. She took a step forward. "I have been meaning to tell you this ever since you arrived for Easter."

MacKenzie quickly set the fork and spoon down where they belonged and then turned back to Hayley expectantly. "Yes, what is it?"

"I sincerely believe . . ."

MacKenzie seemed to be bracing for the worst.

"I believe that you are one of the kindest and most loving mothers I have ever seen."

MacKenzie cocked her head to one side as if she thought she had heard wrong. But as the words began to sink in, her eyes filled with tears and she choked out, "Do you really mean that?"

Hayley nodded. "And I am as proud of you as I am of Dustin. I had my doubts, but you two have turned out to be exceptional parents and Eli is one lucky little boy."

That was it.

MacKenzie could not hold in her emotions any longer.

The waterworks began flowing.

She threw her arms around Hayley, hugging her tightly.

Behind them, Hayley could see Dustin watching the scene. He gave his mother a wink and mouthed the words, "Thank you."

He knew how much this meant to MacKenzie.

From the laundry room came another deafening shriek.

Eli had apparently discovered another hidden candy.

And Hayley could not think of a better way to spend Easter Sunday. With good friends, her sexy husband, her maturing son and his kindhearted girlfriend, and her wild and rambunctious but adorable grandson.

She had a lot to be grateful for.

# Island Food & Spirits
## by
## Hayley Powell

After all of the planning, organizing, and preparation for the Easter holiday, it almost feels like a letdown when the fun and festivities are finally over and I have to go back to my real-world job and responsibilities.

But if I was to be honest, this year was quite a bit different from previous Easters, especially with the sad passing of Raymond Dobbs, who served as our beloved hometown Easter Bunny over the last few decades, not to mention a small tornado disguised as my grandson, who took over every inch of my home for the past week.

I was ready to get back to the routine of running my restaurant and dealing with the day-to-day fires that needed to be put out. But mostly, I was looking forward to spending some much needed quiet uninterrupted time with my husband since we had not had a minute to ourselves for a few weeks now.

So the other night we found ourselves alone, and we decided to have a cozy romantic movie night. Just the two of us. We had settled down on the couch with a big buttery bowl of popcorn between us, ready to start a new Margot Robbie movie that I had been dying to see, when Bruce's cell phone rang.

I instantly knew who it was. No one ever calls Bruce after eight in the evening except my old boss and friend Sal Moreno, chief editor at the *Island Times*, where Bruce works, as a local crime reporter.

After speaking with Sal, Bruce hung up the phone and broke the news that our date night had to be put on hold because he needed to get to Boston for the criminal trial of a man who had island connections. He had to pack and get ready to leave for a flight out of Bangor to Boston at six the following morning.

So much for watching Margot tonight. Instead, as Bruce headed upstairs, I settled on a rerun of *Criminal Minds* and apparently drifted off to sleep in the middle of the episode.

Sometime later I was startled awake by the sound of glass breaking! I struggled to rouse myself, thinking Bruce had come down for a drink and broke another piece from my new glassware collection I had recently ordered from Pottery Barn. As I pushed myself up off the couch and padded to the kitchen, I glanced down at my watch and realized it was four thirty in the morning. I thought to myself, Bruce should have already left before now if he was going to catch a six o'clock flight in Bangor.

As I reached the threshold of the kitchen, I stopped short and slapped my hand across my mouth before I erupted in a bloodcurdling scream.

Standing with his back to me in front of my kitchen sink was a six-foot-tall giant white furry Easter Bunny!

My first thought was: *What is Raymond Dobbs doing in my kitchen this early in the morning?* My second thought was: *Wait a minute, Raymond Dobbs is dead, so who in the world is standing in an Easter Bunny suit in my kitchen at four thirty in the morning? And was he actu-*

*ally eating my leftover potato and ham casse-
role at my kitchen counter?*

Yes, in fact he definitely was, because there
on the floor next to his big bunny feet was my
grandmother's casserole dish lid broken in
pieces.

The Easter Bunny slowly turned around, his
smile and whiskers appearing much more evil
and maniacal in the dark! He suddenly grabbed
a butcher knife from the wooden holder on the
counter in front of him and held it high above
his head as he advanced toward me.

I turned and ran back toward the living room,
where I snatched my cell phone off the end
table beside the couch, and then ducked into
the dining room, crouching down to hide behind
the table. I could see the Easter Bunny scanning the living room, searching for me, before
slowly turning toward the dining room.

Luckily, he did not see me down on all fours
hiding, so he then pounded up the stairs looking for me.

I dashed back to the kitchen, racing for the
back door and freedom, when I suddenly stumbled over something blocking my escape. I
swallowed another scream as my eyes fell upon
a man's body lying facedown in a pool of blood!
There was only one man who had been in the
house with me tonight!

Bruce!

As I bent down to check on him, I heard
heavy footsteps charging back down the stairs,
so I quickly ran to the cellar, securely locking
the door behind me with the key that was dangling from a hook on the wall. Then I frantically
called the police!

Chief Sergio's number two, Lieutenant Donnie, answered the phone. I urgently whispered into the phone for him to please get the chief because there was an armed Easter rabbit in my house, and I believed he had stabbed Bruce, and he was now coming after me, and to please hurry before the marauding bunny found me hiding in the basement!

Instead of advising me to stay calm, that help was on the way, all I heard was silence.

"Donnie, can you hear me?" I spit out, hearing footsteps overhead approaching the cellar door.

*Stay quiet, don't panic,* I told myself.

Just then, Donnie burst out laughing and said, "Hayley, I think you need to lay off some of those special cocktails you experiment with and write about, because I think you may have tested one too many of them!"

And then the phone went dead.

I stared at my phone.

No, he did not just hang up on me!

He was worse than his buddy Officer Earl.

Suddenly I heard the Easter Bunny stalker jiggling the cellar door handle from the other side!

Terrified, I called the police again. Before I had the chance to tell him I was one hundred percent serious, Donnie began lecturing me about wasting taxpayers' dollars on stupid practical jokes, and how I should know better.

I wanted to reach through the phone and wring his scrawny little neck!

The crazy rabbit was now kicking the cellar door, and I knew it was only a matter of seconds before he managed to break through.

With nothing left to lose, I screamed into the

phone, "Donnie, if I'm lying to you, I will personally cook you dinner for the rest of my life!"

There was a split second of silence before I heard Donnie shout, "Chief! There's an emergency at Hayley's house! Stay on the line, Hayley! We're on our way!"

Then the phone went dead again.

The idiot told me to stay on the line and then he hung up on me again!

The cellar door suddenly splintered open, and the giant white knife-wielding Easter rabbit came pounding down the steps as I covered my eyes and screamed and screamed!

That's when I heard someone calling my name over and over again.

It was Bruce!

He was still alive!

I popped my eyes back open, disoriented.

I wasn't in the cellar.

I was still on the couch.

And Bruce was still home. As he reached down and gently took hold of me by the shoulders, I could see the time on his watch. It was not even midnight yet.

It finally dawned on me that it had all just been a wild and crazy dream!

Bruce laughed and said, "Maybe you should cut back on the chocolate peanut butter–filled Easter eggs before bedtime." He pointed to the pile of crumpled-up foil wrappers strewn all over the coffee table in front of me.

I looked sheepishly at Bruce, admitting I may have removed a few handfuls of chocolate eggs from Eli's Easter basket before they left for the airport earlier that day. But I was only thinking of his poor parents. The last thing they needed was Eli on another turbulent sugar high from eating too many chocolate Easter eggs during the long six-hour flight back to California!

Bruce chuckled and gave me a hug. "That's my wife. Always thinking of others."

I certainly learned my lesson. No more overeating chocolate peanut butter eggs while watching *Criminal Minds*. It definitely leads to ghastly nightmares.

I will be sticking to Hallmark movies from now on when indulging with sweets, thank you very much.

Forget the chocolate for now because I have my final potato dish that is the perfect end to your Easter weekend. It uses up your leftover ham, and with just a few simple ingredients, you will have a meal so simple and delicious, you can whip it up any time of the year.

But first, here is a lovely cocktail to serve alongside it.

# Spring Cocktail

*Ingredients:*

3 cups fresh grapefruit juice
1½ cups gin
¾ cup ginger liqueur
1 cup club soda

In a large pitcher combine grapefruit juice, gin, and ginger liqueur. Top with the club soda.

Serve in highball glasses filled with ice.

If you like to garnish, add a grapefruit wedge, serve, and enjoy.

## Easy Potato Ham Breakfast Casserole

### *Ingredients:*

4 cups of your favorite frozen potatoes (I like the ones
    with the peppers & onions in them)
2 cups leftover ham, cut into bite-sized pieces
2 cups shredded cheese, divided
1 can cream of mushroom soup (or your favorite cream
    soup)
½ cup sour cream

Preheat your oven to 375 degrees. Spray an 8-inch pan
with nonstick spray.

Mix all of your ingredients together except one cup of
the cheese in a large bowl until everything is well mixed.

Spread mixture into the greased pan and top with the
rest of the cheese.

Bake for 45–50 minutes or until very hot and melted.

Let rest a few minutes before serving.

# HOPPED ALONG

Barbara Ross

# Chapter One

My nephew, Jack, age six, zoomed around the great lawn at Windsholme, searching under bushes and behind boulders for the brightly colored eggs left by the Easter Bunny. He was beyond revved up, emitting a high-pitched giggle as he held up each egg in triumph, fueled, no doubt, by the handfuls of jelly beans he'd been able to stuff into his mouth before my sister, Livvie, had stopped him.

I was ready with an explanation in case he noticed that the hidden eggs were the same ones he, Livvie, my niece Page, and I had dyed in my mother's kitchen the day before. The Easter Bunny had hidden *his* eggs, I was prepared to say. But it wasn't necessary. Despite the characters drawn on the eggs in wax crayon by his own hand, Jack was far too excited for deep observation, analysis, and the resulting awkward questions.

My boyfriend, Tom Flynn, and our friend Jamie Dawes stood on the long front porch of Windsholme, occasionally providing hints, since they had hidden the eggs only an hour before. Page and I were on the ground, running after Jack to make sure he stayed away from the cliffs, the water, and the physical hazards of Morrow Island, where our mansion, Windsholme, stood. Page was sixteen, far too old to hunt for eggs. Jack was the only child in the family young enough. I watched him run from place to place, feeling sorry that the reproductive capacity of our family had come to such a sharp point. Jack, on the other hand, didn't appear to feel the lack of other children in the slightest. "All the more for me," he might have said.

"Warmer!" Tom shouted as Jack headed toward the worn wooden gate to the old rose garden. Tom leaned over the back of one of the rocking chairs on the porch, a mug of coffee clutched in both hands against the chill of the last day of March. I took a moment to gaze at him in appreciation. Even as he leaned, his back was ramrod straight. Since we'd gotten together the previous summer, he'd let his hair grow slightly longer and cut his gym visits to one a day. "No longer feels the need to sublimate," Livvie had said when I'd mentioned this. Once a day appeared to be enough to keep him in amazing shape. He was a powerful man, average in height, but broad-shouldered, with a strong chest that tapered to a waistline without an ounce of fat. He loved his job as a Maine State Police detective and everything about him proclaimed what he was.

As I watched, Tom stood, stretched, and said something to Jamie, indicating his apparently empty coffee cup. Jamie nodded and the two men slipped inside through the front door. I watched them go, then looked around for Jack.

"Aunt Julia!" Something in Jack's tone made me turn and run immediately. He charged back through the decrepit gate before I reached him. "The Easter Bunny's in the vegetable patch, and he's *dead*!"

"Watch Jack!" I called to Page, who nodded, her expression serious under her cloud of bright red hair. She ran to her brother, while I made my way toward the garden to see whatever it was Jack had spotted.

The garden gate was old and weathered, dry gray wood, barely hanging on by its hinges. At one time, it had been the entrance to Windsholme's formal rose garden, which had been surrounded by a high hedge. The hedge was long gone, as were the roses. My sister had repurposed the garden for the vegetables she grew to feed us and the crew that worked at the authentic Maine clambake we ran on the island during the summer. We had never replaced the hedges with a fence. There were no mammals on Morrow Island—no deer or bunnies, gophers, or squirrels. Only Le Roi, our cat, who was currently at my mom's house where he and I both lived in the off-season. Occasionally, crows or red-winged blackbirds bothered Livvie's crops, but it was a rare occurrence, and a fence wouldn't have kept them out anyway. The old gate stood alone, the sole sentry, simply because no one had ever bothered to take it down.

It was the lack of mammals that niggled at my brain as I sped toward the gate. The odds that Jack had seen a dead bunny, or other animal, were exceedingly small, since there weren't any. What could it have been? Perhaps those gobbled jelly beans had him in such a state that he was seeing things.

The garden was dead and brown, the dirt hard packed. We'd all agreed we'd been lucky in the weather, but though the sun held promise, spring hadn't yet arrived in Maine.

I ran down the garden's central path, looking in both directions for whatever Jack had seen. I caught sight of a bright pink egg on the ground, and then a sky blue one, but no dead Easter Bunny.

I was ready to give up when I rounded onto the smaller path that ran along the left half of the garden. A pile of clothes lay tangled in the dried brown cornstalks. *Livvie doesn't have a scarecrow*, my brain told me, searching for denial. I moved closer.

A man, an older man, lay on his side. He had thin white hair and a white mustache. Much more astonishing, he was dressed in a full morning suit—the dark gray, striped trousers, black coat with tails, white shirt, pale tie, dove gray vest and matching gray gloves worn by modern Americans almost exclusively at very formal daytime weddings. Even more astonishing, just beside his head, lying on its side, was a top hat.

I processed all this and the strangeness of it as I dropped to my haunches and felt for his carotid artery. His skin was warm. Was there a pulse? My own heart was beating so hard I couldn't tell.

When I ran back through the gate, Page and Jack were nowhere to be seen. I hoped she'd taken him in the house. I sped across the lawn, shouting, "Tom!" and waving my hands over my head. He met me on the porch, the space between his brown eyebrows lined with concern. Jamie Dawes, our childhood friend and current member of the Busman's Harbor Police Department, was right behind him. "Call the Coast Guard," I yelled to Jamie. "There's a man in the garden. He's unconscious, either hurt or dead."

Jamie nodded, already pulling out his phone. The Coast Guard didn't have jurisdiction, but they could get to the island fastest with medical help, and they would come.

"Then the Busman's Harbor P.D.," I added though it hardly needed to be said.

Jamie turned away, the call already connecting, as Tom and I raced for the vegetable garden.

# Chapter Two

Shoving aside the old gate, I led Tom through the garden at a run. Jamie was close behind, sounding authoritatively coplike on his cell phone. I rounded the path to the corn patch and stopped dead.

There was no one on the ground. "But, but, but . . ." I sputtered, breathless and pointing. Tom came up by my side, grim-faced, looking down where my finger indicated. Jamie halted soon after.

Jamie spoke into the phone. "Stand down," he said. "I'll call with an update." He jabbed his finger to the screen to end the call, then looked at us. "Busman's Harbor P.D.," he explained. His second call.

"He was right there," I insisted. "I swear." Two rows of the dried stalks, broken and bent, reflected the ghostly outline of a body.

"Not dead then," Tom said.

"But definitely unconscious," I told them. "I felt his neck and he didn't move."

Tom walked to the other side of the corn patch. I could see his blue cotton shirt through the remaining stalks. "Nothing?" I called, unnecessarily. He surely would have said if the man had been there.

"Nothing," he confirmed.

Jamie had turned back, searching along the center path the way we had come. His head swiveled from side to side, though there wasn't much left of the garden, no place for anyone to hide. I started toward the path that ran along the other side of the garden from the one Tom was searching.

We met back up by the cornstalks, where we'd begun.

"We'll have to search the island," Tom said. "If he's hurt or passes out again—"

I described the man, though they weren't likely to come across a different stranger on Morrow Island. When I came to the part about the morning suit and top hat, Tom blinked rapidly, and Jamie opened his mouth and then closed it. I could tell he wanted to ask if I was sure the man was real, but then had thought better of it.

Tom shaded his eyes, looking toward the house. "Should we get Sonny to help?" Sonny was my sister's husband and Jack and Page's father.

Jamie shook his head. "He took the Boston Whaler to the harbor to pick up the rest of the guests before Jack saw the man."

In the heat of the hunt, I hadn't seen Sonny leave.

"I'll take the woods," Tom said. The west side of the island was covered in trees. There was a trail that our clambake guests sometimes rambled along as they waited for their lobster dinners. There were also treacherous boulders and steep drop-offs. At least at this time of year, with no leaves on the trees, the hazards were easy to spot.

"I'll start around the outside of Windsholme and then go to the beach," I volunteered.

Tom looked like he might protest, but then his face relaxed. How dangerous could an elderly, recently unconscious man in a morning suit and top hat be?

"I'll take the dock, the little house, and the cliffs," Jamie said. The east side of the island was the highest, offering sheer, rocky drops to the sea below. A glance at the dock told me it was dead low tide. No one could survive that fall.

We'd nodded our agreement to the plan and turned to walk back down the path when something caught my eye. "Wait!" I waded into the corn patch and picked the item up. We hadn't spotted it immediately because the basket was the same color as the dead stalks. It had a sturdy handle arching over its top. As I tilted it toward me, I saw brightly colored plastic eggs, and foil-wrapped candy. A greeting card sat on the top, a standard Easter card you might buy in a supermarket or pharmacy, not in an envelope. "Did you hide this?" I held the basket up for Tom and Jamie.

They shook their heads.

I lifted the card off the top and opened it. "From the Easter Bunny," it said, in bold, unbunny-like handwriting. Under the card was a small used book. *The Tale of Peter Rabbit* was the title across the top of the worn brown cover. The book looked strangely familiar. Of course, it did. Livvie and I had a newer set of the Beatrix Potter stories when we were small. Jack had it now.

I took a deep breath and my stomach, which had been tight with fear up to that point, unclenched. Whatever was going on here, it was kindly meant. "I'll take it to the house and hide it somewhere until we know what's going on."

We'd started back across the lawn, getting ready to split up, when the noise of an engine came across the water and a small Coast Guard boat headed toward our dock. Jamie sprinted toward it. There followed a conversation shouted over the noise of the engine and the water. I could hear Jamie's deep voice and the answering one, also male, but couldn't make out the words. Jamie waved, mouthed his thanks, and ran back to us. "They're going to cruise around the island, checking the perimeter from the water. They'll call my cell if they see anything. Anyone," he corrected.

A body, I knew he'd been thinking, but then had decided not to say that, either.

Jamie walked back toward the little yellow house by the dock where my sister and her family lived during the summer, his first place to search.

After he left, Tom and I lingered, hugging. I fit perfectly against his chest. He rested his already stubbly chin on my hair. I hadn't known until we started dating that he shaved twice a day when he was on duty.

"Be careful," he said as he released me.

"You too," I answered.

"You have your phone?"

I felt for the reassuring bulk of it in my back pocket. I'd been taking photos of the hunt until it had ended so abruptly. Why hadn't I thought to take a photo of the man? But then I'd been panicked in the moment, running for help. And I never expected him to disappear. "Yes," I answered Tom. "You?"

He shook his head yes and then kissed me, longer and harder than a temporary parting called for. When he was done, he squared his shoulders and stalked off toward the woods.

I turned and crossed the lawn toward Windsholme.

The front door of Windsholme was unlocked, as expected in a home on an island where company was coming. The sounds of pots being moved and bowls being scraped came from the new kitchen just out of sight, along with the voices of my mother, Jacqueline Snowden; my sister, Livvie Ramsey; and our friend Zoey Butterfield, consulting on some aspect of our Easter meal.

I stood in the huge front hall for a moment, thinking what to do next. I didn't know where Jack was and the last thing I wanted was for him to spot the basket I carried. I'd just decided to creep up the stairs to my summer apartment on the second floor to hide it when Livvie came through the front hall.

"Julia! There you are. I wondered if you got lost. Did you dispose of it?"

I was momentarily confused. "Dispose of what?" *Does she mean the basket? Plainly I'm holding it in my hands.*

"The dead bunny or whatever it was." Livvie smiled. "Jack came in telling us the Easter Bunny was dead in the cornstalks. How did it get there, do you suppose? Dropped by an eagle?"

"It wasn't a bunny," I said in a low voice. "It was a man."

"A man? Someone we don't know? What was he doing in my garden and why did Jack think he was the Easter Bunny?"

As quickly as I could, I filled her in on our disappearing visitor, morning suit, top hat, and all. She stared down at me, her hazel eyes growing wider with every sentence. She'd grown taller than me when she'd been in fifth grade and I'd been in seventh, and the height difference had only gotten greater. Broad-shouldered and tawny-haired, she was the image of our late father, I of our petite, blond mom.

"A top hat and tails." Livvie shook her head. "Just like the bunny in Jack's favorite Easter book. So that must be why—"

"Exactly," I said.

"Is he dangerous, do you think?" she asked.

"He's an old man, who was recently unconscious," I answered.

She put her hand out for the basket, glancing over her shoulder as she did. "Jack and Page are with Mom and Zoey in the kitchen. I'll stash this and search inside the house. Until a few minutes ago Page and I were setting the table." She inclined her head toward the formal dining room, visible through a wide archway. "I don't think a stranger could have come in without me noticing."

"Take Zoey with you." I didn't think the old man was dangerous, but there was safety in numbers. Besides, the mansion was massive. Searching from the basement to the old servants' rooms on the third floor would take a good amount of time.

"Will do."

I gave her a quick hug and went back out the front door. I started along the porch. Windsholme had an enormous number of entrances. French doors to the main-floor rooms ran all along the front porch. There was a smaller porch with a side door that went directly into the dining room, and a new set of steps to the renovated kitchen entrance at the back, as well as doors and windows to the basement. All of these had been replaced as a part of the renovation, and I doubted anyone had unlocked any of them except the main front door. For most of my life, Windsholme had been derelict, and though we put up barriers to keep the clambake customers out, for a savvy child with all the time in the world, entrance had been easy. Now, even I couldn't get in without a key.

I rattled each French door as I passed, making sure it was locked. When I got to the end of the porch, I walked along the side of the house to the back.

Windsholme sat at the highest point on the island. The front of the house was three stories, but there were four full stories in the back. I tried each of the basement doors, including the one that had once led to the two-story kitchen. It had been a beautiful room, with the equipment and sinks in the basement, ringed all the way around by a balcony at the main-floor level providing access to closets for linen, shelves for china, and drawers for silver. The woodwork had still been beautiful, dark, and solid, despite ninety years of neglect. Destroying it had been the hardest decision of the renovation, one I still occasionally regretted. But if we were going to use the mansion as an events venue, the kitchen had to be modern. And the service staff would no doubt appreciate it being on the main floor.

I came around the other side of the house and continued along the path that led over the top of the island to the beach, walking fast. Then I caught myself. This wasn't about speed. It was about slowing down and noticing.

My first stop was the playhouse, its exterior a perfect replica of Windsholme. At one time, it had stood on the edge of the great lawn across from the mansion, but the area surrounding it had long since given over to woods.

"Hello!" I called. "Hellooo?"

No sound came from the little house. I went up onto the porch and pushed on the door. It didn't budge, evidently swollen shut by the damp Maine weather. No one had entered it since the previous fall when Sonny and I had closed the island buildings for the winter, I was sure. But, in the interest of thoroughness, I put my shoulder against the painted wooden door and shoved.

The door shuddered and swung open so quickly I almost fell into the front room. The smell of mold and mildew assaulted me, tickling my nose. We'd replaced the siding, roof, and windows the previous year as a part of the renovation of Windsholme. Heated only by a fireplace, which was almost never used, the playhouse had always been dank and needed airing out in the spring. This year the smell was worse than I'd ever experienced. I began to have second thoughts about making the little house airtight.

"Hello!" I called again, for no good reason.

The second room was a bunk room, just the place you'd go to lie down if you were sick or hurt. I was certain there was no one there, but I went through the doorway to check anyway. "Hello?" No answer. The four bunks were stripped and untouched, their blue striped mattresses dusty and clearly unused.

I left the playhouse and continued on the path through the center of the island. The ground leveled off and then began to descend. I heard Tom calling to the man from somewhere to my left, "Do you need help?" There was no answer.

The path to the beach was well-worn. Lots of tourists walked there when they visited for the clambake. I had to stop from time to time to clear a tree branch, the leavings of winter storms. Sonny, Livvie, Tom, and I had hastily cleared up the island from the dock to Windsholme the previous weekend as we readied the island for Easter. But there'd been no need to clean the other paths.

I turned my head from side to side, looking for a man in a top hat. Strong sunlight beamed through the trees. Even though the man was dressed in black and gray, I didn't think I'd miss him if he was nearby.

The path continued downward and split, part of it continuing to our little beach, and part leading to the enormous flat-topped boulder that overlooked it. I decided to go to the beach first. There was a long crevice under the big boulder where someone could easily hide.

The man wasn't there, and the rest of the beach was deserted. He wouldn't have swum for it. Westclaw Point wasn't far, but the late-March water could induce hypothermia in minutes. No one in a morning suit would last even that short distance.

Sighing, I turned up the path that led to the top of the boulder. I didn't think the man would be there, but up higher I would be able to see farther into the woods.

I walked out as far on the familiar granite as I could to where the rock hung over the water. The solid rock was familiar. It was the place where Livvie and I had sunbathed and dreamed, read, and picnicked once we were old enough to roam the island on our own. I sought the stillness there sometimes even now, especially on quiet days in the fall and spring before the clambake opened.

From up here, I could see the shoreline of the island through the naked trees. It was midday; the sun was fully out. The clocks had sprung forward earlier in the month, but the sun was still weak. The dark blue water of the Gulf of Maine contrasted prettily with the multitude of browns of the trees, dead leaves, and soil. But I saw nothing. No one moved.

I looked out across the water at the houses dotting the waterfront on Westclaw Point. Directly across, Quentin Tupper's marble and glass edifice stood as if thrust out of the rock on which it was built. As the old lobster shacks and summer cottages had disappeared, they'd been replaced by new homes that imitated Maine's shingle-style summer houses. Big and prepossessing, yes. Modern, no. Except for Quentin's house. It gleamed beautifully in the early afternoon sunlight.

No lights shone from the interior. Of course not. Quentin wasn't there. He wouldn't be until July first. He was the silent investor in the Snowden Family Clambake, the person who had saved us from certain mortgage default and the loss of the island seven years before. He was unspeakably rich, wealth he'd surprised himself by making when he was in college. Now, he would be preparing his new yacht for the season on the Côte d'Azur.

Which was the reason I wondered why there was a small red boat with an outboard motor bobbing at his dock.

# Chapter Three

Coming over the top of the island I met Tom and Jamie on the path in front of Windsholme.

"Nothing," Jamie said, confirming what we could see with our own eyes. None of us had anyone with us, and if we'd found the man injured, we would have used our phones. "The Coast Guard didn't see anyone from the water, either."

I told them about the little red boat at Quentin Tupper's dock.

Tom shrugged. "There's no one on the island," he said, quite reasonably. "We're free to get on with our holiday."

The sound of the engine of our Boston Whaler caused all three of us to look toward the dock, where Sonny was bringing the rest of the guests for our Easter celebration. We went down to help them to the house.

"Yoo-hoo!" Fee Snugg called, madly waving. I smiled and waved back, pushing the mystery of the man in the cornstalks firmly to the back of my mind.

Our guests were old family friends, old in the sense of longtime, and old in the sense of aged. I tied up the boat while the guys helped the five of them off. Fee and Vee Snugg were Mom's across-the-street neighbors and our honorary great-aunts. Gus and Mrs. Gus Farnham had come with the second group of guests because Gus had insisted on opening his restaurant that morning, as he did at 5:00 a.m., seven days a week, eleven months a year, except in February when he and Mrs. Gus visited their grown children and grandchildren in California and Arizona. Captain George was a longtime clambake employee who piloted the tour boat that brought our customers to the island. He was also my mother's "friend." She would never use, and would never let us use, the word "boyfriend," which I found both endearing and annoying.

"Wee!" Fee closed her eyes as Tom held her tight and moved her off the boat. Both sisters were serious fans of his, especially his physique. "Watch the competition," Mrs. Gus whispered to me, sticking her sharp elbow in my ribs. "They're after your sweetheart."

We helped carry the items the guests had brought; Mrs. Gus and Fee had both baked and Vee had made a salad. Captain George carried a paper bag. "Rolls," he informed me. "Baked them myself this morning." A man of hidden talents. Gus held a bottle of good Scotch whiskey, which he handed to Sonny as he climbed off the boat. Sonny cradled it like a baby.

We all crossed Windsholme's front porch, passing under the flag fluttering on a pole that Sonny and Tom had put up the weekend before. The flag was all pinks, pale yellows, and baby blues, with a bunny chomping a carrot, along with the words "Happy Easter!" Until a few years ago, I would have laughed if you'd told me my mother would have owned such a thing. But since she'd gone to work at Linens 'n' Pantries, the big-box store in Topsham, she'd used her employee discount to buy all kinds of stuff I never thought my stiff-upper-lip, flinty Yankee mother would love. Who knew she had such a soft spot?

None of the new arrivals had seen Windsholme since

the renovation had been completed, so after coats were shed and food stored, I gave them a tour, with Zoey tagging along. I took the group through the dining room, the table set for the day's festivities, with its restored murals of boat building and ice harvesting on the walls. Then we went through the huge front hall to the beautifully proportioned main salon, the ladies' retiring room, and the former gentlemen's billiards room, now refitted as a place for brides to dress. Several times I noticed Zoey casting a proprietary eye over the space, giving small nods of her curly brown head. She and Jamie would be married on the island in June, our first wedding at Windsholme. I could see her artist's eye at work, placing tables, flowers, and decorations in the mostly empty rooms.

Though the main floor rooms were grand, it was my mother's and my apartments on the second floor that brought the biggest response from the other guests. These were our summer homes, and our friends were happy to see us settled.

"It's beautiful!" Fee exclaimed, looking around the old nursery, a room that ran from the front to the back of the house and now served as the kitchen-living-dining space in my apartment.

"It is," Zoey said, and gave me a wink. She'd helped me choose the built-ins and fittings and was more than a little proud of how it had turned out. I'd had my doubts about the dark blue kitchen cabinets, but I had to hand it to her: They were stunning.

Back downstairs in the front hall, our guests went off to help in the new kitchen, where there was more than enough space for everyone to pitch in. The smells of lamb and garlic, onions, and something lemony floated through the house. I lingered and was rewarded when Tom came through looking for me. He took me in his arms and gave me an encouraging squeeze. "Are you okay?"

"I am," I said, meaning it. But then I hesitated. "You believe me about the man, don't you?"

He chuckled, a low, deep sound that made his chest vibrate. "I do. You're not given to delusions." He let me go and looked me in the eye. "Besides, there's the basket." He smiled. "And another witness."

"There's another basket?" Neither of us had noticed the second witness, who was crouched behind the thick leg of the round table that stood in the center of the foyer. His face was covered in chocolate, and he held a headless bunny in his equally chocolate-covered hands.

"So maybe not a completely reliable witness," I said.

With a look at me, Tom bent down to address the perpetrator. "Let's get you cleaned up before dinner, bud." Then straightening up, he added, "And before your parents kill you." Touching Jack lightly and only on the top of his head, Tom steered the miscreant off toward the public men's room, another necessity in our new event space.

They were just out of sight when Livvie stuck her head into the hall and called, "Dinner!"

The huge dining room table, one of the very few original furnishings in the house, easily fit the fourteen of us—Tom and me, Mom and Captain George, Livvie, Sonny, Page and Jack, Zoey and Jamie, Fee and Vee, and Gus and Mrs. Gus. The food laid out on platters and in bowls looked like it should be photographed for a magazine. The lamb, boneless and butterflied, marinated overnight, and cooked on the new grill on the kitchen stove, was the star of the show. It was Sonny's contribution and he'd carved it before we came to the table, his job in the twelve years since my father had died. There was a plate of asparagus in lemony butter made by Zoey and Jamie, roasted potatoes with onions and carrots carefully peeled by Tom and me. Captain George's fresh-baked rolls and Vee's salad rounded out the offerings.

It had been near insanity to have this meal on Morrow Island. We'd had to bring out everything. Most of the furniture we'd ordered for the new business had yet to be delivered along with the pots and pans, cooking utensils, and flatware. Getting anything large out to the island was a laborious and expensive process that couldn't take place over the winter in any case. Zoey was supplying the dishes and serveware, a way too generous thing to do. The set wouldn't be completed until her own wedding, so we'd had to bring dishes out too.

Despite the challenges, Mom and I had wanted the celebration held here. Once the season began, we'd be living upstairs from an event space, and we wanted this moment with our family and close friends. Looking around the table, I reflected that most of us lived private lives in public spaces—Fee and Vee in the Snuggles Inn, their bed-and-breakfast; Zoey, in the apartment over her pottery shop and studio. Though Gus and Mrs. Gus had moved out long ago, they'd started their married life in the little apartment over their restaurant.

When the food was passed and plates piled high, my mother rose. "To our nearest and dearest. Thank you for this meal, for the food, but also for the fellowship." She raised her wineglass. "To old friends in our new home."

"Hear, hear," the captain led.

"Cheers, dears," Fee responded.

We toasted and clinked, one of Jack's favorite things. Across the table from me, I saw Zoey wipe a long finger under her eye, flicking away a single tear. She saw me

watching and gave a wavering smile. She was our most recent recruit, cemented in her status as a friend and boss to
both Livvie and me at her company, Lupine Design, and as
the fiancée of Jamie.

She turned to Jamie on her right and gave him a "he's so
dreamy" look that almost made me giggle aloud. He was a
handsome man, tall, blond-haired with deep blue eyes and
dark lashes and brows. Jamie was a childhood friend. I
didn't feel what Zoey felt, but I could see what she saw.

She didn't have a family. Her father had never been in
the picture and her mom had died tragically when she was
sixteen. She was a genius at bringing other potters and all
kinds of artists together, but the nomadic life she'd led as
she learned her craft and built her business had precluded
scenes like this. I wondered if she'd ever before sat around
a table with friends and family on Easter Sunday.

Sonny's lamb was perfectly cooked, crispy, and tangy
from the marinade, chewy in a good way. It was my father's recipe, and each bite brought back memories of him,
memories of my childhood Easters at my grandparents'
house, surrounded by aunts, uncles, and cousins.

The conversation flowed along with the food and wine.
My mother sat at the head of the table, Captain George to
her left. He leaned in and said something I couldn't hear
that made her laugh. They made a striking, if contrasting,
couple. He was a bear of a man, a polar bear, specifically,
given his long white hair and white beard. His face was
permanently ruddy from a life lived on the water. My petite mother had the refined features of a marble statue.
More and more silver ran through her hair, but it still
gleamed blond in the sunlight.

A year after it had apparently started on a snowy Saint
Patrick's night, the captain and my mother wouldn't define
what was going on between them. Or couldn't. All I knew

was my mother was happier and lighter and I was happy for her. With my father she had lost her love, her partner in life and in business, and her best friend. The grief that had followed her for years like a thin but visible wraith had lifted at last.

Across the table, Tom sat wedged between the Snugg sisters, who took turns offering him food he had already politely declined. His body was his temple, and though he'd graciously accepted the lamb, asparagus, and salad, there was no way the other stuff was passing his lips. He turned to smile across the table at me, rolling his eyes heavenward in a gesture of helplessness. While he looked at me, Fee snuck a spoonful of roasted potatoes onto his plate. Big, strong cop, helpless in the face of the Snugg sisters.

Tom was another of our strays, I supposed. He wasn't estranged from his family per se, just removed. I knew he'd spoken to his mother that morning, sending Easter greetings to the family. He'd left Rhode Island because it had been crowded, so to speak. With three brothers on the Providence police force and his father a captain, he'd come under a lot of scrutiny. And there was the inconvenient fact that his brother had married Tom's former fiancée, which made the family circle feel more like a noose. Even more inconvenient, she hadn't been "former" at the time. I hadn't met his parents yet, but he'd invited them to visit during the summer.

He spotted the potatoes on his plate and shrugged, still smiling.

When the main course was finished, Tom, Zoey, Jamie, and I cleared the table and brought out coffee and the desserts. Vee had made a cake in the shape of a bunny, slathered with white frosting, and covered in coconut flakes.

Mrs. Gus had contributed one of her signature pies, ricotta for the holiday.

Jack stared, entranced, but then squirmed and asked to be excused. He could sit still no longer. Given the amount of sugar he'd already consumed, Livvie granted permission immediately. Jack pushed out his chair and ran into the main salon, where he'd left his toy fire engine. We heard him pushing it around the big, empty floor, a marvelous place to play, making siren sounds with his mouth.

With Jack gone at last, we could discuss the man in the morning suit. In answer to curious demands, I described him in detail. The people around the table, groaning, sitting back, pushing away their plates, denied having any idea who he might be.

"It's a mystery," my mother said.

# Chapter Four

On Monday morning, I was at my desk at Lupine Design. My office was toward the rear of the building on the first floor, a part of the space Zoey had expanded into when the previous tenant died. I was far enough from the production floor, with its relentless pounding sound from the press for the molded pieces, that I was able to conduct business on the phone. Which is what I was doing. A forceful interior designer, responsible for the dining room at a charity show house, was trying, mostly successfully, to get Lupine to donate the dinner service he needed to set his table. He'd offered to provide a small sign with the appearance of a place card, giving us credit and directing people to our website. And further to pay for shipping and insurance, both ways, unless he was successful in selling the pieces at full retail, paying us our usual wholesale price, and donating the rest to the charity.

After checking on timing and making sure we had the necessary items in stock, I took the details and agreed. Our busiest season was beginning to wind down. Our retailers had everything they needed for wedding season, and the web orders had slowed as well.

When she'd offered me the job the previous spring, Zoey had made it impossible to refuse. I would run the business side, she design and production. I was allowed to give input, in terms of sales numbers that might influence the direction of creative work, but her word was law in that area. Similarly, she would weigh in on the practicality and desirability of larger deals and financial decisions, but that was my province.

My only hesitation had been about working with a friend, my best friend in Busman's Harbor aside from my sister. That Livvie was employed at Lupine wasn't a worry. She and I had worked together at the Snowden Family Clambake since we were young teens. Zoey, on the other hand, had had complete control in all areas of Lupine Design since she'd founded it. Was she ready to give up any portion of control? Zoey assured me she was eager to walk away from the business side. It turned out she was telling the truth, something she couldn't have really known any more than I did.

After I finished my conversation with the designer, I opened the Snowden Family Clambake tote bag I carried instead of a pocketbook and pulled out *The Tale of Peter Rabbit*, turning it over in my hands. The book was old. The brown cover showed it had received some childish love, though the pages were intact. The illustrations and text were different than I remembered. I opened it to the title page and nearly dropped it. "For Mary James," the inscription read, "from Beatrix Potter with kind regards and best wishes for Christmas 1901."

The author's signature was the clue. I knew where the book must have come from. Breathing slowly, I put the book back in the bag and returned to my computer.

The one disadvantage of my little office was that the only window was high up in the wall, providing light but no view. I'd gotten pretty good though at judging where the sun was in the sky, and that, and the rumble in my tummy, told me it was nearing lunch. I'd vowed after the Easter meal never to eat again. Clearly a vow that was going to be broken.

I could have stopped at Mom's house for leftovers. The previous evening, we'd laboriously cleaned up Windsholme and brought almost everything back, including the garbage and the dirty dishes. But I had something else in mind.

Calling into the workroom to let my co-workers know I was going out, I hurried to Mom's house and backed my aging Subaru out of the old three-bay garage. I'd been thinking about the man in the morning suit since the day before. Sometimes I would shake my head to clear it, convinced I had imagined him. But there had been the dented cornstalks, the Easter basket, and my fellow witness, the six-year-old.

There was no explanation for the man, no evidence as to how he got on or off the island. But there were two small things. The outboard motorboat at the dock in front of Quentin's house, and now the book. Out on the street, I pointed the Subaru toward Westclaw Point and stepped on the gas.

The Subaru had learned the way to Quentin's house much as a horse learns the way to its stable. Without much thought or awareness, I was soon pulling into the double track that led to the imposing marble and glass edifice.

I had made the trip many times over the past several winters. Quentin had asked me to check on his house, so every couple of weeks, I drove over and looked for plumbing leaks, heat outages, weather damage, and so on. Quentin could have paid someone to do it, or he could have installed a security system that would enable him to check on the house himself. But he'd asked me, and he had done a lot for me, so I'd readily agreed. I sometimes suspected he asked me to do it so I would know I had a refuge if living and working surrounded by family and friends was ever too much.

Quentin and I were friends, inasmuch as anyone could be a friend to Quentin. While he was in college, he had invented a piece of computer code that made most programs run faster. He hadn't done it as work for hire, or sold it, but instead had licensed the code to almost every company that made consumer or business applications. It had made him uncountably rich before he was twenty-two.

It had also made him distant, lacking in trust, never sure if people liked him for himself or for what he could buy them. If he'd grown up rich, he might have had a set of equally rich childhood friends he could trust. If he'd made his money when he was a little older, he might have had an established group of friends who knew him back when. Lacking either of these, he was a solitary individual. He was also a gay man, though I'd never heard him mention a boyfriend or even a date. It was a complicated life.

Quentin had saved the Snowden Family Clambake from a certain demise seven years earlier. He said he'd done it to protect his own interests, most notably his picturesque view across the channel to Morrow Island and Windsholme, but I knew there was softheartedness in the investment. He had said he'd be a silent partner, taking payment on the loan in the years we could afford it, and he'd kept his word. Quentin gave advice only when I asked for it. He'd been an advocate for the renovation of Windsholme but left the decision to my mother about whether to fix it up or tear it down.

At Quentin's house, there was no vehicle in the drive, no lights in the windows, though that didn't prove much since it was midday. The house loomed up, all marble and glass, shiny surfaces, hard and cold, as out of place in the Maine

landscape as a skyscraper or a tiki hut. I often teased
Quentin about the house, calling it his Fortress of Solitude. I found it striking, dramatic, and starkly beautiful.

I entered, not as I usually would have during the summer through the dramatic glass doors that faced the sea on
the other side of the house, but through the door at the
back. As I pushed the buttons on the keypad, I wondered
how many people had the code and when Quentin had last
changed it. Definitely never in the years I'd been looking
after the house.

The door opened into a mudroom that led to a long
hallway. I stopped at the glass-fronted, climate-controlled
bookcase in the hallway and placed *The Tale of Peter Rabbit* among the other signed first editions there. *Thank
goodness Jack didn't get his chocolatey hands on it.*

As I walked toward the front of the house I noted the
unmistakable smell of canned tomato soup being heated.
Immediately after, I heard humming, in a low voice, a
peppy tune. And then the scrape of a spoon across the bottom of a pan.

I considered leaving. I considered calling the police. But
the idea of a burglar cooking soup was too preposterous.
Whoever it was, he was probably a guest of Quentin's.
Normally, that was something Quentin would have mentioned to me, but he was in no way required to.

I came around the corner from the hallway into the
huge, open main room. In the kitchen area at the back of
the space, a tall figure stood in front of the restaurant-
grade stove, stirring. He wasn't wearing the top hat, the
jacket, or the vest, but the gray striped trousers were un-
mistakably part of a morning suit. The strings of a black
apron were tied neatly across his back. He was still humming.

I cleared my throat, not wishing to startle him. "Excuse me."

He didn't jump but turned slowly. "Hello, m'dear." He smiled broadly, not in the least perturbed.

"You-you were lying in my garden Easter morning," I stated, surprised into straightforwardness. Seen vertically, rather than horizontally in the cornstalks, the man was tall, over six feet, and lean, almost thin. He didn't look frail or confused.

"I believe I was," he said.

I was sure it had been him, but the matter-of-factness of the admission nonplussed me momentarily. "Why?" I stammered.

"I saw you with your friends working over there the weekend before," he said. "You left that flag with the bunny on it hanging from the porch, so I thought you might be back for Easter."

There was a telescope by Quentin's big front windows. Through it, I knew the man could see Windsholme at the top of Morrow Island and enough of the lawn around it to spot us as we'd worked outside.

"During the week, I gathered some Easter bits, candy and eggs and such, with the thought that I might offer them as a holiday gift to your family. When I saw you all Easter morning, I brought the boat over but before I could get to the house—"

"You passed out in the garden."

"Quite. I know it sounds presumptuous," he added quickly. "But I only meant to be neighborly. It's the first time I've been alone on Easter in a long time."

His accent was English. I was hardly an expert, but I thought he sounded refined, educated, very BBC. And strangely, I believed him. He was a lonely old man, staying in an area with many closed-up summer homes. We were, arguably, his nearest neighbors.

But why was he staying in Quentin's house? "What are you doing here?" I asked. "How did you get in?"

He wasn't defensive in the least. "I'm a former employee of Mr. Tupper's. He knew I needed a place to stay for the short term between jobs and he offered me this. He's such a kind man, a real lifesaver."

Quentin was a kind man and that sounded exactly like something he would do. I stuck my hand out. "Julia Snowden. Friend of Quentin's. I check on the house."

He took my hand in his own and shook. His hand was soft, but his grasp was firm. "Alfred Minucci. Pleased to meet you." He had a nice smile.

"You stole a book from Quentin," I said, trying not to sound accusatory. "*The Tale of Peter Rabbit.*"

"Oh, that," Alfred said. "If you know Quentin, you know he's quite a magpie. Always has piles of stuff around. I didn't think he'd miss it. A child should enjoy it."

The Quentin I knew was neat as a pin. I'd teased him once about having a living room you could perform surgery in. "That book is a first edition from Beatrix Potter's private printing when she couldn't land a publisher. It's worth one hundred thousand dollars." I put my hand out palm forward when Alfred gasped. "Don't worry. I put it back."

"Thank you. Quentin's collecting has certainly gone up a notch since I worked for him."

"Does it happen often, the passing out?" I asked, leaving the subject of the book behind.

"Only recently," he answered.

"Have you seen someone about it?"

He shrugged. "Between jobs, no insurance. I will as soon as I can."

The soup began to bubble in the pan. "Excuse me," he said, turning off the burner.

"I'll let you eat your lunch," I responded. I went to the drawer next to the refrigerator where I knew I would find what I was looking for. I pulled out a small pad of paper and a pen and scrawled my name and phone number on it. "I live right in town," I said. "Call or text if you need anything."

"Thank you, m'dear," Alfred Minucci responded. "Very thoughtful. But I'm settled for now."

He seemed nice. I liked him. I said goodbye and wished him well and he did the same to me. I let myself out, listening for the click of the lock as I closed the door behind me and went back to the Subaru.

I picked up a chicken salad sandwich at the pizza place in the mini-mall by the highway and headed back to work. Sitting at my desk, I unwrapped the messy sandwich gingerly, careful not to smear mayonnaise on the papers piled around the edges of my workspace. I'd made tea in the kitchen area of the shop and stopped in to the studio while the water boiled. Livvie and Zoey had each given me questioning looks. I rarely left for lunch. I shrugged and went about my business.

I took three bites of sandwich, just enough to quell my insistent tummy, and then called Quentin on my cell.

I followed Quentin's movements with interest, not an easy job. He disdained social media, and though we were friends, he wasn't the type to drop a line or start a chat. My guess was that he and his new yacht were in the Mediterranean, positioning for the season on the Côte d'Azur, which would start shortly. Which meant he was probably six hours ahead, getting ready for or just finishing dinner.

"Hello, Julia."

Success. Wherever he was, he was near enough to a cell tower or a satellite that my call had reached him. "Hi. Where are you?"

"France," he said shortly. I had been right.

Now that I'd found him, I wasn't sure where to start. "I checked on your house today." I chose the most casual, least alarming entrée I could think of.

"Umm, hmm." I could picture him in his yacht's dining room, nodding to indicate a vague interest, but eager to move on to other things. It was likely there were several other screens blinking in front of him.

"There was a man there."

"A man? *In* my house." Now I had his attention. "Julia, this is a terrible April Fools' joke."

I had forgotten until that moment that it was April Fools' Day. "I take it you don't have any invited guests staying there."

"Let me check my calendar." Quentin was capable of telling someone to use his home and then forgetting the invitation entirely. "No," he said. "Not one of mine."

My surprise turned to alarm. "He says his name is Alfred Minucci and you told him he could stay there while he's between jobs."

"Not ringing any bells."

"He's tall and thin. In his sixties, I would guess. White hair, has a mustache, very dapper."

Quentin sighed. "A squatter then." He seemed less interested than I thought one should be when informed there was a stranger living in one's house.

"He says he used to work for you. Both times I saw him, he was wearing a morning suit," I added.

"Oh!" This was an entirely different "oh" from the last, resigned "oh." This "oh" was an indication of sudden alertness, awareness, and memory. "Oh, my." The resignation was back. "I know who it is."

"Is he dangerous, this person?" I asked. "He came over to visit us on Morrow Island."

"No, no, no." Quentin's tone was certain, not in the least alarmed. "Nothing like that."

"Do you want me to take care of it? Call the police, or—" I didn't mention *The Tale of Peter Rabbit*. I believed it had been an honest mistake and I'd returned it, so no harm done.

"No," Quentin said quickly, "I'll handle it."

And that was that. No chitchat. Barely a goodbye. But Quentin wasn't good at small talk. And I supposed he'd rushed off to get the strange man ejected from his house.

# Chapter Five

For the next three days I went about my business. I worked at Lupine Design during the day, went back to Mom's house in the evening, and had long, meandering phone conversations with Tom at night.

He was on a case in the middle of the state. I'd followed it in the *Press Herald*, though Tom was typically tight-lipped. It was a sad, tawdry affair, the suspect apparently obvious. But he hadn't been arrested yet, so Tom and his partner, Jerry Binder, were still on-site conducting interviews with neighbors and gathering evidence.

I'd told Tom about Alfred Minucci that first night and over the next two we chewed it over. Why on earth would a man in a morning suit be squatting at Quentin's house?

Our explanations grew ever more fanciful.

"He works at a tuxedo rental shop," Tom said. "He's been embezzling from them, got discovered, and had to take off in a hurry."

"Wearing the most conspicuous outfit in the store?" I laughed. "Surely, he had his own clothes."

"They make the employees wear the merchandise," Tom continued, still laughing.

"I think he was in a wedding," I countered. "Possibly even his own. He got cold feet and ran away. The bride's a member of an organized crime family. Her father and uncles are looking for him. Alfred fled as far as he could go."

"He walked away with the bride's tiara." Tom got into the spirit of the tale. "He's lying low until he can turn it into cash and escape the country."

"In his little motorboat," I amended. "That's what he was doing on Morrow Island. Dry run before he heads to Canada."

"He didn't get very far." Tom paused, coming back in a more serious tone. "Has the man left Quentin's house?"

"No idea." I was a little miffed about that. But Quentin was under no obligation to report developments to me. He had said he would take care of it. "I'll call Jamie to see if Busman's Harbor P.D. has an update."

"Julia," Tom cautioned. He hadn't been happy that I'd entered Quentin's house after I realized it was occupied. I couldn't blame him.

"Just a phone call," I assured him.

It wasn't too late to call Jamie that night. After Tom and I hung up, I punched in his cell number.

"Julia." The voice was familiar, but not Jamie's.

"Zoey."

"Your name came up on Jamie's screen, so I answered. Were you looking for either one of us or do you need him in particular?"

"In particular," I answered.

"He's downstairs. I'll get him."

Even as she talked, I could hear her footsteps headed down the stairs. "Where are you?"

"Jamie's house." Zoey had a stunning renovated apartment over the studio and store. Jamie had an old sea captain's house around the corner from my mother's. Our backyards were adjacent, and we'd grown up running through them, equally at home in either house. Jamie had three much older siblings. There was a ten-year gap between him and the next youngest. His parents had moved to Florida to be near his sister years earlier, leaving Jamie rattling around in the big old house alone. Lately, he and Zoey had stayed more frequently at his place than hers and I thought they might move there permanently after they were married in June. Which would be good, because I cold-bloodedly had my eye on Zoey's apartment for Lupine Design expansion.

"Jamie! It's Julia for you." There was a muffled sound as the phone was handed over.

"Julia, is everything okay?" Jamie's voice was urgent, worried.

I glanced at the clock. Ten fifteen. Maybe it was late for a call. "Fine, fine," I assured him. "Sorry to call so late." I paused, then decided I might as well get right to it. "The man Jack and I saw on Morrow Island. He was squatting at Quentin's house. I let Quentin know. Did he call the P.D. to report him?"

Jamie hesitated a moment, as if rifling through police reports in his head. "No," he answered with a strong degree of certainty. "Haven't heard from Tupper. Haven't had any squatting reports in the last month, I would say."

"Hmm. I wondered." Quentin had said he'd take care of it. He hadn't said he'd involve the police. Since he knew the man, he probably decided to deal with him directly.

"Do you want me to take a run out there tomorrow?" Jamie asked. It was the police department's quietest time of year. The truly bad weather and the holiday partying were over, the snowbirds and tourists not yet returned.

"No," I answered. "Don't bother." If Quentin wanted to deal with his squatter privately, he should be allowed to do so.

# Chapter Six

I woke up early the next morning, still thinking about Alfred Minucci. Without a car on Westclaw Point he was very isolated. Perhaps he needed groceries or a ride to urgent care to check on his mysterious illness.

Quentin didn't have a landline, so after I brewed a cup of coffee, I poured it into my travel mug and headed to Westclaw Point once again.

As before, there was no car on the sandy track, no lights on inside. I didn't want to ring the bell or walk in, so I went around the side of the house to the deck out front.

The little outboard motor wasn't tied up at the dock, so perhaps Mr. Minucci was gone.

I turned to look inside the house. Quentin's house faced west, but there was enough morning sun that I put my face against the glass and shaded my eyes to see.

The house was quiet. No one in the open kitchen at the back. No one on the couches or seated at the dining table. Perhaps Quentin had "taken care of it." Or perhaps Mr. Minucci was still upstairs in bed. If that was so, I wasn't inclined to bother him. No one had asked me to come here. The empty, cavernous room, plus the missing boat, led me to assume the house was vacant.

I was about to turn away, when I caught sight of something on the white rug in between the white couches. A more careful look revealed a long leg in striped gray trousers. My breath caught. Mr. Minucci must have had another of his spells. I banged on the keypad next to the sliding door.

After what seemed like minutes but must have been seconds, the door clicked open. I pushed through, rushing toward the prostrate body of Alfred Minucci.

He was on the floor, on his back, the top hat not far from his white head. His white shirt and gray vest were stained with bright red blood, and one of Quentin's expensive kitchen knives stuck out just under his rib cage.

# Chapter Seven

Standing well away from the blood that soaked into the white carpet, I inspected the body as best I could to make sure he was dead. An unnecessary but necessary action. Then I called the Busman's Harbor police, who would call the Maine State Police Major Crimes Unit. I also called Zoey to tell her I'd be late to work.

"What's going on?" she asked, suspicious.

"Nothing," I lied. "Just tied up is all."

"Harumph," Zoey responded. "When you get back here you better tell me everything."

I hung up and went back out on the deck to wait. A stiff, chilling breeze came off the water, but something kept me from going to the Subaru. Instead, I huddled on the steps to the deck, staring out at the comforting sight of Morrow Island, with Windsholme at its highest point, standing straight and tall.

Jamie and his partner, Pete Howland, arrived first, followed immediately by an ambulance I knew was unneeded. Jamie asked if I was okay and then directed me to wait in my car while they secured the scene. He knew the state police detectives would prefer to do my first interview. I did as he asked, turning the car on, and running the heat for a few minutes to warm up.

I wasn't sure it would be Tom and his partner and superior officer, Jerry Binder, who would come from Major Crimes. Though Busman's Harbor was in their territory, if they were still on the other case, another team might be pressed into service. I closed my eyes, fervently hoping it would be Tom.

Vehicles kept arriving—the medical examiner's van, the crime scene techs in two cars, and another van. The ambulance left. I wasn't paying much attention and jumped when a hand knocked on my driver's-side window. My heart slowed immediately, and a smile spread across my face when I saw the short brown hair over the expressive brows and warm brown eyes peering into the car. Tom. Thank goodness.

I opened my window. Tom reached in and clasped my shoulder, his hand strong and reassuring. I felt better instantly. Lieutenant Binder was right behind him. They asked me to stay in the car while they inspected the scene and caught up with the officers and technicians inside.

I sat until my bottom was numb. Then I got out of the car, stretched my spine, waved my arms, and got in again. Many of the houses on Westclaw Point were seasonal and empty. Most of the people who lived out there year-round were at work or in school. Nonetheless, the activity at Quentin's house had drawn a small crowd. Jamie and Pete kept people beyond the boundaries of the property and directed traffic.

Finally, Tom appeared at my window again. "You can go back to town. Meet us at police headquarters in an hour." His voice changed. "Are you okay to drive?"

I assured him I was.

Jamie found the crime scene tech who was parked behind me and got her to move her official car, and then forced the crowd on the street to let me out. I recognized a few faces, which undoubtedly meant they recognized me. The news that I was at the scene would be all over before I got back to the harbor.

The multipurpose room in Busman's Harbor's combined police station–firehouse–town hall building was being set up as an incident room when the three of us sat down. Tom and Binder were across the folding table from me, all of us in uncomfortable metal chairs.

Tom had been there for the start of the story, the appearance—and disappearance—of Alfred Minucci on Morrow Island. But Lieutenant Binder hadn't been, and he questioned me closely.

Next, we talked about my first visit to Quentin's house. At times, the din from the people in the room made it difficult for me to hear.

"What did you ask?" I semi-shouted.

"Why did you go to Mr. Tupper's house?" Binder repeated with more volume.

"I look after it during the winter," I said, and left it at that. It was true enough.

Tom cleared his throat, carefully not looking at me, which was all the hint Binder needed. "Was this a regular visit to the house, then?" he pressed.

"No." I wasn't going to lie to him, and Tom knew better anyway. "When we searched Morrow Island after the man in the morning suit disappeared, I noticed an outboard motor tied up at Quentin's dock. There was no reason for it to be there. It made me curious. And I'm responsible for the house." I raised and lowered my shoulders as if there was nothing else I could have done. Neither of them was fooled.

I described my visit, my interactions with and impressions of Alfred Minucci. I didn't mention *The Tale of Peter Rabbit*. It seemed like an unnecessary complication.

"And he's standing at the stove, stirring soup in the whaddyacallit—" Binder groped for the words.

"Morning suit," Tom said, very assured, as if I hadn't told him what it was five days earlier. "Same thing he was wearing when he died."

"Minus the jacket and the vest," I put in. "Which he was wearing when I saw him that first time in the garden."

We continued. I told how Mr. Minucci said he was a guest of Quentin's. I'd called Quentin, who'd denied it, but seemed to finally realize who the man was. Probably was.

"We have a call in to Mr. Tupper," Binder informed me. "No response yet."

"He's in Europe," I said. "On his yacht. Six hours ahead. He's probably asleep."

Binder nodded. "I'm sure he'll be in touch."

I told them about the call to Jamie, when I'd learned Quentin hadn't called the Busman's Harbor police, and my return to Quentin's house.

"Mr. Tupper didn't ask you to go to his house," Binder stated.

"No," I admitted. "He said he'd take care of it. But I thought if he hadn't involved the police and had merely asked Mr. Minucci to leave, Quentin had no way of confirming that he had. I decided to check."

Tom made the low, skeptical noise in his throat again, but this time I was telling the absolute truth.

The detectives made me walk through every second I'd been at Quentin's house that second time. Where I went, what I touched. How long from the time I got there until I spotted the body. How long before I called the police, and so on.

When they were done with the questions, Tom underlined the last sentence in his notebook with a flourish.

"Is there anything else you can tell us, Julia?" Binder asked.

I hesitated, struggling. *Should I say it?*

"One thing." I cleared my throat. "I looked at the body pretty closely. And I don't think the man on the living room floor at Quentin's house is Alfred Minucci."

There was a moment's stunned silence while both of them stared at me. Tom was the first to speak. "You're saying there are *two* strangers in Busman's Harbor wearing morning suits?"

"Yes. They look very alike—tall, thin, white-haired, mustache—but not quite identical." I tried to think what had given me this impression. I'd seen bodies before, recently dead. A corpse did look different from a person in life. But there was something about the dead man's face. His features were smaller and sharper, his nose and chin slightly more pointed. I tried as best I could to describe the differences, but I could tell they thought I was mistaken.

At the end of the interview, they both thanked me and stood. Binder said they'd be in touch. Tom walked me to the door that led from the multipurpose room into the police station beyond. He put a hand on my arm to stop me, then quickly removed it. There was no worry about Binder seeing we were a couple. The lieutenant knew, had known from the beginning. Had probably known before either Tom or I did, truth be told. But the multipurpose room and the police station teemed with activity. People snaked wires for computers and chargers, moved whiteboards, and set up tables and chairs, preparing for a homicide investigation. Most of those people probably didn't know, and I was an important witness.

I turned around to face him. His face was serious, his brown eyes full of sympathy. "Are you okay?"

"Fine," I said, though it wasn't quite the truth.

"How sure are you that it isn't the same man?"

"Pretty sure." I shrugged, but kept my eyes on his, unblinking.

"Okay," he whispered, touching my arm once again. He gave a little smile which I answered with my own. I would return alone to Mom's house. He'd sleep at the Snuggles Inn, right across the street.

"See you soon, I hope," I said, and walked through the door.

# Chapter Eight

The next morning was Saturday. While it would be very like me to put in a few hours at work, especially having missed the previous day, I hung out at Mom's house. I was out of sorts from the whole discovering-a-body experience. Eventually, I dressed in my usual winter uniform of jeans, long-sleeved T-shirt, and flannel shirt over that and went out on the front porch to read. The day was sunny and cool. The porch screens hadn't been put up yet, which made me feel like I was sitting in the street, but I resolutely pulled an old quilt over myself, opened my book, and was soon enveloped in the world of the story.

"Julia!"

I looked up, a little shocked. I'd been so deep in the book, I came to not sure when or where I was. I was even more shocked when I realized who had called me.

"Quentin! What are you doing here? How did you get here? When did you get here?" Then I realized in his world of private jets and hired drivers, he easily could have gotten to Busman's Harbor overnight.

"About two hours ago." He answered the last question. "I've been at the police station since I arrived."

He wore his usual long-sleeved blue button-down shirt and khaki pants, augmented with a navy sweater against the chill. The skin around his eyes was puffy and there was a gray pallor underneath his tan. "I'm not going to thank you," he said, very formally, "for being the impetus for the call that woke me last night."

"Would you rather the corpse had moldered in your house for days or weeks?" I might be in this situation up to my neck, but no one could say it was my fault. I hadn't murdered the man.

Quentin trundled up the wooden steps to the porch and sat down on a hassock across from me. The cushions weren't yet on the furniture. I'd brought mine out with me but he was sitting on bare wicker. It wouldn't be comfortable for long.

"How did it go with the detectives?"

He ran one of his big hands through his abundant dark blond hair. "About as I expected." He didn't say anything more for a few moments while he shifted on the uncomfortable ottoman. I waited him out. I was owed an explanation.

Finally, he began. "When I was in my early twenties . . ." He stopped, groping for the words, then started again. "It was a crazy time. The money was pouring in, but so were the business deals that required my attention. I had good attorneys, but I was the only one who understood how valuable the thing was that I had." His piece of code. "The lawyers understood contracts, but I understood the technology. I had to be an active part of every negotiation. My lawyers were in New York. I moved to the city. At first, I rented an apartment in the Plaza Hotel."

He noticed my smile. "What? It was convenient. My attorneys were in midtown. I was seldom in the apartment and thought having hotel-style amenities would be helpful."

"Nothing," I protested, smothering the smile but still amused. I easily understood how twenty-one-year-old

Quentin, newly rolling in money, would have thought living at the Plaza was "convenient." I could see him there, haunting the kitchens during off-hours like an overgrown Eloise.

"Anyway," Quentin continued, grim-faced, but determined to get through the story, "within a year or so my friends began to graduate from college and drift to the city. It was natural," he said, a little too defensively, "to offer some a place to stay until they got settled. The apartment, not surprisingly in retrospect, became a gathering place, the party house for friends, and friends of friends, and eventually, people no one knew at all."

This part of the story was startling. Quentin never talked about friends. Perhaps this situation had been the beginning of his wariness with strangers, of letting no one get close. Of realizing his money was a double-edged sword.

"The management at the Plaza hated the crowd of young people and the noise. And I hated coming home every night, exhausted, to people and food and clothes and dirty plates all around, the smell of weed hanging over everything, and vomit in the bathroom."

I waited for the story to meander its way to Alfred Minucci. "You asked them all to leave?" I suggested.

Quentin chuckled. "Not exactly. I hired a butler."

This did make me laugh out loud. The picture of poor, confused Quentin, twenty-two years old, trying his best to get out of an awkward and aggravating social situation by hiring an English butler. In a morning suit. "Alfred Minucci," I said.

"Alfred Smythe, he told me his name was." Quentin sat back and relaxed a little. "Anyway, he was brilliant. The presence of someone who was clearly an adult tamped down the party atmosphere enough that I wasn't in danger of being tossed out. He got to know everyone who was living there. He pushed the hangers-on out the door, and then persuaded my friends they either needed to find places of their own in the city or go home to their parents. He helped them find apartments and jobs. He even conducted mock job interviews. He was truly loved."

For the first time as he told the story, I heard sadness and regret in Quentin's voice. I could believe the man he'd described was Alfred Minucci. I'd seen the kindness and the can-do attitude in the twinkle in his eye. "What happened?"

"We went on like that for some time after he cleaned up my life. But in an empty house with his employer rarely present, there wasn't much for Alfred to do. He lived in the servants' quarters in the apartment. During his third year with me, he received word his mother in England was nearing the end of her life. He took off immediately to be with her when she died, and then stayed to deal with her estate.

"When he returned, sooner than I'd expected, he shut himself in his room. He began to drink to excess and to criticize me and my life in shouted conversations through his door whenever I asked him to do anything or simply asked how he was. He came out during the day when I was out of the apartment, shopped and cleaned, and then shut himself back in his room.

"At first, I made allowances. He was grieving. Even when it continued, I could understand his frustration. He was a talented man. He wanted to work for someone who threw parties and brought home pretty young women to cheer up the place. I wasn't ever going to be that person.

"Still, we went on. Each of us more and more unhappy, me reluctant to do what I knew needed to be done. Finally, after one terrific argument, I went to my office in the apartment to write him a severance check and discovered many checks were missing from my checkbook. Going through the account, I saw that since he'd returned from England, Alfred had been helping himself to the household money. There was barely enough of a balance to keep the account open."

"You fired him then?"

"I fired him then. I moved downtown, where my place is now."

I was quiet for a moment, digesting this. "You wouldn't have offered your house here to Mr. Minucci."

"No." He shook his head. "Not a chance."

"But he was here. Or so we assume."

"So we assume." Quentin rose off the ottoman and rubbed his backside. "The detectives have asked me to go to Augusta to identify the body. Not in an official capacity. They're looking for family. But to make sure the man is who I think he is." Quentin rolled his big shoulders. "It's been more than twenty years. I told them I would do my best."

"Did they tell you—" I started, but then thought I shouldn't mention my doubts about the corpse's identity. It might tip Quentin in one way or the other.

Quentin looked at me, brows raised.

"Nothing," I said.

He climbed off the porch and started down the walk. "Wait," I called. "How will you get to your house?"

"My home is a crime scene," he answered. "My sister's picking me up at the police station. I'm staying with her."

His family was local. That's what had brought him to the Maine coast in the first place. I'd known him for years before I realized his parents as well as his sister and her family were living nearby. And though the idea of him staying with his sister and her two young kids made me smile, I was glad he had a place to go.

\* \* \*

Half an hour later, I was still on the porch when Tom walked up the street, obviously headed for the Snuggles. For a man who always stood straight as a rod, he was strangely canted, shoulders slumped, neck sunk toward his chest. He spotted me before I called to him, straightened up, and smiled. He headed toward the porch.

"You look exhausted," I greeted him.

"Thanks. You look beautiful." He glanced around, spotting the same lack of cushions Quentin had, but in Tom's case I scooted my legs over, offering him a place on the lounger with me. He sank down gratefully. "What I am is confused, puzzled, and frustrated," he said. "Not exhausted. Not yet."

I offered him water, about the only thing he drank, but he waved me off. "Any more and I'll float away."

"Why are you confused et cetera?" I asked.

He put a hand on my knee. "Let's start with your Mr. Minucci."

Tom had long since given up pretending it was inappropriate to talk to me about his cases, though since we'd been together there hadn't been one in which I was so intimately involved. "He's not my Mr. Minucci," I protested.

"Might as well be. You're the only one who's called him that."

"Quentin—" I started.

"Quentin knew him as Alfred Smythe." Tom rubbed his eyes. "If it even is the same man."

"You agree that there might be two." I sat up, eager.

He gave my knee a reassuring pat. "Your guy and Quentin's guy from twenty years ago may not be the same guy. But that doesn't mean your guy from Easter morning and Quentin's house five days ago and the dead guy aren't the same guy."

"It doesn't mean they are," I pointed out. "Any of that." I was having trouble following the conversation and I'd been involved in all the twists and turns of the case so far. How would anyone who'd just arrived on the scene understand it?

"We don't know who our corpse is," Tom continued. "But we do know who he is not. He's not Alfred Minucci."

I sat up even straighter. "How do you know that?"

"There was no identification in the house. All we had to go on was the name you gave us. We began a search for next of kin, figuring that would take a while. We found Alfred Minucci right away. He's a barber in South Portland."

I raised my eyebrows at this. "It could be a coincidence."

Tom shook his head. "Could be but isn't. We emailed a photo of the dead man, looking as lifelike as the ME could make him, to the living Mr. Minucci. Turns out he'd cut the victim's hair three weeks ago. They had a conversation about the fact that they had the same first name. No mention of a last name. The man paid in cash."

Tom paused for a moment so that could sink in.

"Maybe his real name is Alfred Smythe," I said. "The dead man, I mean."

"Or the identical one." Tom sighed. He wasn't given to sighing. This case was really bugging him. "We've started making inquiries in that direction. We've also sent fingerprints from the corpse to the FBI and UK National Crime Agency to see if they have him in their files."

"The UK?"

"You said he was English."

"I said he had an English accent. Given the rest of his butler"—I hesitated to call it an act—"persona"—that wasn't right either, but I let it go—"he could have been putting it on."

"Quentin's Alfred was English, too," Tom reminded me.

I took a deep breath and let it out slowly. "You're looking for two men, right? The victim and the man I met."

He smiled, amused and tolerant. "*I* am. I promise. But I don't need to point out the utter lack of probability of two men, both tall, thin, older, walking around coastal Maine in morning suits. Officially, the state police are pursuing all leads, but we're assuming there is only one man, whoever he may be."

I smiled back to let him know I understood. "Officially," I repeated.

"Officially." Tom grunted. "We'll find out who he is. Somehow. And who killed him." Corpses with no name and knife-wielding killers with no identity didn't sit well with him.

"Are you staying in town again tonight?" I cocked my head toward the Snuggles.

"No. The techs are already gone. We've checked with all the neighbors that are on Westclaw Point over the winter. No one had a clue as to who he was or even that there was anyone in Quentin's house. They haven't seen any knife-wielding killers, either, though we've managed to scare them to death. Some families have closed their houses and moved in with friends or relatives here in town or elsewhere on the peninsula. Those remaining on the point are barricaded in their houses."

"They think the murder was random," I said. "Not targeted. What do you think?"

Tom shook his head. "It wasn't a random robbery gone wrong. Quentin has a lot of nice stuff in that house, and none of it was disturbed. We'll take him out there soon to confirm nothing is missing." He paused. "It's my belief whoever the killer is, he came looking for the victim specifically, but he didn't come to kill him. The murder seems opportunistic, the weapon something that was on hand, not brought to the scene. So, someone who had a beef with Alfred, or whoever he was, and poor impulse control." He returned to my original question. "We'll be back in town soon, but for tomorrow, I have to be back at headquarters. There's a lot going on in Augusta." He glanced over his shoulder toward the house. "Your mom home?"

"She's at work. Back at five."

"Hmmm." The hmmm was emblematic of our dilemma. Tom lived and worked in Augusta. I lived and worked in Busman's Harbor. While I didn't love living with Mom and had already been here far longer than I'd ever imagined, I did love my jobs. Besides, Tom hadn't asked me to live in his rented house, or even offered me a drawer. We were a couple without a hangout spot.

*But then . . .* "It's Saturday," I pointed out. Days blended together for him when he was on a case, but at least until summer and the opening of the Snowden Family Clambake, I was a working woman with semi-regular hours and weekends off. Mostly off.

"Good point," Tom said, looking me straight in the eye. "I can probably wind up work by eight or so. Meet me at my place?"

"I'll be there."

# Chapter Nine

By Monday I was back at my desk at Lupine Design. I sipped my coffee, wishing I was somewhere else. I loved my job, but three days away from it had taken a toll. My email inbox was crammed with orders, and questions about pricing, availability, and shipping time. I had monitored my work email and voicemail over the weekend, but I'd only dealt with things that were truly on fire.

The administrative work wasn't my favorite. What I loved was collaborating with Zoey about how to extend popular product lines, when to sunset old ones. On my own, I'd opened new distribution channels and worked on the website, the catalogs, and the limited number of industry shows we participated in. I also loved the budgeting and tracking of finances, sales, and shipping that enabled all the cool stuff to become a reality. But the admin work had to be done. I was supposed to be keeping just this sort of thing off Zoey's plate.

I whittled away at the most urgent emails. Later, when Zoey stopped in to check on things, she found me staring at my monitor holding my head. "Better you than me," she said.

She leaned against the doorframe of my little office, hand-thrown coffee mug in hand. "I gather you were out on Friday because you're up to your neck in this murder out on Westclaw Point."

"Only if you count discovering the body as up to my neck."

She laughed, snorting a little. "Only if. I noticed your car was gone on Saturday and Sunday."

You had to love small-town life. In fact, I'd been back at Mom's before midday on Sunday, because Tom had gone back to work. There weren't any days off so early in an active murder investigation. Saturday night had been an unexpected treat. I wasn't in a position to complain, even if I'd had a mind to. By summer I'd be working fourteen hours a day, seven days a week at the clambake, and Tom would frequently be the one waiting around for me.

Instead of acknowledging Zoey's unasked question, I turned the tables. "You would only have noticed that if you spent the weekend at Jamie's." I pictured the glorious space directly upstairs. All I was awaiting was her official announcement that she and Jamie would live at his house after they wed. I'd already calculated the revenue level we'd have to hit for me to hire an assistant to do exactly the type of work I was doing at the moment.

Zoey laughed before she left, and I returned to the mess in my inbox. But even as I pecked away, my mind kept returning to the dead man at Quentin's house. The man who was definitely not Alfred Minucci.

Tom was being a loyal boyfriend, telling me he believed that the dead man was not the man I'd met. But he'd also listed chapter and verse all the reasons there was probably only one man. Despite my faith in him, I wondered how hard the detectives were looking for another person.

In the studio kitchen, someone was heating up their lunch. The smell traveled around my office and got into my head, reminding me of something. It was a familiar smell, a childhood memory—canned tomato soup. I pictured the man in the morning suit, the one who'd said his name was Alfred, turned to the stove, stirring.

Where had the soup come from? A nonperishable, he could have brought it with him to Quentin's house, though he apparently didn't have a car. And the things in the Easter basket?

There was a likely source, close at hand.

I finished the email I was working on, scanned through it, and then pressed send. I grabbed my car keys and headed to the break room.

"I'm going to Hannaford. Can I get anybody anything?"

I was too late for order-taking. Lunch was well underway. The potter's wheels and molding press were silent in the studio. Nonetheless, I did get a few requests for sweets and drinks. Zoey gave me a look of curiosity, the skin pinched over her nose. I normally ate at my desk, and here I was, headed out again.

"I'm off," I announced.

"Godspeed," she said. Only half in jest, I thought.

Hannaford was our only supermarket, now owned by a big conglomerate somewhere, but still very much a local store. It expanded its hours and variety of goods from June to October when the summer people were in town, and then contracted again in the fall. Otherwise, it was very much like any grocery anywhere.

The big sliding doors clanged shut behind me, cutting off the chilly breeze. I stood and assessed. There were two cashiers working. Pat had been there forever and knew everyone and everything that happened in town. Illana had started full-time in the summer after graduating from Busman's Harbor High. Pat was checking people out, a snowbird couple, obviously newly back in town and stocking up on everything. The husband and wife each had a cart and the pile on the belt was enormous and growing.

I thought Pat was my better bet, so I went off to find the items on my short list and buy a deli sandwich for myself. The old couple were still checking out when I got back. I waited, shifting the heavy plastic basket from one hand to the other, while Pat totaled up their order in between observations about the weather ("I heard it's going to rain") questions about their drive home ("those tolls on the turnpike are too high") and comments on their purchases ("I like the wheat bread myself, but Mick loves the white").

Finally, they were done. I put the basket on the belt while they paid and removed everything from it.

"Julia, how nice to see you."

"Lovely to see you, Pat."

"I heard you were up in Augusta this weekend."

*Sheesh.* Not thrilled to have every aspect of my life reported, but accepting it as part of small-town life, I was more than happy to change the subject. "Did a man come in here wearing a morning suit, like maybe a week, ten days ago?" I asked.

"A mourning suit? You mean like a black armband?"

"No," I answered. "Like formal wear. Like a butler would wear in an old movie."

Illana had looked up from her phone to listen to our conversation.

Pat was incensed. "Why in the name of blazes would someone come in here dressed like that?"

Illana, meantime, had grown even more interested. She came around her checkout station and entered Pat's. On the way, she plucked a bridal magazine from the rack at the front of the store. She turned the pages with a practiced hand and found the one she was searching for. "An outfit like this?" She stabbed the page with a fingernail painted a shade of blue that made it look like she'd slammed her hand in a car door.

"You've seen him?" My heart sped up.

"He came in twice," Illana answered. "I was working Ten Items or Less. Checked him out both times."

"Did he buy soup?" I asked. "Tomato soup?"

She hesitated, eyes rolling upward as she tried to remember. "I think so."

"Plastic eggs, Easter candy, and a card?"

She was less sure. "Probably. Almost everybody bought that stuff last week."

"Did you talk to him?" I asked as gently as I could.

"A little. 'How are you doing?' That kind of thing."

I waited to see if she would remember more.

"I didn't say, 'Why are you wearing that outfit?' if that's what you're wondering," she added, a little defensively. "We don't comment on customers' appearance. Training."

"I'm sure you don't." I rushed to reassure her. "Did he say how he was doing?"

"He was good. He said, 'Very well, thank you.' I remember because of the accent."

"The English accent," I confirmed, though I was certain it was the same person, falling into the obvious trap. How many men could there be in our little town running around in morning suits? I had to admit, Lieutenant Binder had a point. There was probably only one.

Illana nodded. Pat had listened to the whole conversation, open-mouthed. "Wait a minute," she said. "Is this the man who was murdered on Westclaw Point?"

I answered honestly. "The police aren't sure."

"I heard you found him." Pat made it sound like an accusation.

"I heard he was chopped into little, tiny bits." Illana's voice was faint.

Before I could correct this bit of misinformation, Pat chimed in again. "My sister's brother-in-law and his family live out there. He thinks the killer tried to break into their house the night before the murder. He said the point was crawling with cops, state cops, marine patrol, warden service. With dogs. He and his family have moved in with my sister in town. They have five kids. Teenagers. All I can say is the police better find the killer soon, or there's going to be another murder. At my sister's house."

The town was unsettled and afraid. There was still no one behind me in line, though I could see and hear a few other shoppers moving through the aisles. I loaded my groceries into my Snowden Family Clambake tote bag and handed Pat my credit card.

"The poor man," Illana said, turning the conversation back to the corpse.

"Did you notice how he got here?" I asked Illana. "When he came."

She shook her head. "No, but he left in a taxi."

I wanted to kiss her, but I was sure they didn't do that with customers, either. "Is there any chance that the man who came the second time was different from the man who came the first?"

"No, Julia." Illana didn't say what she was obviously thinking. Neither did Pat. At Hannaford they didn't call customers crazy to their faces.

Training.

There were two taxis in the Hannaford parking lot, not an unusual occurrence. While the summer season was a busy one for taxi drivers, off-season business consisted mostly of bringing people without cars, especially senior citizens, on errands and then waiting while they completed their tasks.

I knew both taxi drivers. Odie Barnes was unpleasant generally and didn't like me in particular. My ex-boyfriend Chris had been a competitor of his in the taxi business. In Busman's Harbor, the drivers, full- and part-time, were mostly a friendly lot, passing riders they were unable to accommodate to one another. Odie, however, regarded every other driver as the enemy. Somehow, two and a half years after Chris and I had broken up, and months after he'd left town, Odie still saw me as the enemy.

The other driver who was parked in the Hannaford lot, Kelly Bush, was friendly and chatty. Naturally, I wanted to approach her first. I hesitated a moment. I'd been wrong about which cashier to talk to. But then I marched resolutely to Kelly's cab, a low-slung older sedan painted copper and white, with a prominent taxi sign on the roof.

Kelly was happy to see me and invited me to sit in the cab with her out of the wind after I'd stated my mission.

"Yes!" she said. "The man in the penguin suit."

"You gave him a ride?"

She nodded, the brim of her pink baseball cap moving up and down. "Twice," she confirmed. "The first time I picked him up at the train station in Portland. We stopped here on the way to Westclaw Point for him to pick up some groceries. The second time he called me directly and I picked him up at that ugly glass and marble house."

"Did he tell you his name?"

"Alfred."

I'd been expecting her to say this, but the name still took my breath away. "Did he give you a last name?"

"Not that I remember. He paid in cash. I give a discount for that."

"Do you remember the dates?"

She removed her phone, which was mounted on her dashboard. "I keep a log." She tapped on the screen and scrolled with her finger. "I picked him up in Portland on March fifteenth. I picked him up at the glass house, brought him here, and took him back on March twenty-fifth."

March twenty-fifth fit exactly with Alfred's story of seeing us out on Morrow Island and being motivated to buy the Easter stuff.

"The time you picked him up in Portland, did he seem to know where he was going? Had he been to the glass house before?"

Kelly thought about it for a moment. "I don't think so. He had the address, but he had me going slowly as he looked for the house from the cab. You know how crazy the house numbers are on Westclaw Point Road, and some of the places are hidden by hedges. But once he saw the house, he seemed to recognize it. He went right in, no problem with the keypad. Was he not supposed to be there?"

"It's Quentin Tupper's house," I said. "They may have known each other in the past." *Not really an answer.* "Did he have luggage when you picked him up in Portland?"

"Only a small leather valise. I didn't even bother to put it in the trunk. He kept it with him in the back seat." She looked at me sideways underneath furrowed brows. "Wait a minute. Is he the guy that got murdered?"

"The police haven't identified the victim," I said, which didn't fool her for a second. "Have you seen the man or given him a ride *since* the murder?"

Kelly shook her head no. "I liked him," she said, her voice low.

"I liked him, too. Have you spoken with the state police detectives yet?"

"No," she answered, suddenly wary. "They've been bugging my dispatch, wanting to speak to all of us drivers, but I've been avoiding . . ." Her voice trailed off.

As the former girlfriend of a former taxi driver, I knew what the problem was. "The trip from Portland was off the books," I said.

She stared at her lap again. "I put a business card on the bulletin board at the train station in Portland and added a note saying anyone coming to the peninsula could schedule a ride. When that happens, if they pay cash, I don't always report the money."

I put a hand on her solid arm, a gesture of support. "They're the Maine State Police, not the IRS. They don't care about the money. You have to talk to them."

"I will," she promised. "I have to run this ride home." She pointed toward Hannaford, where her passenger was no doubt shopping. "I'll go right after."

"Is it possible," I asked, speaking slowly, "that it was two different men in penguin suits you picked up for those rides?"

"WHAT? Are there two of them? Is one still running around here?" Kelly's voice rose as she spoke, ending in dog whistle range.

I had gone too far. "No, no, no," I rushed to reassure her. "It's my fanciful idea. The state police don't think there are two of them."

Her body relaxed a bit, her shoulders coming down from around her ears. But when I said my goodbyes and got out of the cab, I heard the locks thunk closed behind me.

# Chapter Ten

I checked my phone as I walked to the Subaru. Tom had texted that he and Binder were back in town. Could I come to the police station for a chat?

"For a chat?" I wondered aloud. Had they already found out I'd been talking to people at Hannaford? I hadn't even left the parking lot.

I dropped my purchases off at Lupine Design, including my sandwich, and told Zoey I had to go out again. She looked more amused than annoyed. We'd only been working together since October, but she knew I'd get the job done no matter what.

The bullpen that held the single desk all six Busman's Harbor sworn officers shared was deserted. The three on the daytime shift were either out on duty or at lunch. I wondered if "out" meant normal duties or if they were still involved in securing the crime scene and other murder-related activities.

Tom and Lieutenant Binder, the only people in the vast multipurpose room, stared at something on a single computer monitor. I was sure there were many others working on the case—out in the field and at headquarters in Augusta. But I worried how the terrified citizens of Westclaw

Point would react to the quiet atmosphere in the almost empty incident room.

Tom looked up, spotted me, and grinned. My heart sped up. I grinned back.

Sensing Tom's movement beside him, Binder looked up, too. "Julia. Thank you for coming." He swung his chair around, as did Tom, and then Tom brought a chair over for me. He placed it on their side, so we formed a little circle. This was new. Over the years, they had both accepted my help with local cases, Binder earlier and more graciously than Tom. But our conversations had always been across a table, me clearly on my side, not theirs.

"Quentin came to Augusta yesterday and attempted to identify the victim," Binder said.

I didn't miss the "attempted" or the "Quentin." It would have been "Mr. Tupper" in the past. "I take it he couldn't."

"He said our victim 'could be' his former butler, whom he knew as Alfred Smythe. He couldn't be more definitive than that." Tom waved his hand in a gesture of dismissal. "It's been more than twenty years."

"But really, would that matter?" Binder challenged. "They lived together, saw each other every day for—what, three years, did Tupper say?"

"Tupper was young, busy, and at an age where he was probably pretty self-involved," Tom countered. "People change. The years between age thirty and age fifty may not matter so much for identification purposes, but between fifty and seventy?"

Binder didn't look convinced. This was something else that was new since I'd been with Tom. When dealing with the public, they naturally fell into a sort of good-guy, bad-guy routine. Binder kindly, even avuncularly, asked the soft questions, the ones that put anyone—victim, witness, even suspect—at ease. Tom, with his intense physicality, taut as a rubber band, was a natural for the bad guy, the one who asked the intrusive questions and demanded answers when necessary. But when it was just the two of them—and me—there was much more give-and-take to the partnership, despite their differences in age and rank. They asked each other's opinions; they pushed back and tested ideas. I could see why Tom was loyal to Binder. There was respect there, and it went both ways.

"We took Quentin to his house today," Tom told me, "to see if anything was missing or if he could identify any objects as not his own, presumably the dead man's."

"And?"

"Quentin confirmed what we thought. Nothing was missing. As to the squatter's belongings, there wasn't much. A few pairs of boxers, undershirts, and socks, a small leather valise."

"The valise was all he had when he came to town," I told them. "He arrived in Portland on the train."

"We know that," Binder said. "But how do you know?"

I filled them in on my afternoon, including Kelly Bush's promise to come into the police station. "But how do you guys know about the train?" They obviously hadn't followed the same trail I had.

"We found a ticket way under the bed in the guest room at Quentin's house during our first search. We followed up with the station in Portland." Tom looked at me. "Before you ask, he paid cash."

"Where did he get on the train?"

"Boston, but then he would have," Tom answered. "He'd have to change trains, and probably train stations, in Boston no matter where he was coming from."

"We know he was in South Portland because he got his hair cut by Alfred Minucci before he came here," I said. "Was he there long?"

Tom went to a whiteboard on the other side of the room, dragged it over to where we sat, and flipped it over. There were already the beginnings of a timeline on it. The train ride from Boston to Portland was there, as well as the haircut, which occurred on the same day.

"He must have come in on the train and found the barbershop somehow and taken a taxi or car service to it, but we haven't found the driver yet," Tom said. "If your Kelly Bush picked him up at the train station the next day, he must have stayed somewhere that night. We'll ask the Portland police for help tracking that down." Tom added the date for the taxi ride to the whiteboard as he spoke. "The train station was probably just a convenient place to meet an out-of-town taxi."

"From what Julia learned from the cab driver, he arrived in Busman's Harbor, stopping at Hannaford, and ending his trip at Tupper's house," Binder said, as Tom added information to the board.

"He deliberately came here. He didn't pick the house randomly." I recounted Kelly's description of the ride down Westclaw Point Road. "He *must* have a connection to Quentin. He was looking for the house and he had the keycode."

"Tupper said he's used the same four-digit keycode, his birth year, for everything except his financial stuff, for decades," Binder told me.

"Which means it wouldn't be hard for someone else to figure out," Tom said.

Lieutenant Binder nodded his agreement.

"Alfred told me he saw us on Morrow Island preparing the house for Easter. That could have been on Saturday the twenty-third or Sunday the twenty-fourth," I added, moving on with the timeline.

"I think he would have seen us on the twenty-third,"

Tom said. "Sunday we were working mostly inside Winds-holme."

"He went back to Hannaford on the twenty-fifth," I told them. "Then he came out to Morrow Island on the thirty-first, Easter, when Jack and I saw him in the garden." This information was already on the timeline.

"I saw him at Quentin's on April first," I said, "and he died—"

"April fifth, shortly before you found him," Binder supplied. "Very shortly, according to the medical examiner."

I swallowed hard. This was new information. Had I just missed the killer? I stared at the increasingly populated timeline. "There's only one problem with this," I said. "You're assuming there's one man."

They were nice enough to give me the respect of remaining silent.

"In other news"—Binder shifted, either uncomfortable in the folding chair or uncomfortable with the turn the conversation had taken—"we don't know who the dead man was, but we do know some of where he's been and what he's done."

"His fingerprints lit up the FBI's database like a pinball machine," Tom broke in, impatient to give me some good news. "This guy has been wanted for multiple offenses across many years. Here and in Britain, which is why the feds and the UK National Crime Agency have tracked him. Offenses like stealing from employers and unauthorized use of credit cards and checks."

"Crimes that fit with being an assistant or a butler," I said.

"And," Tom added, "get this one. More recently, only in the U.S., trespassing. Unauthorized use of former employers' homes."

"Exactly what happened at Quentin's house. But if

they've investigated, why don't they know who the man is?" I asked.

"He was never caught in the act. The homeowners returned and found their homes had obviously been lived in. The fingerprints tied the cases together."

"But these former employers, they must have called him by a name, checked references, collected tax documents," I protested. "Once the FBI knew the cases were connected, the homeowners would have been interviewed."

"Early on, the man was hired through an agency," Binder answered. "That's how Quentin found him. The employers paid the agency, who paid our victim, so it was the agency's job to check all that stuff. Lately, he seems to have been working directly for his employers, but for cash, under the table. The agency still exists, but no one who works there now was there when this guy was active. The people there are cooperating, but the dead man's records, from over a decade ago, are gone. We're trying to track someone down from the old days."

I thought about the corpse. I pictured myself looking down at him. Then I reran the other images of Alfred I had—lying in the garden at Windsholme, cooking at the stove in Quentin's kitchen. "Was there more than one set of fingerprints? In Quentin's house, I mean."

"Yours," Binder said with a smile. "On the front keypad and in the living room."

I was confused. Those prints were from the morning of the murder, the only time I'd used the front keypad. "My fingerprints should have been lots more places. I've been checking the house since Quentin left in mid-October. I know I opened the drawer next to the refrigerator when I was there on the first of April. I touched a pad of paper and a pen. And was there a tomato soup can in the trash? Alfred's fingerprints should be on it."

"The soup can was neatly stacked in the recycle, ready to go to the dump. The paper label had been removed and the can thoroughly rinsed." Binder squinted at me over his ski-slope nose. "I can have the techs check the inside of that drawer, but frankly, I'm not looking for you or your prints. The crime scene techs said they'd never seen a cleaner house. The only prints were the dead man's, and precious few of those."

"None on the knife?" I confirmed.

"The dead man's," Tom said. "And smudges, like the killer wore gloves."

I remembered the dove gray gloves Alfred had been wearing the first time I'd seen him, in the garden on Morrow Island.

"Where is Quentin now?" I asked.

"We left him at his house. It's no longer an active scene," Binder said.

I thought about Quentin's story. Alfred Smythe had been a lifesaver. Whoever he was, he'd known a great deal more about being a butler than twenty-one-year-old Quentin had about being a butler's employer. But then things had changed. The formerly cheerful, competent, uncomplaining servant had become a critical, miserable drunk and a thief.

I'd liked Alfred when I'd met him, but then I supposed that was what con artists did. They were probably all charming. "But you're still looking for someone else," I said, with hope in my voice that I already feared was unwarranted.

Tom gave a quick, automatic, almost involuntary shake of his head, but it was Binder who spoke. "Julia. Of course we are. We're looking for the killer."

He knew that wasn't what I meant.

"Besides," he said, "if there were two men in morning suits, how did the other one get here?"

# Chapter Eleven

The weather changed as I walked back to Lupine Design. An unending ceiling of clouds covered the sun and the wind whipped up. It was the kind of quick transformation we experienced every April but were somehow always surprised by. From a block away, I could hear waves as they hit the town pier, until the sound disappeared in a howl of wind. It wasn't raining, at least not yet. I shivered in my quilted vest and walked toward Lupine Design as quickly as I could. A cold, fat drop struck me on the head as I hurried through the front door.

I didn't check in with Zoey but went straight to my desk and tried to bury myself in my work. The rain drummed on the windows in wind-driven sheets. My mind kept drifting back to the question of the second man. Lieutenant Binder had asked: If he existed, how did he come and go? How indeed.

Finally, I threw down the pen I was using to take notes and turned off my computer. I couldn't concentrate enough to do the detailed work my job required. The noisy rain had stopped. I popped my head into the studio. "Headed out again!" Zoey, deep in conversation with Livvie about a piece about to go into the kiln, barely looked up.

I drove slowly out of town, over the swing bridge to Thistle Island and over the nameless plank bridge from Thistle Island to Westclaw Point. When I got to his house, Quentin's car wasn't in his drive, but I hadn't expected it to be. He had an antique wooden-sided station wagon that was lovingly stored over the winter in an environmentally controlled facility. Binder and Tom had dropped him off and he'd come and go by taxi while he was in the area.

I watched through the glass in the back door as Quentin slowly made his way down the long hallway, determined to tell whoever was knocking to get lost. When he caught sight of me, the corners of his mouth turned up in a reluctant grin. "Come in."

"Which is worse, the murder investigation or spending time with your sister's kids?" I teased as I followed him down the hall.

He didn't answer but gave a grunt of acknowledgment.

The big, open living space looked much as it always had, except the white carpet and the white slipcover from the couch were missing. Both were undoubtedly in Augusta, being analyzed or already in an evidence locker.

I made myself at home, bustling around the kitchen to make us both tea. I tried not to look at the empty slot in the knife block, but my eye kept returning to it. I wondered if I'd ever feel the same way about the house again. I wondered if Quentin would.

When I set his mug in front of him, Quentin inhaled the steam and finally answered my question. "The murder investigation is worse. Far worse. To have a man murdered in my 'Fortress of Solitude' is horrible." His lips curled up when he'd said the name I jokingly used for his house, but only momentarily. Quentin was deeply unhappy.

"I heard you couldn't positively identify the body." I

said it with sympathy, but also to prompt him into saying more. Never one for personal disclosure, Quentin seemed to need to talk.

"No."

Not an expansive answer. "Couldn't identify to a certainty for the police, or didn't recognize at all?"

"Hard to say." Quentin had both of his big hands clasped around the mug, though the room wasn't cold.

"Did you *feel* something when you saw him?" I pressed.

"That's just it." He shivered visibly. "I felt nothing. And I should have felt something. Alfred was an important part of my life. Even after our falling-out, I never lost sight of the fact that he'd rescued me at a time when I was vulnerable and alone. That's why him stealing from me was so devastating. But I looked at that body and felt nothing. Not love or gratitude, not hate or betrayal. Nothing at all."

*Because it wasn't him.*

I stayed with Quentin for as long as he seemed to want my company, though I couldn't find another topic to distract him. Not even talk of the yacht engaged him, and normally it would have been a subject I couldn't get him off.

When I left, I hugged him and suggested he take a nap. He hugged me back and said, "Thank you for coming by, Julia. I appreciate it more than you can know."

I sat in the Subaru for several minutes. Seeing Quentin like that had been deeply disturbing. He was another victim of this terrible murder.

My mind returned to Binder's question: If there was a second man, how had he come, and how did he go?

*The little motorboat.* Surely, it was the way the man I'd met, Alfred, had come and gone from Morrow Island. It could have and would have taken him elsewhere along the shore. More important, the red motorboat wasn't at the dock when I'd arrived the day of the murder. The dead man hadn't removed it. Likely the other man did. The killer.

The boat wouldn't have gone far. It was too small for much but moving along the shoreline. If the killer had taken it, he'd probably arrived on Westclaw Point in some kind of vehicle, parked it well away from Quentin's house, and made his way there on foot to surprise the victim. Alerted by the sound of my car turning into the drive, he might have left in the little boat. If that was the case, he would have ditched the boat somewhere along the shoreline near wherever he'd left his vehicle.

I drove slowly, peering into yards, looking for the boat at someone's dock. If a house was far off the road and I was sure no one was in residence, I drove right down the driveway like I owned the place.

Most of the houses were locked up tight, several with their shutters closed against winter storms. Occasionally a house was occupied with lights on against the afternoon gloom. I looked down those driveways but didn't stop to ask about the motorboat. People were on edge enough without me stirring the pot.

The police would have talked to all of them anyway. They had searched Westclaw Point by land and the marine patrol had searched from the water. But I had an advantage. I had seen the boat. I knew what I was looking for.

There were plenty of boats pulled up in yards or parked in driveways, covered in canvas, or wrapped in shiny white plastic. There was no mystery where a man who arrived alone in a taxi might have got a boat, if it was indeed Alfred who'd first taken it. It was an easy matter to walk into any of these yards, unobserved by the nonexistent neighbors, and ease a boat into the water. He would have gotten wet in the process. The water was breathtakingly cold. But he could have done it.

My heart banged when I saw a boat the right size and shape in the yard of a house way down the point. How extraordinarily easy it was to hide a boat in plain sight. I parked the Subaru and crept toward it. One push on the canvas cover revealed a bright blue side. I didn't know whether I was more disappointed or relieved.

At the end of the point, I pulled into the parking lot of Herrickson Point Lighthouse and sat watching the gray waves, full of roiling sand and seaweed, washing onto the beach. The point was deserted except for a few noisy gulls, looking for clams or periwinkles washed ashore at the tideline.

The boat had to be somewhere. It couldn't have gone far. Any direction from the point led to open water and the little outboard wasn't big enough for that. It lacked power and range. Of course, whoever it was—the victim, the killer, or the other man—could have simply untied it and let it drift. It could be anywhere by now.

There was another answer: Morrow Island. My gaze drifted from the waves to the island, with Windsholme, barely visible, standing at the top of it. The boat had made the trip before, carrying Alfred on Easter Sunday.

The rain began again, blurring my view of the island as it cascaded down my windshield. I started the Subaru, turned on the wipers and defrost, and headed back to work.

It was late enough by the time Tom finished in town that he stayed for dinner. Mom was still at work, her late-shift day. Tom and I raided the fridge and threw together a meal of leftover vegetable soup, bread, and a salad of whatever was in the crisper. We ate at Mom's old kitchen table with the scratched and dented wooden top. Despite the lingering clouds, the days were getting longer. We didn't bother with the overhead light.

Tom was plainly exhausted. Dark circles ringed his eyes and the skin was drawn tight across his nose and cheeks. He kept his body upright, a resting pose for him, and made a valiant effort to give me his undivided attention.

We talked of this and that, got caught up on conversations with friends and family. I spoke about my job. He didn't talk about his. I could tell the trivial nature of the conversation was making it difficult for him to stay awake.

"I drove down Westclaw Point today looking for the little boat that was tied up at Quentin's dock," I said.

That got his attention. His head jerked up. "You don't think we did that—and more, to try to find that boat?"

"I'm sure you did," I assured him. "But you didn't know exactly what you were looking for. I saw it. Twice."

"Tell me you didn't get out of your car."

I wasn't going to lie to him. "Just once, to check under a tarp."

His head dropped to his hands. "Please don't do that again. We're doing all we can."

"Are you? Because the lieutenant pretty much dismissed the notion of a second man."

"Of course there's a second man. There's the killer." He was losing what was left of his tattered patience.

"A lookalike man." I wasn't going to let him get away with that. He knew what I meant.

He sighed. If he hadn't been so tired, I would have assumed the sigh was for my benefit. "Promise you won't do anything like that again."

"I think whoever took the boat must be on Morrow Island."

"Seriously, Julia, the marine patrol has circled it every

day since the murder. They've disembarked and searched on foot."

"Okay." I didn't want to give in, but he was plainly too tired to discuss it. I scooched my chair closer and put a hand on his shoulder. "Where are you working tomorrow?"

"Here in town."

"It's too late to check into the Snuggles." It was the off-season and Fee and Vee were undoubtedly already in their nightclothes, settled in front of the TV. "You should stay over. I don't like the idea of you driving home."

His gaze drifted up the back stairs toward my room. The one with the twin bed that had been there since my childhood. I could have bought a grown-up bed and in-stalled it anytime since I'd been back at Mom's house. But despite how long I'd been there, I'd always viewed the sit-uation as temporary.

"Your mom—" he started.

"You can stay in the guest room," I clarified. I didn't think my mom would be in the least disconcerted to find him in the kitchen in the morning, but I worried he would be. "I know you keep a bag in your car." If he raced out of town for a case, he never knew how long he'd be gone. There was always a gym bag with clean clothes and a toothbrush in his trunk.

"Okay." He knew I was right. It was an hour to his apartment on dark back roads.

I stretched out a hand to him. He took it and kissed it gently, then went outside to get his bag.

Logistics. He and I were always negotiating the logis-tics.

# Chapter Twelve

In the morning, I came downstairs to find Tom and my mother chatting amiably in the kitchen. Mom had brewed coffee and a mug of the milky beige drink sat in front of her on the kitchen table. Tom, always abstemious, held a mug of hot water with a piece of lemon floating in it. Le Roi circled his legs, leaving white and gray cat hairs on his navy blue pants. Tom bent his head and greeted the cat. "How ya doin', big guy?"

"Morrow Island," I blurted. "We need to search it again."

They looked at me with eyebrows raised, their expressions so alike I laughed.

"What about it?" Mom asked. She was coming into the middle of a conversation.

"The body in Quentin's house. The killer took the little motorboat that was tied up at the dock. He's on Morrow Island."

"Julia," Tom said, with a patience I could charitably label as exaggerated. "I told you. The marine patrol has searched the island."

"That little boat would be easy to hide," I insisted. "There's shelter on Morrow Island, and fresh water. We turned it on for Easter."

"Windsholme is quite secure," my mother reminded me. During the renovations, we'd installed strong doors and windows, good locks, and alarms. The mansion had far more security now than had ever existed in any building on the island before. We'd never felt the need before. But if we were to leave furniture, appliances, and the place settings and cookware to stock a catering kitchen on the island over the winter, more care had to be taken.

"But other places on the island aren't secure," I pointed out. "The dining pavilion. Livvie's house. There are plenty of places to hide." Some of them not so comfortable during cold April showers, but there and accessible. "Besides," I played my ace card, "he's been on the island before. At Easter, when Jack found him in the garden."

"He isn't there now. *He's* in a drawer at the medical examiner's office," Tom said.

"I'm going with you," I persisted. "Even if the island has been searched before, I know every inch of it, every hiding place. You need my help."

Tom didn't look happy, but his resistance was crumbling. "I expected nothing else."

He had a murdered man, a town in an uproar, and no good leads that I could see. Action was better than inaction. Even if there was no one on Morrow Island, he would be glad to check it off his list.

He walked into the dining room to call Binder and tell him what was up, letting the swinging door close behind him. Mom finished her coffee and put her mug and a plate with toast crumbs on it in the sink. She went to the back hall and pulled on her jacket but didn't leave.

Tom returned from the dining room with purpose in his step.

Mom looked from one of us to the other. "Be careful," she said, and left for work.

\* \* \*

We circled the island in the Boston Whaler before we pulled up at the dock. I wasn't in favor of the circling and said so to Tom. It might telegraph to anyone on the island that we were coming, giving them time to hide or hide better. But Tom insisted. If we saw any signs of occupation, like the little red motorboat, or smoke from a fire, he would call for backup and we would have to wait.

As Tom steered the Whaler, I searched the shoreline for signs of habitation. If anything big moved in the woods, it would be human. There were no other large animals. A young moose had once swum over to the island, to the delight of our lunchtime customers, but he hadn't stayed long.

The day was gray and breezy. We'd come dressed in sweaters covered by windbreakers, but I still shivered as the boat cut through the cold water. Tom's black windbreaker said STATE POLICE in large white letters on the front and the back.

When we tied up at the dock, I jumped out and started toward the little yellow house, the place where my mother's family had spent their summers from the time Windsholme was abandoned during the Great Depression until it had been restored. When the clambake was in operation, Livvie and her family stayed there now. I knew from experience the house was easy to break into despite the precautions we took.

Tom put a hand out to restrain me. "We'll look for the boat first. If it's here, the killer may be here. We'll stay together." He spoke in a low voice, his tone serious, especially on the last point.

"If the boat isn't here, it doesn't prove the killer isn't. He could have set the boat adrift," I pointed out.

"Then he's trapped," Tom said. "Unless he's brought

enough food for a long stay, he's in trouble. But then, the murder didn't show much forethought, either, so it's possible." Tom paused, considering. "I still want to look for the boat. If he's here, he already knows we are. It's not going to change anything. We might even see him in the open if he tries to change locations. And if he gets to his boat before we do, we'll hear it. I'll call the marine patrol to pick him up. They're at the town pier and they have much faster boats. Let's go."

As we'd circled the island, my eyes had been on the shoreline as my brain ticked through every place where you could land a boat and haul it easily into the woods. "This way," I said, and led Tom along the flat piece of shoreline where our clambake fire pit stood to where the trail started through the woods on the west side of the island, the one he had searched on Easter Sunday. The trail wasn't used much, by either our summer visitors, the staff, or the family. It was more efficient, more comfortable, and prettier to go up over the top of the island by Windsholme and then down the other side to get to the beach. The trail wasn't in great shape, and particularly not so in the spring, when there had been no maintenance of it since the previous fall.

Without leaf cover, it was easy to see from the trail down to the rocky shore. Around this part of the island, it was flat enough to land a boat and haul it in between the trees. A red boat would have shown from the water, but not if it had been covered. There were plenty of gray and beige tarps around the island that someone could find and use to hide a boat.

Tom walked ahead of me, frequently waiting to hold an overhanging branch out of the way. We didn't talk, focusing on the search. In addition to looking down at the shoreline, Tom also glanced frequently up the hill behind us, as if he expected to see someone in the trees, watching. We were certainly sitting, or rather slowly moving, ducks, particularly me in my bright blue windbreaker. But the killer at Quentin's house hadn't used a gun. *There are guns in many of the locked-up summer houses on Westclaw Point*, my brain nagged, *there for the taking.*

Tom's jacket clearly said he was state police. Surely, anyone would know if they killed us, more officers would come. It would be much more sensible to slip away in the boat than to confront us. *But is the killer rational?* my brain chimed in again. Tom had talked about opportunism and poor impulse control. *Tom wouldn't let you come if he thought it was dangerous*, said the best side of myself.

We stopped at several places where I pointed out large boulders or thick stands of evergreens where a boat might be hidden. We circled those, walking carefully on last fall's leaves, still wet and slippery from the previous day's downpour. We saw nothing, no boat, and no signs of one.

Finally, we reached the little beach on the north side of the island, my best bet as to where a boat would be. I was sure it was where the man had landed when he'd come to the island on Easter Sunday—whichever man he was. It was the most obvious place, a cove protected from the current and flat ground to haul a boat out on.

The sand showed no signs of anything large being dragged over it, though I thought the rain the day before might have obscured the marks. The space under the huge boulder that hung out over the beach was empty.

"Darn." I hadn't realized how much I'd been counting on finding the boat here.

Tom merely nodded. He was used to setbacks. "Where to now?" he asked.

There was no point in searching the east side of the island. The cliffs rose dramatically from the rocky shore.

No one could land a boat there, much less drag it up after them. I pointed to the wide path that led over the top of the island and back to the buildings.

"Okay," Tom said, and we started toward the top of the hill.

We reached Windsholme and kept going. As we walked through Livvie's garden, I couldn't stop myself from looking at the place in the cornstalks where I'd first seen the man. I shivered as we exited through the broken gate. Without the sun and the joy of watching a six-year-old hunt for brightly colored eggs, the garden was dead and gray. Not a nice place to be.

Tom looked up at Windsholme. "That place is huge. Let's leave it for last. We'll start down there." He pointed to the little house by the dock.

When we got there, the two padlocks we left on the door over the winter were in place, undisturbed. The regular lock in the door was still secure, too. Tom waited for me to use the keys I'd brought to unlock the place. As the door opened, he stepped in front of me, going in first. "The locks are fine, but there's no way to check all the windows," he said in a low voice. A part of the house stuck out over the water so we couldn't walk all the way around it. I didn't see how anyone could get in that way, but I understood his caution.

Inside the house was colder than it was outdoors. It had never been heated except by its fireplace, which lay empty and broomed clean. The building could provide someone with shelter, but not much.

The long main room was divided into kitchen, dining, and living spaces. The picture window at the end framed blue-gray water that went to the horizon. The casement windows on either side of it were shut tight. No sign of disturbance.

In the living room, not a pillow was out of place and the crocheted throw my father's mother had made was neatly folded on the back of the sofa. No one had been here.

"I'm going upstairs," Tom whispered.

I shrugged. No point in begging to go along. "In addition to the two bedrooms and the bath, there are crawl spaces under the eaves," I told him.

He was down in a couple of minutes, and we set off back up the path.

The next stop, the dining pavilion we used for the clambake, would provide even less of a refuge. It consisted mostly of a long, open porch. The only place inside that could be locked, the small kitchen, still was. The door was so flimsy it could easily be knocked down, but it stood just as we'd left it the previous fall. Tom insisted on checking behind the bar and under the counter in the gift shop, but I could tell it was pro forma so he could tick them off his mental checklist. When he was finished, we walked up to Windsholme. We circled the house, checking the many windows and doors on the first floor in the front and the basement in the back. Nothing seemed amiss.

Leaving me on the long front porch, Tom stepped away to make a call. "I've asked Lieutenant Binder to gather a few officers and the marine patrol and come along," he said when he returned. "I didn't want to drag the whole gang out here if there was nothing, but the mansion is huge, and I'd like others here for the search."

"We haven't seen anything since we've been out here," I said. "What made you change your mind?"

Tom looked up at the imposing façade of Windsholme. "I don't want the two of us in that labyrinth of a house, targets for an ambush by an impulsive killer. The odds are low he's in there, but if there's any chance at all, I want backup."

We stood, looking around for a moment, considering what we might do while we waited. I pointed across the Great Lawn. Without leaves on the trees, the playhouse was just visible from where we stood. "We haven't searched there," I said.

It was the perfect place to hide, with a fireplace and bunks. The bare mattresses would be cold and hard but better than sleeping in the open April air. No smoke came from the chimney now. We'd passed within forty feet of it when we'd returned from the beach. Focused on Livvie's garden, we hadn't stopped to search it.

Tom grabbed my elbow to stop me moving forward. I immediately saw what he had seen. The door to the playhouse was slightly ajar. "Julia," Tom muttered under his breath. He didn't have to warn me. My stomach was trying to climb up my throat.

We watched as the door opened more fully and a tall, older man came out, waving a white handkerchief tied to the end of a stick. He wore a morning suit.

The man walked toward us slowly, deliberately non-threatening, waving the flag. The elbow of his other arm was bent, his hand at shoulder height, plainly visible. He was coming to talk.

"Julia," Tom warned again. I looked over and his gun was drawn, something I'd seen only once before in the seven years I'd known him. I took a big step backward.

The man continued to advance until Tom ordered him to stop. He was within shouting distance.

"Hullo, m'dear," the man in the morning suit called. "Remember me?"

And then he fainted dead away.

# Chapter Thirteen

Tom quickly searched the unconscious man for weapons and then handcuffed him. As he did, the man's eyes fluttered open. He turned his head toward where I stood on the porch. "Hello, Julia."

"You fainted," I informed him.

"Yes." He looked at Tom. "Do you think I might, um . . ." He nodded toward the porch. No doubt it was uncomfortable on the hard, wet grass.

Tom hauled him up and walked him to a rocker. "Stay there," Tom directed. "A boatload of state police will arrive in a moment." Tom motioned with his left hand for me to move away.

The flag of truce still lay on the lawn where the man had dropped it. "I want to confess," he said to Tom.

"You wish to confess?" Tom confirmed.

"I do." Alfred's voice was calm, determined.

Tom straightened up. "I'm placing you under arrest for the murder of the unidentified man at 101 Westclaw Point Road." He clicked his phone to record as he recited Alfred's Miranda rights. Then he moved a few steps away to call Lieutenant Binder.

"You want to confess," Tom said to Alfred when he returned. He'd hung up from his call, but still held the phone, recording.

"I do," Alfred said. "I want to make a clean breast of it."

Tom looked toward the water. There was no boat in sight. "Why don't you start at the beginning."

I moved into Alfred's sight line. There was no danger from him. He looked at me as he spoke.

"In the beginning," he said, "I was an actor by the name of Alfred Smythe."

"In the beginning, you were born," Tom corrected. "And your name then was—"

"Alfred Dingleberry."

I smiled. I couldn't help it. Alfred smiled, too. "Now you see why my stage name was Alfred Smythe. I changed it legally."

"And where were you born?" Tom asked. Alfred had kept up the English accent throughout the encounter so far.

"Bristol, United Kingdom," he answered. "I'll save you the trouble. In 1958."

"Thanks. Clears that up." Tom had just the slightest bit of skepticism in his voice. Everything the man told us would need to be verified.

"I had a good run," Alfred continued. "In the theater in England. Never a leading man, mind you. But as a jobbing actor. I had a particular look, a particular talent. I often played a butler when there was one to be played." He paused so we could appreciate that. "I was young for those roles back then, but it's easy to age people for the stage."

"I'm confused," I admitted. "Are you a butler or are you playing a butler?"

"In good time," Alfred said, and continued. "Like most young men I longed for more. TV, movies, even. I had a good agent, auditioned, and auditioned, but nothing like that came my way. Until I was offered a good part in a western being made in Italy. I was the leader of the bad guys. My Italian was terrible, but it would be dubbed before release.

"I went to Italy and made the movie. One thing led to another, and I stayed ten years. I was always the bad guy, but the main one. It wasn't Hollywood money, but it was good steady work and I loved living in Italy." He stopped again and cleared his throat. "I was assigned a stunt double." He looked up and held my eyes.

So that was who the victim was. It had to be. The man had been his double. Professionally.

"In the beginning I wasn't much at riding horses, or anything physical. I learned over time. As I became more successful and was paid more, my double did more, standing in for me for lighting tests and distance shots and the like."

"And this man's name was?" Tom led him on, looking for the identity of the victim.

"Charles. Charlie Bridgeworth. He was English, too. A couple of years younger than me." Alfred paused and coughed. "M'dear, do you think I could have a glass of water?" He addressed me but then glanced at Tom to be sure it was okay. I looked to Tom, too.

"Sure," he said.

I fumbled with the lock on the door to Windsholme, then rushed inside to turn off the alarm. In the kitchen, I grabbed one of Lupine's ceramic mugs. I let the water run a bit, so it would be fresh, tapping my foot with impatience. I didn't want to miss anything on the porch.

When I returned, going as quickly as I could without spilling, Tom and Alfred were waiting in silence. Evidently, Alfred didn't want me to miss anything, either.

I gave the mug to Tom, who helped the handcuffed man drink it down. When he was done, Alfred said, "Thank you," and continued with his confession. "Eventually, I got homesick. I was in my late thirties, unmarried, not settled. My mother was in Bristol, alone and doing poorly. I thought it was time to get on with things. The producers were disappointed but wished me well. Charles wasn't happy and let me know it. I recommended he take any future roles that might have come my way, but the producers were excited about using the opportunity to try something different.

"When I got back to England, I took some time getting my mother settled in a sheltered accommodation. When I finally got back to London, I found I'd been forgotten there as an actor. My connections had atrophied, my agent had died. I worked as a waiter and then a bartender for a while, hoping something would come up, until it became clear that nothing ever would. I began to think about something else. Finally, it struck me. 'You've played a butler so many times, surely you can be one.'

"It wasn't hard. I presented myself to an agency desperate for people who were presentable. My bartending and waitering experience cut some ice. The term 'butler' had fallen out of favor. By that time, most people were looking for 'assistants.' But there were certain people, Russian oligarchs, oil billionaires from the Gulf States, who wanted a butler in the British tradition. The woman at the agency said, 'It was like you were sent from central casting.' Little did she know how true that was.

"The first few assignments went well. The foreign businessmen and their families were often not in residence. I even squeezed in a few auditions."

Alfred took a deep breath as if willing himself to go on. Had we come to the heart of the matter already? Unless I was calculating wrong, we were still in a part of his story from decades ago. Before he'd gone to work for Quentin.

"At one audition, the casting director looked at my sheet and said, 'You've already read for this part. Two weeks ago.'

"I didn't understand at first. I tried to persuade her she was mistaken, but she acted like I was trying to sneak in for a second audition even though I hadn't been called back.

"By the time I got back to my place of employment, I'd figured it out. Charlie was pretending to be me to take advantage of my London theater experience. There was no other explanation. It gave me the creeps, but I let it go. A fat lot of good it would do him. I wasn't booking jobs based on my name, either.

"Another few months went by. Then one day, when I got back from visiting my mother, my employer met me at the door, waving a piece of paper in his hand. He accused me of writing unauthorized checks on the household account. I was mortified. I argued. I demanded to see the checks. I protested the handwriting wasn't mine. But the checks were made out to me, Alfred Smythe.

"As I slunk out of the house, my few belongings, including my uniform, in my valise, the family driver called me over. He'd heard what happened. Everyone in the household had. He told me that he'd seen me come and go the day before while I was supposed to be at my mother's and had thought it odd. He'd accosted the fellow to get a better look. It wasn't me. Now, in the wake of all the hubbub, the driver thought he'd seen the man pretending to be me coming and going from the house several times before.

"Of course, it was Charlie. I knew instantly. He was an inch taller than me, but of the same build. His features were sharper, at least they were then, though age has a way of smudging and softening. His natural hair was lighter, but that was easily addressed. And he'd been trained, professionally, to ape my posture, gait, and movements.

"I realized Charlie had been luring me out of the house. With messages left with other servants claiming he was my employer and needed an errand run. And most recently with the false audition. He'd also taken advantage of my normal absences, such as the weekend just past when I'd been with my mother."

"It's diabolical," I said, awed by the inventiveness of the deception. It seemed like a lot of trouble. A lot more trouble than getting and holding a job.

Tom looked at me sharply, reminding me I shouldn't be interrupting in the middle of a confession.

"I begged the driver to tell our employer what he'd discovered, but he refused to get involved. The story was too unbelievable. He feared he'd be accused of covering for another servant and get painted by the same brush.

"I ran away," Alfred continued. "I was terrified by the whole situation, unequal to confronting it, not sure what I could do about it. I ran to New York."

Alfred stopped to catch his breath. He was pale and a thin sheen of perspiration gleamed on his face. He was plainly uncomfortable in the handcuffs, but he squared his shoulders as well as he was able and went on.

"In New York, I was an even hotter commodity, a true, experienced English butler. The first agency I contacted took me on and helped me get a green card. I became friendly with one of the women there, Isla was her name. At another time and place, we might have . . ." His voice trailed off and he sighed. "Well, be that as it may."

"In New York you went to work for Quentin Tupper," Tom prompted.

"He was my first employer there," Alfred confirmed.

"So young. So lacking in social skills, so overwhelmed by work and money. I thought I could really help him."

"You did," I assured him.

"We went along very happily until I received word that my mother was dying. I stayed in England for three months, spending her last days with her and then tying up her small estate. When I came back, Quentin was furious. I'd been generally unpleasant, insulted him, and stolen his money."

When Alfred paused again, I looked out at the water and spotted a boat just coming around the end of West-claw Point. The marine patrol bringing Lieutenant Binder and the state police. It had to be. They'd be here soon.

Alfred continued his slow, deliberate confession. "I knew what had happened, but there was no point in telling Quentin. It would make me sound crazy. He didn't really need me by then anyway. I'd cleaned the vipers out of his nest and got him settled in his house. He was a young, single guy who no longer entertained. He didn't need a butler.

"Quentin let me go, but he didn't report me to the agency, merely told them I was surplus to his requirements. Isla helped me get another job. I confided to her what had happened and told her I wanted to use another surname for the next job. Strangely, she believed me and helped. I always called myself Alfred so I would answer when my employer or anyone else addressed me. I was at the next job for three years before Charlie Bridgeworth showed up again and ruined it all. It went on like that for over a decade."

Alfred looked out at the water. He must have seen the marine patrol boat with its load of state police officers coming toward the island. "Sometimes Charlie would disappear for years at a time, and I would begin to relax and be happy. Then there he'd be, sneaking into the house and ruining my life."

Alfred's story made me queasy with sadness. I knew about identity theft, with its terrible financial and bureaucratic consequences. But to have your physical presence stolen. It was awful beyond imagining.

"The agency fired me finally," Alfred continued, his voice matter of fact. "Even Isla couldn't defend me. There had been too many complaints. It was affecting their reputation. I started taking only jobs where I could be paid under the table, doing any sort of domestic work, mostly as a one-man band, the only paid help in the household. I was a housekeeper, a nanny, a cook, a dog sitter, a carpool driver. You name it. My only requirement was that I got a room.

"The anonymity helped keep Charlie away. It may also have been that my employers weren't nearly as attractive as targets for theft. They were the type of people who would notice instantly if thousands of dollars were drained out of their bank accounts.

"I thought I'd dodged Charlie Bridgeworth, that he was out of my life for good. Then, two months ago, Isla called. Out of the blue. We hadn't spoken in years. She was retired by then, but still spoke occasionally with her former colleagues. She said the agency was getting complaints from my former employers that I was staying in their vacation homes without authorization.

"She told me where Charlie had already been discovered. He was working his way through the homes of my former employers, backward. I figured he'd inevitably come to Quentin's house. It was easy enough to find the address on the web. I quit my job, came here, and waited.

"It was a lonely existence. I hadn't lived entirely alone since I entered domestic service. I cleaned the house thoroughly every day, to atone for borrowing it. I watched your Easter preparations through the telescope. I longed for a family. That's when I decided to join you. I brought the basket as a gift."

The marine patrol boat was closer, Lieutenant Binder clearly visible in the bow. Would Alfred keep talking when a half dozen state police arrived? Tom must have had the same concern and urged him on. "You were saying—" he prompted.

"The fainting spells are new. I've only had them for a few months. I haven't seen a doctor, but I sense I am at the end of my life. That has made me reckless. And angry. Seething about the waste and the betrayal."

"You planned to kill Charles Bridgeworth." Tom said it casually, like it was an obvious conclusion.

"No!" Alfred's response was immediate and vehement. "Only to confront him. To discover why he has done this to me and to demand that he stop.

"He did come," Alfred continued, calmer now. "You know that. I had taken some pains, as Julia observed, not to make my presence in the house obvious. I was in the kitchen. I heard the alarm code beep, the door opened, and he strolled in, easy as you please.

"As prepared as I was, as much as I expected him, I was stunned. It was like looking in a mirror. The years had softened his features, making them even more like mine. Our hair was now both thinning and white. He may even have lost that extra inch. He was dressed identically to me.

"When he saw me, he was furious. I had meant to confront him, but he screamed at me. He said that *I* had ruined *his* life when I left Italy. Ever since, he'd been forced to live off my leavings, the scraps of my life. He was still as angry as he was that first day in Italy, when I told him I was leaving.

"But *he* had ruined *my* life. I was the one who had the right to be angry. I realized right away that he was crazy.

I'd always kind of believed that. It was obsessive, what he did to me. The fight went out of me. I wanted him gone.

"But then, in his fury, he grabbed a knife from the block in the kitchen and came after me. He kept repeating that I'd destroyed his life. I was fighting back, yelling that he'd destroyed mine. I managed to get the knife away from him and I . . . killed him with it."

Alfred stopped talking.

Lieutenant Binder charged into my view, followed by half a dozen officers. I hadn't even heard their boat dock.

# Chapter Fourteen

It was fully dark by the time I staggered out of the police station. Tom and Binder still had work to do and would for a while. Nonetheless, Tom insisted on walking me back to Mom's house. When we got there, without speaking, we sat on the lounge chair on the front porch. I hadn't put the pillows away.

"What will happen to Alfred?" I asked. "What will the charge be?"

Tom shrugged. We were sitting side by side, close enough I could feel him move. "Ultimately, the district attorney's office will decide the charge. Will they buy the story that it was self-defense? I don't know."

"What do you think?"

He stretched his legs out in front of him and leaned back on his hands. "Strictly off the record and under the banner of 'the girlfriend exception,' I don't think the murder was premeditated. There are better ways to kill people. But whether it was self-defense, or an impulsive attack driven by years of abuse, I don't know."

"Why didn't Alfred call the police and turn himself in immediately if it was self-defense?" I asked.

"We asked him that," Tom said. "He told us he jack-rabbited out of fear, afraid we would look at the wreckage of his life and believe he'd planned it, an execution."

"Jack-rabbited." I laughed despite my tiredness and the stress of the day. The adrenaline was seeping out of my body. "I see what you did there."

"You liked that?" he said, and put his arm around me.

I snuggled in, leaning against his hard chest. "I did. Since he ran, why didn't he keep running?"

"He didn't have a vehicle, only the boat, so he went to the nearest place he could. He knew the marine patrol would be looking, so he set the motorboat adrift as soon as he got there."

"How did he expect to get off the island?"

"He hoped your family had boats stored there, even a kayak, but you don't. He knew the water was too cold for him to make it to land swimming, so he stayed. He had very little food, just some energy drinks and protein bars he had stored on the boat."

"Where was he when the marine patrol searched the island?" I asked.

Tom laughed. "On the roof of the playhouse. The marine patrol doesn't have dogs and evidently no one thought to look up."

"If he meant to surrender, why didn't he do it when the marine patrol searched the island? Or flag them down one of the many times they circled it?"

"He said he didn't know them. They frightened him. It was when he saw you that he decided to surrender. He liked you."

"I liked him, too." I did. I couldn't think of Alfred Smythe without feeling the weight of strong regret sitting on my chest. "And I feel badly for him. It would be so awful to have your life stolen, to constantly be looking behind you. If I were his attorney, I'd do everything I could to verify his story, to help a jury understand what happened to him."

"It's a double-edged sword," Tom said. "It could also convince a judge or a jury that he planned the murder. My best guess is there will be a plea deal and premeditated murder will be off the table."

I sighed. "But he'll still go to prison, real prison, not the county jail."

"It's almost a certainty. Unless whatever's causing the fainting gets him first."

I'd thought of that, too. I shivered.

Tom squeezed me tighter. "Are you going to be okay if I leave you?"

What I really wanted was for us to lie back on the lounger, wrapped in each other's arms, and not move for the rest of the night. The full force of the day was hitting me. The tiredness crept from my limbs to my chest and to my head. The world was an increasingly fuzzy place and I needed him to be the rock I held on to.

I didn't say any of this. Instead, I said, "Of course!" in as sprightly a tone as I could manage. The man had a job to do, a job he loved. He would always have that job.

"Okay then." He kissed me hard, helped me up, and led me to the front door. "I'll call tomorrow."

# Chapter Fifteen

Our Memorial Day barbecue was at Livvie and Sonny's house. Everyone was there, Fee and Vee, Gus and Mrs. Gus, Mom and Captain George, Jamie and Zoey. And Tom.

Busman's Harbor was coming alive. The snowbirds were back. Summer families used the three-day weekend to open their cottages. There were pansies in the traffic circle on the highway and the restaurants were bustling.

Our little gathering had the feeling of endings and beginnings. I'd finished my work at Lupine Design that week. For a while, I'd been juggling two jobs as I hired staff for the Snowden Family Clambake and made sure Lupine was well set up so I could leave it for the summer. Getting the clambake underway had been challenging. Not only did I need staff for the twice-a-day lobster meals, but there was also Windsholme to consider. I was feeling good, getting close. A few more servers and a host to cover me when I was working events at Windsholme were all I needed. The clambake would open on Father's Day weekend.

Tom and I stuck much closer together than we usually would have at a family event. He knew everybody quite well by now and normally would have mixed on his own. But he'd just wrapped a big case on the other side of the state, and I would move out to Morrow Island the next weekend and begin working seven days a week shortly after. A sense of time running out kept me close by his side.

Jamie and Zoey were sticking close, too. Their wedding was three weeks away, the first event at the renovated Windsholme. It had been a logistical nightmare. They both had guests flying in from all over the country. But the worst of the planning was behind them. Now they just wanted to be wed.

Mom and Captain George seemed to stick unusually close, as well. I even saw him—gasp—holding her hand. I would have teased her about it, but I knew she would hate it. They were facing separation as well when Mom moved out to Windsholme. Not entirely, because George would pilot the tour boat that brought our guests to the island. But the very nature of the job demanded that he end and start his days in town, while she ended and started hers on the island.

Quentin had returned to the Côte d'Azur. He'd be back in town in a month or so.

Tom had news of Alfred Smythe. Sadly, he had been right about nearing the end of his life. His fainting spells were actually a form of seizures brought on by a brain tumor, advanced and aggressive. He had declined treatment. He was living out his days in a prison hospital. Alfred Smythe would never stand trial.

As Tom told the tale, the others made noises of sympathy, but they had never met Alfred. I felt sad, which surprised me given the circumstances and short nature of our acquaintance. I felt terrible about the shadow life he'd been forced to lead, the desperate act he'd committed, and the lonely death he faced.

"Can I visit him?" I asked Tom.

"If he'll allow it."

Livvie called us to the picnic tables. The meal was simple, burgers and dogs, potato salad and green salad, one of my favorite meals of the year. We'd been lucky with the day. May in Maine could be cool, but a bright, warming sun was shining.

As I moved toward the tables, I met Captain George coming the other way, with Livvie close on his heels. He pulled us behind the shed where Sonny kept the lawn mower and his tools.

"I want to talk to you girls." His tone was grave. "I want your permission to ask for your mother's hand."

"What?" My mind boggled. But then I saw his face and amended, "Congratulations."

"Good luck!" Livvie, much quicker with the right response, gave him a big hug.

"You didn't need to ask us," I told him. "Mom knows her own mind."

He pushed back the hank of long white hair that had fallen over his brow. "I don't have to, but I want to. She won't agree if she thinks you don't approve. Do you?"

"Of course," Livvie assured him. "We just want Mom to be happy."

As the three of us made our way back to the party, my mind whirled. What would Mom's answer be? How would this work? Mom had been without a partner for twelve years and the captain had never been married or even lived with another person as far as I knew. If she said yes, would they live at Mom's house? One thing was clear, it was time for me to move on.

I put my hand on Tom's shoulder to steady myself and swung my leg over the picnic bench to sit beside him. He was reassuringly strong, a bulkhead in a storm.

The future swirled before us. Maybe it was already here.

## Sonny's Grilled Lamb

*In the novella, I've given the job of grilling the main dish for the Easter meal to Sonny Ramsey, a job he's inherited from Julia and Livvie's late father. Lots of families have lamb for Easter dinner, though probably not nearly as many people do it on a grill. This dish is amazing, a true crowd-pleaser, and it frees up your oven for other important parts of the meal.*

*In reality, the recipe comes from my late friend Peter Wright. Peter made it every Fourth of July for years, while he and his wife, Ruth Ferguson, threw a marvelous backyard party. We make this dish to this day, and always enjoy it.*

### Ingredients for the marinade

¼ cup olive oil
¼ cup tamari or soy sauce
¼ cup lemon juice
2 tablespoons Worcestershire sauce
1 3-inch piece of fresh ginger, peeled and chopped
4–6 large cloves of garlic, chopped
1–2 teaspoons hot sauce (optional)

### Ingredients for the meat

1 boneless, butterflied leg of lamb
salt
ground black pepper

## *Instructions*

### 24 to 72 hours before grilling

Prepare marinade in large plastic bag or non-reactive bowl. Salt and pepper the lamb all over and add to marinade. Close bag or cover bowl and put in refrigerator for at least 24 hours or, preferably, for 2–3 days, turning every 8 to 12 hours.

### On the day of grilling

Remove the bag or bowl containing the lamb and marinade from refrigerator and allow to come to room temperature before grilling.

Prepare your charcoal or gas grill to a medium-high heat. Remove the lamb from the marinade and place it on grill, cover, and cook, turning every five minutes or so until cooked through to desired doneness. (Medium rare will record a temp of 135 degrees on an instant-read thermometer.)

Remove from grill and allow to rest at least 20 minutes before slicing to serve.

Dear Reader,

I hope you enjoyed reading about Easter with the Snowden family and friends and the mysterious man in the vegetable patch on Morrow Island. If this is your first introduction to the Maine Clambake Mysteries, there are eleven standalone novels, starting with *Clammed Up*, and as well five previous novellas.

I found the Easter basket theme that ties the three novellas in this book together to be a challenging one. Everything I thought of—severed head in an Easter basket—was decidedly not cozy. Eventually, the idea of the bunny caught in the vegetable patch—like Peter Rabbit!—came to me.

I know why my Easter Bunny wears a top hat and tails. It comes from one of my favorite stories told by my father. When he was small, maybe five or six, he heard a noise outside just after dawn on Easter morning. Hoping to catch the Easter Bunny in the act of leaving the basket, he got out of bed and sat at the top of the stairs. Through the transom over the door, he was thrilled to see a top hat bobbing down the front walk. When the door to the house started to open, he lost his nerve and darted back to bed.

I don't know how many years later it was that my father figured out that he'd seen the top of his father's head as his parents returned at dawn from a formal party. But after my dad witnessed that scene through the transom, he said forever after he pictured the Easter Bunny wearing a top hat, and thus I do, too. (The top hat in question is in its original box in my guest closet along with the original bill of sale from Macy's in Herald Square. I have no use for the hat, but I can't seem to get rid of it.) My son, Rob, has pointed out that when he and his sister, Kate, were young we read a book over and over that had an Easter Bunny in a top hat on the cover, reinforcing the family tradition. None of us can remember the title.

So, we had a man in a morning suit and a top hat lying in the vegetable garden on Morrow Island while the Snowden family celebrates their first holiday in the renovated Windsholme. But how did he get there? Why is he there? And what happens to him? That's the fun part that I get to make up.

Writers get by with a little help from our friends. The idea of an acting double was born at a retreat of Maine crime writers during a brainstorming session with Brenda Buchanan, Robin Facer, and Julia Spencer-Fleming. Sherry Harris, my Wicked Author blogmate, read the manuscript and, as always, was truly helpful in her suggestions. My friend Annette Holmstrom, an expert in rare and collectible books, supplied the Beatrix Potter details. Thank you all!

I'm always happy to hear from readers. You can reach me at barbaraross@maineclambakemysteries.com, or find me via my website at www.barbararossauthor.com, on Facebook www.facebook.com/barbaraannross, on Pinterest www.pinterest.com/barbaraannross, and on Instagram @maineclambake. You can also follow me on Goodreads at https://www.goodreads.com/author/show/6550635. Barbara_Ross and on BookBub at https://www.bookbub.com/authors/barbara-ross.

I wish a Happy Easter to all who celebrate the holiday with family and friends. And a lovely Sunday to those who will be at home with a good book. Eat a chocolate egg for me!

Sincerely,
Barbara Ross
Key West, Florida

# MEN

# AND

# MISCARRIAGE

## A Dad's Guide to Grief, Relationships, and Healing After Loss

## AARON & MJ GOUVEIA

Skyhorse Publishing

Skyhorse Publishing books may be purchased in bulk at special discounts for sales promotion, corporate gifts, fund-raising, or educational purposes. Special editions can also be created to specifications. For details, contact the Special Sales Department, Skyhorse Publishing, 307 West 36th Street, 11th Floor, New York, NY 10018 or info@skyhorsepublishing.com.

Skyhorse® and Skyhorse Publishing® are registered trademarks of Skyhorse Publishing, Inc.®, a Delaware corporation.

Visit our website at www.skyhorsepublishing.com.

10 9 8 7 6 5 4 3 2 1

Library of Congress Cataloging-in-Publication Data

Names: Gouveia, Aaron, author. | Gouveia, MJ, author.
Title: Men and miscarriage : a dad's guide to grief, relationships, and
   healing after loss / Aaron & MJ Gouveia.
Description: New York, NY : Skyhorse Publishing, [2021] | Includes
   bibliographical references and index. |
Identifiers: LCCN 2021016166 (print) | LCCN 2021016167 (ebook) | ISBN
   9781510763609 (hardcover) | ISBN 9781510763616 (ebook)
Subjects: LCSH: Miscarriage--Psychological aspects. | Father and child. |
   Grief.
Classification: LCC RG648 .G68 2021  (print) | LCC RG648  (ebook) | DDC
   618.3/9--dc23
LC record available at https://lccn.loc.gov/2021016166
LC ebook record available at https://lccn.loc.gov/2021016167

Cover design by Daniel Brount
Jacket photograph © Getty Images

Print ISBN: 978-1-5107-6360-9
Ebook ISBN: 978-1-5107-6361-6

Printed in the United States of America

For our unborn Alexandra.

# Contents

# Contents

# Introduction

THERE'S A PRETTY SIMPLE EXPLANATION AS TO WHY NO ONE hears much about how men are impacted by miscarriage, infertility, and pregnancy loss. It's because hardly anyone has ever bothered to ask them about it. This book sets out to change that because the answers are not only crucial for men, but also for society as a whole.

Going through infertility and pregnancy loss means becoming a member of a club you never wanted to join.

The very first time my wife, MJ, told me I was going to be a dad was in late 2006. I'd had a bad day at work and MJ was late to meet me at the restaurant for dinner. Not being on time is a major pet peeve and instantly puts me in a horrendous mood, yet as I snarkily shot not-so-thinly-veiled barbs her way as we waited for our menus, she seemed unfazed. Amused, even—which only served to ratchet up my annoyance even further.

"You know, being late isn't always bad," she said, coyly.

A smarter twenty-seven-year-old man who was newly married and actively trying for a baby would've picked up the innuendo, but alas, I was not that man. Instead, I launched into a diatribe about the importance of punctuality and how being on time means being respectful of other people. As I blabbered on,

I saw the playfulness fade from her eyes which had begun to roll all the way into the back of her head as her lovingly constructed plan fell to pieces.

"You're not listening! Being late isn't always bad. *Late!* Get it?"

But I didn't get it.

"I'm pregnant, you moron!" And with that she slapped a gift bag down on the table between us. I didn't open it right away because my entire being was trapped under the weight of the news she had just delivered. The silence lingered for what seemed like an eternity as I eventually rediscovered my fingers and slowly reached toward the bag to find the tiniest Boston Red Sox and New England Patriots jerseys I had ever seen in my life. With raised eyebrows and wide eyes, I shot her a look that silently screamed *Really?* and she nodded her head with a smirk.

I bolted up from my chair and shouted, "Hey everybody, I'm gonna be a dad!" A total cliché, but I gave not a single shit as I screamed so loud the guy next to me dropped his soup spoon. With tears spilling from my eyes, I got down on my knees in the middle of the restaurant and hugged my wife, then put my face right to her belly and whispered, "I already love you so much. I can't wait to be your dad and I'll always take care of you."

As well-intentioned as that promise was, it was a lie.

A week or so later I fielded a phone call from my sobbing wife in her work bathroom as she stared into the bowl at something she couldn't readily identify but still knew was very bad. One doctor visit later our worst fears were confirmed and just like that we were no longer expecting. Poof, gone in an instant. A future of endless possibilities replaced simply by an abrupt end.

It happened just before I headed out on a road trip with my dad and a couple of buddies to spend fifteen hours in the car traveling to Indiana to watch our beloved New England Patriots play in the AFC Championship game against Peyton Manning and the Indianapolis Colts. I had been so looking forward to that trip because we had just told my parents they were going to have their first grandchild and my dad was so excited at the news. Excited is an understatement, actually, he was damn near over the moon. A huge part of that is because it meant carrying on the ridiculously over-the-top Patriots fandom that runs through my family for another generation. We are a superstitious sports family and I remember thinking that with all the good juju new life brings, our team just had to win this game and continue on to the Super Bowl.

But suddenly all that joy was gone—literally flushed down the toilet. We had already started planning for this baby despite only being at the eight-week mark. We were thinking of names and picking out colleges and designing nurseries, but now there was just this emptiness. As rapidly as everything had been put into motion, the grinding halt and grim realization of being on a road to nowhere was beyond jarring. I no longer wanted to go on my road trip, partly because I didn't want to leave MJ alone, but also because, at that moment, I felt deeply ashamed. I still can't really tell you why or of what, but I can tell you it was an inordinately heavy guilt and fear. Feeling like something must be wrong with my DNA that made the pregnancy not take. Feeling like a jerk for having told our family and friends that we were going to have a baby and now suddenly being a liar. Feeling like less of a man and more of a disappointment at the thought of telling my dad I failed at my only true biological imperative. Feeling like a selfish prick for focusing on my own feelings when clearly this was a time to focus on my wife, whose body was literally housing this drama.

Yes, I ended up going on the trip at the urging of my wife. No, I didn't tell anyone immediately because I just couldn't bring myself to do it. Yes, it absolutely was terrible juju as the Patriots lost by blowing an eighteen-point halftime lead. Yet as horrible as I felt, I had no idea how the ensuing and unexpected long-term fallout would take an emotional toll, impact our marriage, and chip away at my mental health.

Fast forward to today and we have three healthy children, for which I'm immeasurably grateful. But MJ was pregnant a total of eight times and lost five pregnancies to get here. Eight pregnancies in nine years after overcoming my infertility issues, first trimester losses, a gut-wrenching second trimester abortion (much more on this later), and a round of IVF in which the sole viable egg mercifully took.

It sounds like a lot to go through but we actually consider ourselves extraordinarily lucky.

As this book proves via the people brave enough to talk about pregnancy loss, abortion, and infertility, we are far from alone and there are people who have had it way rougher. But we didn't know that because very few people actually talk about this.

To be brutally honest, it was extraordinarily difficult to write this book for that exact reason. When I floated the idea in my network and on social media, the enthusiasm for it was off the charts. Everyone, both men and women, went on and on about how a book like this is terribly needed and they even enthusiastically agreed to be interviewed. However, time after time, they would inevitably fail to show up when it was time to talk via phone or Zoom. Some said they were too busy. A few said they just couldn't bear to recount the pain. Others simply said nothing at all. I completely understand why, because it involves reliving some of the most painful, traumatic, and personal moments of their lives to be published in a book for all to see (even though I offered anonymity). I had initially hoped to interview roughly fifty people but quickly learned that was not going to be possible in my time frame, because the shame and stigma attached to these topics is a powerful force. In the end, between a survey we sent out and in-depth interviews we conducted with those who did agree to speak with us, we heard from sixty-six people in total and personally interviewed nine of them.

To the folks who backed out or declined, please know there is zero ill will and I hope reading the stories of others makes you feel less alone. But I'm damn grateful for the people who did decide to share with us because, without them, what you're reading now simply wouldn't have been possible.

The main takeaway from writing this book is there exists a thick blanket of shame covering these issues that very few people want to talk about. And yet, while they don't want to be the ones sharing, they do want more of a conversation and more light shed on these shadowy, taboo topics. The reticence to discuss miscarriage, infertility, and abortion certainly exists for women, but in some ways it may even apply more to men for a host of reasons spanning basic confusion, the toxic belief that men are supposed to suffer in silence, and believing infertility and pregnancy issues are solely for the realm of women. After all, it's her body this is happening to so what right do we have to complain? Also, if no one asks men how they're doing following a loss then that signals they're not supposed to feel anything. Men wonder if they're allowed to grieve. And what are we even grieving? Is a miscarriage like losing a baby that's already been born? Aren't we supposed to focus on our partners instead of ourselves? Because feeling upset is one thing but openly admitting to that hurt and letting people in (especially a therapist or counselor)? Now we're "simps" and "pansies" who can't handle our own problems.

It goes without saying that's all bullshit, but it can be nearly impossible to realize that at the time.

Biological sex and rigid societal gender roles shouldn't dictate whether or not men are allowed to feel emotion. We're human beings and the men in this book have bravely stepped forward to talk about something that barely ever sees the light of day. They not only discuss their own fears, hopes, struggles, and how this impacted them mentally and emotionally, they also talk about how their families and relationships were impacted. And the women who were interviewed provided invaluable feedback because many (heterosexual, in these specific instances) men feel they're being noble by stuffing away their feelings and looking after their partners, but those partners are wondering why the heck they're not feeling anything. They report feeling alone in the experience because men are trained not to show any emotion, so many women think they don't care.

If anything, this book confirms the self-fulfilling prophecy I suspected was at the heart of the disconnect surrounding this topic. Men feel the need to be silent and strong, women interpret that silence as being unfeeling or nonplussed, and both parties are left feeling guilt, shame, uncertainty, and resentment.

This book will tackle miscarriage, infertility, and abortion as seen through the eyes of men and women. We tried to interview men and women from all walks of life, ethnicities, ages, sexual orientations, and locations to get as broad a cross-section as possible. I wish we had gotten more people of color and LGBTQ folks and I certainly reached out to those communities for inclusion, but at the end of the day 11 percent of our respondents were from an underrepresented minority group. Also, the reason

I keep saying "we" is because my wife, MJ, will be intermittently offering her voice throughout this book because that duality of perspective is essential to take a nuanced look at this issue.

After all, no one wants to hear about these issues solely from a straight, white man absent the fundamentally necessary opinion of the woman who was at the center of it. Justifiably so, I might add.

You may not like or agree with everything in this book. It's raw and honest and that can be tough for many people. But if the only thing that comes out of it is that a handful of people going through hard times feel less alone, then mission accomplished. If it gets one man to open up to his partner or to seek help via counseling, that's a win. Even if it just gets some guys to take a few steps back from the edge because they realize what they're feeling is normal and that they're actually allowed to feel, I'll take it.

Sunlight is the best disinfectant and it's time to drag this conversation out into the open air so we all feel a little less alone and a little more empowered.

\* \* \*

*I only knew one person who had a miscarriage when I had mine. Growing up, everyone told me about all their ailments that came along with pregnancies, but no one told me how up to 50 percent of pregnancies end in miscarriages.*

*I've been pregnant eight times in nine years: the culprits being four miscarriages, one abortion, male infertility, and IVF. Going through each one was extremely painful, but while I'm a very private person (the polar opposite of my husband), I've decided now is the time to start talking about it. We should be open about what we went through so others will feel less guilt and shame. Especially* men. Women talk among their friends and family and generally have better support systems compared to men who have few outlets where they can speak openly about their feelings. Whether it's toxic masculinity, fear, societal expectations, or a combination of all those things, it's time to unpack it so we can start to move beyond it.

The feeling of isolation is a powerful force. Technically I had no reason to feel alone when I went through these journeys because I had a solid support network in place, yet alone is exactly how I felt. Alone with thoughts, questions that no one had answers to, and alone because I had no idea where my husband stood while all of this was going on. He was stoic for all of our losses until he'd see me getting upset, but then he'd go in the polar opposite direction and try to make me laugh. A sense of humor is great and all, but I was in no mood to laugh and I didn't need a court jester—I wanted a partner. While he took his feelings to his blog to write and share with the world, I wanted him to share with me. I wanted him to talk to me about each loss and why he seemed to lack any emotion (or so I thought).

When we talk about miscarriages and reproductive health, it's usually about women having their physical and medical needs met. But we never hear doctors, nurse practitioners, or other medical professionals ask us how we're doing emotionally. I felt my emotional well-being was never met by doctors or my husband. Because honestly, if I had these strong emotions then why wasn't my husband feeling the same? Men are human beings and have feelings. The child is half theirs. Yet Aaron spent his time trying to make me smile, promising that we could try again soon, and sharing with anonymous Internet strangers instead of me, his wife.

When I had my miscarriages and abortion, not one professional asked if I was okay or if I needed to talk to a support group

or mental health professional. That was very frustrating personally, but looking back now, what is even more frustrating is no one
asked Aaron if he was okay either. He was not okay. It took years
of healing on both our parts to talk about it together. I felt resentment that his needs were better met among his online readers,
which was not the case. He actually did want to talk to me and
had strong emotions, but didn't want to burden me with them. I
was the one who was going through it, so why would he want to
talk to me about it? He could see I was struggling with everything
we went through but I couldn't see that he was trying to spare me,
I just saw cool disinterest. A little communication would've gone a
long way at the time.

The reason this book is so important is because it brings a
topic out of the darkness. By talking about something so common
yet so shrouded in shame and mystery, it has the potential to help
so many people. Especially men. Men have a hard time expressing
their feelings due to being raised in a culture of toxic masculinity.
They are told from a young age to "man up" and be the rock of
their family. This is not a good mindset and I didn't need a rock.
Women want an emotional partner, an equal. Someone they can
talk to and get emotional feedback from, especially during a miscarriage, abortion, or infertility.

I have to believe if more men knew what women truly wanted
they would see that being an unfeeling mass of granite is not the
answer. And their emotional well-being, as well as their relationships, wouldn't suffer.

Yes, this book is mainly for men. However, I'll be adding perspective because no book on this subject can possibly be complete
without input from the women who are physically and emotionally enduring this trauma. Also because it was astounding to
recall these events with Aaron and realize that our recollections

*were often vastly different—as varied as our perspectives and approaches to what was happening in our lives.*

*In this book, as in life, we're better and stronger together.*

# Chapter 1

## *Know the Statistics*

BEFORE WE WORK ON OVERCOMING THE STIGMA OF MISCAR-riage, infertility, and pregnancy loss, it's important to have a thorough understanding of what we're dealing with. Largely because there's a lot of guilt around these topics and much of that guilt stems from myths and misunderstandings surrounding the prevalence and causes of pregnancy loss.

Miscarriage is defined as the spontaneous loss of a pregnancy before the twentieth week, and occurs in roughly 10 to 20 percent of known pregnancies[1], according to the Mayo Clinic. But in reality, that number is likely much higher since many miscarriages occur so early in the pregnancy that women often don't even realize they're pregnant. That means some researchers claim up to half[2]—yes, 50 percent!—of all pregnancies end without a living, breathing bundle of joy. The reason people likely feel so alone when it happens to them isn't because it only happens to

---

1  "Miscarriage - Topic Overview." Mayo Clinic, accessed Nov. 25, 2020, https://www.mayoclinic.org/diseases-conditions/pregnancy-loss-miscarriage/symptoms-causes/syc-20354298

2  "Miscarriage: Risks, Symptoms, Causes and Treatments." Cleveland Clinic, accessed Nov. 25, 2020, https://my.clevelandclinic.org/health/diseases/9688-miscarriage

a select few people, but because only a select few choose to talk about it.

As for what causes miscarriages, far too many people assume it's genetic or something they've done during the pregnancy. According to a 2015 survey[3] of more than 1,000 men and women, more than three-quarters of respondents said miscarriages are caused by a stressful event and nearly two-thirds thought lifting a heavy object contributes to miscarriage. Going to work and strenuous exercise are also common reasons people list, but the fact is none of these things cause women to lose a pregnancy. A miscarriage is simply the abnormal development of the fetus. In the overwhelming majority of cases, according to the Mayo Clinic, chromosome problems result from errors that occur by chance as the embryo divides and grows.

This is important because thinking your everyday, routine activities are why you're not fulfilling your dream of having children is dangerous on many levels. In our 2020 survey of fifty-seven people, guilt about miscarriage was ever present. While nearly half (46 percent) of men felt guilty and partially responsible after a miscarriage, 59 percent of women said they felt like they were to blame. Understanding how miscarriage occurs can alleviate some of that guilt and shame surrounding these losses.

Also, just for your information, having sex while pregnant is not a cause of miscarriage, either. In an unintentional moment of levity following our first miscarriage, I mentioned to MJ that I was harboring major guilt because we had had sex a week or so before we lost the baby and I was sure that played a part. While I tried hard to make my wife laugh and smile again after being

---

3   Bardos, Jonah et al. "A national survey on public perceptions of miscarriage." *Obstetrics and gynecology* vol. 125,6 (2015): 1313–20. doi:10.1097/AOG.0000000000000859

so unimaginably sad, I won't pretend it didn't hurt a little to hear her cackling hysterically at the thought of my manhood being so imposing that it could possibly have any negative impact on an 8-week-old fetus.

When it comes to infertility, a lot of people automatically think of it as a problem mainly among women (you'll notice this theme over and over again throughout this book). But the truth is while about 11 percent of women of reproductive age experience infertility issues, 9 percent of men are in the same boat.[4] After one year of having unprotected sex, 12 to 15 percent of couples are unable to conceive. After two years, 10 percent are still without a living baby.[5,6,7] And while fertility decreases with age in both men and women, the decline is much more rapid in women as they are roughly half as fertile in their thirties compared to their twenties. After age thirty-five (which is considered "advanced maternal age"), the decline in fertility is nothing short of precipitous.[8]

When male infertility does arise, it usually has something to do with the testicles, according to the National Institute of Child Health and Human Development. Between 10 and 15 percent of men who are infertile experience a complete lack of sperm,[9]

4  Chandra, A., Copen, C. E., & Stephen, E. H. (2013). Infertility and Impaired Fecundity in the United States, 1982–2010: Data From the National Survey of Family Growth. National Health Statistics Reports, 67, 1–19. Retrieved February 7, 2018, from https://www.cdc.gov/nchs/data/nhsr/nhsr067.pdf

5  American Urological Association Male Infertility Best Practice Policy Panel. (2010). *The optimal evaluation of the infertile male*: AUA best practice statement. Retrieved January 7, 2016, from https://www.auanet.org/documents/education/clinical-guidance/Male-Infertility-d.pdf

6  American Society for Reproductive Medicine. (2012). *Optimizing natural fertility*. Retrieved May 31, 2016, from https://www.reproductivefacts.org/news-and-publications/patient-fact-sheets-and-booklets/documents/fact-sheets-and-info-booklets/optimizing-natural-fertility/

7  Gnoth, G., Godehardt, D., Godehardt, E., Frank-Herrmann, P., & Freundl, G. (2003). Time to pregnancy: Results of the German prospective study and impact on the management of infertility. *Human Reproduction*, 18(9), 1959–1966.

8  Practice Committee of the American Society for Reproductive Medicine in collaboration with the Society for Reproductive Endocrinology and Infertility. (2013). Optimizing natural fertility: A committee opinion. *Fertility and Sterility*, 100(3), 631–637.

9  American Urological Association (2008). *A basic guide to male infertility: how to find out what's wrong*. Retrieved June 11, 2012, from https://www.auanet.org/guidelines/azoospermic-male-best-practice-statement.

which can be caused by a hormone imbalance or a blockage. Men experiencing infertility often produce less sperm than normal, as 40 percent of men with infertility issues suffer from varicocele (pronounced VAR-i-koh-seel), which is an enlarged vein in the testicle.[10] In addition to there needing to be enough sperm, they also have to be good swimmers. Unfortunately for men like me (more on this later in the infertility chapter), motility (how the sperm moves) and morphology (how the sperm are shaped) are the culprits.

But perhaps the most frustrating part of male infertility is that in 50 percent of the cases, the cause of the infertility cannot be determined.[11] And as we all know, most men don't do so well when they know something is wrong but they can't identify it to try and fix it.

Abortion is perhaps the least understood but most controversial subject we'll tackle in this book. Far too many people believe abortion is a form of birth control used primarily by sexually promiscuous young women (and women of color, at that), when in reality abortion rates have been falling for years and the legal procedure is one had by women of all ages, races, and economic statuses.

Nearly one in four women in America will have an abortion by the age of forty-five, according to researchers at the Guttmacher Institute. Also, despite what many think about young people, the abortion rates for adolescents between fifteen and nineteen years old declined by 46 percent between 2008 to 2014—the largest decrease of any other group. Abortion rates declined during that span for all groups, but the largest decreases

---

10  American Urological Association (2008). Report on vericocele and infertility. Retrieved June 11, 2012, from http://www.auanet.org/guidelines/male-infertility-azoospermic-male-(reviewed-and-amended-2011)

11  Jose-Miller, A. B., Boyden J. W., & Frey, K. A. (2007). Infertility. *American Family Physician*, 75, 849–856.

came from non-white women. In fact, nearly 39 percent of women who get abortions are white—the largest group listed in the study. While never-married women accounted for nearly 46 percent of all abortions between 2008 and 2014, 45 percent were either married or in a relationship and cohabitating. Fifty-nine percent had at least one prior birth and 23 percent were college graduates.[12]

The bottom line is lots of women from lots of different backgrounds and circumstances have abortions for lots of different reasons. Reasons, by the way, which are no one's business except for her, her partner, and her doctor. My wife's abortion while trying for our second child in 2010 was due to Sirenomelia (a.k.a. Mermaid Syndrome, where the legs are fused together and body parts like the kidneys, anus, and bladder are missing), but that doesn't make her reproductive health decision any more or less credible than another woman's. Perhaps if we stop the condemnation at the outset there would be far less shame associated with this legal medical procedure in the long term.

\* \* \*

*All of these statistics about miscarriage, infertility, and abortion are well and good. But what doesn't get touched on is how you and your partner are too often treated as statistics.*

*I love numbers. Hell, I worked in banking for ten years. But I hate statistics—the formal calculation of where you should fall in a category. It's information without emotion and it's very black and white. When I had my first miscarriage, we became one of those statistics. Then Aaron and I became another statistic when*

---

12   Rachel K. Jones, Jenna Jerman, "Population Group Abortion Rates and Lifetime Incidence of Abortion: United States, 2008–2014," *American Journal of Public Health* 107, no. 12 (December 1, 2017): pp. 1904–1909.

*our unborn baby was diagnosed with Mermaid Syndrome. The doctors told us it was 1-in-100,000 odds of that condition developing during pregnancy. We became a statistic when I decided to have an abortion following that terminal diagnosis, and then we became a statistic once again when we couldn't get pregnant. It seemed we were statistics no matter what we did with our reproductive health.*

*"Miscarriages happen, try again next month. Many women have miscarriages," the nurse told me when we spoke on the phone after I started to bleed with my first pregnancy. There was no emotion in the call, no sympathy. Just "shit happens" and "better luck next time." I became a statistic at that point and stayed one in the eyes of the medical field for the next decade.*

*To all the partners of people going through pregnancy loss, it's normal and natural to gather information and be informed. I would never dissuade anyone from that. But even if you're statistically minded, please don't perpetuate behaviors that continue to make us feel like we're just a number. We don't want to hear about the percentages and the likelihoods—at least not from the people closest to us who serve as our support structure. We get that enough from the doctors.*

*So come armed with statistics, but more importantly, come with your ears open and your arms outstretched in embrace. That's what we really need.*

# Chapter 2

# *Toxic Masculinity: Recognize It, Understand It, Battle It*

Toxic masculinity is any cultural norm that is associated with harm to men themselves, as well as to society. So guys, every time you've refused to ask for help because you don't want to seem weak, told someone you don't want to talk about your feelings because that's "gay," or refrained from providing comfort (or seeking it) from a male friend for fear of being thought of as a "pussy," you've been bathing in toxic masculinity.

And whether you're intentionally or unintentionally swimming in these waters, you're likely drowning and don't even realize it.

These are the cultural norms and ridiculous societal expectations that are strangling generations of men and festering as the root cause of so much unnecessary pain, fear, guilt, and shame most men feel but never discuss. And in the context of miscarriage, infertility, and pregnancy loss, the default settings of modern manhood are traps that not only cause men harm, but also cause their partners suffering as well. The notion that men

7

have to suffer in silence when all we really want to do is scream and cry at the top of our lungs. The idea that we have to be the intractable rock that weathers the storm when we really feel like letting the waves carry us out to sea. The mistaken belief that we have to suck it up and fix our own problems when what we really need is a helping hand or at least the tools for the job. In each one of these scenarios, everyone is getting hurt—men because we erroneously believe shutting down emotionally is the correct course of action, and women because they're left with a partner who has morphed into an emotionless drone at one of the most emotionally vulnerable crossroads in life.

Benjamin, a thirty-six-year-old from Salem, Oregon, spiraled into a deep depression and experienced suicidal ideation (thoughts of suicide without the accompanying desire to carry through with it) after his wife lost two pregnancies in 13 months. He knows he is a rarity in that he's a man who was described by his therapist as an empath, cops to his feelings, explores them deeply, and publicly discusses them both in person and online. Yet the struggle to be himself and allow himself to feel things openly is forever being stifled due to toxic masculinity.

In Benjamin's mind, how could he, as a man, not allow himself the emotional bandwidth to grieve after losing one child at the 15-week gender scan and then enduring a stillbirth 13 months later at nearly 37 weeks due to Trisonomy 13? Suddenly he was filled with frustration and anger at life. Add to that his two best friends moving across the country, the death of a step-mother, losing three grandparents in rapid succession, and the couple's therapy dog dying all in the same general span of time, and he came face-to-face with an often overwhelming emotional obstacle that men aren't generally equipped to handle.

"Talking about this isn't natural for a lot of men so we're always fighting an uphill battle. My wife understands it and is encouraging, but she doesn't do deep feelings like I do so there were a lot of times when I was just sitting in it by myself."

That feeling of isolation is unfortunately common for many men, myself included. It's also something that's self-inflicted due to stereotypical gender expectations.

Societal demands on men call for them to be strong, silent, and self-sufficient. Never ask for help, never talk about how you feel, suck it up, rub some dirt on it, quit yer bitchin', and walk it off. Our role is that of protector, rock, fixer. Now don't get me wrong, many of those things on their own are not negative. Strength is a positive, as is being self-sufficient and a problem solver. But, as with most things in life, the key is moderation. Be strong but don't let a performative flex become the main goal. Give yourself what you need to get by, but if things get too overwhelming remember that asking for help is not weakness and no one can do it all by themselves. And emotional vulnerability, not some mandatory masculine stoicism, might very well be what your partner needs to see from you to begin processing the grief together.

After MJ lost the first couple of pregnancies, I went straight into "Protector Mode." I stuffed any feelings of loss and heartbreak way down deep and committed myself to taking care of her and her needs. I did that because it was her body this was happening to, that's what men are supposed to do, and—most notably—I realized while everyone was asking how MJ was doing, hardly anyone was asking me. I internalized that as proof that I didn't deserve to be feeling bad about anything because real men don't worry about their feelings. This sentiment is shared by the respondents in our survey, as 95 percent of men said they were more concerned with their partner. In contrast, only 13 percent of women said their main concern was for someone other than themselves (totally justifiable, by the way, but still notable for the contrast).

\* \* \*

*The most revelatory part of writing this book is getting the glimpse into Aaron's head that I never fully got when we were going through this. Aaron is writing in hindsight about his emotions and while he says he hid them and went into "protector mode," all I remember him doing is falling into a depressive state.*

*My life was already complicated by mental health issues and Aaron was (and still is) my rock. Except, at that point, I was watching a tsunami bury my rock deep into the murky and seemingly endless abyss of despair. With each miscarriage it got a little worse. Then came the abortion that saw sadness coupled with intense anger at the universe. Finally, the infertility rendered him barely recognizable to me. As I saw the love of my life struggle with finding a balance between what the world expected and what our family needed, I felt completely helpless to stop the freefall.*

*It doesn't help that the doctors and nurses we saw never asked how we were doing emotionally. We saw many doctors and specialists over the course of ten years and not once do I ever remember them asking Aaron about his mental health and how it could impact him or me.*

*Some may say it was an oversight, but I know now it was a form of toxic masculinity. The male doctors had blinders on. Why would they ask if Aaron was okay? It wasn't his body. He had to be strong for his hysterical wife who just had a string of miscarriages. Why should he have feelings—he was raised in a "man-up" culture. Crying is for women and girls.*

*I asked him to go see someone but he told me he was fine. "Fine" is our family's go-to word when things are supposed to be good but aren't. This put a huge strain on our marriage. I felt he was pulling away from me, that he didn't want the family we had talked about, and he was no longer my support. All because of a stereotypical "strong and silent" ideal men try to live up to without even stopping to think about why.*

\* \* \*

Vernon, forty-two, of New Jersey, and his wife lost twins at 19 weeks following a cervical issue. Prior to that they endured multiple first-trimester losses, but losing two babies at the same time nearly halfway through the pregnancy was "very, very rough." While some members of his family did check in on him, Vernon said he was craving conversations with other guys who had been through similar losses because he couldn't shake the feeling that these losses were "an indictment on me as a man." He even took the added step of attending a parenting conference where seemingly every topic under the sun was discussed at length, but never pregnancy loss and how to deal with it as a man.

"Men don't talk about it. Maybe it's machismo or maybe because it's not our body and it's not us who is literally losing the baby, but we have a part in this whole process and it's not just a women's issue. But in general, guys think it's all about her and our feelings don't matter."

Vernon was able to push through the veil of toxic masculinity and eventually wrote an article in the *Washington Post*[1] detailing his thoughts on the loss of his twins, with raw honesty and

---

1  Gibbs, Vernon. "Fathers Suffer From Pregnancy Loss and Stillbirths, Too." *Washington Post*, April 23, 2018, https://www.washingtonpost.com/news/parenting/wp/2018/04/23/a-father-finding-his-way-after-loss/

emotion. Yet even in that piece, some stereotypical male thinking is evident when he writes that he was overjoyed to find out they weren't just having twins, but twin boys. "I'll admit that as a man, I felt that my ability to make more men somehow made me more manly." I know it seems harmless to so many people but it's this line of thinking that plants the seeds for the toxicity that has the potential to pose serious problems for men down the road. Because oftentimes the same men who feel more masculine for creating more men and seemingly valuing them over girls are the ones who think of themselves as less masculine if they express heartbreak or admit they need a hand following a tragic loss.

Thankfully for Vernon, his wife is a psychiatrist so he has never felt shame about asking for help when necessary. Yet after that piece was published, he steeled himself for an onslaught of judgment and barbs about not being a "real man," but said he was pleasantly surprised to find no negative feedback. Instead, other men quietly thanked him or privately confided in him that they too had gone through a similar situation and were grateful to feel a little less alone.

The problem gets even worse with infertility because, to be blunt, it feels like a direct attack on our manhood and virility. When I found out there was a problem with the morphology of my sperm, it felt like someone took a sledgehammer to my pride. You can be the most woke and down-to-earth man in the world but the second some doctor tells you there's something wrong with your swimmers, you shut down and circle the wagons. At least I did. My frazzled and paranoid mind went to places I cringe at describing, to the point that I asked my (very supportive) wife if our oldest even belonged to me since my sperm was so screwed up. Pro tip, fellas—accusing your wife of infidelity just because you're insecure about your own infertility issues never leads anywhere good.

If you really stop and think about it, it's patently absurd. I spiraled into an instant depression simply because my sperm wasn't up to snuff. It's the same level of absurdity as thinking men aren't really men unless they watch football or drink beer or work on cars. Yet that toxicity is so powerful that as soon as I found out I had an issue, I automatically labeled myself as defective and pathetic and crawled into my shell of self-loathing at the exact same time that my wife needed me so we could form a plan of attack and get to where we needed to be. And while curled up in the fetal position with my partner in life trying to help me, I lashed out and insulted her instead of taking her hand and allowing her to be my strength when I needed someone to lean on.

Pushing past societal expectations of men and the comforts of gender stereotypes isn't easy, but it's almost always a game-changer in a positive way. If men are asked how they're doing they're free to respond openly and honestly. If they freely express themselves then their significant others suddenly realize they have a partner in feeling all the same grief, shame, fear, and sadness they're experiencing. And maybe, just maybe, in all that conversation, a man can find the space to admit it if he's not coping well and that he needs help. But none of that happens if men (and women) cling stubbornly to the rigid and restrictive gender roles that suffocate progress and growth, so it's imperative to sit with the uncomfortableness of being dominated by toxic masculinity and then get ready to truly do the work to extricate yourself from its clutches.

# Chapter 3

## *Miscarriage Sucks No Matter the Stage and Everyone Grieves Differently*

I F A MISCARRIAGE OCCURS BEFORE THE FIRST ULTRASOUND, does it even really count?

Yes, that's something I actually wondered. Along with *Am I even allowed to grieve with a loss this early?* and *Can I even consider this a loss?* Maybe it's because I knew people who had lost second trimester pregnancies when little hands and feet were actually formed and, in one heartbreaking instance, a couple who had lost their sweet little five-year-old girl. Now *those* were losses, I reasoned, because there was something tangible there. Mourning the loss of something I could readily identify as a human baby made sense, and certainly the loss of a living, breathing child is a horror beyond anything I can comprehend that calls for the deepest ocean of grief and sorrow. But a loss of a collection of cells? An amorphous blob with one tiny, flickering pulse of a heartbeat on some flimsy black ultrasound photo that resembled a large blood clot more than it did a baby? I told myself there's no way I get to be upset about that—especially compared to the much more grievous losses others endured.

What I failed to realize at the time is: There's no right way to mourn. No acceptable or unacceptable standard to which people must adhere. That whether it's a chemical loss at 6 weeks or a stillbirth at full-term, we're allowed to navigate and define our respective levels of hurt.

That first loss was deeply painful despite coming at just the 8-week-mark, and hurt more than I ever let on. I never truly dealt with it because I didn't think I was allowed. In part because I was a man and this was my wife's issue, but also because it was so early. I didn't have a name picked out, we didn't know if it was a boy or a girl, and I hadn't felt the kid kick. And yet the undeniable truth was that I was a mess. A shit show. An abject disaster. I pretended otherwise but I'm not a very good actor, and in hindsight, I can honestly say the loss of that first pregnancy impacted me just as much if not more than the baby we would go on to lose a few years later at 18 weeks.

\* \* \*

*Aaron trying to be the "rock" proved to be the thing that hurt our relationship the most. He thought he was doing the right thing but in reality, it was killing us. He wanted to be stoic for me but instead he came off as cold, callous, and uncaring and I thought he didn't care about the baby I had already begun bonding with. Our baby. I know it kills him to hear it but that hurt more than the loss of the child itself. He is supposed to be the person who loves me yet he refused to show any kind of emotion about what was going on at the time.*

\* \* \*

It took a few years and some professional help to see it, but I was mourning the loss of what could have been, because one of the saddest things imaginable is the idea of unrealized potential.

Of our survey respondents, 75 percent experienced first trimester losses. Whether we want to admit it or not, many men start planning out the future the moment that pregnancy test confirms new life is present. My mind immediately went to one day having a Field of Dreams moment on the Fenway Park outfield as my son (I was adamant it was going to be a boy even though we didn't find out the sex beforehand with any of our pregnancies), the starting first-baseman for the Boston Red Sox, invited me to play a game of catch after winning his first World Series ring. I pictured his first words, first steps, teaching him how to ride a bike, Little League games, his first date, high school graduation, and his college graduation as the youngest Pulitzer Prize winner in history. Sure, I had thought about these things before when discussing starting a family with my wife, but that was in the abstract. This was real. It was happening. And somehow, in a way I'll never understand, my mind and heart automatically and instantaneously grew to accommodate this new life that was only weeks old.

Yet the second and third trimester losses, which accounted for 14 percent and 5 percent respectively in our surveys, are just as mind-numbingly painful.

David, forty-seven, from California, said the first early miscarriage his then-girlfriend (now wife), Penelope, went through caught them so unprepared they didn't really have time to dwell on the negatives because their heads were spinning from all the upheaval. However, when they decided to commit to one another and try again for a baby, they embarked down a road of infertility and miscarriage so bumpy that David says he and his wife legitimately lost count of just how many early miscarriages they experienced. Yet they remained hopeful, even positing that famous actress Brooke Shields reportedly had a dozen miscarriages before successfully having a baby, so if she could do it so could they.

But then came the second trimester losses and David hit his tipping point.

"We went through so many of those first trimester losses that I honestly don't remember how many there were. Because that's what this does to you—it makes you forget and it makes trauma the baseline. Eventually it feels like Stockholm Syndrome. When the first trimester miscarriages happened, it was this valley, but it was a place where I was already low and I just expected to feel that way forever. But the second trimester losses were where we raged at the fucking universe because we made it past that arbitrary twelve-week goal and then we lost anyway. It all just seemed like such a hopeless crapshoot."

That feeling of arbitrary randomness is an especially vile pill to swallow for many men because we like to control and fix things, but you can't fix the universe's random fits.

When receiving a Sirenomelia diagnosis while trying for our second child and hearing from doctors that the odds of it occurring are 1 in 100,000, I experienced a much different feeling than the previous losses. While the first trimester miscarriages left me shell-shocked and terribly sad, this one had me seething because there was nothing that could've been done. Nothing. Doctors still aren't even sure how it occurs and simply say it happens randomly for no reason whatsoever. Even more irritating was that you could tell they were intrigued because most of them had never seen a rare case like this. The rational part of my brain understood it as intellectual and academic curiosity, but rationality was not in my wheelhouse back then. So after going through two early losses we finally made it past the point where everything is supposed to be fine and suddenly the wheel of fortune simply steamrolls us for no earthly reason?

Fuck. That.

I was mad. Really mad. But ironically, this was actually a little easier for me to deal with because part of toxic masculinity is men learning to make anger their default emotion. And my anger was white hot, putting me in very familiar (yet very dangerous) territory. The deep sadness I felt with the first trimester losses was unexpected, unsettling, and profoundly uncomfortable. But I was accustomed to rage and, in a weird and destructive way, it felt comforting. To curse God and the universe and rail wildly against the fickle finger of fate. Unfortunately, all that railing and screaming into the void was accompanied by an uptick in drinking, distancing myself from my wife, and other destructive behaviors that toxic anger brings.

Another important factor to consider is that some people will not grieve the loss, and that is also an acceptable reaction (albeit one that comes with its own unique pangs of guilt and confusion).

Dr. Amy Walsh, an emergency medical doctor, wrote about her experience having a miscarriage in *Parents* in 2018, describing how she felt guilt that she didn't feel guiltier following her loss.[1] Perhaps because of her medical training, Walsh took comfort in the fact that her body knew there was something wrong with the pregnancy and took corrective action to rectify the situation, bringing her logical mind some peace as if order had been restored. She wrote, "During the first several weeks after my

---

1 Walsh, Amy. "I Didn't Grieve After My Miscarriage & Learned It's OK to Feel OK." *Parents*, July 27, 2018, https://www.parents.com/pregnancy/complications/miscarriage/i-didnt-grieve-after-my-miscarriage-learned-its-ok-to-feel-ok/

miscarriage, I kept waiting to feel the intense grief I had seen my patients experience, heard my friends share, and read about in newspapers, magazines, and blogs. It didn't come. So I waited a bit more. Negative emotions arose, but intense grief wasn't one of them. I remember thinking, *Am I a monster for not feeling worse? Or am I in denial and not fully experiencing my grief?"*

Some people move on much more quickly than others. Some people might not have truly wanted that baby in the first place, and experienced relief upon losing it. It's unfortunate that these folks feel guilty for not feeling more guilt, and it's proof that we need to remove all expectations and arbitrary restrictions on what is and isn't acceptable when going through this very personal and emotionally diverse set of circumstances.

The end result is everyone hurts—in their own way, at their own pace, and at varying levels. It's important not to turn these losses into the Grief Olympics and to remember everyone is in the same sad boat. Honest and open communication with your partner goes a long way toward healing and understanding, and it's vital for both people to know what the other is feeling and why. The way one person reacts to an early loss versus a miscarriage later in the pregnancy, and vice versa, will not always be similar and everyone involved needs to know that's perfectly okay. It's also vital to know that if you're not depressed and raising your fist to the sky in anger, that's fine too.

The important thing is to communicate how you're feeling with your partner so you know where the other one stands and no one is left guessing and assuming the worst. I failed miserably in that regard and it cost me dearly.

\* \* \*

*Whether it's a blue line, pink line, plus sign, or digital, you have two feelings when you get the news—excitement and/or fear. I was in the first camp. I was over the moon and couldn't wait to tell Aaron, except we were both at work and this was not an announcement fit for a phone call. So I hatched a plan. I would surprise him at a restaurant. I couldn't even focus at work the day I found out, I was too excited.*

*Later that night we met up at a nice restaurant and I brought a bag of baby things, including the test that said "pregnant" on it (yes, I always used digital tests). He was so confused why I was giving him a bag of baby things. It wasn't until he reached the test that it really hit him. We were pregnant!*

*A week or so later, when I was at work, I started to feel off (a feeling I would soon learn was the end of my pregnancy). First, it started with a telltale cramp, then a feeling like you have the start of the flu. For many years, before I talked about my miscarriages, I thought I was the only one who had these symptoms. The more people I opened up to, I came to find out many women feel these symptoms before they lose their pregnancies.*

*I immediately ran to the bathroom and panicked when I saw blood. I tried to collect myself but I was still crying as I came out of the bathroom and my staff was very worried about me. I proceeded to tell them what was going on and they were very sympathetic and understanding. They did the best they could to console me, but it was too late. I was too devastated.*

*I called Aaron, who worked an hour away, to tell him what was going on. I was in hysterics so, being the supportive husband he is, he immediately told me everything would be okay. Yet somehow, I knew that wasn't going to be true.*

*Driving an hour home that night was the hardest drive I've had to take by myself. The next day I booked a blood test with my*

OB to confirm what we already knew—we lost the baby. Getting the call about the blood work was what I expected, but what I didn't expect was how I would be treated by the nurse. "You lost the pregnancy, but you can try again next month." No condolences, no affection, and no emotion. It was robotic and, to me, uncaring. I didn't want to try next month. I wanted that baby. I wanted all of that potential and all the future I had already begun to imagine.

If the loss of the baby wasn't bad enough, I had a huge interview with my manager the following day as I was going for a promotion. I tried to cancel it because my head just wasn't in the right place, but he refused. I was upfront and honest with him about what was going on which was when he coldly told me the job wasn't for me and he wasn't going to wait around for me to start a family. It wasn't just his unsympathetic nature that was troubling, but punishing women in the workforce for being pregnant—or even thinking about getting pregnant—is yet another form of toxic masculinity and misogyny. I was already feeling guilty for my body betraying me and this compounded things because I was the breadwinner at the time and I felt like I failed my family twice.

To make things worse, after each miscarriage I felt Aaron and I grow apart because we didn't communicate with each other. If I could give myself marriage advice after each miscarriage, I would have not been so hard on myself, avoided blaming myself and Aaron (yes, I blamed him for the miscarriages), and made sure we talked about it. It was like we just let the miscarriages happen and define us, taking control of our lives. We were both too hurt and sad to talk about what we wanted to do, which made the whole thing feel even more out of control.

One of our later losses was a "silent miscarriage" toward the end of the first trimester. I remember having to go in for a D&C (dilation & curettage—a medical procedure to remove tissue from *the uterus). The doctor put me on birth control to make sure I didn't get pregnant to safeguard my health, yet I didn't tell Aaron about it for months. I was too ashamed to admit I failed at giving him a baby. I should have told Aaron that I was feeling ashamed, embarrassed, and stressed about getting pregnant and not staying pregnant, and I definitely should've told him I was on birth control. In my head I was sparing him but it ended up hurting him even more when my period would come that month and I'd see the hope fade from his eyes.*

*Communication. Communication. Communication. We'll write about it five hundred more times before this book is finished.*

\* \* \*

Wow. I just found out my wife didn't tell me she was on birth control for four months while we were trying to get pregnant and I was blaming myself for it not happening. So yeah, definitely communicate. Holy shit. I'm gonna need a moment.

# Chapter 4

# *Infertility Is a Shit Show for Everyone*

"**W**AIT, YOU MEAN IT'S *MY* FAULT?"
Those were the ill-fated words I uttered while sitting in the fertility specialist's office the day we found out the morphology of my sperm was the reason we were having such a hard time with this whole pregnancy thing. I was shocked and appalled. I wasn't shocked to find out there was an issue (because you don't end up at a fertility specialist when everything is smooth sailing), it was more so that I was the cause.

I frantically tried to convince myself it couldn't be my fault. After all, I already had a son. But more than that, I mean hey, I'm a man. A provider. More specifically, a provider of sperm. Copious amounts of baby batter, spraying like a fire hose to my lucky wife. And surely that sperm is a paragon of health. Strong sperm. Super sperm. Sperm that most likely dons a cape or wields a hammer, able to bust into eggs via sheer will and a stern glance. Sperm that swim so fast they'd make Michael Phelps blush.

I asked the doctor to check again but I knew as soon as I saw his furrowed brow that it was a stupid comment. However, I remained undeterred in my pathetic ignorance. Getting more desperate by the second and feeling everyone's eyes on me, I tossed up a Hail Mary.

"Can I have another shot? I actually don't think I really got all of it last time because I was distracted. Just one more chance and I think I can get you a better batch!" That was just about the moment I really heard the words coming out of my mouth and decided to take a time-out. But that was the official beginning of my infertility journey and the start of our path down IVF (In Vitro Fertilization) Avenue. Unfortunately, it was also the onset of one of my deeper depressive episodes due to the knee-buckling level of guilt I had just been saddled with knowing my sperm were to blame for our predicament.

As MJ pointed out earlier, doctors might have brilliant medical minds but their bedside manner can be garbage. Case in point, the droll gentleman who gave me my diagnosis could have been a little more understanding. I get that they deal with this stuff day in and day out and they need to move quickly, but this is deeply personal and stunning news to hear if you're on the wrong end of it. So it doesn't matter how many times you've broken bad news to patients, because it's likely always the first time they're hearing it and they're dealing with the flood of accompanying emotions. That's why it's incumbent upon doctors to avoid sounding like condescending turds while making you feel even less significant than you already do.

I remember how the news was broken to me very clearly.

"Well, basically, the shape of your sperm is a little off and they're confused. Instead of swimming to the goal, which is the egg, they're off running around in circles some place they're not supposed to be. So all we're going to do is make sure the best ones are in the right place at the right time."

Golly gee, Captain Kangaroo. Thank you for that wonderful explanation. Now, I know I didn't go to medical school, but I'm sure even my feeble, state-college-educated mind could've handled a slightly more comprehensive explanation. But hey, at least this way I was not only talked down to but the very essence of my manhood was insulted. I remember picturing my bamboozled, knuckleheaded sperm personifying the Three Stooges. Moe, Larry, and Curly absentmindedly smacking each other around over in the corner like a bunch of drunken frat boys.

But on an even deeper level, I felt shame because I wasn't pulling my weight.

Women have to do everything during pregnancy. It's her egg inside her body which completely morphs like the coolest Transformer ever in order to accommodate and shelter new life for nine months. The morning sickness, the cramps, the cravings, the mood swings—all of it is on the woman. My only job, the only role I have to play, is to literally plant the seed. But after hearing that news it was clear I couldn't even get that right.

Unfortunately, with the passage of a little time came the all-too-familiar anger. I was seething by the time I got to the car, wallowing in an unctuous coating of sadness, shame, self-pity, and fury. MJ, on the other hand, was actually in a great mood because she's a very Type-A, black-and-white person. To her, this wasn't a problem, it was a solution. We had found the issue which allowed us to come up with a plan of attack so, in her mind, it was time to breathe easy and be thankful. But seeing how pissed off I was rubbed off on her and because I refused to open up and she couldn't see where I was coming from, we were two pissed off people trapped in a car together getting angrier by the second.

That's when I decided to ask her if Will, our then-four-and-a-half-year-old son, was actually mine.

There are lots of things you shouldn't say to your wife. "Are you actually going to wear that?" "Have you put on weight?" "You sound just like your mother." I only wish I had asked any of those questions instead of the one I actually asked. But as a "go big or go home" personality, I decided to vault myself right to the top of Asshole Mountain by essentially asking my wife if she had cheated on me, gotten pregnant with another man's baby, and then lied to me about it for nearly five years.

Luckily for me, some part of her realized the nastiness I was projecting was coming from a place of deep hurt. Which, I assume, is why I'm still alive to tell this tale.

But that awful comment wasn't even what had her really upset. She told me what truly hurt her the most was that I would've been fine as long as she was the problem. Being "defective" (which is how I began referring to myself) was fine and forgivable if the problem was on her end, as long as I was fine and dandy. She asked me if I'd judge her negatively or hold it against her if she was having problems physically, and I said of course not. She asked if I'd still try to comfort and console her so that she'd keep going down this road to complete our family. Again, I nodded my head. So why then, she asked, could I not let her console me? Why couldn't I allow her to help ease my pain? Why was it okay for me to suddenly be talking about not giving Will a sibling simply because my feelings were hurt?

I didn't have an answer. All I knew was I was in searing pain but the only thing that seemed like it would hurt more was to admit how much it hurt and try to get some help. The only thing I could manage at that point in time was to assure her I wouldn't stand in the way of starting IVF, but little did I know that would be a whole other process.

Jeremy understands IVF all too well. The forty-six-year-old from Connecticut went through years of infertility treatments with his ex-girlfriend in the late 1990s. Between her advanced maternal age (she was forty at the time) and his male infertility—"I have plenty of swimmers but the pond is shallow"—they were having a hard time fulfilling their dream of expanding their family. His wife was fifteen years older than he was and already had a daughter, but Jeremy said he wanted a biological child of his own to "be there from their very first breath and see myself in their face."

Despite his friends trying to cheer him up at the outset of their IVF journey by telling him making babies is the fun part, Jeremy said he quickly found out that was far from the truth.

"Sex became a chore that slowly but surely sucked all the life out of it. I showed up at UCONN (the University of Connecticut) once a month and jerked off into a little cup. I had sex when I was told to, which wasn't often because I was saving up my sperm for my doctor visits, and tried not to whack off too much in between. I felt like the fun had been taken out of things but I did what I thought I was supposed to do."

After a year of unsuccessfully trying, both their hopes for a child, along with the relationship, came to an end. Jeremy's story is unfortunately not uncommon, and most people who have been through IVF have similar battle stories to recount. I know I do.

First of all, the mere process of sperm extraction for me was an absolute nightmare. Yes, a nightmare of my own making, but still a nightmare nonetheless. Mainly because the first time I stepped into that daunting, sterile, cold room I knew pretty much right then and there that I wasn't going to, ahem, rise to the occasion. They pointed me toward an outdated collection of adult materials that didn't so much induce excitement as it did pitiful laughter at the absurdity of it all, and after about fifteen minutes of hemming and hawing I packed it up and told them this wasn't going to work. For me, the thought of walking into that strange building and entering a room for the express purpose of depositing my future children into a cup was unacceptable. Mainly because all I could think about was the inordinate number of guys who came (pun very much intended) before me.

The doctors and nurses tried to impart the importance of doing the samples at the office, but I just wasn't having it. The compromise was to extract the sample at home, but they'd mail me a list of instructions for the big day. I remember laughing at the thought of instructions being mailed to me to get me to masturbate. I mean, instructions? For this? I may not know how to put together IKEA furniture or fix a car engine, but if there's anything I can figure out on my own, it's this. Yet when I opened the envelope, I was met with a list of requirements I had to follow to the letter.

I could only use the sterilized container provided (as if I were going to use MJ's Tupperware). My name and date of birth had to be written on the cup. I had to absolutely and unequivocally bring photo identification when dropping off the sample (I don't even need ID to vote). But most importantly, I had to have the sample delivered to the lab within one hour of collection without exposing it to excessive light and keeping it at body temperature the entire time.

The office was forty minutes from our house without traffic. That meant I had to jerk off into the cup and immediately drive to drop it off. My oldest son Will was four years old at the time and anyone with a four-year-old will tell you privacy is not something kids that age value. Hearing him shouting, "Dada, what you doing?" from downstairs while I tried to coax his future little brother or sister out was not the ideal situation. Then, when I finally did manage to complete the task at hand, Will desperately wanted to know what was in the paper bag as he tried to repeatedly grab at it.

But then came the car ride.

The instructions specifically said I had to keep the sample at body temperature. But it was hot that day and Will needed the AC on in the car, so I had to come up with something. And that's why I spent the forty-five-minute ride to the doctor's office sitting on a bottle of my own spunk and keeping it warm like a giant Emperor Penguin. How's that for a visual? Sweet dreams.

But as bad as I thought I had it, MJ had it worse.

You see, I'm deathly afraid of needles. My kids handle their vaccinations better than I can deal with a flu shot, so I cringed when I found out MJ would have to take two months' worth of subcutaneous and intramuscular shots. As the doctor described how she'd have to stick herself in the belly I tried not to retch, but it was the shots she'd need to take in her butt that stopped me dead in my tracks.

"You'll have to give her those," the doctor said to me.

I went wide-eyed and thought about running from the room. Me? Give shots? I was physically ill as I tried to explain to the doctor my debilitating fear of needles along with the litany of reasons I couldn't possibly perform this endeavor. But when MJ stared me down and reminded me that she was the one putting her body through hell and she was the one who'd have to be repeatedly jabbed with sharp objects and she was the one whose body chemistry would be changed by the copious amounts of medication that came with this process, I shut my mouth. I was making it all about me when she was the one who'd be doing all the heavy lifting. But still, I had no idea how I'd ever be able to stick anyone with a needle.

The first few attempts, well, they weren't so good. But eventually I got the hang of it and so began our daily routine of me sticking my wife with sharp objects.

All of it led up to a five-day stretch in November 2012 when the doctors extracted eggs. All I really remember when it came to eggs was the more the better. The more healthy eggs that can be retrieved the better the chances of fertilizing them and successfully implanting my not-so-great swimmers in them, and then putting them back in MJ's proverbial oven to bake for nine months.

After the retrieval, we were sitting in the recovery room with two other women—all of us separated by curtains. The doctor spoke to both women before she got to us, and we could hear everything. The first woman was told she had retrieved fourteen eggs, which seemed to please her although she wasn't thrilled. A few minutes later, the doc told the other woman she retrieved six eggs—news that caused her to start crying hysterically, apparently because that number was way too low. Judging by these two interactions, I figured any number higher than six eggs at the lowest end would be a good thing.

But when it was our turn with the doctor, we discovered we had three eggs. Just three. And when we went back in five days later, the news got even worse.

The doctors were technically able to fertilize two of the eggs, but in reality only one embryo was viable. They implanted both, but basically gave us a snowball's chance in hell of the second one taking. So after all those shots, all the pain, and all the time devoted to expanding our family, it amounted to a single chance of a successful pregnancy. Even the doctors called the whole thing "not exactly ideal."

While I silently raged at the woman crying over six eggs, I tried to take solace in the fact that, at that moment, we were pregnant again. At least for the time being.

With our spirits low and nothing to do but wait a few weeks to see if the pregnancy was "sticky," I was pretty down. As negative and pessimistic as I can be, I'm actually the glass-half-full person in my marriage. But even though I kept reassuring MJ that everything was okay, well—fortune hadn't exactly favored us the last few years in this department. Still, I soldiered on believing the universe had to owe us one.

And then suddenly it seemed it was happening all over again.

I was at the gym about to hop on the treadmill when I looked at my phone and saw four missed calls from MJ in a three-minute span. Then the phone rang again. When I heard the pain and anguish in her screams my heart sank and my knees gave out. I couldn't make out everything that was said, but I heard "spotting" and "clot" clear enough. I bolted out of the gym trying to calm her down, all the while feeling hope disappear over the horizon once again.

Walking into a doctor's office for that final ultrasound and diagnosis is hell—especially for repeat visitors. At that point we had been through the wringer so many times and knew the drill, so we had pretty much resigned ourselves to our fate. We walked, teary-eyed, to the exam room and held hands. Nothing more could be said or done. I gave her a look that told her I love her more than life itself, and that everything would be okay. We have a beautiful, healthy son. And that's a lot more than some other people have. But I also told her I was proud of her. After you've been hurt that many times, it's excruciatingly painful to even put yourself on the line again for more disappointment. All those times we had to tell our friends and family we lost another baby.

All the empty cribs that had to be disassembled and baby clothes that had to be stuffed back in the drawer. Trying to be happy for all the other people you love in your life who have kids, when a part of you just wants to curl up and cry because you can't have that kind of happiness one more time. And, for me, the pain and guilt of knowing it's all my fault because my boys aren't great swimmers.

Amazingly, the spotting she'd experienced turned out to be normal and we were told everything was indeed okay. That baby, our one-in-a-million shot, turned out to be our middle son, Sam. But the road to that point was so horribly stressful and fraught with disaster that I wondered how people could possibly do multiple rounds, over and over again, without being completely and totally demoralized.

David doesn't have to wonder. He and his wife, Penelope, spent a grand total of six years and untold thousands of dollars going through IVF treatments that all seemed to end with miscarriage. Their problem wasn't getting pregnant, but staying pregnant, and the treatments plus all the losses (they both stopped counting when they got to double digits) led to some hellish times that they were able to get through because of their open communication style and sense of humor.

"It started out as 'we're going to get through this' but with year after year of losses it absolutely does turn defeatist. At the end we were still doing the treatments because hey, we had come this far, but even though neither of us voiced it we both just assumed it wouldn't work. It felt like we were just lining up for more punishment."

The couple's plan was to have one biological child and then adopt a second son or daughter. However, as the rounds of IVF piled on top of one another without success, David said they began to consider the possibility of a biological child a lost cause. So they finished up the final IVF procedure and, before even finding out the results, decided they were going to send a "fuck you" to the universe by putting the necessary money down to start the ball rolling on adopting a child.

"The phrase 'writing a check to the adoption agency' became our way of saying that we're going to do something no matter what. And that was exactly our message—that we were showing the universe we're having a kid despite all the roadblocks and obstacles."

Two days after writing the check, they were pregnant with their now twelve-year-old twin boys.

These are not isolated incidents, it's just that very few people are talking about male infertility—an issue referred to by some as a severely unacknowledged problem. A comprehensive study published in 2017 from the Hebrew University of Jerusalem found that sperm count among men in North America, Europe, and Australia declined more than 50 percent between 1973 and 2011.[1] The report states, "These findings strongly suggest a significant decline in male reproductive health that has serious implications beyond fertility and reproduction, given recent evidence linking poor semen quality with higher risk of hospitalization and death. Research on causes of this ongoing decline and their prevention is urgently needed." If you're not only alarmed by those findings but also bewildered as to how you didn't know about a public health crisis that affects this many men, you're not alone. It's just one of those things that simply isn't discussed, and men are suffering in silence because of the silence.

---

1 Hagai Levine, Niels Jørgensen, Anderson Martino-Andrade, Jaime Mendiola, Dan Weksler-Derri, Irina Mindlis, Rachel Pinotti, Shanna H Swan. "Temporal trends in sperm count: A systematic review and meta-regression analysis." *Human Reproduction Update*, July 25, 2017, doi:10.1093/humupd/dmx022. Link: https://academic.oup.com/DocumentLibrary/humupd/PR/dmx022_final.pdf.

Yet even when you find out this is an international problem, it feels like the universe purposely screws with you by sitting you next to pregnant women at restaurants or forcing you to be around families with young babies.

I can't sit here and tell men who are struggling with infertility that it's not difficult. It is. Hell, simply going to the doctor in the first place is a gargantuan obstacle for a lot of guys. This was something I refused to do for far too long, all because I was scared they'd actually find something wrong. And if that diagnosis does come, you're going to feel a ton of emotions that won't all make sense to you. Even worse, you might be thoroughly ashamed of them. But it is essential that you sit with these feelings, discuss them with your partner, and work through them. Is it going to be an ugly slog? Most likely. But it's vital that men know they are far from alone, and that starts with entrusting all those feelings of anger, inadequacy, and guilt with your partner so they know where you're coming from. And if not your partner then a friend, relative, counselor, priest—just talk to someone you trust who can serve as a sounding board. It's normal to feel emasculated when someone tells you your sperm doesn't work correctly. It's okay to be confused about how to act and what to feel. It's fairly standard to be so mad at the world you want to scream. But it's not okay to bottle that all up, stuff it down, and never deal with it in a healthy way, because it will have disastrous consequences of the mental health and relationship variety.

Remember that in the absence of actual discussion of your feelings with your partner, human beings will fill that void with the worst-case scenario every single time.

\* \* \*

*Any type of infertility is hard to deal with, whether you're a man or a woman.*

*Aaron was not in a good place during the journey to have our second baby. He would have been better able to handle it if it were me and not him having the infertility issue. He writes from a place of experience and how it should have been handled, looking back. He writes knowing the "man-up culture" hurts everyone and not just the men, but what he cannot fully grasp is how it hurts their partners as well.*

*How do you help someone who just received a negative diagnosis? Give them some space to grieve, be supportive and understanding, and be there for them if or when they do want to talk. After all, it is a blow to their "manhood," according to our culture. And while I know that's a bunch of crap, society puts pressure on these men to be providers, to bring forth children, and to be protectors. Just like I, as a woman, feel societal pressure to be thin and the perfect mother, men are under the gun in other ways. I gave Aaron time and space to grieve about his loss, but I also called him out when he was not being nice and when I thought he wanted to give up. It's not an easy balancing act.*

*Most importantly, they need to be helped through this, not blamed. I know that sounds easy, but going through infertility is like being in a pressure cooker and you start to think some thoughts you might not ordinarily have. At the end of the day, you love this person and want a family with them, so blaming them will only make them talk less, be less likely to seek help, and blame themselves when, in reality, most men have blamed themselves enough. Blame can eat away at your relationship. It will be difficult because most men don't like to be open with their feelings, but keep communicating with them, talk, touch, and reassure them that you are not holding them responsible.*

*Giving someone the room to grieve can be hard. When we see our loved one in pain we want to help, but sometimes the only way to help is to not say a word and just be there for them. Aaron did not want to talk when we found out he was suffering from infertility. He kept his emotions to himself and I watched him turn from an outgoing person to someone who beat himself up daily over our struggles. But while I gave him space, eventually there comes a time when action is needed.*

*People can say horrible things when grieving—Aaron was no exception. When he asked if our oldest was truly his, I tried not to take offense but that one hurt me. I learned quickly he was looking for an outlet for his feelings, but there are healthy outlets and there are truly problematic ones. As partners, we want to guide them to a healthy outlet. They are also trying to work on getting past the grief. They are grieving the loss of potential children, their relationship, and possibly their self-worth. Especially the last one. Our culture is tied into their manhood and their manhood often consists of having children. Offer to talk through it with them, offer to see someone, or talk to a trusted friend. The trick is you can't let it get to a point where you're an emotional punching bag because nothing good comes of that and it's completely unacceptable for men to believe women are there simply as props for their journey or emotional pincushions. It's the world's crappiest tightrope but it's important to keep moving forward.*

*Infertility is a roller coaster of emotions. One minute you think you can handle it and the next you think your chance of becoming a parent is never going to happen. When I could not get pregnant in 2012, I thought for sure it was me. Why wouldn't it be me? I had always been on the sicker side of things with thyroid issues, Crohn's, allergies, ADHD, etc. On top of everything else, I'd made the choice to have an abortion. I felt I was being punished for it—like karma finally coming back around to make me pay up. I had no idea at the time how common it is and that lots of people go through it but no one talks about it.*

*I found it a relief when we discovered the problem was with Aaron, but that relief was only because we finally had answers to so many questions we'd had for the last year. But he was devastated. I could not figure out why he was so unhappy with the diagnosis as we left the doctor's office, and the truth didn't come out until he started lashing out at me. He was mad that it was him and not me. I remember feeling so betrayed that it was easier for him to accept the infertility if it was me, which I thought was petty and ugly.*

*The journey of IVF is not for the faint of heart. It was shots, money, and talking to people about the most intimate things in our relationship. I wasn't sure about it at first, but eventually came around. Aaron, on the other hand, was not truly on board. I remember calling him at work and making sure he wanted to do this because we needed to put the money up for the medication for the IVF. I remember him going back and forth on the decision about it. He finally agreed to it, but it broke my heart to have a partner who was not 100 percent committed to it. He eventually came around on the whole process but it took us many months to come to terms with everything.*

*It was even more difficult when it came time to have our third baby because he definitely was not on board going through the process again. Once again, I felt heartbroken and alone. While he reluctantly became part of the conversation, his first reaction was not acceptance and even though he ultimately agreed to it his heart wasn't in it and he wasn't fully communicating his feelings. It's difficult to talk to someone who does not feel the same way you* do about expanding your family, and you know that it will turn into a fight. I hate conflict, and try to avoid it if at all possible.

Turns out he was just scared, as was I. Scared the shots wouldn't work, scared the embryos wouldn't take, how it could easily be all for nothing and end in another unbearable miscarriage, and how was I going to handle all the IVF with a preschooler.

It sounds cliché, but hope and joy got me through at that point in time. Women can't "fix" a man, so at a certain point, I no longer worried about how Aaron was feeling because he wouldn't talk to me and I was determined to get myself in the right headspace to have our second baby. I was happy to take on everything like giving myself the shots and driving an hour each way for blood work whenever they asked for it. All the while, Aaron was not even talking about the idea of a second baby. Not only that, he actually refused to give me shots at first. I felt absolutely alone. I was lucky to have family support me through this process but while my husband was physically present, emotionally he was a million miles away.

When it came time for the extraction, we got three viable eggs—this was not acceptable to me. I wanted a dozen eggs and I wanted them all to be healthy. I was shattered emotionally, but of course in Aaron style he told me it would be okay and that we only needed one to take. Even though he was citing statistics and making sense, I had never been so mad at him because, in my mind, he was repeating things the doctors were saying which meant he wasn't on my side. He wasn't feeling my hurt because he wasn't as invested. Then came the call from the doctor saying only two fertilized. I was still pissed there were only two but I was relieved we were at least pregnant for the time being. In typical male fashion, Aaron decided that was the moment to say "I told you so," which just made me more upset and resent him even more.

*While we waited with fingers crossed, I found it incredibly difficult to balance a preschooler, Aaron's emotional well-being, and my own self-care. On top of all the things going on, some people just weren't kind in what they would say to me. Someone told me to give up, others told me the child we already had was enough and to not even try for more, and others would give me statistics about how it would not be successful because of my age and history. I was lucky to have a close group of friends and family who supported me through the process and thought it was worth it, but I was still appalled at what others thought they had the right to say to me.*

*Our oldest was my biggest cheerleader. He asked all the right questions, gave me space if I needed it, and was always helpful when it came to giving the shots (he never touched them, just watched as a spectator). Aaron and I made sure he was informed with age-appropriate information. Even the most mild-mannered and well-meaning child has his moments, after all he was four years old. It was hard balancing my mental health with everyone in the house. Going through shots for IVF does not make you the picture of mental stability. I had mood swings all the time and spent most days in the house so as to not bother anyone with my unbalanced hormones.*

*It's not easy balancing everything while going through this journey. But as we hit all our milestones, Aaron started to get invested in the pregnancy and cautiously excited. Eventually he told me he was really, really scared and I said, "Of course you are, but I am too and I feel like I've been doing this all by myself!" He was very apologetic and we had a long conversation about how he was afraid to let himself care too much about the baby before it was a done deal. Also, how he felt like less of a man because resorting to IVF meant he wasn't able to perform his manly duties, and all of that was impacting his self-confidence. I didn't like or understand everything he was saying but it was a huge relief that at least I knew where he was coming from and that he did actually care and want this.*

*Guys, I can't stress this enough—you have to get over this macho crap. Sometimes you don't even realize it's hurting you but it definitely is. And it's hurting your partners and your family as well. No human being is better off alone and isolated. No one should have to suffer in silence and solely take on the weight of the world. That makes zero sense and if you roll your eyes at terms like toxic masculinity then you're going to be in trouble because it's virtually impossible to fix a problem you refuse to see. Infertility is too emotionally draining a process to put up with extraneous nonsense.*

# Chapter 5

## *Dealing With and Moving Beyond Abortion*

THERE ARE FEW ISSUES MORE EMOTIONALLY CHARGED AND controversial than abortion. It spans politics, religion, sex, toxic masculinity (men trying to legislate women's bodies), women's rights, and it has even resulted in deadly violence on multiple occasions by anti-choice religious extremists. Because of this extra "baggage" abortion brings with it, it can often be that much harder to deal with when you're personally going through it.

And when you're a journalist and a blogger who puts his life on display for the world to see, it can get even more complex.

MJ had two miscarriages before our first son was born, but as the spring of 2010 drew near, we finally had a stroke of luck as MJ not only got pregnant but stayed pregnant past that all-important 12-week mark. Unlike with the three past pregnancies, we didn't tell anyone this time around because miscarriage makes you gun-shy. Shortly before my son was born in 2008, I started a parenting website called The Daddy Files, in which I (terribly) chronicled the life and times of a new father. Although

41

my early writing was cringeworthy and atrocious in hindsight, it was a handy resource for me to return to while writing this book because I could go back and see exactly what I was feeling at the time.

We found out MJ was pregnant in April of that year yet I completely forgot about it at least a couple of times during that next three months. I know it sounds horrible but I had been so mentally scarred by the previous miscarriages that my brain refused to recognize her pregnancy as some sort of weird defense mechanism. Because even though I would never have told MJ at the time, I was convinced that pregnancy wasn't going to get to the 3-month mark so I was trying to protect myself by not getting my hopes up. Is it a wise idea, when your wife wants to talk about planning and hopes and dreams, to say "about what?" No. No it is not. She had it out with me one day because I suggested we go to the bar and cut loose a little and I couldn't understand why she was just glaring at me like I was the biggest idiot in the world. To her (rightfully so), it seemed I wasn't taking the pregnancy seriously and was having second thoughts about having another baby, but in reality I was just scared and trying not to set myself up for disappointment. There was an HBO documentary about twenty years ago called *Band of Brothers*, all about World War II paratroopers and how they survived the war. I distinctly remember one of the characters saying the only way to survive and maintain the bravery and fortitude to fight in battle after battle is to convince yourself you're already dead. Sadly, that was my mindset—to pretend there was no baby because we had already lost it. I thought about the two previous times we got excited, told friends and family, and started throwing around baby names only to have to tell everyone bad news a few weeks later. It's exhausting and terrifying and I wanted to avoid our hearts being smashed into a million pieces again.

But yes, it would've helped if I had let her in on that. Here's what I wrote back then:

> MJ is thirteen weeks pregnant and we had an ultrasound and blood work today to look for any genetic abnormalities. My heart raced as the ultrasound tech put the jelly on MJ's stomach and prepared for a look-see. I told myself not to be surprised when there was no movement, no heartbeat. I readied myself for MJ's breakdown. For the disappointment that would haunt us for months. For the mourning of what should have been. But there was our baby, complete with a flashing heartbeat. Holy shit. The head, the little hands, the feet, and a perfectly healthy beating heart. All there. Moving around, looking like a creepy little holographic alien. Or in other words, everything is normal. And that's when I realized this baby is a go. A green light. It's on! I know it's still possible that things could go wrong, but at this point the doctors said we're largely out of the woods as far as miscarriages go. Which means I can concentrate on this baby and all the wonderful things in store for us. I'm really, really excited. And although we're not finding out if we're having a boy or a girl, this kid was incredibly stubborn and refused to move for the ultrasound tech. Specifically, the kid would not—under any circumstances—spread his/her legs.

I'm not sure I was overjoyed as much as I was relieved. It felt like the world's biggest weight had been lifted off my chest and I could breathe again. Looking at MJ, who had put up with my dour and detached personality the last three months, I was in tears as I picked her up and spun her around in a bear hug, all smiles. We skipped out of that office in celebration and immediately told all of our friends and relatives the good news, in addition to posting it on my website. I even remember making a stupid and crass attempt at humor about the baby not spreading its legs.

Less than twenty-four hours later I was not laughing.

No sooner had I pressed publish on my blog post announcing the pregnancy than we received a call from our radiologist's office asking us to come in as soon as possible for another appointment out of concern for the issue with the legs. They told us not to worry and not to jump to any conclusions, and that follow-ups were fairly common just to rule things out and take a closer look. But the quickest way to get people to worry is to tell them not to worry.

MJ was very freaked out and already in tears, and I wasn't close behind. I had been prepared (well, as ready as anyone can truly be) for this bad news just twenty-four hours ago, but I lowered all my defenses when they sent us out of that office with a clean bill of health. Feeling the familiar tentacles of fear reach out for you after you thought you vanquished the monster is terrifying beyond belief. Suddenly I was right back in that dark place with the worst thoughts, but now with the added shame of having stupidly and gullibly let my guard down when I knew better. I told myself this was all my fault and I would never forgive myself if the worst actually happened.

I was working as a journalist at the time so the way I snapped out of my panic vortex was to immediately start to research— which was, coincidentally, one of the things the woman from the radiologist's office had warned us not to do. I used to make fun of those people who flocked to WebMD to self-diagnose their health issues, yet suddenly I was one in full force. While it gave me a sense of control in that I felt like I was preparing for whatever might be ahead, there's also no doubt I was simultaneously terrifying myself. Soon I was neck-deep in articles about Down Syndrome, Cerebral Palsy, and Cystic Fibrosis. I also came across a few articles on something called Sirenomelia (a.k.a. "Mermaid Syndrome"), which is a rare congenital deformity in which the baby's legs are fused together, but I didn't worry so much about that one as the odds of encountering it are 1 in 100,000.

Our visit to the radiologist's office the next day was among the worst days of my life.

I don't pray, but I hoped like hell the first thing we'd see was that kid spread eagle. MJ could barely keep it together but admitted to me she was expecting the worst. I tried to do what a friend had suggested and unleash the power of positive thinking to the point I had it all planned out in my head. The tech would smile and reassure us, showing us the baby's legs were separate and flailing away. MJ would shed small tears of relief and I would say "See? Told ya so!"

But, it didn't work out that way.

When the fuzzy image came into focus, it looked exactly the same as it did the last time. MJ asked if the legs were separated but even I could see the answer to that. And when she saw, she lost it. I gripped her hand as tight as I could and told her it doesn't mean anything yet. After all, this was only the ultrasound tech. We hadn't even seen the doctor yet. He would take a look and find that everything was okay. I refused to shed a tear and I convinced myself the doctor would come through for us. I was going to will this baby into acceptable condition. I clung to that.

The doctor came into the most tense room imaginable and immediately started asking MJ a barrage of questions about her health history. It became abundantly clear that while this guy might be an expert in examining ultrasounds, some etiquette and sensitivity classes would've also been a worthwhile investment. With deft skill but horrible manners, he viewed the baby from every possible angle as MJ and I struggled to keep our shit together. Then he stopped and looked at us.

"The fact that the legs do not separate and won't move is highly unusual. It leads me to believe there is some kind of lower extremity defect."

Hell is sitting next to the person you love most in this world and listening to her wail hysterically because her heart just broke into a million pieces. Hell is watching her entire body convulse with sobs as she screams because she's being tortured with grief. For as long as I live and no matter how many children we have, I will never forget that sound. Ever. I tried to hug her, to hold her hand, to console her in any way I could. But she just pushed me away and screamed at me to leave her alone. In that instant I was completely powerless. My baby was sick and there was nothing I could do. Nothing. I couldn't even hold the baby to comfort it. My wife was making sounds like a wounded animal who wouldn't even let me near her and I couldn't make her feel better no matter what. The pain of two miscarriages, the flood of hope, and then the onslaught of unimaginable pain just when we thought we were free. That feeling of helplessness is paralyzing and it will rock you to your core.

To make matters worse, our doctor told us that while he clearly saw a problem, it was too early in the pregnancy to pinpoint the exact cause. That meant there was nothing else for us to do for the next month other than let the pregnancy progress despite knowing something was severely wrong, and then go to specialists in Boston to get an official diagnosis. A month. Four weeks of just waiting around filled to the brim with anxiety and dread to hear the extent of what's wrong with our baby.

Speaking of our baby, MJ ran out of the office at that point because all she wanted was Will. To hold him, comfort him, and presumably exert some level of control in a situation where we had none. So somehow I found my legs and used them to walk her to the car, drive her home, and then go to my aunt's house to pick Will up. I settled her in and told her I'd be right back with Will, went outside to the car, and started driving. I managed to get around the corner to where I knew she couldn't see me, and then I lost it.

I pulled the car over to the side of the quiet back road I was on, put it in park, got out on the side of the road and fell to my knees to have what I can only assume was a full-blown panic attack. I was wailing and then sobbing so hard I couldn't catch my breath to the point I was seeing black at the edges of my vision. I didn't care who saw me or how I looked. I didn't care about anything other than potentially losing our baby. That feeling of unadulterated, wild desperation is unlike anything I've ever felt and it scared the living hell out of me. For what seemed like a damn eternity but was probably only a few minutes, I punched the earth and kicked the car and had a full-on breakdown the likes of which I hope to never again feel. And, referring back to the chapter on toxic masculinity, I purposely did it out of sight of my wife because it seemed even more shameful to let her into my sad, terrified world.

I honestly don't remember what the next month was like. Will kept us relatively sane because despite how much pain we were in, we had a child who needed our love and attention. So MJ went to work, I went to work, and we cared for Will. I don't recall much discussion about the baby during that month because we both knew it was over. Whatever the diagnosis ended up being, we knew it was not going to end with us having another baby. We just wanted the nightmare to end so we could try again. Or maybe not try again. Neither of us could think through the pain.

When we went to world-renowned Brigham & Women's Hospital in Boston, we got our diagnosis. It was, in fact, Sirenomelia and our case was "not one that is compatible with life." In addition to the problem with the legs, our baby had no kidneys, no bladder, and no anus. A handful of babies with Sirenomelia do survive and one managed to live to twenty-seven years, but the doctors said our baby was already dying and there was zero chance of making it to birth. So, armed with that information, we were given a choice. MJ's life was not in imminent danger so this wasn't considered an emergency; however, they said it's obviously never optimal for the mother's health to have a dead or dying baby inside the womb. The next time they could get us into the hospital for a termination would be in two weeks, which would bring us to just shy of 19 weeks and doctors said there would be a fifty-fifty chance of being able to perform an abortion. If not, we'd be looking at a stillbirth. The second alternative was sending us to an affiliated clinic for an abortion in the next couple of days.

Those are not good choices. For us it was like choosing whether we wanted to drown or burn in a fire—either way the outcome was going to be the same. So, after a lot of discussion and soul-searching, MJ chose to have an abortion at the clinic because, at the end of the day, she just couldn't bear the thought of having a stillbirth, so she made the decision she felt was the most merciful. As a Catholic, that was an incredibly painful decision for her to make and I supported her 100 percent. But all the support in the world doesn't make it any easier.

We had to go to the clinic two days in a row. The first day consisted of cervical softening and dilating, performed with medication and small dilating sticks, called laminaria or Dilapan, that are placed in the cervix. Laminaria are thin sticks made from a special seaweed material that widen as they absorb moisture from the body. Dilapan are synthetic sticks that work in the same way. The laminaria stays in the cervix overnight and prepares your body for the next day's surgical procedure. The second day was for the actual surgical procedure to terminate the pregnancy. Things went fine the first day, although I noticed a couple of people on the sidewalk holding anti-choice signs. But they were about 40 feet away from the parking lot (I wasn't aware Massachusetts had a 35-foot buffer zone in front of clinic property at the time) and they weren't being disruptive so I didn't pay them much attention.

When we came back the next day, it was a different story.

This time, in addition to the people from the previous day, two older women had taken up residence across the street with large signs about Jesus and they were shouting across Harvard Street as loud as they could. "YOU'RE KILLING YOUR UNBORN BABY!" was the one we heard the most and the loudest, as I did my best to hustle MJ into the building. I was shaking with anger at those religious zealots who think shouting at perfect strangers in the name of God is an effective use of their time, because their words had gotten to MJ and she broke down once again into an inconsolable mess. I barely had time to calm her down before her name was called and she was whisked away alone (partners weren't allowed) into surgery. But before she left, I gave her a wordless look as I motioned out the window with my arms shrugged that silently pleaded *Can I go confront those*

49

*monsters outside?* She had the faintest hint of a smile and simply nodded, before we kissed goodbye with tears in our eyes.

Maybe she knew it or maybe not, but it was that exact moment that MJ found a way to help me pick myself up and start walking out of the darkness of depression.

I turned on my cell phone camera and crossed the street to peacefully but sternly confront the people who had shattered our world on one of the worst days of our lives. As a newspaper reporter, I knew my rights and what I could and couldn't do, and as I stood on a public sidewalk at a safe distance from them asking them questions they had no salient answers to, I began to feel better. I was angry, for sure, but I was also filled with a sudden sense of purpose for the first time in a long time. It was like that first sip of water after you've been in the sun all day and forgot to drink anything. As I let them know exactly what I thought of them and their "Christian" ways, I thought about how good it would feel to show the recording to MJ so she'd feel better.

I went for a walk to clear my head and when I got back to pick MJ up, there was a patrol car and the protesters were gone. MJ, still groggy from surgery, smiled and said, "What'd you do?" I showed her the video and she started crying again, but this time it was because she was grateful I had stood up to them for her. For us. And then, much to my surprise since MJ is an extremely private person who doesn't understand my need to chronicle everything on social media, she said, "This makes me feel so much better, and I think it will make other women who have been through it feel better too."

She was telling me to tell our story, so I did.

I had been a journalist for more than six years at that point so I was used to my byline being noticed and occasionally I'd get invited on television to talk about the news. But none of that could've prepared me for what happened after I published my encounter with the anti-choice protesters. It was the very first time I went viral and suddenly our story was everywhere. Salon, Jezebel, The Young Turks, Gawker, Slate, Alternet (remember, this was 2010), and more than one million views on YouTube. Neither MJ nor I were prepared for the overwhelming nature of that kind of attention and, as you can imagine, there were nay-sayers out there. Cruel, callous, religious anti-choice extremists who called us murderers and killers and told us we were going to hell. Some truly nasty stuff that made me think perhaps this wasn't the best of ideas.

But then I got the first of what would be hundreds of online comments and emails from women all over the country who not only lent us their full support during a tough time, but thanked us for standing up to bullies and for sharing our story. The comment was "From all of the women who had to walk through a line of protesters alone on one of the hardest days of their lives, thank you." Suddenly everything was worth it. With each new comment and email from people baring their souls and wishing they had had someone with them that day to stand up to vile behavior, I felt a sense of purpose and peace that helped me get back on track. In a flash I could see a path forward via helping others and using what little platform I had developed to be an advocate for people who, for whatever reason, couldn't advocate for themselves at the time. Although we still had a long road ahead, helping others helped me get my life back and it just might have saved my marriage, because it wasn't too long after the events of that summer that I got up the guts to see a counselor for the very first time in my life.

But abortion is such an emotional and far-reaching issue it can negatively impact people just by being adjacent to it.

Zachary (name changed upon request), forty-six, is originally from the United Kingdom but has spent years living in Brazil. In 2014, he and his wife found out they were unexpectedly pregnant with their second child but received bad news at the 3-month mark that the pregnancy was no longer intact. Zachary said his emotions were already complicated because he had never planned on having another child, but suddenly he was also dealing with a hospital visit for a D&C. A hospital that was "basically a maternity hospital" where their son had been born three years prior.

More to the point, this hospital was in Brazil where abortion is illegal in almost all circumstances. Although they weren't having an abortion, Zachary said the doctors and nurses treated them coldly and were highly suspicious that they had done something to end the pregnancy and skirt the abortion laws, which are punishable by jail time. He was already "shell shocked" at the pregnancy news and he didn't know how to help his wife, who wasn't getting the care she needed simply due to the suspicion of having aborted her baby.

Eventually a friend came in and took charge, demanding better care and ultimately getting it. But the entire ordeal was a "nightmare" that took years for the couple to move beyond.

"I was always pro-choice but this episode in our lives reinforced this view because by making abortion illegal you're also essentially making miscarriage illegal, as if that were really even possible. We weren't even having an abortion but no one should be treated like criminals by hospital staff at one of the lowest points of their lives."

If you're looking for a silver bullet solution to getting past abortion, it doesn't exist. The situation MJ and I went through is certainly unique and not everyone can or wants to solve this problem by becoming a national media story. But the point is, I needed to feel something besides the unique brand of pain and loss that accompanies abortion. I needed an outlet that would give me a way to describe what I was feeling combined with an opportunity to turn our terrible situation into something good. The biggest takeaway from this ordeal was that if you can't handle your own depression and properly care for your own well-being, it's virtually impossible to try to take care of someone else. I thought by focusing all of my attention on MJ I was being heroic, when, in actuality, I was being selfish and shortsighted. Deciding to find a way out of the hole I was in made me a better husband, father, and person and until I worked on myself there was no way I could be the kind of truly supportive partner my wife needed.

Abortion is a legal medical procedure and it's no one's business besides a woman, her partner if she chooses to include them, and doctors. The shame and guilt associated with it is nuanced and complex, so make sure you find help in the form of a counselor or therapist that is equally multifaceted. And guys, while women ultimately do and must remain in control of their own bodies to which you are not entitled a say, that doesn't mean this is an issue of which you can just wash your hands. The repercussions from abortion can and will impact you, not just her, and failure to deal with those issues will turn into a time bomb. Find an outlet that gives you the relief you need to work through it and make sure whatever plan you make involves your significant other.

\* \* \*

*"Damned if you do, damned if you don't."*

*This is the position I put Aaron in back in 2010, when we were pregnant with our second baby, who had an abnormality, and we were facing the prospect of an abortion or having a stillbirth. I desperately wanted his input on what we should do. Have the abortion? Deliver a stillborn? Which is more merciful? Which is most responsible and doesn't make me a horrible mother? Could I really risk my soul burning in hell if I chose abortion? I kept asking Aaron what he wanted me to do and all he kept saying was that he'd back my decision 100 percent no matter what I chose. Yet that infuriated me because I was so desperate for someone else to make the choice.*

*We hear all the time it is a woman's body so she makes the choice whether or not to have an abortion, but I wanted someone to give me the relief of not making the choice. I wanted Aaron to make it so I could take my sadness, anger, and frustration out on him and not myself. It is selfish to want to put someone in that situation, but I was tired of feeling the pain, sadness, and heartbreak of not being able to hold another baby. I was tired of feeling in general.*

*I would ask Aaron what he wanted to do and all he'd say was it's "my body and my choice," which is true and technically the answer we should all want to hear from men. But at the same time, I did not impregnate myself. It took two people to get to this point. All I wanted was for him to give me a glimpse into what he was feeling or thinking. I felt he was being cold and callous with me every time we spoke about the baby.*

*As I sat in the waiting room for the nurse to call my name, I felt so alone. I felt no one knew what I was going through. Aaron supported me wholeheartedly but ultimately he left the final decision up to me. Did I make the right choice? Should I have delivered a dead baby? Should I have kept the remains and not donated the baby to science so doctors might better understand this rare condition? There were so many questions that morning and I felt like they were all resting on my shoulders. I just wanted one choice not to be mine. It is further complicated by the fact that I was raised strictly Catholic and opting for an abortion goes against everything I was raised to believe.*

*I was taught that abortion is evil and hell is a very real place—not only for me but for my unborn child. I truly believed I would go to hell and that I would never be accepted back into the church. I felt even more alone in that regard because Aaron is an atheist who absolutely can't stand organized religion, so it was like I was taking all of the existential risk and he had nothing to lose. He never said that, of course, but he wouldn't say anything other than he was supportive of whatever I decided. Suddenly the unconditional support of my husband became frustrating and a bad thing, just in case you're wondering how upside-down things can get during times like this.*

*After the procedure, in the recovery room, I looked around and saw many women in the same position as me. As I glanced around the room it was the first time in six weeks I didn't feel so alone. I realized I was not the only one who had made the hardest choice of her life and there were women just like me who were navigating these uncharted waters too. I didn't know a single one of them but I wanted to pay back those women for making me feel less alone. I wanted to tell my story. I wanted to share with the world what I went through. It is extremely hard for me, considering I am a very private person, but I was suddenly filled with an overwhelming desire to make sure no one going for an abortion ever felt this alone again.*

*Yet I could not even hear the word "abortion," never mind say it myself. I made Aaron and my friends and family say "termination" or "procedure" or any other word except the one I still worried would send me to hell. I remember Aaron talking on the phone to a dear friend of ours when he didn't know I was around, and when he said abortion I immediately started screaming and crying. If I'm being perfectly honest, it's still tough for me to hear and say that word even eleven years later.*

*To say my Catholic faith did not play a role in my choice for an abortion would be a lie. I fought hard with my upbringing and the local church where I was raised. I thought for sure if I went through with the abortion I would go to hell and my baby would too. That I would be punished for the rest of my life. It took me looking back a few years later to realize I had made the right choice. It helped hearing personal stories from other women who had been down that path, as they gave me the strength to do the right thing and stand by my decision.*

*As I stated earlier, I felt so alone in my journey. From my husband to my family to my coworkers, everyone was supportive but none of them would dare offer advice because abortion is such a charged issue. I remember a male colleague taking the time to call me on the phone to tell me his story about his wife and himself. He described how it tore them up inside and I still can remember hearing the pain in his voice. All I remember is getting off the phone and crying. He was one of many people sharing their stories about abortion and pregnancy loss to help support me. My boss gave me two paid weeks off from work. One week to recover from the procedure and a week to recover emotionally. I was grateful but, at the same time, thinking I'd be fine after a week was pretty ridiculous. I vividly recall the day I got back to work a woman my age and my same due date came in with her belly on display and I lost my mind. I could not stop crying. Needless to say, my staff sent me home.*

*It's interesting how my staff and everyone in my close circle was fully supportive at every turn, yet I felt utterly alone. I'm eternally grateful I had the right to make my own choice but that doesn't change the fact that it is an incredibly lonely and terrifying thing to be the sole decider of something that, in my mind, could have everlasting repercussions.*

*For anyone in this situation, cut through all the clutter and choose what is right for you and your family. And after you make that choice, ask for help. My problem was I never asked for help and I constantly doubted whether or not I had made a huge mistake. I stopped seeing my therapist, stopped talking about the situation, and refused to acknowledge what was going on. I was too grief stricken to think straight. This doesn't sound very feminist of me but, at that moment, I needed Aaron to step up and tell me what to do. In situations like this one, right and wrong really gets thrown out the window. It's not fair to expect him to decide an issue the women in his life have always told him is their choice, but at the same time I needed more than "whatever you want." He thought he was doing the right thing by leaving it up to me, and I thought he was being callous and cold. We needed better communication and a real conversation, but it's all taking place in this surreal moment when you're losing your baby, you're paralyzed with fear, and no one knows what's the right and wrong thing.*

*To anyone facing a similar situation, talk it out. Seek outside help. And remember you are not alone. People have been through this before. Ask them for their advice. I wish I had not stopped seeing my therapist, I wish I had gone to the websites and online forums to talk about my feelings, and I wish we had immediately entered couples' therapy. We would have been able to talk out our feelings with a neutral party and gained a better perspective. Time eventually provided us with the insight we needed, but we were lucky our marriage stayed intact through all the chaos to get to that point.*

# Chapter 6

# *It's Not Your Fault,*
# *Skip the Blame Game*

ONE OF MY FAVORITE MOVIES OF ALL TIME IS *GOOD WILL Hunting*, starring Matt Damon and Robin Williams. Damon's character, a rough-around-the-edges boy genius out of South Boston, has a tortured past filled with physical and emotional abuse at the hands of foster parents. He is forced to see a counselor, played by Williams, by court order and spends months grudgingly working through unresolved issues. At the end of the movie, there's a powerful scene between the two where Williams tells Damon not to blame himself while embracing him until it pierces all the hurt and all the trauma, and Damon collapses into Williams's arms releasing all of the anger and guilt and shame he's internalized over the course of his life. As he holds Damon, he keeps repeating "It's not your fault, it's not your fault, it's not your fault." That always resonated with me and it's the first thing I think of when talking to men who all seem to at least partially blame themselves while harboring major guilt regarding their situations.

58

Nearly half—46 percent—of the men we surveyed said they felt guilty following a miscarriage, infertility, or pregnancy loss. The number of women who admitted feeling guilty was even higher, at 59 percent. The majority of people who spoke to us reported feeling like they had done something wrong in their lives and that what was happening to them represented punishment being doled out by God or Karma or the universe. They also believe they should've done something that would've avoided losing the pregnancy. Feeling targeted by unseen forces trying to punish you is normal and natural, especially for people who go through multiple losses and years of infertility while seemingly everyone around them has a million babies. But everyone in that boat needs to remember one thing.

It's not your fault.

As difficult as it is to believe when you're in the trenches, this is not something that's punitive. That's easy to say now, but I absolutely and unequivocally believed I was being punished somehow. So did MJ, who thought all the bad luck was due to the necessary abortion because she was going against her faith. For me, it was the fact that I got a girlfriend of mine in college pregnant and she ended up having an abortion, and I was convinced the miscarriages, and especially the Sirenomelia diagnosis, were some sort of payback. Or worse, that that pregnancy had been my shot at having a healthy baby and I blew it. Or perhaps because I had been such a misogynistic piece of crap in my younger days and now this was the price I had to pay. And the reason so many people think like this is often because of one sentence many of us going through this hear quite a bit during the journey.

"It's just bad luck."

Sometimes you know exactly why a miscarriage or loss took place, and that's hard. Really hard. But then there's the other end of the spectrum. The times when you have two seemingly healthy people trying to get pregnant and failing, or getting pregnant and losing the baby over and over and over again. So you go to the doctor and you see all the specialists and you keep asking why it's happening. Then, after all of that time and money and pain, you realize something awful—they don't know why. There might not even be a medical reason why. So they chalk it up to bad luck. Coincidence. Universal randomness subject to the whim of fickle fortune.

And even though it's not their fault, you just want to choke them for saying it. Because in the absence of a concrete medical explanation for what's occurring, our minds will fill in that blank with the darkest, most outlandish, logic-defying figments our imaginations can concoct.

David went to several doctors who all said his sperm was fine. All of his wife's tests said she was fine, too. The couple eventually called this process "kicking the tires" and compared it to bringing your car into the shop when it wasn't running quite right without a reason why. All of the specialists running all of those tests for all of those years and not a single one of them ever explained why they were losing so many pregnancies. It was enough to make David blame someone in whom he didn't even believe.

"You think there has to be some reason this is happening and there just isn't, so even though I'm an atheist I reverted back to my Catholic upbringing and got so mad I started blaming God. There really is a nice little tossed salad of negativity and guilt that flashes through there."

When Vernon and his wife lost their twin boys at 19 weeks, he recalled feeling responsible without really knowing why, saying, "I thought *what did I do to deserve this?* I mean, I thought I was a good man and provider but all of a sudden I remember thinking that maybe this was happening as an indictment of me as a man. There must have been something I could've done to prevent this outcome."

Charlie, forty-one, from South Dakota, is a father of three boys but he and his wife didn't feel they were done. The second and most recent miscarriage at 10 weeks occurred in 2020 during the COVID-19 epidemic, which meant he wasn't allowed in the room to be with his wife when they found out the bad news. The end result was Charlie not only grieving the miscarriage, but also experiencing the additional guilt of not being able to be present by her side in the hospital.

"I was considered non-essential due to COVID, which meant I wasn't able to be more involved at the health care facility with my wife. I was working full-time and supporting our family as an at-home father but I was disappointed because I've always been there for my wife in tough situations. But suddenly I'm not able to attend checkups, hear the heartbeat, etc. I felt distant since I wasn't able to attend the ultrasound or be at her D&C surgery."

As if these examples aren't bad enough, the guilt with late stage losses can be even more dizzying and tragic.

Jennifer, forty-one, and her husband, Matthew, live in North Carolina and have a four-year-old son, Miles. In 2018 they were preparing to welcome a sibling for Miles into the world when disaster struck at 37 weeks. Despite having had an ultrasound just two weeks earlier at which point everything was fine, Jennifer said she was at a senior seminar project presentation about a week later and realized she hadn't felt the baby move for a long time.

After some vigorous exercise on her part and lots of water to get the baby to shift, she convinced herself she had felt some slight movement from the baby and went about her day. Besides, all of the pregnancy journals she read said that the baby's movements would be fewer and farther between as it ran out of room so close to delivery.

A weekend passed with no movement. Then Monday. Then Tuesday. Jennifer said she talked to her loved ones who all said, "I'm sure it's fine," and reminded her that babies move less often the closer it gets to the delivery date. Besides, Jennifer said she wasn't in any pain, her blood pressure was totally normal, and she had no other symptoms that signified trouble. Still, she was concerned so she made an appointment for that Thursday just to be on the safe side.

That's when the couple abruptly found out there was no heartbeat due to a knot in the umbilical cord. Unimaginable, earth-shattering, worst-case scenario news the likes of which no human should ever have to deal with, and yet here they were right in the thick of it at 37 weeks with a baby whose time had already expired. Jennifer said they were waiting to find out the sex when they finally learned it had been a girl. They named her Nora.

To say there is guilt involved would be the understatement of the century, she said.

"I felt so much internal guilt for not going to the hospital immediately when I had the 'lightning bolt' moment after not feeling the baby move for a while. Even though my midwives assured me that typically once the mother senses the lack of movement it's already too late, I felt so much guilt that I had pushed myself too hard during the pregnancy. Surely I drank too much caffeine which made her overactive and led to the knot.

Maybe it was because I had gotten the flu that winter and taken medication, even though it was doctor-approved. I knew something I did had to have caused this tragedy."

Jennifer said her husband, Matthew, is incredibly supportive and involved, but prefers not to talk about these issues or show much emotion. Nevertheless, Matthew broke down upon hearing the news and eventually admitted that he was also blaming himself for failing to heed a dream he had before the couple knew there was anything wrong with the pregnancy.

"Matthew dreamed that the baby had died and it was his fault because he had not installed the showerhead properly. I also had a dream that it was a girl and we named her Nora Claire, which was odd because that wasn't even a name on our list. Neither one of us told the other about these dreams until after we found out, and he felt tremendous guilt for not telling me to go get checked."

Of course the rational part of our brains knows human beings can't possibly blame themselves for not raising the alarm in real life over what occurred in a dream, but rationality is not always present in the abyss of grief.

Whereas Jennifer's horrific ending came out of the blue, Benjamin's experience with loss at just shy of 37 weeks was expected for months. With a Trisonomy 13 diagnosis at 20 weeks, he and his wife knew they were likely fighting a losing battle by carrying their baby, Jonah, to term but they felt it was the right thing to do. The situation was made even more difficult by the advice of their initial team of doctors to terminate the pregnancy immediately after the Trisonomy 13 diagnosis.

All parents in impossible situations like this think about a variety of factors when trying to determine how to proceed, chief among them what is going to cause the least amount of suffering for baby and mother. When it came to me and MJ, our decision was to terminate because we saw it as the most merciful path for the baby that also preserved MJ's health for future pregnancies. But for Benjamin, it was important to bring the baby to term and give Jonah a chance to overcome steep odds.

"Going through a 'genetically imperfect' pregnancy is an experience that no one should have to endure. Things like being pressured by seemingly the entire medical community to terminate all the way through week 32, trying to decide if you should finish the nursery while being told your child won't make it to birth or, if he is lucky enough to make it that far, that he won't come home. But parents need to be able to choose their own path because even with the acceptance of Down's syndrome, it is still not accepted that the lives of genetically imperfect babies have value from a medical resource perspective. So being prepared to hold the line and fight for every step is a necessity."

As an extra gut punch, Jonah ended up being a much larger baby when he was delivered, to the point that the preemie clothes Benjamin brought for him didn't fit. Not wanting to leave him even for a second before Jonah was delivered to the morgue, Benjamin had to put him in a whale onesie that was far too big for him. Even worse, he and his wife were then told they had to buy a second urn because the one the funeral home picked out wasn't big enough.

"That's something I'm always going to hold on to. I should've been more prepared."

The bottom line is people expect mothers to be out of their minds with grief and blaming themselves for everything when a tragedy like this occurs, but they don't automatically assume that about fathers. But let me and the brave people who spoke to us about this topic be very clear—men are grieving, too. Men are out of their minds with worry and panic, too. Men are scared and confused and silently blaming themselves, too. But, for a host of reasons, we don't feel like we're allowed to show it or discuss it at all.

Every parent in situations like these needs to know this is not their fault. Parents can do a lot and moms are borderline superheroes who can accomplish more than should be humanly possible, but none of us can stop genetic imperfections. Not a single one of us can prevent fetal abnormalities that sometimes occur before women even know they're pregnant. No parent can wave a magic wand or pray hard enough to separate a tiny baby's legs that are fused together or prevent an umbilical knot from forming. If you try to shoulder that responsibility all by yourself it will inevitably crush you and grind you to dust. I can't tell anyone how to dig their way out of that hole filled with grief and shame. We're all unique and the journey toward the light is going to be different for all of us. But what I can impart is the universal truth that can be used to get up off the mat.

It's not your fault.

* * *

*But it was my fault! I knew for a fact that I somehow deserved this because I had sex before I was married, I had an abortion, I wasn't kind enough to people, I didn't go to church enough, maybe I was a puppy killer in a past life . . . whatever the reason, I knew it was on me. Hell, it was Aaron's fault, too. It was everyone's and everything's fault. I blamed myself, the world, and anyone or anything else I could find.*

*Now, of course, the truth is no one deserves blame when it comes to pregnancy loss or infertility. Not you and especially not your partner. While I mostly blamed myself, Aaron took a sizable portion of the blame as well. It is hard to accept that things happen, especially when you want something so desperately. It's so easy to blame yourself and those closest to you for a million reasons, but it does not help anyone. It breaks you down emotionally and physically. It eats away at your relationship. And it can negatively impact your mental health.*

*I got stuck in a rut and I couldn't get out of the mindset of blaming myself and Aaron, to the point that it threatened our marriage.*

*I am not a crier by any stretch of the imagination, and I only remember breaking down two times during my five pregnancy losses. The first one when I broke down was in front of Aaron, when we found out our baby's condition was not compatible with life. At that moment, I was mourning the loss of what could have been, but most of all I was feeling I let my whole family down, including Aaron. Aaron wanted to do anything in his power to make things better, but he was powerless to fix it.*

*The second was being graveside of my late stepfather, begging him not to let me have another miscarriage, because I was not strong enough to go through another one. Yet even then I was blaming myself because here I was at his cemetery plot, crying in the rain begging with audacity for another healthy pregnancy, when I already had a healthy child at home. I felt selfish and small knowing other people weren't as lucky as I was, but I still couldn't help feeling the way I felt.*

*I was so desperate; I was doing everything in my power to have a healthy pregnancy. I even reverted to my Catholic roots. I prayed, lit a candle, and went to church a few times all to have good luck.*

*When all these attempts failed, I fell into a depression and accepted a fundamental truth—I was to blame and I deserved it. How could I be so childish in thinking these things could help? The irony was I had friends going through similar situations and I would comfort them and be strong for them while telling them all the right things and good advice that I refused to accept for myself.*

*I went into a deep depression every time I had a miscarriage. It was even worse when I had the fetal abnormality and the abortion. Instead of talking about it and continuing to see my therapist, I threw myself into my work, which is not healthy because I shut myself off to my husband and, in large part, to my oldest son at home. I closed the door on Aaron, who was my rock and the one person in the world not judging and making me feel bad.*

*I should have been forthcoming with my feelings. I should have trusted Aaron, a friend, or my therapist. Instead, I hid everything I was feeling and pretended I had no feelings instead. I noticed many of my friends who had lost pregnancies and dealt with loss and infertility did the same thing. I knew they told people just enough to get them to eventually leave them alone, but they never truly let people in or let anyone know how bad things really were.*

*For anyone going through pregnancy loss or infertility, please do not take on the burden of blaming yourself or your partner. You did not deserve it. Your past experiences are not coming back to haunt you in the form of punishments related to your pregnancy. Open up to someone. If you think your partner is grieving too and you think that you are off-loading on them emotionally, then go to a trusted friend or therapist. Talk to someone. Get help. Otherwise, it will only eat you up further.*

# Chapter 7

## *Guys, This Can't Be Fixed*

I'M NOT A HANDYMAN BY ANY STRETCH. I DIDN'T HAVE A TOOL-box until I was thirty, my wife knows more about car repair than I do, and anything I've fixed around the house has been minor and required detailed YouTube videos to accomplish. However, I consider myself an emotional fixer/problem solver.

When MJ would come home from work and tell me she had a bad day because her manager was condescending to her, I'd ask if she addressed it with him. I'd mention how going to human resources might help. I suggested making a list of all the things he did that were problematic so that she'd have it with her when she addressed him so she didn't forget anything and it would give her a paper trail if necessary. If she mentioned that she was feel-ing sad or angry I'd ask her when was the last time she exercised, tell her we could go for a run right then and there, and remind her to eat because she gets pretty hangry. Headache? I was always on hand to ask her how much water she'd had that day and offer to fill up her glass so she wouldn't be dehydrated. Basically, if she had a problem, I had a potential fix (or seven or eight) that

I wasn't shy about offering. Because there's nothing women like more than men trying to fix their problems, right?

One day MJ snapped and said, "I'm not looking for your fixes because you can't fix everything. Sometimes I just want to complain about stuff and know that you hear me and sympathize!"

I'm not sure exactly the reason why, but when things go wrong in the babymaking department, many men immediately shift into Mr. Fix-It mode. Perhaps coming up with a plan and offering solutions is an attempt to exert control over an uncontrollable situation. Or maybe it's because men aren't taught to outwardly display compassion, empathy, and gentle understanding, but they are expected to fix shit when it breaks. But whatever the case, a lot of men have to learn that sometimes just talking about a problem and having someone listen—I mean truly and actively listen—is the real solution.

Daniel, a fifty-three-year-old Seattle resident, and his wife, Laura, have seven children—six together ranging in age from four to seventeen as well as a twenty-eight-year-old son from Daniel's previous relationship. While some would consider that many kids an eye-popping number, Daniel and Laura endured several first and second trimester miscarriages along the way, including one in 2012 as parents of four.

While stopping short of saying he felt resentment during those times, he did say he felt "hamstrung" as a man trying to comfort his inconsolable wife following one of the losses.

"It wasn't because I had failed as a man or a father or anything like that, but because I couldn't do anything to help her. The only thing I could do was be there and it's really hard as a man to just be there and not have a list of things I can do to make her feel better. Acknowledging this kind of loss and just sitting with it is extremely difficult, but it's also probably the best thing anyone can do. It's tough but there's healing in just acknowledging the pain and letting it sit there."

But an even harder truth, according to Jennifer, is the fact that people who go through trauma, such as losing a baby at 37 weeks as she did, can't be "fixed." The person Jennifer was before the loss is simply not the same one who emerged from the ashes, and not even a supportive and loving husband like hers can do a damn thing about it. Because while well-intentioned men want desperately to protect their partners from the despair and soul-shattering grief, they need to realize that's an unfortunate but mandatory part of the journey.

"You can do all the right things but it doesn't take the grief and pain away. You just have to learn to live with that."

But I found out the hard way that talking about that, trying to fix things by talking about that future joy too soon, is also problematic.

MJ was devastated about losing the baby. So was I. The rational part of my brain told me that there was still time to have another healthy baby in the future, but I wish my brain also could've figured out that that's not what MJ needed to hear at that moment. She snapped at me and told me she didn't want a future baby, she wanted this baby that we lost. She asked if I even cared about what happened since I had already seemingly moved on to having another baby at some point down the road. Of course I cared and I was devastated, too. I was just logically looking at the next steps so we could inch closer to our goal, but in her mind I was callously skipping over the hurt she was very much feeling in the present. It was impossible for me to see how flippant the "we'll just try again" message was sounding to someone deep in the weeds of misery, and I wish I'd had the presence of mind to stop trying to solve everything for her when all she wanted was for me to climb in the weeds with her and let her know she wasn't alone in her sadness.

I don't care how big and tough you are or how handy you are with a hammer or circular saw. Guys, you can't repair this. It feels empowering to have a list of solutions and go down the list checking them off. I get it. It's a defense mechanism. Because the only thing scarier than the fallout from the miscarriage is the unassailable fact that the only thing that truly even comes close to fixing what's ailing you is time. Sorry to pull the old "time heals all wounds" card because that's not even necessarily accurate (time creates enough scar tissue so the wound isn't fatal but that's a far cry from healed), but taking the time to sit with the grief and tangibly deal with it is the only true way to move forward. Which is terrifying, but essential.

Just know that it's not so much a fix as an evolution and a new normal. Be there. Sit with the hurt and the vulnerability. Listen just to listen. That's what will help mend more than anything else.

\* \* \*

*You can't fix a broken heart, and I was so brokenhearted with all our losses and infertility. But while I knew no one could fix it, Aaron was hell-bent on trying.*

*Aaron is an emotional fixer. He needs to find a solution for all my problems, even if they don't involve him. I love him to death but this is one of his most annoying qualities. Some problems have no solution—only talking it out or time is needed to help heal the problem.*

*Our losses and infertility were no exception. All he wanted to do was talk and fix the problem, which translated to him wanting to fix me. But I couldn't be "fixed." I wanted a partner in grief and a co-commiserator, not a repairman. I wanted to know Aaron felt something. I wanted him to feel the way I was feeling, but all I got was a one-sided conversation full of unsolicited advice that just made me feel worse about myself.*

*I remember vividly the day we found out about our pregnancy abnormality. I was inconsolable. I refused to talk about it and all I wanted was our oldest close to me. I wanted to hug him and feel all the potential he held in that moment. I remember Aaron leaning over and whispering in my ear it will be okay. I knew he was lying and he couldn't fix the problem, but here he was trying to promise something that no human being can guarantee. All it did was make me angry. Angry he thought he could fix a problem which had no solution, and furthermore, a solution I knew could only eventually come from me and from time.*

*When I made it clear there was no "fixing" me, Aaron took it hard because he felt like that was me saying I didn't want to talk about anything with him. Which was true, in a sense, because I wanted someone to grieve with me and not mend me. And guys, a little word of advice, please don't let the words "we can try again" or "it was just not meant to be" escape your lips. I know we can try again. I know how babies are made. And I know it wasn't meant to be since it's clearly not happening. These things might seem like kind tidbits, but they are not and it would be great if we just dropped those terms from our vocabularies.*

*So, what should be said? I wanted Aaron to tell me how much he hated life at that point, because that was how I was feeling. I wanted to know how angry he was with the whole situation. But because men are the fixers of the relationship, he was giving me lines of bullshit instead.*

*Men, you do not need to be the fixer. Be real with us. Be sad and mad as hell. When someone is emotionally tapped out and frayed beyond belief, curled up in the corner, they don't need a lecture or pithy advice. They need you to get down there with them, wrap them up, and tell them you feel it too. That doesn't make guys less manly, it makes them men who truly care. Men who can access their grief and feelings and the emotional intelligence to actually help the situation. The baby was part you—let us know the grief and hurt is part yours as well.*

# Chapter 8

# *Ladies, He's Hurting Too*

"**D**OES HE EVEN GIVE A CRAP? IS HE FEELING ANYTHING AT all? Because he's not showing it."

That's not a direct quote from anyone in particular, but more an amalgamation of all the comments I've seen and heard from women who are in relationships with men while experiencing miscarriage, infertility, and pregnancy loss. That might be one reason why less than half (47 percent) of the women we surveyed said they felt fully supported by their significant others following some kind of traumatic episode. The long-held stereotype of men harnessing every ounce of stoicism they can as they steadfastly sip their whiskey in the corner while women outwardly wail and scream and express their sorrow does have some truth to it, but it's also a woefully incomplete snapshot of reality that lacks any and all nuance.

The short answer is: Yes. Most of the time, men are hurting too. But the long answer is complex and must consider societal expectations based on gender, the fact that men and women are allowed vastly different levels of emotional bandwidth with which to operate, and the simple fact that everyone grieves and displays emotion differently.

It's not fashionable, in this day and age, to expect people to feel sorry for you or understand your plight as men (especially a straight, white man like me). Please know that I'm not asking anyone to dry their eyes, pat us on the head, and weep with pity for men as if we're downtrodden victims. That's not the case and we've collectively earned much of the scorn we're now facing for our historical misdeeds, misogyny, and patriarchal monstrosities. But what I am absolutely asking you to do is to really stop and consider where most men are coming from and try to imagine things from our point of view as it relates to pregnancy loss.

Imagine being a 20- or 30-something man who was raised in a stew of patriarchy, misogyny, and Neanderthal antics. Picture being part of a gender that controls everything—we get paid more, promoted faster, hold more leadership positions, occupy political office in far greater numbers, etc.—yet is seldom taught how to control our response to anger, resentment, or rejection in a healthy way. Men are raised to believe they are kings of the universe, yet so many of us grow up lacking any kind of mastery of our full range of emotions, to the point a not-so-insignificant portion of us are essentially emotionally stunted.

Then a miscarriage or male infertility pops up. Suddenly we are smack in the middle of a maelstrom of feelings and we've either rejected or never been offered the tools we need to deal with it in a healthy way. For years we've been taught to be hard and strong and never show weakness, but suddenly that's backfiring because our strong and silent act is being mistaken by the person we love as indifference or apathy. Now we're taking a vicious one-two punch, first from the loss and then from the realization that so much of what we thought we knew about being a man is wrong.

We're told to ask for help but we don't even know what that looks like. We're told to talk to someone but the male friends we'd ask for advice are in the same boat, fighting the same battles, and would likely spew back the same rhetoric we've already internalized. In the absence of answers, people generally resort to what they know, and unfortunately what most men know is—be strong, be silent, be a rock, and suck it up.

However, I do think there's a certain "damned if we do, damned if we don't" factor that men are negatively impacted by.

Case in point, Jennifer said her husband, Matthew, was totally supportive and would do anything she said and get her anything she needed, following the loss of their daughter at 37 weeks. Although he's a man who prefers not to show his emotions outwardly, Matthew was "freely emotional and expressive in the moment," and took the lead on communicating with the funeral home and setting up the cremation. But once the immediacy of the moment was over, things changed.

Matthew moved into "keep busy" mode while Jennifer sank deep into grief. As she sought to find ways to remember and honor their lost daughter as well as seek out help in the form of counseling, religion, and yoga, Matthew preferred to "push it all down" and quietly stay busy on projects around the house.

"He's not an initiator so it was difficult and, at times, I have felt resentment that I have to be the one to bring our daughter up and talk about her to be her memory keeper and keep her legacy alive. I know he wants these things too and is appreciative of the initiative I take and the voice I give her, but it frustrates me that it is always just me. I know he doesn't want to upset me but it would have helped me know we were both grieving the loss of our daughter because I know he grieves, but I don't always know it in real time and I certainly can't help him through it if I don't see or hear about what he's thinking or feeling."

But during this process, Jennifer began to notice something. While she had previously existing protective factors such as friends, community, and mental health resources that were already built up and in place to help her through the tough times, her husband had nothing. His family is a collection of people who don't air their emotions and he wasn't keen on counseling, either. She realized with horror that Matthew, like many other men, had no existing support structure whatsoever.

"It disappointed me that no one pulled him under their wing like other moms did for me. In fact, I realized people rarely even asked how he was doing. That's really unfortunate."

Many men resemble ducks on a pond—looking all composed above the water but kicking like crazy just underneath the surface. What seems like simply fixing a car in the garage or taking extra trips to the gym can actually be a coping mechanism. I know the stereotype is men and women are different species from different planets and all that crap, but the truth is men and women just receive vastly different societal messaging from this very screwed-up planet. In fact, one British study of 323 men found that although they displayed less "active grief" compared to women, men were more vulnerable to feelings of despair and difficulty in coping eight weeks following the loss.[1]

So what can the partners of these emotionally hesitant men do? Well, first of all know you are not the one responsible for solving his emotional issues. Be concerned, be open, and be available, but ultimately getting help is on him. One thing Jennifer

1   J. E. Puddifoot & M. P. Johnson (1999) Active grief, despair and difficulty coping: Some measured characteristics of male response following their partner's miscarriage, *Journal of Reproductive and Infant Psychology*, 17:1, 89–93, DOI: 10.1080/02646839908404587

did that was effective was send her husband articles she thought were helpful in processing his grief, and she found inviting him to accompany her to support groups was more apt to work than suggesting he go on his own. Sharon Covington, director of psychological support services at Shady Grove Fertility Center in Washington, DC, agreed with Jennifer's approach. She said in a 2015 *TIME* article that she had tried organizing men's support groups but inevitably not enough men would show up to keep the group running. The trick, she said, is convincing men "you're not grieving memories, you're grieving the hopes and dreams you had for this baby. You have to make the loss real to you and find a way to express it."[2]

Also, since 95 percent of the men we surveyed said their top priority was to be focused on their partners, it's important to point out studies like the one from the *Journal of Psychosomatic Research* that found the women who struggle the most with depression six months after a miscarriage had partners who were less likely to speak openly about the loss.[3] So if men are truly concerned about the well-being of their partners first and foremost, the data says one of the best things they can do is talk openly and honestly with their partners about what they're feeling.

In the end, everyone involved needs to know one simple truth. Whatever is pushed down will eventually rise up at some point. The trick is to make it a healthy free flow of feelings and not a volcanic eruption of anger and unaddressed grief.

2   Sarah Elizabeth Richards. "Men Are the Forgotten Grievers in Miscarriage." *TIME*, Aug. 3, 2015, https://time.com/3982471/men-are-the-forgotten-grievers-in-miscarriage/

3   Beutel M, Willner H, Deckardt R, Von Rad M, Weiner H. Similarities and differences in couples' grief reactions following a miscarriage: results from a longitudinal study. J Psychosom Res. 1996 Mar; 40(3):245–53. doi: 10.1016/0022-3999(95)00520-x. PMID: 8861120.

\* \* \*

*Men have feelings. Of course they do. They are every bit as complex emotionally as women; don't let anyone tell you differently. The real difference between the sexes isn't that men lack complex emotions, they simply don't enjoy the same safe spaces that women do to talk about them. And sometimes even when they do have those spaces, they're conditioned not to use them. Aaron's demeanor towards me after a loss was not what I liked or needed, and while I know it wasn't intentional it was ultimately harmful for both of us.*

*In my opinion, he was aloof and uninterested. Again, not intentionally because I know he felt something for the baby we lost and he was trying to express his feelings, but he didn't know how and I didn't understand the forces he was up against. He was raised to be the protector and the fixer. Women can show emotion to their friends, family, and even strangers. People are more apt to ask women if they are okay and what can be done for them, but they almost never ask the men. Why? Because men are meant to be strong and not speak about feelings. Women are raised to show emotion. We can process complex emotions without resorting automatically to violence or anger from grief.*

*Men need to be up front about how they feel when it comes to pregnancy loss and infertility, because women will not interpret that silence very well. We hear that deafening silence from men and view their over-the-top need to protect as a sign they don't care, but that's not the reality of the situation. They have strong feelings of grief, loss, and anger just like we do. Even though I'm a woman, it took a long time to realize I'm also affected by toxic masculinity because I didn't comprehend the societal restrictions under which they operate. And I underestimated just how firm that stranglehold is on them to never show emotion. I expected Aaron* to understand me and where I was coming from, but I never gave any thought to the battles he was facing because, as a woman, I had simply never been through them.

I don't ever remember Aaron crying over any of our losses. But I distinctly remember the jokes he would crack after each one, how he would tell me it would be okay (but it never was okay), and him telling me we could try again. I remember how pathetic I thought it was and how angry it made me, when all the while he was feeling the same as I was, but just felt he couldn't talk about it.

I recall having a huge fight when I was about six months pregnant after we had gone through IVF. I was into my third trimester yet he had refused to even acknowledge the pregnancy and, in one case, literally forgot I was pregnant when he offered me a glass of wine. I finally had enough of him not taking it seriously and I snapped. I called him some very awful things that day and told him he was not being a good partner or father, because he refused to connect with the baby. I unleashed all the anger I had been harboring and let out a tidal wave of hurt, frustration, grief, and anxiety because it was the first time I'd had a chance to let it all out.

At first he was confused, then angry, and then suddenly he cracked too.

Maybe it's because he saw how hurt I was but he broke down and admitted he was scared that we would never actually bring the baby home with us from the hospital. He was convinced there was something wrong with the baby at all times and that there was zero chance it would survive. Through tears, he told me that he couldn't get attached to the idea of a baby that was never going to be because the pain would just be too great after all we had been through. It was in this moment that we were finally on the same page. I was having the same feelings and it was keeping me up at night. *This was the first time in many years he was talking about his feelings with me.*

*I realized then that he was living in a whole other world I knew nothing about, and that partners of men need to understand we don't always know the whole story. If we want them to be open and communicate their feelings, we must be willing to at least try to understand that world and the pressures that come with it, before we can battle it. But the biggest relief I had that day was knowing men are hurting too, and we simply need to give them the outlet to talk absent judgment. We need to help them open up about their feelings of loss, grief, and whatever else they are feeling even if we don't truly understand their perspective.*

*Also, once Aaron knew that what I truly needed to be taken care of and protected was for him to get on my emotional level and be honest with me, that helped a lot. That way he was still being the "protector" but he was also showing me he was emotionally invested, which comforted me in ways he couldn't have achieved prior to that. And while this feels like a little bit of a sexist generalization, you can't wait for them to get it. You can't drop hints at what you want and think they're going to pick up on them. If I could do it over again, I'd have that blunt blow-up moment with Aaron much sooner to save ourselves a lot of time and heartache.*

# Chapter 9

# *Communication Keeps Relationships Alive*

For those who get married in the United States, there is a 39 percent chance of divorce.[1] But for the folks unlucky enough to go through miscarriage, infertility, and other traumatic losses, studies show they are at increased risk of divorce or separation. Compared with couples who had pregnancies that went as planned, those who experienced a miscarriage were 22 percent more likely to break up while that rate for those who went through a stillbirth increased to 40 percent more likely.[2] Marriage is hard enough, but when major events test and strain even the best of relationships, they're either going to get stronger or fall apart.

That's why establishing a baseline of open and transparent communication is so unbelievably essential if the goal is to be in the former category and not the latter. This isn't just advice that's relevant to those going through traumatic losses, either. To avoid

---

1 Luscombe, Belinda. "The Divorce Rate is Dropping. That May Not Actually Be Good News." *TIME.com*, November 26, 2018, https://time.com/5434949/divorce-rate-children-marriage-benefits/

2 Gold KJ, Sen A, Hayward RA. Marriage and cohabitation outcomes after pregnancy loss. *Pediatrics*. 2010;125(5):e1202–e1207. doi:10.1542/peds.2009-3081

being among the 39 percent of Americans who get divorced, creating a two-way street where partners can communicate openly is the surest protective measure there is to safeguarding a relationship.

Jeremy knows the statistics all too well, because he and his ex lived it.

In addition to Jeremy's infertility complicating the relationship, his girlfriend's advanced maternal age (she was forty at the time) added to the struggle of getting pregnant. One unexpected side effect was that he said the monthly IVF injections he gave to his then-girlfriend made her gain a significant amount of weight. Although Jeremy says he didn't negatively judge her, it became an issue for her self-esteem, which, combined with her idea that she was too old and barren to give him what he wanted, made her more and more jealous and bitter to the point "we both began to question whether or not there was going to be a future here." Compounding problems even more was the cost of treatments, totaling thousands of dollars in their attempt to have a baby.

"You have to find somebody who you can talk to and get everything that you are feeling out into the open in a healthy way," Jeremy reflected, noting that he and his ex-girlfriend didn't have that foundation from which to build. "It seemed like I was just supposed to do whatever needed to be done to support her and I was just supposed to suck it up. Because that's what men do, right?"

After a year of unsuccessfully trying, Jeremy waved the white flag and they were soon separated. Three years later he met a woman and they had a daughter together, but that relationship also ended a few years ago. To his point, sometimes the agony of miscarriage, stillbirth, and infertility doesn't create the fault lines, it just exposes and exacerbates the ones that were already there but hidden from sight.

Zachary, the UK native living in Brazil whose wife miscarried at the 12-week mark, said he was "sick to his stomach" that his wife was hurting so badly and there was nothing he could do about it. But, at the same time, he was also feeling a tremendous amount of guilt for something he had failed to communicate to his wife before the pregnancy occurred.

"I really didn't want another child and I felt very guilty that a part of me was relieved when we lost the baby. So I was feeling guilt because of what had happened and our experience at the hospital, but also because of my reaction."

Between losing the pregnancy, being mistreated at the Brazilian hospital by nurses and doctors who suspected them of secretly aborting their baby, and Zachary's after-the-fact admission that he had no desire to have another baby, the result was a noticeable distance in his marriage. They stopped talking as much, ceased having sex altogether, and danced around the issue for four years until they were honest with one another and got everything out into the open. Although they are still together and "in a great place" now, failing to adequately communicate with one another was a near fatal blow to their marriage.

Sometimes miscarriage isn't the main problem, but it creates larger problems in relationships that then cause major strife.

When Daniel's wife, Laura, had a miscarriage at the age of forty in 2012, he wanted to get a vasectomy. After all, the couple already had four kids together and her miscarriage at 8 weeks had been particularly scary with Laura experiencing blood loss and an alarming amount of ectopic pain in her side that sent her to the emergency room and had him concerned about her health. However, when Daniel voiced these concerns he discovered that although his wife was scared, she felt strongly she didn't want that to be how her pregnancy journey ended and she had every intention to keep trying.

"I was scared to lose her. This is my wife, my partner, my best friend, and the mother of my children and I was scared that if we kept trying it was going to have long-term health effects. I had wanted to get a vasectomy earlier but she was opposed to it, and there was some resentment there on my part because if she let me get the vasectomy we wouldn't be in this situation. We already had so much and I thought we needed to be thankful for what we've got."

Laura said she understood her husband's concerns and appreciated them, but figured he'd come around when she imparted how important it was for her to keep trying. But, for the first time in their relationship, he was firm in his objections.

"I wasn't used to Daniel saying no and so there was major conflict for about a year," she said.

One thing that previously helped the couple gain and communicate greater insight into each other's point of view was participating in a 2004 study from the University of Washington about miscarriage. They were required to fill out journals and record their thoughts together, a process that helped validate their feelings and emotions and allowed them to better understand the other's perspective and process it. For Laura, who is adopted, it helped her explain to her husband how she views birth with a biological family as joy, while adoption is about loss.

"With adoption, biological parents are losing a child for whatever reason, the child loses the opportunity to be raised by its biological parents, and the adoptive parents are often undergoing some kind of loss, hence their need to adopt. Behind all adoptions there is loss. I just love the joy of having kids and I couldn't let this be how it ended."

Even if there's a difference of opinions on things like choosing adoption, communication to determine perspective can lead to understanding. For Daniel, that window into her reasoning softened his stance and the couple went on to have two more children.

The perfect couple doesn't exist and there's no one way to get through this minefield of miscarriage, infertility, and pregnancy loss. Everyone is different and there's no silver bullet or right or wrong way to navigate a path through pain and emotional trauma. However, after being involved in men's discussion groups and online dad groups and hearing this anecdotal evidence, I do absolutely believe that couples who excessively communicate are going to fare a whole lot better than those who keep to themselves.

David and Penelope describe themselves as "chronic over-communicators" and despite going through so many rounds of IVF and miscarriages that they literally lost count, their marriage never really suffered. In fact, it improved.

"We just wear everything on our sleeves and we're very good at expressing whatever emotion is happening, even if it's negative. The saving grace for us is we were both feeling the weighted blanket of depression but we were under it together. I hate to be cliché and say adversity brings strength and all that crap, but after everything we went through we realized we walked through fire and came out stronger because of it."

David, a self-described atheist, reverted to his Catholic upbringing and blamed God during the darkest days of depression following the string of losses he experienced, but faith was not a factor in strengthening his relationship. However, shared faith and religious beliefs absolutely can help some couples get through tough times.

Vernon and his wife were devastated after losing twins at 19 weeks but a couple of factors saved them from becoming a divorce statistic. First of all, his wife is a psychiatrist so Vernon fully understands and appreciates the importance of added communication during tumultuous times. But also, the couple's Christian faith helped insulate them against the gnawing depression and sadness that is always threatening to creep in at all times.

"We're both faith-based people who go to church and read scripture so our faith helped us stay together. I actually feel like we became even closer after our loss. There was this feeling of being in it together, and if it doesn't work then we'll try again. Even if kids aren't in the cards we'll do everything we can to make it happen."

A huge challenge arises when couples aren't on the same page. For instance, in my marriage to MJ, I am usually the over-communicator while she holds it all in and internalizes everything. She's very private; I'm exceedingly public. She wants to move on before anything has really been dealt with, while I'm a dweller. In tough times, she tends to resort to her Catholic roots, while I am adamantly opposed to organized religion (especially Catholicism). We are truly opposites in so many ways, except for the fact that we both love each other dearly and would do anything for the other.

Still, that doesn't make it any easier to effectively communicate while in the throes of trauma and loss.

Further complicating matters is the fact that I was so shaken up by our string of losses that I stopped being able to communicate appropriately with MJ. Usually I'm the one perpetually attempting to pry her feelings out of her while she tells me she's "fine" over and over again while desperately trying to change the subject; but after everything piled up I just couldn't do it anymore. I had lost the energy to deal with my own problems, never mind hers, and the end result was no one tending to our communication needs and both of us internalizing everything and letting it fester.

As a professional writer, my solution was to show her how I was feeling by getting it all down on paper. Some guys put all their feelings into work so they don't have to think about it. Others pour everything into a hobby so they don't go insane. And then there's me. Overweight, deformed sperm, couldn't get a pregnancy to stick, couldn't protect my unborn baby from a genetic abnormality, and couldn't console my wife, whose own mental health was in jeopardy. I was scared, I was confused, and I was savagely angry. My defense mechanism was unrelenting, superfluous self-pity to the point it almost led to a divorce. Woe was me, all day, every day. If MJ initiated sex she was met with, "Why bother? I'm fucking defective," knowing it would end in a fight, that ultimately I would try to blame on her. Did I want to fight with her? Make her feel bad about herself? Feel bad about me? No, of course not. But anger was a comfort to me. It was the devil I knew and it was far less terrifying to me than being vulnerable in front of the person I cared about most. No matter how much I wanted to throw my arms around my wife and tell her I was in a tremendous amount of pain, I couldn't bring myself to have that conversation with her.

But strangely, I could do it in writing.

The blog I started in 2008 became the place where I eventually was able to share those thoughts and once I turned the faucet on, it all came pouring out. I know it sounds odd that I couldn't have these conversations face-to-face with my wife out of pure embarrassment but thought it was acceptable to write it all down and publish it for total strangers on the Internet to read.

I'm still not sure I can adequately explain it, but the thought of having to speak those words to MJ at that time just cut too deep. Also, I hid behind the rationale that by publishing my struggles I was helping others in the same boat. That might have been true and I hope it was, but the raw truth is that I did it because I was afraid to be that vulnerable in person with the love of my life. Still though, I was briefly happier because I felt that I had found an outlet and, as an added bonus, it was a way for MJ to see what I was thinking and get some insight into my state of mind.

However, she didn't see it that way. Instead of being relieved that I was sharing, she was incensed that I could share personal information with an audience of Internet randos but not my life partner.

There isn't much criticism I can legitimately throw MJ's way during this time, and I fully admit most of the problems were squarely on my shoulders. But I do think she could've cut me a little more slack in this area, because I was desperately trying to find a way to shake off the handcuffs of toxic masculinity and I thought this was a way to do that and a step forward. Was it ideal? No. Ideally I'd have simply realized I can be as vulnerable as humanly possible with the person who loves me the most in this world. But nothing in life is ideal. It was, however, worth it.

Eventually MJ saw I was trying to reach out and speak to her and even though she was less than thrilled with the manner in which I chose to do that, it ultimately led to couples counseling, counseling for both of us individually, and a renewed commitment to our marriage. Being battle-tested is not the most fun or enjoyable way to divorce-proof a marriage, but the fires you walk through together and the scars you collect as a couple really can be used to your advantage.

*  *  *

*I asked myself a thousand times why Aaron could not talk to me
about our losses and infertility. All I wanted him to do was grieve
the way I was grieving. I wanted him to talk to me about how he
was feeling. Why would he talk to strangers? I wanted the level of
support he was giving out, but instead I received silence. I never
considered how differently people grieve. When you go to a funeral
there is some type of closure to the death. When you have a loss of
pregnancy or infertility, there is no wake or funeral to mourn the
loss. People do not get to say goodbye to their loved one, it's more
like a loss of potential. Aaron and I were no exception. There was
no family grieving with us, no wake or funeral. We could not say
goodbye to our baby. We had to sit in the doctor's office hearing
the news and go back to our house to grieve by ourselves. There
lies the problem: we grieved by ourselves, not together. I grieved by
throwing myself into work and became angry at the world, including taking it out on Aaron.*

*I would yell and scream at him for the stupidest reasons. I
remember having a fight over shoes, right after one of our miscarriages, because he put them in the "wrong" place. I started throwing the shoes down the hallway and when he told me I was being
unreasonable I'm pretty sure I threw a broom at him, too. At that
moment in time and with him not opening up to me at all, the only
way I knew how to communicate with him was through my anger.*

*There was another time I was so upset, sad, and disappointed
that I refused to let him come to the doctor's office with me for
the ultrasound to confirm the miscarriage. I wanted to spare him
from the pain, from seeing the blank ultrasound screen. I wish I
had talked to him about my decision before it caused a rift in our
marriage. Of all the things we went through, this hurt Aaron the
most. All he wanted was to be there with me and have a sense of*

*closure, but all I did was block him from it out of some misguided notion that I was actually helping him. Aaron deserved to come with me, the baby was his, too.*

*But mostly I was angry with Aaron for talking to other people instead of me. Even though he was clearly trying to get me to read it so he could communicate with me in at least some way, I refused to look at his blog. In my eyes, his being able to write everything down and hit the publish button, but not have an actual conversation with me, was unforgivable. To make matters worse, he was gaining quite a following and people asked me all the time if I read his latest blog post. I would shrug my shoulders and tell them no, because it was his business and not mine. In hindsight, that wasn't the case but at that moment all I saw was my own anger. I should have been reading his writing because, while definitely not perfect, it was the only way he could communicate to me from within the cloud of his own depression. He was in pain and he was reaching out to me, but I was ignoring him. It has taken years for me to come around on him penning such private pieces, which has now turned into a book that's going out to an even wider audience. Honestly, the whole thing still weirds me out but I've come this far, so why stop now?*

*Once I started reading his blog and getting into his emotions surrounding our losses and infertility, I began to see how he felt and how he was grieving. It was not easy to read. These were our most personal moments and emotions on display. He always asked me for permission before he posted and I'd say "fine," but I am a very private person and I don't like publicizing my emotions. But after reading them and coming to terms with what was written for the world to read, we were finally able to talk. I won't sit here and pretend it was all healthy communication at first, but it was a start. And in doing so, I realized I was upset at him for being able to so eloquently and honestly express (albeit in written form) our most intimate details of our miscarriages and infertility, when I could not find my own words to heal. I was downright angry. I knew what he was writing since he'd always run it by me first, but it was hard when I really started to read it. It meant I had to come to terms with all my emotions and we had to start to communicate about the ocean of melancholy that was between us.*

*As we started truly talking with each other we realized we were both grieving, but in very different ways. And one was no better or worse than the other. It was not in the way we each wanted the other to grieve, but you don't get to judge how others do it. I wanted to forget the pain of the experience and he wanted to get it all out on his blog. There is no one way to grieve a loss, but what is important is communication.*

*If you can't find a way to communicate on your own, try couples counseling or write out your feelings or do interpretive dance. It doesn't matter what form it takes, what matters is that the communication happens. Even if it's horrible and messy and seemingly unproductive at first, beginning to communicate is the key. In hindsight, even though Aaron had his blog, I wish we had sought professional help to talk it out. I'm grateful we eventually made it to the other side, but there's no reason it had to take years of fighting and resentment to get our marriage back.*

\* \* \*

Some people believe "getting back to normal" is the trick to making sure things get back on track when it comes to rocky marriages. For most couples, especially ones that already have children, that includes the daily grind of caretaking, household chores, and going to work. However, work can all too often be an escape hatch for people who don't want to deal with their emotions regarding loss.

Jennifer said busy lives and packed schedules can be the enemy of progress and open communication. That was beginning to be the case after she and her husband Matthew lost their baby at 37 weeks, when Matthew would keep himself busy with projects instead of joining her at counseling, church, yoga, or in conversations aimed at keeping their daughter's memory alive. But then came COVID and instead of escaping to work every day, Matthew was suddenly home with his family.

"In a way, the COVID quarantine has saved us because it has forced our lives to slow down and forced us to focus on our family. I have shared and he has seen me grieve more than ever and it has connected us on a deeper level. If life had continued at our fast pace I fear it would have pushed a wedge between us because we never took time to process together. I am much more comfortable sitting with grief than he is but he has seen what that looks like now so maybe that has been helpful to him."

But, on the flip side, Jennifer said she also was forced to reexamine her own actions post-loss regarding how she was viewing Matthew's handling of the situation. She said she had an "A-ha!" moment listening to a Brené Brown podcast about high divorce rates among parents who lose children, when a guest said it's not so much about the loss of the child but rather the way spouses judge the other's grief that pushes them apart. "After that I immediately apologized to Matthew because I was certainly judging his level of grieving for not being like mine," Jennifer said.

Just like most men can never truly understand what it's like to lose a life they felt literally growing inside them, most women have no idea what it's like to live in the pressure cooker of toxic masculinity, where admitting any kind of weakness is a cardinal sin. In the end, both sides don't have to fully understand each other because that would be impossible, but they do need to listen. They need to empathize. They need to be considerate of the other's point of view. But that only comes about if both people are willing to talk, share, and be open about their experiences.

The thread that connects all these examples is that if you don't make the effort to communicate in some way, things are going to go south very quickly. If you haven't been communicating important information like whether or not you truly want to have kids, then continuing to isolate and put up walls during the emotionally fraught time following a loss could very well be the death knell of your relationship. In the end, it matters less the form of communication (talking, blogging, letters, carrier pigeon, smoke signals) than the act of actively communicating because, first and foremost, the effort needs to be there. Sometimes one person might have to initiate and carry the heavy load at first until the other finds their way out of the darkness, but it's worth it.

* * *

*My form of communication is to shut down and bury myself in work. With each passing loss Aaron and I went through, the deeper I dug into my work. I was working so much that I would get to my office before anyone was up and come home after everyone went to bed. The grief and failure of all the loss and infertility was too much to bear, and I couldn't face Aaron. Even though he was always my biggest cheerleader, every time I saw him I felt like I was letting him down.*

*So working myself to the bone became my preferred method of grieving. But while it became a surefire way to forget about everything going on, it came with consequences. I entered a spiral of depression because I refused to have any feelings about it or talk about it, even with the person I trusted the most. We have always struggled with communication in our relationship, even before we had losses and infertility, because we're such different personalities. Aaron loves to talk but it's never been high on my list of things to do. I didn't ever like to express myself and Aaron should've been a lawyer, the way he hammers away and dramatically makes his points. But as communicative as he is, he has a tendency to try to trap you in arguments until he "wins." Neither of us is right or wrong, we were just raised differently and we're different people. But the end result was that nothing was being accomplished, especially when we were both in pain and unable to express how we felt about the losses and infertility.*

*As time passed and I began to get help, it started to become clear my way of grieving was not healthy. I apologized to Aaron about my behavior and even though I gave him hell about his writing, at least he was talking and communicating with people and getting the support he needed. I was not.*

*Eventually we started couples counseling which was rough at first but did set us on the right track. I see my counselor regularly, Aaron was seeing his own counselor, and we still go to counseling together when things get rough. Eventually the fights decreased in frequency and intensity and while we're not perfect, we're worlds better now than when we started. With three kids there isn't always a lot of time for communication, but we try to fit it in after the kids go to bed and before I fall asleep, as well as at dinnertime. Sitting down to dinner at the table was mandatory for me because that's when I want my family to share things that are happening and talk about the good and the bad. Aaron's family never did nightly dinners, which is fine, but I feel very strongly sitting down together at the table breeds conversation and strengthens the family via improved communication, and that's something we implement even now all these years later.*

*But however you do it, find the means and a time to make communication a priority. The real trouble comes when you stop trying.*

# Chapter 10

# *Your Mental Health Is At Risk, So Seek Help*

B OTH MEN AND WOMEN ARE AT RISK OF DEVELOPING MENTAL health issues following struggles with miscarriage, abortion, and infertility. While this is in no way meant to dismiss the very real and devastating negative mental health impacts on women, I'm focusing on men because there are tomes of research and no shortage of resources already in place to help women get through this incredibly tough time. The same cannot be said of research into how men are impacted by these events, and men certainly don't have anywhere near the same level of resources to help them should they find themselves in the dark recesses of depression following a loss.

To be extra clear, women generally have the harder time and the more difficult struggle. This isn't meant to be a competition or to belittle the pain men go through, but it's important to note the obvious that the people who house the pregnancy and whose bodies are physically altered are naturally going to bear the bigger burden. That having been said, both women and men are absolutely impacted by pregnancy loss, but they are impacted quite differently. Research shows men most often feel that their role is primarily one of support for their partners, which often ends with them failing to recognize their own feelings of loss. They report feeling overlooked and marginalized in comparison to their female partners, whose pain is typically more visible. Studies also indicate that while men tend to have less intense and shorter-lasting levels of negative psychological outcomes than women, they are more likely than women to partake in potentially destructive behaviors such as increased alcohol consumption or drug use.[1]

"No, I never sought any help. It's just not a thing that I even considered because she was supposed to be the one that was having a hard time, not me." These words from Jeremy, who experienced multiple miscarriages (including a late-stage loss) and years of infertility, perfectly sum up what so many men feel when the subject of their mental health arises.

Jeremy and his ex-girlfriend went through so much turmoil and anguish trying to get a pregnancy to stick, that after a while, he said he was just "done." Done with feeling worthless, done with the pain, and done with trying to be strong. After coming home from the doctor's office and hearing Creed's hit song "With Arms Wide Open," written by Scott Stapp after finding out he was going to be a father, Jeremy lost it. When he was supposed to be getting some Advil at the store for his recovering girlfriend, he instead found himself at his local bar for a quick beer. The beer turned into a metric ton of tequila and an ill-advised drive home which he was lucky to have survived without

---

1  Due C, Chiarolli S, Riggs D W. The impact of pregnancy loss on men's health and well-being: a systematic review. *BMC Pregnancy Childbirth.* 2017;17(1):380. Published 2017 Nov 15. doi:10.1186/s12884-017-1560-9

injuring himself or others. Upon exiting the car in a stupor and failing to deliver medication to his girlfriend, Jeremy said he started throwing up in his bushes while simultaneously realizing he had hit rock bottom.

"I handled my feelings the only way most men know how, by drowning them as quickly as possible. Of all the stupid stuff that I've done over the years, it remains one of my most shameful moments. I completely failed as a partner because I didn't know how to handle what I was feeling. But I just didn't know how to step up and say that this stuff messes men up too."

While Jeremy chose to seek temporary comfort in the bottle instead of getting professional help, Zachary said he avoided counseling because he thought talking to a couple of friends was enough. He says he did not suffer any negative mental health impacts but admitted he did not feel free to openly express what he was feeling at the time because "my wife was the one who had to deal with the medical and psychological consequences, so I had to deal with the daily stuff and just be seen to be normal."

Benjamin had a terribly tough time with the first miscarriage at 15 weeks, but the stillbirth just shy of 37 weeks sent him and his wife over the edge, mentally. They say couples that share common interests and do things together stay together, but simultaneously falling into depression only made he and his wife grow apart in many ways.

"My personality has changed, still to this day, to a much more cynical, intense, colder perspective, and I'm still fighting to get that back. My wife understands that and is encouraging, but she was fighting her own battle with depression. It's definitely been a shot to my perspective on life in general and it's just a really long road."

Benjamin had no history of depression prior to these losses, and therefore no concept of what being depressed would feel like. Noting that he experienced suicidal ideation during this time, things were made worse by the fact that he knew his wife needed his help but he was in no position to help himself, never mind someone else. He was able to talk to family members and friends who helped convince him it would be beneficial to see a counselor, which he said helped immensely. The only problem is Benjamin had to stop seeing his counselor when the couple changed insurance providers two years ago, and he hasn't been able to find another provider who is accepting new patients, takes his insurance, and is a good fit. Hooray for the American health-care system!

Backing up for a moment, it's imperative for people to know how negatively many men, including myself, view counseling, therapy, and mental health problems in general.

In my case, one of the most hurtful and ignorant things I did that set the tone for not only my terrible approach to self-care but also my wife's approach occurred at the very beginning of my relationship with MJ when I told her therapists were "quacks" and counseling in general was a "pathetic crutch for people who aren't strong enough to solve their own problems." As ridiculous as it sounds, I wasn't saying it to be malicious—I simply and truly believed it as fact. I said it with the certainty of knowing that grass is green and the sun is hot. At that point in my life, during my mid-twenties, I had never spoken to another person about their mental health or experiences with mental health counseling, and therefore viewed it akin to voodoo.

The problem was I didn't know MJ had undiagnosed bipolar disorder. What I mistook as her being a workaholic at an internationally renowned bank was actually not her desire to get ahead in her career, but prolonged manic episodes that kept her operating at superhuman levels. She wasn't choosing to work ridiculous hours and forego sleep and meals, her brain was holding her captive and forcing her to do it. And those ruts she got into which seemed to be more frequent and longer-lasting? Well, I just chalked those up to bad moods. Maybe even that time of the month. I'd later learn she was also hearing voices that were not only telling her she wasn't worth it as a wife and mother and compelling her to run away and never come back, but also whispering suicidal ideations. And the reason it was undiagnosed was because I had stated so firmly and unequivocally at the start of our relationship that anyone who needed help with their mental health was pathetic, so she saw no reason to get an official diagnosis. One of the most dominant parts of MJ's bipolar is unceasing and constant paranoia and believing everyone is judging her at every turn, and along I come—the person who is supposed to love her fully and without limits—and tell her right from the start anyone who needs help with their mental health is less than.

When I think back on the number of years MJ suffered unnecessarily because I offered a Neanderthal take on something I knew nothing about, I break down in tears. I now know a lot more about bipolar and I've witnessed firsthand the Herculean effort and the never-ending tweaking of medications on my wife's part just to get to and maintain a serviceable level of being, and I'm eternally grateful she has the help she has. But while I'm a true convert today, that doesn't change the fact that for more than half a decade my own wife went untreated and waged a war with her own mind simply because I had basically told her I'd think less of her as a person.

This archaic and dangerous outlook I had on seeking help and going to counselors is not unique to me. It's something many men share and it is literally killing us.

According to 2015 research from the National Center for Health Statistics, 9 percent of men in the United States experience daily feelings of anxiety or depression, yet less than half (41 percent) take medication for it. Even fewer (25 percent) speak to a mental health professional to seek help.[2] The end result is men being just as prone to anxiety and depression as women, but far less likely to seek help for their problems, and committing suicide at a rate 3.7 times higher than women.[3] So when we talk about men, their mental health, and imparting the importance of asking for help, it's vital to realize we're starting not just from a deficit, but so far behind the eight-ball we can barely even see the pool table anymore.

That's where my journey began—unintentionally preventing my bipolar wife from getting the help she needed while simultaneously having no idea how to deal with my newfound grief from the loss of several pregnancies and trapped under the weight of my own admonishments of anyone too weak not to solve their own problems.

I started drinking way more, especially when I'd get frustrated or nervous thinking about the miscarriages and the potential heartbreak involved in trying again. I also started smoking cigarettes again after having quit in college, as a bridge to get me through the times when I couldn't drink. I stopped working out, I ate every single one of my feelings, and the weight I put on while denying I was in a depressive episode made me feel even

2 Blumberg S J, Clarke T C, Blackwell D L. Racial and ethnic disparities in men's use of mental health treatments. NCHS data brief, no 206. Hyattsville, MD: National Center for Health Statistics. 2015.

3 Hedegaard H, Curtin S C, Warner M. Increase in suicide mortality in the United States, 1999–2018. NCHS Data Brief, no 362. Hyattsville, MD: National Center for Health Statistics. 2020.

worse about myself, which I didn't even think was possible. MJ noticed it, my parents noticed it, my relatives noticed it, and my friends noticed it. Yet every time I became aware that someone else had clocked me on their radar, I'd just double down on the harmful behavior that was hurting me in the first place.

In some way, I guess the pain and the misery was the point. I felt guilty about the miscarriages, I felt solely and irreparably responsible for the infertility, and so in a maelstrom of uncontrollable sadness, self-pity, and anger, I wanted to tear myself down to the lowest possible level as some sort of penance for all of these things which were clearly my fault. But at the same time, I adamantly refused to admit anything was wrong. Because if something was wrong with my mental health and I needed to go talk to a stranger to fix me, then any amount of manhood I had left would be instantly obliterated.

But finally, MJ did something that she almost never does in our marriage. She gave me an ultimatum—either I go get some help or she'd leave me. I was beyond furious but I didn't bother to ask if she was joking because MJ doesn't bluff. I knew she meant it and I knew my entire future and the well-being of my marriage and family was on the line.

Yet even with the rest of my life hanging in the balance, I still couldn't completely pull the trigger. So I attempted to slow play it by agreeing to go to counseling but stipulating that I had to find the right person for me. I told MJ I was doing research and getting recommendations for counselors (I wasn't), which bought me a week or so. When she caught on to my ruse, she took it upon herself to find a counselor accepting new patients who took our insurance and demanded I call for an appointment in her presence. But I couldn't do it. I realized it wasn't that I wouldn't do it, I literally couldn't. Picking up the phone and dialing those numbers and speaking the words to some receptionist that I needed an appointment because I needed help handling my own thoughts, well, it was a bridge too far. I broke down in tears in front of my wife and told her everything I was feeling and that I couldn't make the call, not because I don't love her, but because it just wasn't in me to do at that time.

In that moment—the first one that resembled any kind of honesty and transparency regarding this topic between me and my wife—she saw that I was telling the truth. She didn't like it and she certainly didn't understand it, but she saw I was being real with her. So she made the appointment for me and, in fact, had to make all of those early appointments on my behalf because I wasn't strong enough to do it for myself. It is horrifying to look back and see the hypocrisy of believing I was a "real man" for not getting help, yet that same masculinity wouldn't even allow me the strength to make a phone call that would markedly improve my life.

Yet even when the appointment was on the calendar, I still fought it. I canceled once because I said I wasn't feeling well. I canceled the next because of "work." And even after I went the third time (under threat of divorce should I have decided otherwise), my approach to getting help was all kinds of wrong.

I went into that counselor's office determined not to like him, and to outsmart him, which was equal parts shortsighted and ridiculous.

Hell, even when we eventually went to couples counseling, I still had the wrong mindset. My goal should have been to repair our relationship, open up a broader channel of two-way communication, and work toward repairing our marriage and reconnecting on an honest, emotional level. But you know what I did? I went in trying to "win." And by that I mean I judged the effectiveness of our early counseling sessions by how many times the therapist seemed to agree with me and my point of view. So when MJ asked me what I thought of our first session, I said "I thought it went great, I won five to two." World's Most Obvious Spoiler Alert: I am not smarter than most therapists. In fact, on this topic, I was very dumb.

But while that initial therapist I saw ended up genuinely not being a great fit for me, I did open up ever so slightly during the session about our losses and our situation. It wasn't some huge breakthrough moment or epiphany with an angel choir singing in the background, but even if I didn't want to publicly say it, I had to admit to myself I felt slightly better afterward. A little less burdened. A little more heard. And it wasn't full of psychobabble nonsense or Freudian theories as I had imagined—it was just a normal conversation. It was like talking to a friend over a beer. Simply by walking in that door and following through, I had dispelled so much of the stigma that existed solely in my head as the result of toxic masculinity and ignorance.

Eventually I found a counselor I liked and I saw him fairly regularly until he quit to take another job during the COVID pandemic in early 2021. And even though I'm very much pro-therapy and absolutely plan on finding someone else so I can continue my progress, writing this chapter has made me realize old habits die hard and it's been a month since I was supposed to call the referral he gave me, but I haven't yet. Because the thought of starting over and being vulnerable with someone new is still scary for me, proving this is not something of which you're just magically cured. I have to work at it every single day and untangle myself from all the bullshit I internalized when I was younger.

The interesting part is that while I was paralyzed with fear when it came to getting help for myself, I became a great ally for

MJ in her mental health battle. I was supportive of her going to counseling, I made sure she got to her appointments, and I was even called on by her doctors to help them treat MJ because she wasn't telling them important information so they relied on me coming to sessions and giving them the entire picture. I remember patting myself on the back at the time and thinking that this totally covered me from a mental health perspective because I was helping with my wife's struggle, but in hindsight learned that wasn't the case at all. I was fine with beating back the stigma of mental health struggles as long as it wasn't me who was struggling and as long as I could see myself as her white knight in shining armor. It's one of the more insidious parts of toxic masculinity that reinforces the idea of men always needing to come to the rescue, and it was a way for me to focus on someone else rather than myself.

I hope any men reading this (or partners of men who are clearly struggling and need help) understand that asking for help is not weak. It is actually the epitome of strength. One of the tenets of masculinity I hear most often is that "real men" take care of their families no matter what. To that end, there is nothing in the world more manly than asking for help to be a better man and husband for the people who need you the most.

\* \* \*

*My first introduction to the mental health system was when I was nine years old, and my parents were going through a divorce. They wanted me to have a safe place to talk about what was going on in my house. I remember hating it as a child, but as I grew older, I realized everyone needs a safe place to talk about their feelings without being judged. A sympathetic ear is a good thing, especially if you are going through a tragic event.*

*Asking for help is not a sign of weakness but a sign of strength. It has taken me years to realize I was not weak for asking for help but I, like many others, find making that ask to be very difficult.*

*Before I finally asked for help following my miscarriages, I was at one of my weakest points in my struggle with mental illness. I could not work, I was destroying my marriage and relationships with my family and friends. I was not in a good place. I was drinking, thinking about leaving my family, and at risk of losing everything.*

*I should have sought help after the first two miscarriages, but I thought I could handle it. I was strong and independent. Plus, the way I figured it, it's not like I lost a baby at birth or anything so I had no right to whine or complain. I had family and friends who supported me. I had my network, my support group, and that should be enough. I did not need to see someone about how I was feeling, period, end of story.*

*But the miscarriages took a much bigger toll on my mental health than I realized. I was so depressed and angry. I took it out on anyone and everyone around me to the point it slowly ate away at my soul. By the time my oldest was born, I could not enjoy the pregnancy, birth, or taking care of him. I went into such a deep postpartum depression without really knowing what postpartum depression was, and it only got worse the longer it went unchecked. By the time he was nine months old, the black hole of depression was too great and I fell all the way in. I stopped eating, I slept all the time, and I was angry with my new baby thinking he was the cause of it.*

*I remember the night like it was yesterday: It was November and a very dark, moonless night. I was walking up to the front door of our condominium and suddenly the thought of turning that doorknob and walking inside was just too much. I fell to the* ground in a puddle of tears because I didn't want to go home and I was disgusted because I knew not wanting to go home and see my family was the worst thing a wife and mother could ever feel. But despite knowing I was a terrible person for feeling it, the truth was I did not want to see the family I helped create. Given the choice, I would much rather have stayed in the freezing cold than seen the smiling face of my husband and baby. All joy had been taken out of me as I let a tidal wave of depression wash over my life and threaten to drown my family as well. It had won, I had lost, and it was the first time in years I realized I not only needed help, but I needed it now. Desperately. Because suddenly I was terrified with the knowledge that it was possible at this point for me to hurt myself or the people around me.

I went to see my primary care physician the next day and told him what was going on, at which point he prescribed me antidepressants and told me to seek immediate help through the mental health system. I was and continue to be one of the fortunate ones who have great health insurance and access to mental health benefits, so I was able to find one the following Monday and get in on Tuesday.

Even though I knew I needed help, it was still difficult to admit defeat (yes, that's how I looked at it at the time). I felt like a failure—I failed the people around me and I failed myself. Aaron had previously asked me to get help, but I refused it. Hell, he needed help too but he was stubbornly refusing to go, so why should I? I thought if I just work harder at my job, all my problems would go away. And to make matters worse, Aaron, my partner in life, had said something years prior about only weak people needing therapists and counselors, and it had just stuck with me—I was terrified to let him down or appear weak in his eyes. Even though he had changed his tune and was begging me to go get help and despite being raised to believe that caring for your mental health is just *as important as looking after your physical health, the paranoia of being pitied or looked at as weak had a grip on me.*

*I struggled for months and even years because all I could hear were his words echoing in my mind. I knew better and I'm not the kind of person who lets her husband dictate what she believes, but I loved him and valued his input. Also, I'm stubborn and I really thought I could handle the depression. I thought I was stronger than the pain and the hurt. I really thought no one was noticing, at least at first, and I laughably believed it wasn't that bad. But it was bad. My job was suffering, my home life was falling apart, and it was impacting my friends and extended family. My staff was picking up the slack and covering my mistakes. Aaron was also working full-time but because I was spending so much time away from home he was also doing most of the parenting duties like morning pickup, afternoon pickup, and making dinner. But he was struggling too, and neither of us would admit there was a problem or go get help, until I cracked wide open that night in November.*

*People who think they are hiding their depression are only fooling themselves. Friends and family notice when you aren't yourself and despite how many times you tell them you're fine, they know you're not. Do not lie—to them or to yourself. These people are your friends and family and if you're lucky enough to have people willing to help you, take it. Because not everyone has that lifeline and privilege. There are medications you can take and counseling you can seek. I had to learn the hard way and hit rock bottom before I realized there was a problem. By the time I realized my drinking became high risk, I was ignoring my family and my job was suffering.*

*Drinking seemed to be the easiest escape from the pain I was feeling. It was socially acceptable and no one would say a word if I would drink with them, even if it was too much and I overindulged.*

*Also, I was the life of the party when I drank (or so I thought). I remember a time after the abortion when I was in an especially dark place because I had blamed myself for having to end the pregnancy. I was at a wedding rehearsal dinner and saw a woman who was due a week after me. I lost it. I called my best friend and cried. She told me it would be okay and that I just needed to take my mind off it. She told me to go have a couple of drinks and enjoy the wedding we were at in Boston. We had an opportunity to let the stress of the last few weeks go and have a good time. I took it to heart and began downing martinis by the glasses. By the time I realized how many I had, the damage had been done. I was a hot mess; stumbling, crying, and making a complete spectacle of myself. I was lucky enough the bride and groom took it in stride, but the next morning I realized it was one of my lowest points and I needed more help than I was getting.*

*Before the wedding I really thought it was all in good fun. The drinking was just to relax and dammit, I earned it. But the truth is it resulted in some dangerous activity. It became harder and harder to stop drinking and to control the pain and depression. The deeper I fell into the rabbit hole, the harder it was to stop drinking. I would make up excuses to drink: Baby was up all night, long day at work, and so on. Anything to escape the pain, no matter how temporary that escape was. I was already going to counseling once a week and on medication, but it wasn't enough. I needed to be honest with the people around me and with my medical team. I booked an emergency appointment that following Monday. They increased my medication, and I went to counseling twice a week. They urged me to stop drinking because it was making things worse. Drinking always makes things worse.*

*As I was self-absorbed in work and drinking, my other duties were being neglected. As I said, Aaron was holding down the home* front basically on his own, making sure everything was taken care of, including our oldest son. He tried to tell me I needed help and that he was scared, but I ignored him. I wish I could have told people, Aaron included, what I needed, but I was unable to communicate it. All I know is that it was easier to stay by myself than to be with people and talk about how I was feeling. I felt they were judging me and wouldn't understand what I was feeling, but this couldn't have been further from the truth. People, and especially Aaron, wanted me to talk. He wanted to be there for me but didn't have the skills to help. He would have benefited from counseling at that point, both to deal with my situation and to begin tackling his own demons. Many people don't have the skills to help or understand what you are going through but the important thing is to let them try. Sometimes it really just starts with a friendly ear for listening.

Looking back now, I needed Aaron to be my support and give a little tough love. One of the things he told me he loves about me is how independent and strong I am, so he let me go about my daily life as though nothing had changed because he was cling-ing to the notion that I was strong enough to handle everything. He also acted as if we never had a loss, to the point I sometimes wondered how much of it was real and how much was in my head. He didn't intentionally gaslight me or anything, but his way of coping through silence and determination to go back to life as normal made me question whether anything bad even happened. Thinking that he cared so little about our losses made me strug-gle with depression even more. It made me wonder if I was being too emotional. And then the more outgoing he became online, the more depressed I became. How could he confide in strangers but not me? Aaron was getting some help in the form of writing for his blog. He was talking about his feelings and not feeling so alone. But I was not communicating my feelings and I had no outlet. I needed Aaron to offer me couples counseling. I needed him to carry me into the office if it came to that. I feel if we had done couples counseling, we would have had a much easier time with life in general. I don't think I'd have fallen down the rabbit hole of drinking and we both could have begun communicating our needs. It would have given us a safe place to talk to a neutral party and help guide our feelings. Instead, he went online to a support group (which was the right fit for him) and I buried myself in work and drinking. None of which is good or healthy.

Aaron and I both have the ability to see mental illness from a variety of perspectives. He went through it with me with my bipolar, postpartum depression, and general depression. I went through it with him suffering through depression after each loss. However, I finally hit my breaking point and went and sought help on my own accord. He did not. He became moody, sad, and withdrew from his favorite activities. Knowing from my own personal experience about mental health, I realized he desperately needed professional help.

I tried to talk to him about how he was feeling but he consistently stonewalled me. He told me I didn't know what I was talking about and that if he needed help he'd get it. Even though the mental health system did wonders for me, in his mind it was for the weak. He thought he could control this and even though I knew that was impossible, there's very little you can do if the other person refuses to get help. Yet at the same time, depression is bigger than one person can handle. It eats you up inside. Depression was taking my loved one away from me and I couldn't stop it. All I saw was a shell of my love—ashes of his former self. I needed to help but I was still struggling myself and I didn't have the training.

But I knew someone who did.

I started with talking to my own counselor about Aaron because I needed an outlet for myself if I was going to get him the help he needed. I needed a plan and a foolproof way to talk to him because, like many men on this subject, he is stubborn and woefully misguided. This is how they were raised. Not to show emotion, to be strong, and that depression is for the weak. We live in a "man-up" culture where emotions are for women and make you weak. I knew it would be an uphill battle to get him help, but it was also essential to get him in front of a mental health worker because he was miserable and only getting worse.

I knew I couldn't just jump right in and tell him he needed help. He would insist he didn't and that he was fine (I'm guilty of this line too), and refuse treatment while simultaneously retreating further into his depression. With help from my counselor, we talked through how I should approach Aaron and get him the help he needed. I started asking how he was feeling, if there was anything he wanted to talk about, or if something was bothering him. Once I realized he wasn't going to open up to me, I went back to my support network and asked for emergency help. She offered to see us together under the guise that he was being brought in to help me. It wasn't my proudest moment lying to him like that, but desperate times call for desperate measures. She saw both of us a couple of times, and it seemed to soften Aaron a little. He saw it wasn't so bad to talk to someone about feelings or emotions, and started to see the benefit. By the end of the second session, I don't even think he realized it but he was doing most of the talking. A few weeks went by and I asked if he would like to go see someone himself. It was a no-go and he instantly clammed up again. It wasn't until I hit my wit's end and ran out of options that I did what I try never to do in our marriage—give him an ultimatum. I told him he needed help or I would leave and take our oldest with me, because I could not live with someone who was so toxic. I wanted to be there for him with all my heart but I just couldn't any *longer. It was not healthy for Aaron, it was not healthy for me, and I'd be damned if I was going to let it impact my son.*

*He reluctantly agreed. I figured he would have run to the next counselor he could find to avoid me leaving, but he didn't. He danced around the issue. He demanded to pick out the counselor to "find the right fit," yet he was finding a million excuses not to even call. He either didn't like their name or the office was too far away or pick any other possible excuse. I finally had to take the matter into my own hands. I called the insurance company, found a person for him, and booked the appointment.*

*I wish I could say this was the magic bullet and he walked into that office and lived happily ever after, but that's just not true. He went to the appointment but he was furious at me for forcing him to go. I don't think he spoke to me the day before, day of, or the day after his appointment, but eventually he softened to the idea. He still didn't like the idea, but eventually came around.*

*It's hard to find a balance between your mental health and your partner. It took Aaron and I years of separate counseling and couple counseling to get to a place where we can feel stable mentally and physically. Our marriage is stronger, but it all starts with communication and understanding.*

\* \* \*

Oh my god. All these years later and I just learned that MJ tricked me into her therapist's office by telling me it was vital for me to go to better ensure her health. I honestly didn't know that until she wrote it on these pages. Wow. Well, I'm glad she did it and the other moral of the story is clearly—marry someone who is much smarter than you are.

# Chapter 11

# *How to Navigate Stupid and Insensitive Comments*

WHEN GOING THROUGH MISCARRIAGE, INFERTILITY, AND loss, the good news is people will want to help. The bad news, however, is most of them will have no idea what to do or say. The result of that confusion is often well-intentioned but ridiculously insensitive comments that only make matters worse.

From "Well, at least you have a kid already" to "Phew, you dodged a bullet," the things people say to those going through loss truly boggle the mind. The difficult part is most of them are friends and family and you know (or at least you're pretty sure) they mean well, but they're nervous and unsure of what to say and do. And nervous people often keep talking and talking until they step on a landmine and blow up everyone's day.

When Vernon had to break the news to his family members that his wife lost the twins she was carrying at 19 weeks, it was understandably tough. Vernon is a religious man who values faith and uses those beliefs as a way to comfort himself and others during difficult times, but even he wasn't ready for what his wife's grandmother said. "Maybe those two boys were going to be rascals, and God wanted to spare you the pain of raising them. He knows what you can handle and maybe you weren't ready for this burden. He has great things planned for you," she told him.

This was a beloved family member who loved the couple completely and without reservation, which is why Vernon generously called her comment "sweet, but very straightforward" and moved on to other matters. But it has to be jarring to believe in a loving God and then hear someone say that same benevolent deity hastily ended the potential for two human beings to come into the world at the halfway point of the pregnancy simply because they might've been "rascals" or a "burden."

Given that I was very public with our losses and was developing an audience of readers at the time who were sharing our journey, I ran into other people injecting their religion into my grief quite a bit. Churchgoing folks love to tell you they'll pray for you, which bugged me because they believe God is omnipotent, which means God has a plan for us all and therefore the miscarriages and infertility would be part of God's plan. So that means the same God that forced us to go through these miscarriages is the one they're praying to for help with the same miscarriages. None of it made sense to me. But ultimately I let that one go because even though I'm a nonbeliever, I knew they were basically just saying they'd be thinking about us and I appreciated that.

However, some people took it too far in my opinion when they tried to "comfort" me by telling me that losing the pregnancies is all part of God's plan or that our unborn babies were in a better place with God. Those comments were the ones I couldn't let go. Yet when I requested they respect the fact that I'm a nonbeliever and I found it insulting and hurtful that they would tell me to be happy about God taking away our very much wanted children, most of them just doubled down. Some even scolded me for being an atheist and then implied that my lack of faith in God might have been the reason the pregnancy ended. I could live to be a million years old and I still wouldn't understand how anyone could possibly think foisting their personal religious beliefs on someone who doesn't share the same faith, and then insulting them by blaming their atheism for the loss of a pregnancy, is a good idea. It's hurtful, narcissistic, selfish, obnoxious behavior that hurts instead of helps people going through a tough time.

Daniel and Laura have seven children now, so most people don't associate them with pregnancy loss. When she experienced her most recent miscarriage she already had five kids, and remembers some people in her circle of friends and acquaintances making offhand comments that it probably wasn't as big of a deal because she had so many children at home.

"I remember feeling like I'm not supposed to feel devastated because I already had so many children and I should shut up and be grateful. But for me, that last one was actually more devastating than all the previous ones."

In fact, Laura said she has known for a fact other people in her life have had miscarriages and have specifically avoided talking to her because she has so many children so they think she couldn't possibly understand the pain. Working as an elementary school teacher, she recalled hearing rumors one of her coworkers had a miscarriage and when Laura saw her sneak away into a supply closet looking frazzled, she went in to comfort her. Laura said the woman was shocked to hear she had also had a miscarriage and assumed she didn't know anything about the experience simply because Laura was a mother of seven.

The best approach, Laura said, is simple honesty and the avoidance of platitudes. Laura told her she had gone through several miscarriages and it was really sad. The other teacher started talking about how she was okay and she and her husband could try again and all the other things people tell themselves and hear from others in that moment. So Laura softly but firmly repeated, "Yeah, but it's still sad," and finally the woman cried, thanked her, and admitted that yes, it is definitely sad.

"Don't try to appease people or make them feel better. Just acknowledge what they're going through and validate that emotion. That's the best thing you can do in that moment."

Unfortunately, when it comes to many men, we get it all wrong in this regard. Due to a mixture of toxic masculinity and the misguided notion that we should bottle up all our feelings and never talk about them with anyone because showing sadness will end up with the revocation of our "Man Card" (whatever the hell that is), too many of us come off as emotionally stunted simpletons, offering up ill-advised jokes instead of genuine comfort and reassurance.

I remember being so nervous and afraid of what to say to MJ to make it better that I resorted to humor. Or, more specifically, I resorted to default guy humor. Looking back, it is abhorrently cringeworthy to think that I winked at MJ and tried to cheer her up by assuring her that "at least we get to have fun trying again." I repeat, I suggested to my wife, who had just undergone a D&C and had the life literally scraped out of her, that it would be "fun" for me to get right back up in there and have sex with her as soon as possible. That it would be "fun" to have a couple months' worth of shots in her body and have sex on command in fleeting windows of time as we attempt to play Beat the Clock. Because sure, that's what women want to hear after a surgical procedure involving their genitalia following an episode where their bodies betray them. So to any men reading this who might think this is an innocuous idea or that it's cute, please don't. I was an idiot and I'm shaming myself in this book so you don't have to follow suit.

David agreed that talking to other men can be especially frustrating during these times. He said he could see it was hard for his wife and close family to talk about as they hemmed and hawed for the right thing to say following any of the dozen or so miscarriages he and his wife, Penelope, endured. But things got so much worse when other guys would try to talk to him about what was happening.

"Most of them just had no frame of reference or experience with anything going on. One friend tried to reassure me by telling me I had 'dodged a bullet' following a miscarriage. Honestly, it's kind of a joke because we haven't figured out how to express these thoughts yet. There's no playbook on how to help somebody who is going through this. The truth is there's just no Hallmark card for miscarriage."

He also recalled one friend who made the annoying mistake of trying to bring up the miscarriages of others, which made it seem like some kind of contest. "Never say 'Well, my sister had two miscarriages and now she has two beautiful kids.' Honestly, I don't give a shit about your sister's kids. I'm worried about myself," David said.

Eventually David stopped confiding in people until he and his wife befriended another couple with whom they instantly clicked. The wife was a child and family therapist and her husband was smart and kind, and David ended up having a conversation with him during which the man simply listened and let David know he was there for him if he ever needed to talk. For the first time, he was talking to another man who wasn't offering solutions or trying to fix the problem, but instead simply acknowledged he was going through something difficult.

"That helped me get to a point where I was comfortable letting other people know what I needed to hear, which was 'I'm sorry you're going through this and I'm here if you need me.' That's all that's needed. I don't want to hear about your offer to get me drunk or that it happened to your sister. Just notice the trouble and the hurt and be there."

The terrible things people say in these situations has become such a problem that a simple Google search of "stupid things people say after miscarriages" yields nearly five million results, with pages upon pages of distressed people on the receiving end of comments venting about them on the Internet and warning others to avoid them at all costs. But unfortunately, for those folks who have been there, it's a safe bet that the majority have heard at least one, if not multiple, of the following.

"You probably shouldn't have told everyone you were pregnant." Great. That's really helpful. As if would-be parents don't feel bad enough that the joyous news they recently shared with Mom, Dad, Grandma (who only has a few months to live), and all of social media now has to be shamefully and painfully walked back, now they have someone blaming them for sharing that good news in the first place. This is not only unproductive, it's also a terrible form of victim blaming and it should not ever be uttered. There is no right or wrong time to share the news of a pregnancy (more on this in an upcoming chapter) and making someone who already feels terrible feel even worse is diabolical.

"Maybe you shouldn't have gone to the gym or to work so much." Again, more victim blaming. The people who say these things might think they're being helpful and giving the grieving party some helpful advice if there's a next time, but in the moment it's going to be seen as a tactic that shames the woman and erroneously puts the blame on her for the miscarriage when scientifically that is not the cause.

"Well, look at the bright side, at least you can get pregnant." This one truly irks me for several reasons. First of all, it sets everyone out on the path to the Grief Olympics by implying infertile people clearly have it worse and that somehow losing pregnancy after pregnancy is "lucky" compared to simply not being able to get pregnant. The fact is everyone in either situation is going through hell and pitting different factions against the other does nothing to help anyone.

"Maybe it's time to take a break." Nine times out of ten, the person saying this is not only *not* a doctor, but they're probably not *your* doctor. Chances are the folks who have been going through repeated miscarriages or infertility have seen an abundance of doctors—esteemed professionals with years of training who are paid a lot of money to be intimately familiar with the case histories of their patients and best practices. So all those who lack medical training and are without firsthand knowledge of the person who has likely been poked, prodded, and examined countless times, can keep their medical opinions and diagnoses to themselves and leave their unsolicited advice at the door.

"Why do you call yourself a mother/father of two when you only have one kid?" Why in the name of all things holy would anyone want to pick this hill to die on? Yet, it happens. Laura has been questioned with raised eyebrows and rolled eyes when she corrects people who say she's simply a mother of six. When that happens, she responds by saying, "I have six living children, one loss of twins, and three other miscarriages." Some people try to argue that she should only count her living children, but what's the point of even making that argument? Why battle a person who considers their lost babies in that count? There's absolutely no harm in it and picking a fight about it is insensitive and cruel.

So what should people say and do in these situations?

Just listen. Show up when welcomed, be there, sit with the pain, and acknowledge the hurt. Don't pretend that you have to understand or fix the problem, and stop thinking the problem can be fixed. This is a perfectly acceptable time to feel sad and terrible and the people going through it simply need someone to sit with them in all of that misery and acknowledge that it's real and it sucks and it's painful.

This is a sensitive topic and most of the people who say misguided things aren't trying to be malicious or hurtful. Most of them care and want to help but don't know how, so they end up putting their foot in their mouth and unintentionally causing even more hurt. While it feels awkward, don't be afraid to tell people exactly what you need because it'll help you get better and they'll likely be very grateful for the direction so they can stop hopelessly scrambling for the right things to say.

\* \* \*

*"It's not the right time in your career."*

*That's something my boss said to me after my second miscarriage when I asked him for some time off to recover. To this day I'm not sure if he thought he was helping or if he was purposely being a jerk, but to say that to someone going through hell is tone deaf at best and absolutely appalling at worst. Not to mention none of his damn business, as my manager. But whether it's an example of toxic masculinity thinking he had the right to dictate what was and wasn't appropriate in my life, or he was just ridiculously thoughtless, I learned then and there that people say some truly dumb stuff following pregnancy losses.*

*Now that I think about it, some of the most hurtful comments came from the men in my life. I remember coming out of surgery from a D&C because I had a passive miscarriage, and the doctor told me that I needed to take a break from trying to have a baby because I may not be able to successfully deliver another healthy baby. I was literally in a post-surgical fog and he's telling me this when my husband wasn't even around. This was the last thing I wanted to hear at that time and it was the most hurtful thing anyone could have said. The nurses tried to comfort me but it was too late, I was hysterical.*

*Women were better, but still problematic. I worked in banking and communicated with the public regularly, and some of my regular customers who knew I was pregnant felt the need to comment on my pregnancy, especially after my miscarriage. They would tell me it was God's plan (I was struggling with my religion already), it was for the best, that I'm lucky I could even get pregnant because their daughter couldn't and had it so much worse. These were hurtful because as soon as I thought I had a handle on things, someone would say something insensitive and bring me back down.*

*And since I'm never one to dodge blame, I need to hold myself responsible for some ignorant and insensitive comments I made. I recall talking to my friend who lost her very first pregnancy right before my bachelorette party. My first question was if she was okay, but I was barely done letting her answer before I asked her if she was coming to my party, and laying a guilt trip on her when she wavered. I told her it would be fun and she could forget about the pain of losing the baby if she just went out with me and got wasted. I wasn't married and had never lost a pregnancy so I didn't have the proper perspective, but the way I acted was so mean and insensitive. All I did was think about myself and not about the pain she was feeling. All I could think about was losing* my good friend during an important moment in my life, but gave no consideration to her loss. To my friend's credit, when I had my first miscarriage, she did not say a word about how terrible I had made her feel the first time she lost her baby. She was a kind ear for me to listen to me talk about how I was feeling. She also gave me advice on how to navigate work insensitivities, rude comments, and unsolicited advice.

In my opinion, the hardest place to deal with these kinds of comments is at work. As progressive as my company was, all it takes is one bad manager who doesn't get it to really make life hell. My male bosses had stepped in it so many times that I eventually had to call human resources and document my boss's inability to give me time off, which they eventually granted me after a hassle. I was one of the lucky ones who had the option to call and was taken seriously. If you do not have the support of human resources or a supportive boss, seek it out in other ways. When I reached out to my unsupportive boss and didn't get anywhere, I relied heavily on my staff to help me get through the most emotional time of my life. At the time of my second miscarriage, I was working with a strong staff of mostly women who had at least one miscarriage each in their lifetime. They fully understood where I was in my grief. If you do not have a strong network at work, reach out to human resources. They are there as the go-between for you and the company.

Outside of work, I knew there would be one or two comments from people who meant well but would say the wrong thing. Some of the most hurtful was "at least you can get pregnant" or "it was God's plan" or "it was meant to be this way." I didn't want to hear these comments. These people wanted to be nice and helpful, but all they were doing was being hurtful. One of the ways I dealt with insensitive comments was to ignore them. That worked fine for people I didn't see often, but it was a disastrous way to handle those who I saw regularly. I didn't tell anyone how these comments made me feel and, as a result, I internalized the comments and started to believe some of them. Maybe I should just be happy that I can get pregnant. Maybe this truly was God's plan for me. That one got to me most of all because, at that point, I hadn't been to church in years and I began to believe I was being punished for not being a better Catholic. A few people had warned me not to marry an atheist so I even wondered if Aaron was responsible for God punishing me. Words have consequences and many do not fully comprehend the fallout from their words.

As time passed, I began to realize I wasn't to blame and neither was God. When people would make a comment that perhaps stress or me working too much caused the miscarriage, I would come back with the facts about pregnancy that proved those people were wrong. I would tell them what Aaron and I had gone through. I have been pregnant eight times, miscarried four times, opted for one abortion, and blessedly had three live births. This usually changes their tune quickly. They suddenly realize they stepped into a minefield of emotions and I get the quick apologies for their unkind words or they shrug their shoulders and walk away. Either way they have learned a lesson. Hopefully they will think twice about what they say to people grieving a loss through miscarriage, abortion, or infertility, and I urge anyone reading this to do the same.

I also recall the unsolicited advice I received from strangers at my job and well-meaning family members. Some were supportive but most were harmful and hurtful. "Don't get pregnant too soon after miscarriage or it will happen again," "Well it's because you ate soft cheese, we know how much you love your cheese," and "You work too much." I would die inside every time. I was already dealing with all kinds of guilt and I didn't need any more, whether from people I either knew well or from casual acquaintances. For anyone going through what Aaron and I went through, just ignore it if you can and do not internalize what people say. And if it's coming from people close to you, politely but firmly let them know how it makes you feel so they'll adjust how they address you. Know that it was not your fault. Your eating habits, work habits, and how soon you get pregnant after a miscarriage do not matter.

Find your network and a supportive group of people in whom you can confide. People who are not going to make judgments and are willing to have a kind ear for listening. Even if it means taking a step back from friends who simply refuse to understand. I cut a few people out of my life after my miscarriages because they became toxic. I even took a step back on a family member who told me part of the reason I had a miscarriage was that I was "too skinny." Surround yourself with people who give you hope and comfort, not nightmares.

People will always make stupid comments and give unsolicited advice but being prepared for it can help. I didn't think people could be so evil with their language, but I was so wrong, as even the most well-intentioned people can say the wrong things. You are going through one of the most miserable experiences of your life. Emotions are high and raw; you are more susceptible to people hurting you than you were before. Just be aware of it. It's okay to not like someone who just said an awful thing to you about your miscarriage, abortion, or infertility.

*You come first.*

# Chapter 12

## *Social Media Makes Miscarriage Really Public and Really Hard*

THE QUESTION OF WHEN TO TELL PEOPLE YOU'RE PREGNANT is a deeply personal one that has no correct answer. But when you've experienced a miscarriage and gone through the process of unringing that bell to people both in person and on social media, it gets even more complicated to the point that it's very possible your mind will change with each pregnancy. I understand that is deeply unhelpful, but it's also the truth.

The prevailing wisdom is to wait to announce pregnancies until the twelfth week because the chances of having a miscarriage drop to 5 percent for the remainder of the pregnancy.[1] But when you're an innocent and inexperienced young couple who are bursting at the seams to shout this good news from the rooftop, waiting nearly three months seems like a Herculean task. That's why many first-timers buck traditional norms, throw caution to the wind, and tell everyone they can as soon as they

---

1  "When Is the Best Time to Announce Your Pregnancy." *Healthline.com*, https://www.healthline.com/health/pregnancy/when-to-announce-your-pregnancy. Accessed January 27, 2021.

find out. They tell people in person. They catch the tearful, joyous reactions of soon-to-be grandparents on video. They post the cutest, most Pinterest-perfect pregnancy announcements that rack up hundreds and maybe thousands of likes, courtesy of everyone from close relatives to that bitch from high school you keep on your Facebook just for moments like this one. Everyone is thrilled, cups overfloweth with joy, and all is right with the world.

Until it isn't.

Imagine going to an 8-week ultrasound only to find there's no heartbeat. That's horrific enough for would-be parents, but when there's already been a pregnancy announcement made, suddenly it's grief on top of grief because now people need to think about how to walk back the announcement. So much shame, guilt, and humiliation rushes right to the surface and threatens to erupt and suddenly people have to consider their own heartbreak along with a strategy for dealing with everyone else's by telling expectant grandmas and grandpas, not to mention coworkers and the wider social media world, that the pregnancy has ended.

The social media component might be the hardest part. It used to be that the media outlets were the only ones with designated platforms, but not anymore. With Facebook, Instagram, Twitter, TikTok, and every other social media channel out there, everyone is now their own individual media platform. A lot of people share what they eat for breakfast and dinner every day, making the pregnancy journey a social media goldmine and an easy and effective way for people to keep their friends and relatives who live anywhere in the world updated on the latest news. But no one ever mentions what to do when that news is absolutely devastating.

In our interviews with people for this book, most of them started off telling family and friends right away about the first pregnancy as soon as possible, but then fell into the "once bitten, twice shy" camp. That's to say they excitedly made big announcements very early on in the pregnancy before they experienced losses, but after going through the agony of walking it back, they played their cards closer to the vest. And who can blame them? But even though they're all generally in the same boat, there are some minor differences in how they approached this topic and various things others should consider when making their own decisions.

Zachary and his wife in Brazil only told their parents about the pregnancy for fear of something going wrong. So when things did take a wrong turn at the 12-week mark, they only had to tell each of their parents. The couple had his mother-in-law come to the house to be on hand to help him with their other child and take care of his wife while she recovered, while he notified his parents via telephone. "I tried to keep emotion out of it so it was a very matter-of-fact conversation with my parents. Fortunately we really hadn't told anyone she was pregnant so we didn't have to tell them about the miscarriage."

Another trend that we found among people who had been through this in the past is having a plan in place in case things don't work out favorably.

Benjamin and his wife learned some tough lessons from losing their son at 15 weeks, so when they received a Trisonomy 13 diagnosis at 20 weeks with their unborn baby Jonah (who ultimately was stillborn at just less than 37 weeks), they were grimly more prepared. They brought both mothers together and told them in person and told both fathers over the phone immediately because they weren't readily available in person. But that still left social media.

"With Jonah, after we received his diagnosis, we took a day to sit with it, tell our immediate family members, and process all the information. Then we created a private Facebook group to give updates to everyone who wanted to join."

This can be an effective alternative when you simultaneously need social media to connect with loved ones but don't want the crushing emotional weight of announcing terrible news to such a public audience. Creating a closed online group where you're insulated from fringe acquaintances and even strangers making potentially problematic comments is something that helped people like Benjamin immensely during an unbelievably emotional time when you feel a responsibility to provide worried friends and family members with updates, but don't want to put yourself on display.

While Benjamin received a diagnosis at 20 weeks and had time to prepare, Jennifer lost her baby at 37 weeks suddenly and without warning, which brings up an entirely different set of circumstances. Stunned by the news and unable to think about anything other than her grief, she enlisted the help of her parents and two close friends to reach out to people in her social sphere and let as many of them as possible know what was going on to avoid Jennifer receiving messages or phone calls that would unintentionally upset her. Once she had been home for about a week, she did decide to post the news on social media mainly to avoid people asking whether or not she had had the baby yet.

Despite having no appetite to post on social media in the initial aftermath of what happened, Jennifer said that feeling did change with time. Not long after losing Nora, she joined a Facebook group devoted to mothers who lost babies in the late stages of pregnancy. She didn't post there much at first because she was looking for reassurance—the need to be around other women who understood her pain who could prove that there was hope for eventually getting through a loss of this nature. Then, with time, Jennifer felt the urge to speak out.

"I started posting on my personal Facebook page at first because I felt I had to say something and that my putting it out there would diffuse the questions. But now I share because I want people to know how significant this has been to my life and that she is my daughter and always will be. I feel a strong need to keep her memory alive as part of our family, and speak for her since she isn't here to tell her own story or live her own life."

After having a baby in 2013 with no difficulty, Vernon and his wife experienced three early miscarriages and then lost twins at 19 weeks. When they found out they were pregnant with their current twins, they were warned by doctors they were likely in for a turbulent pregnancy due to preexisting cervical issues, so the couple took no chances. They told their parents early on in the pregnancy but swore them to secrecy and told precisely no one else, including going on a social media pregnancy blackout.

"On Facebook, no one knew until we had the kids. When they were born and we knew they were healthy, we posted pictures and most of our friends and relatives said, 'What? We didn't even know you were pregnant!' With the previous losses and her surgery, we just felt much more at ease that way. We knew we were going to hit bumps in the road and so this was our way of swerving around them. It's like driving down the street with no seatbelt versus wearing one, and we felt a little more in control. Like we had done something ahead of time to prevent another loss."

David and Penelope had so many miscarriages they took it a step further.

"After so many losses we just stopped telling people we were pregnant. I mean everyone. Penelope has a super close relationship with her mom and she didn't even tell her. I stopped telling my parents and stopped making any notification part of the process. Hell, I wouldn't even tell people at work why I needed to leave when we were doing treatments. Radio silence."

And who can argue with that? Certainly not me. I do, however, have a slightly different outlook that likely puts me in the minority.

Social media is a double-edged sword in that it is both the bane of my existence and my saving grace. My relationship with social media is complicated, maddening, beautiful, and ridiculous, but I can't deny that it helped me get through some of these losses and provided me with an essential outlet when I wouldn't agree to counseling. Maybe I'm just an over-sharer but I find value in commiserating with others who have been there before. I find it cathartic to be with a group of people, most of them strangers, but still feel this kinship like you've truly found your people who understand what you're going through. And while I've been raked over the coals, torn apart, and even ridiculed on the front page of a Nazi website because of social media, I've also been helped immeasurably by it.

The women (and some men) who wrote to me after I shared our experience in front of the abortion clinic really got me through that ordeal. I was so angry and so low at that point that I truly feared I wouldn't be able to pull myself out of it and get back to being myself, but the encouragement and support I found on social media wrapped me up, kept me warm, and gave me a sense of purpose. The various parenting groups I joined online were also an essential outlet for me, because it was far easier for me to open up to strangers on the Internet than it was to the people in my life or a therapist. I've told nameless, faceless people a few incredibly intimate details and thoughts that I still, to this day, haven't told anyone else. I did it because everyone else was sharing too and there was a level of trust and acceptance there I didn't think I could find anywhere else.

Were there bad times and huge complications caused by social media? Of course. Trolls who called MJ and I murderers for having an abortion. People who doxxed us and published our address and phone number. Then they'd call my parents at home and tell them they raised a baby killer. Internet randos with too much time on their hands who contacted my employer and left one-star ratings for my place of work online. The dark underbelly of social media and the Internet can be a truly disgusting hellscape of inhumanity and cruelty, without a doubt. But the thing is, at least for me, almost all of that dissipates immediately after getting just one heartfelt email from someone who needed to hear what I had to say. People who felt utterly alone and wondered how the hell anyone gets through what they're going through, only to find my story on the Internet and, if not gain hope from it, then at least they were comforted by the fact that they weren't the only ones out there feeling the same things.

But mostly I wanted to tell people we were pregnant right away because, if the worst-case scenario did play out and we lost the baby, then at least we wouldn't be so alone.

The one time I waited and told nobody with the pregnancy we lost before we had our third son, Tommy, I mistakenly believed it was good that I hadn't told anyone because then there was no one to disappoint with harrowing news. But I soon learned the main benefit of my plan was also the worst part—it meant we had to go through the aftershocks of the miscarriage totally alone. I understand that's a positive for some people, which is why this topic has no correct answer and is entirely dependent on personal preference. But for someone like me who already kept too much bottled up inside, the worst thing that could've happened was to feel even more isolated because we didn't tell anyone.

One unexpected part of social media that did help me involved celebrities. That's a strange and uncomfortable thing for me to say because while MJ consumes television shows like *Inside Edition* regularly, I abhor celebrity gossip media and usually dismiss it completely. Yet I remember in 2010 when singer Pink went on *The Ellen Degeneres Show* to announce she was pregnant, she said she was nervous because she had had miscarriages in the past.[2] We had already gone through our fair share of losses at that point and even though Pink didn't get too far into the weeds on the show, she talked about it. She spoke the uncomfortable words no one wants to hear to a national television audience. Just that one act of bravery struck me as monumental and I felt appreciative that this wasn't just an "us" problem.

Judging by our survey, I'm not the only one who feels this way. Not only did 84 percent of women report feeling comforted by celebrities sharing their stories of pregnancy loss on social media, but 71 percent of men said they appreciate the transparency from the rich and famous as well.

Zachary said, "I admire their bravery and it helps me realize that we are not alone. I have even used examples of famous people talking about their own miscarriages to start conversations about ours." Charlie agreed and said, "More prominent people in our society can help those who are unsure of themselves or the ones feeling guilty because it lets them know they are not alone with this struggle."

---

2  CNN staff. "Singer Pink Announces She Is Pregnant." CNN, November 22, 2010. https://www.cnn.com/2010/SHOWBIZ/Music/11/17/pink.pregnancy/index.html

The most recent high-profile celebrities openly discussing these kinds of losses are supermodel and author Chrissy Teigen and her husband, famous musician John Legend. In September 2020, Teigen lost her unborn son Jack at 20 weeks due to a partial placenta abruption. She posted intimate and raw photos of herself in the hospital—sobbing, hooked up to monitoring equipment and oxygen, and she and Legend holding Jack—on Instagram on September 30 announcing the news, saying, "We are shocked and in the kind of deep pain you only hear about, the kind of pain we've never felt before. We were never able to stop the bleeding and give our baby the fluids he needed, despite bags and bags of blood transfusions. It just wasn't enough."[3] Teigen's post went internationally viral because of its personal nature, the fact that this kind of loss is seldom discussed, but also because she chose to include photos of herself and Legend in the process of grieving and while holding their stillborn son. The last part earned the couple criticism from some corners of the Internet from people who thought it was too personal and inappropriate to show photos of a dead infant. However, Teigen took those people to task by authoring an exceedingly candid and personal account of the loss on Medium, which featured an in-depth retelling of the events of that day and her rationale for choosing to share it with the world.

"I had asked my mom and John to take pictures, no matter how uncomfortable it was. I explained to a very hesitant John that I needed them, and that I did NOT want to have to ever ask. That he just had to do it. He hated it. I could tell. It didn't make sense to him at the time. But I knew I needed to know of this moment forever, the same way I needed to remember us kissing at the end of the aisle, the same way I needed to remember

---

3  Teigen, Chrissy. Photos of Teigen, Legend, and Son Jack in Hospital. *Instagram*. September 30, 2020, https://www.instagram.com/p/CFyWQLWpJ3u/

our tears of joy after Luna and Miles. And I absolutely knew I needed to share this story. I cannot express how little I care that you hate the photos. How little I care that it's something you wouldn't have done. I lived it, I chose to do it, and more than anything, these photos aren't for anyone but the people who have lived this or are curious enough to wonder what something like this is like. These photos are only for the people who need them. The thoughts of others do not matter to me."[4]

Regarding the pictures, specifically, I went wide-eyed when Teigen explained that it was her mother and her husband, and not a professional photographer, who snapped them.

When I read her account of what happened I was equal parts awestruck at the couple's bravery, tearful at them having lost the baby halfway through the pregnancy, grateful they decided to share their journey for the benefit of others, and bewildered at how Legend was able to take those pictures while actively grieving himself. Pictures of stillborn infants have always been a hot topic in the media and online, with lines drawn in the sand about the appropriateness of taking them, but more specifically, whether or not pictures like that should be shared on the Internet. My personal take is people should do whatever will bring them peace and closure, as Teigen and Legend did. Yet I couldn't help but wonder what if that had been me? If MJ had demanded that I take pictures of my dead son when I was actively riding the world's worst emotional roller coaster. I'm not sure I would've had it in me, nor am I sure how I'd react seeing those pictures pop up at random or with Facebook's "On This Day" feature every year later. I hope that Legend looks back on them now with a mixture of melancholy and appreciation, but I'm not sure my

---

4 Teigen, Chrissy. "Hi." Medium. October 27, 2020, https://chrissyteigen.medium.com/hi-2e45e6faf764

skin would've been thick enough to withstand the criticism from online commenters at such a low point.

Jennifer and her husband Matthew lost their baby at 37 weeks, and she admits she has mixed feelings about celebrities like Teigen and Legend sharing their stories. Jennifer also decided to have pictures taken of her baby daughter, Nora, in the delivery room but, unlike Teigen, she has not shared them on social media. Jennifer said she admires Teigen's bravery but admitted it can often be overwhelming to stumble across posts like that.

"It can be very triggering. It's been especially hard to see the negativity around the images shared by Chrissy Teigen because we had pictures taken in the hospital and they are the absolute treasure of my life. They are all we'll ever have. I have them displayed in my home and I've shared with friends but I haven't yet shared them on social media for fear that someone would only see a dead body instead of my precious daughter that I only got to hold for thirty-six hours before having to hand her over to the coroner in a wooden box. That image is one that haunts me."

Another high-profile celebrity recently in the news for this unfortunate topic is Duchess of Sussex Meghan Markle, who lost her second pregnancy in the summer of 2020 and wrote about the loss in a *New York Times* column that November. While Markle shared far fewer details of the loss in her piece compared to Teigen, a member of Britain's prim and proper (not to mention tight-lipped and exceedingly private) Royal Family speaking out about such a personal topic sent a powerful message about the benefits of addressing pregnancy loss in the cold light of day.

For me, the lasting impact of Markle's op-ed was a story she recounted of being in New York City for the first time in a taxi, and seeing a woman sobbing her eyes out on a public street corner. Markle's first instinct was to stop the cab, get out, and check to make sure she was okay, but her cab driver told her New Yorkers live out their private lives in public spaces and someone would eventually check on the woman. But all these years later and crying uncontrollably in a hospital bed following a miscarriage, Markle wondered what if no one did inquire that day.

"I wish I could go back and ask my cab driver to pull over. This, I realize, is the danger of siloed living—where moments sad, scary, or sacrosanct are all lived out alone. There is no one stopping to ask, 'Are you okay?' Losing a child means carrying an almost unbearable grief, experienced by many but talked about by few. In the pain of our loss, my husband and I discovered that in a room of a hundred women, ten to twenty of them will have suffered from miscarriage. Yet despite the staggering commonality of this pain, the conversation remains taboo, riddled with (unwarranted) shame, and perpetuating a cycle of solitary mourning. Some have bravely shared their stories; they have opened the door, knowing that when one person speaks truth, it gives license for all of us to do the same. We have learned that when people ask how any of us are doing, and when they really listen to the answer, with an open heart and mind, the load of grief often becomes lighter—for all of us. In being invited to share our pain, together we take the first steps toward healing."[5]

It sounds so simple, yet "Are you okay?" is what's largely missing in the pregnancy loss conversation. For women, yes, but especially when it comes to men. Markle, in her piece, said she came to this realization while staring at her crying husband, Prince Harry, the Duke of Sussex, who was at her bedside trying desperately to hold together the "shattered pieces" of her heart when she asked him if he was okay. And sure, the majority of

5  Markle, Meghan. "The Losses We Share." *New York Times*. November 25, 2020, https://www.nytimes.com/2020/11/25/opinion/meghan-markle-miscarriage.html

men desperately need to work on figuring out how to build and utilize the emotional vocabulary to communicate that they are not doing well in those instances, but before that can happen they need to be given the space to do so. They need to know that it's acceptable for them to be despondent and that they're supposed to hurt. They need someone to ask them if they're okay.

That's part of the reason I value online and social media interactions so much, especially in these times of isolation and social distancing, simply because the more you join in and the more people with whom you interact, the mathematical probability of someone asking you how you're doing rises. We need that right now, and the more often public figures like Markle and Teigen put the issue front and center, the more often the question will be asked.

Speaking of celebrities, it's not just high-profile women who are speaking up about infertility and miscarriage. Although their numbers are small, some male celebrities have taken the torch and run with it, which is a huge step in the right direction.

Benjamin, whose wife lost pregnancies at 15 weeks and just shy of 37 weeks, has mixed feelings when it comes to celebrities sharing their losses with the world. On one hand, he sees the benefit others get from it and applauds those brave enough to share. But on the other hand, he hopes that what they are doing is helpful for them and not just for everyone else.

The one example that sticks out in his mind is that of Marquise Goodwin, a wide receiver in the National Football League, who was playing on the San Francisco 49ers in November 2017 when disaster struck. Goodwin's wife, Morgan, had made it to the second trimester with their first pregnancy and the couple was cuddling on the couch for the night, taking it easy because Morgan had been diagnosed with an "incompetent cervix." That meant they had a fifty-fifty chance of delivering a baby prematurely, but the first trimester had come and gone so they were feeling hopeful.

The night before his game against the New York Giants, Marquise had received permission from the 49ers to leave the team hotel and be by his wife's side. Morgan got up and went to the bathroom and immediately began screaming for Marquise, who entered the room only to see the amniotic sac escaping. Although doctors did everything they could, the couple ultimately had to terminate in the wee hours of the morning on November 12, just hours before Marquise was scheduled to play.[6]

Inconsolable with grief and holding their fully formed but stillborn infant son, Morgan told her husband to go play in the team's game that day and dedicate his performance to their son. Marquise refused but Morgan was insistent, and so eventually he made his way to the stadium through a fog of grief and sadness the likes of which are only known to the poor souls who have been in that situation. During the game, Goodwin caught a long touchdown pass and then fell to his knees overwhelmed with emotion. Later that day he took to Instagram and announced their loss, explaining that his reaction after the touchdown had been to honor his baby boy.

"When Marquise Goodwin collapsed in the end zone after scoring a touchdown on the same day he lost his son, I knew exactly that feeling," Benjamin said. "While I'm not the person who needs to read other's stories about a thing to feel it because I'm an empath, I connected with Marquise at that moment. Just trying to move, using muscle memory to hold it together, and then letting it all out despite everything around you. I lost it watching that. I still do to this day."

But perhaps the highest profile man to talk about miscarriage is Facebook Founder and CEO Mark Zuckerberg.

In 2015, Zuckerberg and Priscilla Chan announced Chan's pregnancy in a Facebook post. However, instead of the pregnancy being the focus, it was Zuckerberg's admission that he and Chan had been trying unsuccessfully for three years to start a family and had endured three miscarriages along the way that made international headlines. He wrote, "You feel so hopeful when you learn you're going to have a child. You start imagining who they'll become and dreaming of hopes for their future. You start making plans, and then they're gone. It's a lonely experience. Most people don't discuss miscarriages because you worry your problems will distance you or reflect upon you—as if you're defective or did something to cause this. So you struggle on your own. In today's open and connected world, discussing these issues doesn't distance us; it brings us together. It creates understanding and tolerance, and it gives us hope."[7]

While I do not consider Zuckerberg any kind of hero and have a sizable list of problems with Facebook that have been well publicized and I won't get into here, I still give him credit for speaking out about this. As a human being this is far from easy, but to be a man and tackle this is rare. And necessary.

Not to mention Facebook is where I found a lot of support in groups set up solely to help people who have been impacted by infertility and pregnancy loss. For as many problems as I have with what the Facebook platform has become, there's no disputing the fact that it has helped connect millions of people who

---

7 Zuckerberg, Mark. Facebook Pregnancy Announcement. *Facebook*. July 31, 2015, https://www.facebook.com/photo.php?fbid=10102276573729791

have positively impacted one another in a myriad of ways. To this day I haven't met many of the dads who helped me through tough times in person, but I'm forever changed and helped because I had access to their listening virtual ears, their lived experiences, and their camaraderie. And to have the man who made that community possible essentially tell us he's one of us and he gets it? That was meaningful. It's meaningful any time a man uses his platform to let other men know it's okay to be vulnerable and to struggle. The more examples of men like that we can point to, the more we chip away at the stigma and the more normal it becomes for men to embrace their feelings in an honest way.

\* \* \*

*I was and still am a late adapter to social media—I just got an Instagram account in 2020. I think it has to do with the fact I am an intensely private person who wonders why the world feels the need to share what they're having for dinner every night. My husband, on the other hand, is an extremely public person on social media. Which is interesting because while I guard my life online, I'm actually very social in real life, whereas Aaron shares everything online but is a total introvert in person. Anyway, the bottom line is I would be lying if I said this had not caused a problem in our marriage. In fact, it still does sometimes. Social media plays a huge role in our lives, and that was even more true when we were trying to get pregnant. Aaron wanted to share all the things going on with our lives and, to me, those details were too private to share on social media.*

*I have always been in the camp of not telling anyone you are expecting until you hit the 12-week mark. Aaron, on the other hand, wanted to tell everyone right away. It makes for an extremely hard conversation about when to announce the pregnancy and also when to post it to social media. There is no good choice when it comes to making the announcement because each pregnancy is different. I know for Aaron and myself every time we became pregnant, we would have the conversation of when to announce, who to announce to, and when to post it to social media, and the answer was a little different every time.*

*The very first time I found out I was pregnant, I just assumed we would keep it to ourselves because that's what I had always believed people were supposed to do. But then I saw the excitement in Aaron's face and I got caught up in the excitement, so we proceeded to tell all of our family members and close friends. But I kicked myself when we had to go back to tell them we lost the baby a short time later. I was so embarrassed, confused, and stressed. I shouldn't have had those feelings, but I did. Even though social media wasn't nearly as prevalent then as it is now, I was happy we had not posted anything on Facebook, which has a far greater reach. I would have felt even worse.*

*There is no right or wrong way to announce your pregnancy and I don't judge anyone who announces via social media. However, I choose not to. But with Aaron feeling so strongly in the opposite direction, I decided to leave it up to him and gave him permission to announce the news. To be honest, I don't even remember which ones were announced and which weren't.*

*The only one I remember announcing online was our last pregnancy, but that was after our 8-week ultrasound where we saw the strong heartbeat and had the blood test to back up the proof it was a healthy pregnancy. We went all out for that announcement by getting our other two boys involved in the story. We had just had a blizzard that dumped more than a foot of snow, so we told everyone on social media we were expecting our third snow angel in September with a picture of Will and Sam making snow angels. It felt good at the time, even for me. But I was still nervous because of all our previous losses. In fact, there were times I refused to even let him tell anyone, let alone post it to his media channels.*

*Our seventh pregnancy was one of those we chose not to tell anyone. We had no reason not to tell anyone but just felt it was best for everyone that we waited. Maybe because if something happened, I didn't want to hear the comments about it being time to stop trying or maybe I'm too old. In a way, it made it easier to handle the loss of the pregnancy when it happened. No one knew and I didn't have to see everyone's disappointed faces and looks of pity. It was just me and Aaron at first and, with the exception of telling one trusted friend, I shut everyone out and I was grateful Aaron hadn't posted it online.*

*However, I could see how he was struggling with the silence and that he needed an outlet for his grief, and I didn't want to be the one taking it away from him. I don't pretend to understand it but Aaron is a public person who needs the connection to other people who have experienced the same thing or been in a similar position, to know he was not alone. That's the difference between us—I take solace in talking to one trusted confidante, but he needs to be virtually surrounded by people who make him feel less alone.*

*Social media can be cathartic for someone like Aaron. He sought out help through people in groups who experienced losses similar to ours, while I avoided all forms of social media because I prefer one-on-one interaction. This is why social media has caused fights in our house and disruptions to our marriage. How do you compromise when you both feel strongly about your point of view and have diametrically opposed coping mechanisms for your grief? You can't just say "do your own thing" because if he did that then my private business would be aired out to tens of thousands of his followers, and if I made him keep silent then I'm knowingly harming his mental health. Neither way is right or wrong, they're just different. We're different. It makes finding a way through it tough on everyone.*

*I need to be a private person who shies away from the lime-light because I am extremely uncomfortable with people making a fuss about me. I pulled away from Aaron and the people clos-est to me, never mind posting something to social media. I felt exposed being on social media and my paranoia was through the roof because people on Twitter and Facebook will judge you incessantly. Simply put, I am not nearly thick-skinned enough. I must give Aaron credit; he has a thick skin and can take what the Internet throws at him. He loves to argue and jump into the fray on politics and all the important yet controversial topics, and he defends his position ferociously and unceasingly. He also does a great job at shielding me and our family from the aftermath of his choices when it comes to social media. And the truth is, despite my criticism about the Internet and social media, it probably saved Aaron from getting severely depressed. It gave him an outlet to vent, talk, and be creative. I was jealous at first because I wanted to be enough for him and the reason he lifted himself out of his funk, but eventually I realized social media gave him something I just wasn't able to provide at the time, because I was consumed with grief.*

*Yet even though I refused to discuss what I was going through online, I did find some comfort in other peoples' stories about miscarriages, abortions, and infertility. Many might call me a hypocrite because I turned to the Internet for strength while simul-taneously judging Aaron, who had done the same thing but in a different way. I wanted to stay anonymous so I made a fake profile* because I was still too embarrassed of everything. I'd use social media in spurts, jumping online and searching out groups that made me realize I wasn't alone in my grief, and then I'd retreat and go grieve by myself.

As time has passed the pain of the loss has gone away for me, but it is never forgotten. Every time I hear a story about a loss, abortion, or infertility, it brings me back to the exact moment when I heard the news myself. For the longest time I avoided reading articles that had to do with public loss, because it was too painful to read.

But then came 2010 and the abortion, and suddenly everything changed for me.

I felt so violated and angry at the women who had screamed at me outside the clinic that day, and I became more incensed than I ever had felt before. Although my initial reaction was to fade into the background while Aaron wrote about our experience, I was feeling the unfamiliar urge to speak up myself. I'm not a writer and I'm certainly not a skilled public speaker so this was new territory to me, but sparked on by a burning anger I couldn't douse, I told Aaron I was going to write a piece for his website giving my two cents.

When it was published, I had no idea what to expect. Were there awful trolls? Definitely. And they really are awful. But there were way more notes of gratitude and shared experiences and people rooting me on, and suddenly I saw a glimpse of why Aaron shares so much of himself and our life. In an instant I had gone from being the person who lurks and finds comfort in the online stories of celebrities experiencing loss to the person doing the sharing and putting herself out there.

I scurried back to my shadows in the background after that and haven't come out much until now, but it was long enough to *witness firsthand the importance of people telling their stories and sharing their lived experiences for the comfort of others. I'm no Chrissy Teigen or Meghan Markle, but over the years I've gained a genuine appreciation for how open they are and how important it is for so many people to see their struggles and vulnerabilities.*

*If you're in a relationship where one of you is private and the other wants to share, there's no easy answer. My advice is to talk through it because you may not realize the reason your partner wants to share isn't narcissistic, but actually altruistic. Even if you struggle finding a balance and solution, at least you're having an honest conversation and recognizing where the other person is coming from. That's more than half the battle.*

# Chapter 13

# *Don't Allow Loss to Be a Thief of Future Joy*

O NE OF THE MOST UNEXPECTED AND UNPLEASANT THINGS I discovered about pregnancy loss is that it doesn't just ruin things in the present, it causes future pain people don't even consider until they're going through it. Namely, once you've experienced this kind of loss, you'll never feel the same unadulterated joy upon finding out you're expecting again, and happiness and excitement about expanding your family will be harder to come by.

This kind of loss, especially repeated losses, is insidious because it robs you of future happiness. The fear of losing a pregnancy because previous ones haven't stuck can be debilitating, and the same goes for couples who go through infertility treatment for years. Like dogs chasing fire trucks, some people spend so much time trying to reach a goal they eventually come to view as unattainable that it becomes impossible to enjoy any positive news.

"We spent so long trying to get pregnant that when we were, we didn't know how to enjoy it," said David, whose wife, Penelope, had a series of miscarriages while the couple went to fertility specialists for years. "Pregnancy was a blip for us because we were always waiting for the other shoe to drop, to the point we weren't even ready for our twin boys when they did come because we were so prepared for failure."

I felt what David described on a visceral level, to the point MJ nicknamed me "Eeyore," the downtrodden, pessimistic donkey from *Winnie the Pooh*, because I refused to get excited about (and sometimes even acknowledge) the fact that MJ was finally pregnant. After going through all the loss and the trauma, why would I? Why get excited about something that's going to end in disaster? This impacted our lives in countless ways, from arguing about if or when to announce the pregnancy to undermining our marriage because eventually I began to wonder if we should stop having kids altogether just to avoid the heartbreak.

The other thing no one tells you about is the complete inability to be truly happy for other people who get pregnant or have healthy babies. Obviously, this isn't true for everyone, but some folks need to be prepared for the horrific reality that sets in when you realize you're virulently enraged by someone else's happiness.

This one is exceptionally tough because most people love babies and celebrating new life should be automatic. But what if you've lost a pregnancy? Or two? Or twelve? What if suddenly three of your friends announce they're expecting while you can't get or stay pregnant? What if that one woman at work with seven kids is now pregnant with her eighth and says, "My husband jokes that I get pregnant just from looking at him"? And what happens when you're in public, minding your own business, and suddenly you see a mother or a father holding a newborn? A newborn that would be the exact same age as the baby you lost?

MJ skipped out on a few baby showers and we avoided certain gatherings where we knew babies would be during the times that it was too tough for us mentally. While I'll always feel slightly guilty for missing out on milestones and celebrations with people we genuinely love, I'm not sorry we exercised some strategic self-care. But the big thing for me was feeling like I was losing some of my humanity and compassion. During the time when MJ had the abortion, I was a journalist and was always plugged into the news. I remember hearing about a local case in which a drug-addicted mother with six or seven kids was fighting the state for custody and had gotten pregnant yet again. Even though addiction runs in my family and I was ordinarily very understanding of what drug and alcohol problems can do to people and their families, I found myself cursing this woman and judging her negatively because she had more kids than she could handle and the state was constantly taking them away, yet MJ and I were struggling with loss after loss for a kid we so desperately wanted to love and care for. Losing that empathy for others who were clearly struggling and unnecessarily pitting them against us was so off-base, and yet that's what happens when you're in the throes of these losses.

Benjamin and his wife lost two pregnancies—in the second and third trimester—in the span of 13 months. In a piece he authored called "Angry Faith" following the loss of his sons, he spoke about the joy going to church used to bring him, but how that happiness was so much harder to find when he'd look around the sanctuary and see young families.

"It took us several months to go back to church let alone sit through an entire sermon. I couldn't pay enough attention to the message to absorb anything that was said, so I looked around at the congregation while I processed things and regretted it, every time. Among the couples and families was one who always sat to my left on the other side of the sanctuary—younger, newer parents with a little one easily under a year. It broke me down, watching them hold and occupy their little guy while we would never get to know our baby."[1]

He went on to describe the anger pouring from his heart like a broken faucet that can't turn off, and I'm not sure I've ever related to something so much in all my life.

When MJ told me she was pregnant for the very first time it was one of the most stunning and amazing emotional experiences of my life. It was 100 percent joy, love, happiness, and excitement and if they could bottle that feeling and sell it, it'd be the number one drug in history. Everything was possible, the future was limitless, and for a brief moment everything was truly good in life. And if you're a man reading this who hasn't experienced that yet, the closest comparison I can make is if you're a huge sports fan for a long-suffering franchise and suddenly your team wins a championship (yes, I tend to relate things back to Boston sports teams, so sue me).

But just like no other titles will ever make me feel like I did when the Boston Red Sox ended an eighty-six-year championship drought in 2004, all the pregnancies following our miscarriage left me feeling incredibly apprehensive with an overwhelming sense of foreboding. Like walking around with a guillotine attached to me, just waiting for the bad news to come and the blade to drop.

---

1  McCartney, B J. "Angry Faith." *Still Standing*. December 16, 2017, https://stillstandingmag.com /2017/12/16/angry-faith/

The first couple of our miscarriages were rough. We told family and friends *really* early—basically as soon as we found out. We saw the tearful hugs and witnessed the "I'm gonna be a grandparent!" screams of joy and told brothers and sisters and best friends and passed around indecipherable, grainy ultrasound pictures joking about who the amorphous blog looked like (everyone said me which was kind of hurtful, but I digress). I was a newspaper reporter at the time and when I made a mistake in a story, it ate away at me because I'd have to issue a correction in the next day's edition. I loathe being wrong so having to issue a public declaration that I screwed up for all to see was something that made me crawl out of my skin. Yet here I was issuing what seemed like the ultimate correction, except with a lot more shame involved.

That was 2006 and 2007, so social media was still in its infancy—the one saving grace of our first couple of losses was that they weren't widespread to a huge audience.

Yet even when MJ got pregnant for the third time, I still wanted to tell everyone immediately. I don't know why, maybe it's because I'm a journalist at heart and breaking news seems to be in my DNA. But she made it perfectly clear that while she respected my opinion, we were not announcing anything until the 12-week mark this time. Struggling with undiagnosed bipolar disorder at the time and the paranoia of thinking everyone was judging her and out to get her, of course this made sense. She had been pregnant twice, we told everyone twice, and we had to tell everyone "sorry, just kidding" twice. It sucked. I know I'm a writer and I'm supposed to be more poetic than that, but it just really sucked. Seeing my dad, who was itching to be a grandfather so badly, get all excited and then having to tell him to put his hopes on hold was pretty devastating. So when MJ dictated the rules, I didn't put up a fight.

The same rules were in place for the pregnancy that ended with an abortion. I wanted to tell everyone but MJ was adamant about waiting 12 weeks. But after we got to 12 weeks and still received the terrible news, that's when something inside of me changed. I vowed I would never put myself in that situation again, no matter what. I went from wanting to tell everyone everything right away, to being so jaded that, if I had my way, we would've hidden MJ away in a room somewhere so we never had to announce anything until we knew for absolutely certain the baby was healthy.

By 2014, we had two boys after experiencing four losses and were questioning whether we should have another. Or, more accurately, I was questioning it. MJ absolutely did want a third and so our marriage was pretty tense as we talked and talked without coming to any kind of conclusion. That April, the question seemed to answer itself when MJ found out she was pregnant again.

Even though spring technically begins in March, winter in New England doesn't actually end until some point in April. There's always one day when you know for sure you're in the clear and Mother Nature isn't going to unexpectedly dump a foot of snow on the entire region. After months of freezing temperatures, snow, ice, and brutally cold wind that hurts your face and makes you wonder why people choose to live here, there's always one day in April when the sun busts out and releases the whole region from winter's icy grip. One day winter just gets its walking papers and nature is suddenly blooming with budding light green leaves in their infancy. People leave their houses in shorts without jackets, exposing translucent skin that hasn't seen the sun in an uncomfortable amount of time, and a notoriously unfriendly region of the country collectively smiles while taking in deep breaths of unadulterated spring.

I had taken Will to a local hot dog stand in my hometown, across from my former middle school. It was actually the school where I met MJ for the first time. As we ordered dogs and fries and I watched Will play on the monkey bars across the street from the school where I was unknowingly roaming the halls as an eleven-year-old with my future wife, I was overcome with nostalgic bliss and calm. It was right at that moment a panicked MJ called me and screamed "COME HOME NOW! I'M FUCKING PREGNANT!"

I was stunned. Our talks about whether or not to have a third had yielded no concrete answers, yet suddenly biology seemed to answer for us. While I smiled, hugged her, professed excitement, and said and did all the right things so as to not upset her, I was terrified. In an ironic reversal, she was actually feeling really optimistic and was okay with telling people, but it was me who refused. So we told nobody the news. Not a soul. A decision that initially seemed very wise because when we went to the ultrasound and once again found ourselves staring at a blank screen, I felt vindicated and patted myself on the back for having the wisdom to keep my mouth shut for possibly the first time in my life. It was our fifth loss in seven years.

We kept that secret from everyone. No parents to tell, no relatives to notify, no social media announcements to retract. And for a while I convinced myself it was a good thing that I hadn't gotten my hopes up and gotten everyone excited. As if I spared both us and them.

But after a few months I realized I had made a mistake. All I had done was block any joy or positivity from entering our lives, for fear of the pain. I couldn't see that the pain was now simply part of the equation and would always be no matter how many times we went through this. It's there, it's not going anywhere, and in trying to avoid it completely I failed to realize that not letting in the sunlight for fear of deepening the darkness is a losing strategy for everyone. Good news is good news no matter when it's shared, and if we do get saddled with another loss then that sucks, but it doesn't mean we should simply never be happy or celebrate. And in that rare moment of clarity I also realized that getting through grief can be a lot easier if you don't shut out the people who love you.

So, a few months after we lost that pregnancy and I was able to collect my thoughts, I wrote a blog post about it and published it with MJ's permission. Although some people (namely our family members) were put out that we hadn't told them, it helped me immensely to get the news off my chest, put it out into the world, and feel that familiar support from folks. The other important thing it allowed me to do was figure out how I truly felt about having a third child.

I have to admit, my initial split-second reaction when I got that phone call from MJ was shock. Pure shock. And fear. But with the benefit of several months' hindsight, I was able to see the larger picture and gained perspective I severely lacked in the moment.

At the time, the rational part of my brain knew we'd struggle to afford the baby. Also, we were in a rented duplex at the time and literally didn't have another bedroom for a third, so I wondered where a new baby would sleep. I was flummoxed about what I would ever do with a daughter. Hell, I was mystified how I'd handle three boys. But with time comes clarity and, looking back even just a few months later, the things that stood out to me weren't all the negatives. Instead, I recalled getting the phone call while I was across the street from my old middle school where MJ and I met, and remembering how MJ and I danced in the snow in that parking lot shortly after we were engaged. Instead of seeing my oldest in the rearview mirror and the picture of Sam on my phone and thinking, *why am I volunteering to be outnumbered*, I remembered how many times Will had asked for another sibling and how excited MJ got every time the subject came up.

Time has a way of not only healing, but shifting perspective. So a few months after we lost that pregnancy, I did an exercise with myself. I thought about what I would do if MJ called me and told me she was pregnant again. I tried to put myself in that scenario once more and test how I'd genuinely feel about having another kid. I thought about exploding diapers and sleepless nights and reliving the newborn phase all over again, with all the pros and cons that accompany it. I thought about money problems and lack of space and whether my heart could grow three sizes to accommodate a third child.

And then I busted out laughing. Not a giggle or a chuckle, mind you. I started belly-laughing my ass off. Uncontrollable bursts of hearty laughter usually reserved for my favorite comedies. Will was next to me at the time and looking at me like I was nuts, but for the life of me I couldn't stop. I was laughing so hard I started crying, yet I was also wearing an ear-to-ear grin. I was laughing because I quickly realized I had answered my own question. Not only would I be ecstatic about having another baby with the woman I loved most in the world, but I was no longer going to allow the darkness to win the day. There would be no more shutting everything and everyone out just because there was a chance it would end poorly. Every single thing we do has the potential to end in disaster and the only thing accomplished by encapsulating ourselves in a hermetically sealed bubble was letting grief and fear win. The simple truth is even though I had good reason to be afraid, I didn't like who I became when I insulated myself in that fear. It left me sad, depressed, and unable to see any kind of hope on the horizon. So, I made a conscious decision to be cautiously optimistic if that call ever came again. I'll never be a Pollyanna type of person who sees sunshine and rainbows at every turn, but I refused to let past grief turn me into a lesser husband and father.

Later that year, the call came again for real and I put theory into practice. We made sure our support systems were in place and our counselors were on speed dial and tried to focus on the positives. After going for an ultrasound visit and finding the heartbeat was strong at 157 beats per minute, MJ and I announced our eighth pregnancy at only the 8-week mark. Despite being nervous beyond words, we chose to take the opportunity to celebrate a win right then and there, because as several of the people we interviewed for this book sadly proved, the risk never really goes away. Yet even in all of that joy, I received several messages from people that said, "Aren't you announcing a little early?" Pro tip, folks: Don't do that. Especially when you don't know the couple's history. Believe me, people who have lost repeated pregnancies have done every calculation and examined the pros and cons from every angle. Just respect their decision, celebrate with them, and even if announcing early isn't what you would've done, keep your dissenting opinions to yourself.

I can't sit here and tell you I was suddenly able to flip a switch and be positive all the time following all of our losses. There were days I lost that battle in a big way because the power of positive thinking isn't a panacea that erases nearly a decade of pain and trauma, and I was cold and distant to the people in my life who were able to get and stay pregnant during this time. And strangers I encountered who were either new parents or pregnant? I was usually so angry I was foaming at the mouth and had to leave the premises.

There was one time coming home from one of our losses that MJ asked if we could eat at The Cheesecake Factory. It was the absolute last thing I wanted to do because I wasn't just upset, I was coming unhinged, and had no desire to be around other human beings. But MJ asked so I pulled into the parking lot and off we went. When they sat us directly next to a pregnant woman and her husband, I went apoplectic. I literally shouted "*NO!*" at the hostess, who was clearly taken aback. MJ apologized on my behalf and said it was fine and gave me the "sit the hell down" look, so I did. But I was already done for.

I was close enough to hear their conversations and naturally it was about the baby because she looked like she could go into labor any second. Even though it made no sense and defied any and all logic, I was horrified at them for flaunting their anticipatory glee in our faces. The rational part of me knew they weren't doing anything wrong but anger had completely taken over and I couldn't help uttering "Wow, are you kidding me?" and "Give it a fucking rest already" in a not-so-quiet voice that had them nervously looking over at me with furrowed brows and quizzical expressions. I didn't even make it to our food being delivered before I shot up, slammed the table with my palms, looked directly at them and said, "I can't take any more of this bullshit!" and stormed outside.

Never in my life had I felt that kind of intense animosity toward a perfect stranger. I walked around in frantic circles outside, equal parts terrified and furious beyond compare, took one last look at the couple through the glass, and threw up all over the sidewalk. MJ came and ushered me to the car but I remember being shocked at how angry I felt toward people simply for expecting a healthy child, but even more saddened by how I was losing the ability to feel joy for others.

But by the time MJ was pregnant with Tommy, things had changed. The difference was making a conscious, daily decision that I would at least try not to let grief be a thief of joy, and that we had dedicated ourselves to trying to be happy and surrounded ourselves with resources to prop us up should we fall. Easier said than done, for sure, but when the alternative is prolonged misery and an absence of joy, there really was no other decision for us.

Men, just remember that it's totally normal to be apprehensive about having more kids and about putting the body of the person you love through hell and back. And if you've found that previous losses and traumas have left you feeling unable or unwilling to even consider future happiness, you're not broken or defective. You're a human being feeling completely expected emotions. These are valid, founded fears and you should give yourself permission to feel them. But again, you need to communicate those feelings and talk through them with your partner and/or a counselor if you're going to come to any kind of conclusion or move forward.

\* \* \*

*It is hard not to let miscarriages, infertility, or an abortion leave you jaded for your next pregnancies. I am no exception.*

*You are robbed of the joy of having butterflies in the stomach when you take the pregnancy test after your missed period, you are robbed of the joy of going to your friends' baby showers because it's just too painful, and you are robbed of all the futures that baby* could have had. As an extremely empathic person I have always taken great joy in the good fortune of friends, yet with each loss the pain became more than I could handle—the pain of reliving my own trauma and the hurt that comes with losing the ability to feel joy for the people you love.

Nothing compared to the very first pregnancy test I took. I was so excited in the store I was shaking with nervous anticipation. It must have shown because the cashier wished me luck. When it finally came back positive there was no feeling to describe how happy I was. But for every action there is an equal and opposite reaction, so when the baby was suddenly gone it seemed the only thing more powerful than the joy I had experienced a short time ago was the searing pain from having it callously stripped away. I took a lot of pregnancy tests after that day but none of them were ever truly joyful like that first one. The thrill and glee was replaced with trepidation and stress. What if it came back negative? Even if it is positive, what if we lose the baby? How would I tell Aaron about another miscarriage? Miscarriage means only being able to look at the next obstacle while completely losing sight of the finish line.

How does one come to terms with or recover from miscarriage, infertility, or abortion to have joy again in pregnancies? The answer is different for everyone. Mine was hearing the heartbeat, getting past the 12-week mark, and finally allowing myself to buy clothes and diapers for the baby. But even after hitting some of those milestones, there's still trouble. I still don't think I've gotten over the blood clot I saw at 8 weeks with our middle son. Even though it all eventually worked out, there was no sigh of relief the entire pregnancy. Picture a 32-week panic attack and that's what I was living every single day. Yes, I had great doctors and partners in place who knew how to handle me and I'm forever grateful for their support, but I never believed Sam would be healthy. Not until

*I saw him, held him, and listened to his breathing. That's the after effect of repeated loss—the complete inability to experience happiness or optimism.*

*I let getting pregnant and staying pregnant control my life. I let it take over, like a parasite, to the point that I could not be happy for anyone in my life who was pregnant. It got so bad I started to want people to feel the pain I was feeling. This was a low point for me, no doubt. I am a very happy person and love people, so imagine the emotional trauma that has to take place for me to actively wish harm upon them simply so they'd know how I felt. I was skipping baby showers (I love baby showers) because I was having anxiety over going. I would cry every time I would get an invitation in the mail for a baby shower and it would send me into a depression spiral because I wanted it to be me, not them. I wanted to be a happy, pregnant person. Looking back now it was so selfish to act and think that way. I was not being fair to the people around me; I was making it all about me. Worst of all, some of those showers I skipped were for friends who ended up having miscarriages and never told anyone until they felt comfortable enough talking about it. When I think about the missed opportunities to help other women through a terrible time, it makes me sick to my stomach.*

*How did I overcome all these negative harmful feelings? Friends, family, Aaron, and mental health providers helped me talk my feelings out and come up with solutions, based on where I was when these feelings struck. It's not easy to control your feelings, but it can be done and managed.*

*Everyone is different. You might keep your empathy intact and never go down this road. I hope you don't. But if you do, just know it's okay that you may never have the same unadulterated, blissful feeling as the first positive pregnancy test. However, the trick is trying to pick your spots and find joy at some point in the pregnancy. It will take time and it might not happen at all, but just make sure you seek professional help. You may not have gotten to the point in your grieving process to be happy about it. As I said before, it took me years to accept what has happened to us. It wasn't until I was done having children that I realized how hard it was to find joy in the pregnancy.*

*If you are finding yourself drowning in grief and struggling to connect with your happiness and empathy for others, it is not only acceptable to go and get help from a trusted friend, family, or mental health provider, it is essential. Make sure you do what is best for you and your family.*

# Chapter 14

## *Try Helping Others to Help Yourself*

*"Service to others is the rent you pay for your room here on Earth."*
—Muhammad Ali

Some men get to a point where they are clearly suffering but can't admit anything is wrong. In those instances, sometimes the only way they can help themselves is by helping others. This certainly doesn't apply to all men and I try not to stereotype, but the fact remains that our culture conditions men to be dismissive of their own emotions and hesitant in sharing them for fear (even if subconsciously) of looking like less of a man. But coming to the rescue of others? Well, that's what men are supposed to do. It shouldn't be this way and I wish it weren't—but I'm not naive about the reality of the situation. So if a little psychological manipulation is what helps get some guys on the road to improving their mental health, so be it.

I just learned, in the course of writing this book, that I fit into this category. Ten years ago, I was hurting immensely but

163

refused to get help. MJ, who had been recently diagnosed with bipolar disorder, was also hurting but she did put a support system in place. She urged me to do the same but I couldn't see through the toxic fog and my own outdated notions of manhood to put myself in a position to get to that place. Not being able to stand by and watch me spiral, MJ and her counselor came up with a plan (unbeknownst to me) to ask me to come in for a dual counseling session under the auspices of me helping MJ with her mental health struggles. The way they framed it for me was that I was going to be a second set of eyes and ears for her counselor to report back on what was really happening at home so MJ could get to the root of her problems more efficiently.

Normally, as you've learned by now, it would take an act of God to get me anywhere near a counselor's office, but since they made me think I was helping my wife, I agreed. It was truly a perfect plan because it catered to two things most men love: protecting loved ones and fixing problems. And so I went for two or three sessions. I had no idea it was a ploy to soften me up and introduce me to counseling and get me used to talking to a mental health professional. And while I don't usually advocate for lying to your spouse and tricking them into something, I have to admit that looking back all these years later, it was a vital first step toward getting me to a healthier place.

As long as I thought I was helping my wife, I was happy to talk to someone. My lasting memories of those sessions included being happily surprised that counseling seemed to be a friendly conversation as opposed to more of a clinical interrogation, and that even though I thought I was there for MJ it felt really nice to have someone ask me questions about how I was feeling. That was the first time anyone aside from immediate family members had seemed to acknowledge that I was part of the equation.

Now that I think about it, I believe I probably talked more than MJ in that office for the time we were in there together. Even though they got me there under false pretenses and it would still be another year until I got up the intestinal fortitude to enter counseling on my own, I realize now that that experience was the impetus for me getting on the right track and overcoming a significant barrier.

While I required a little subterfuge to set me straight, things are always better in less extreme situations when couples don't have to dabble in deception to get results. Out of all the people interviewed for this book, an example that stuck out of helping others to help yourself was David and Penelope, who struggled with infertility and pregnancy loss for so long that they literally went from being mentees to mentors.

After starting fertility treatments in Washington, DC, and then moving back to California, the couple was trying to get pregnant every other month and either failing, or getting pregnant and then having a miscarriage. Eventually they decided to join a group called Mind Body, based out of Boston but operating nationally, which was an in-person program limited to eight couples that runs for ten weeks. The goal is to give couples a place to vent and express their feelings with people who are going through similar problems, as well as teach them stress alleviation techniques like yoga and meditation.

David said he went through so many losses and rounds of heartbreak that he eventually stopped telling friends and even family, even when the couple did get pregnant. But in the Mind Body group he was able to voice and feel things he couldn't express to other people in his life.

"I used the group as a psychological tool and it all comes back to men being able to express their emotions. It was about showing me the tools I can pick up and use to fix myself. That changed my idea of what counseling is for because I realized doctors aren't going to fix me, they're going to give me the tools and show me how I have to fix me. And that made everything more palatable."

Yet even in that group—an intimate setting in which all the participants were bonded by the trauma of infertility and pregnancy loss—he said toxic masculinity was still very much present and problematic.

There's one point in the ten-week session, according to David, that the couples are separated for private discussions. So, for heterosexual couples, the women would all go off together and talk and the same for the men, as this was supposed to be a place where everyone could vent without fear of their partner hearing. After, when he regrouped with his wife, she described all the women crying, hugging, and supporting one another with transparency and honesty as they bared their souls. That, however, was a far cry from what David experienced with the other men.

He said the conversation among the men focused mainly on complaints about the doctors and specialists, and everything they were doing wrong. He said it felt like they were examining a car that needed to be fixed and trying to look under the hood to pinpoint all the potential problems. There was absolutely no crying and no emotion.

"It was sadly hilarious how cliché it was because here's an environment where the doors are closed and men can say and do anything they want, yet they're doing that stereotypical guy thing where you're trying to solve a problem instead of actually discussing how they're feeling," David said.

The couple was in the group so long they were actually chosen to be mentors to new arrivals and lead the group—a role David said was a "bittersweet honor." When it was his turn to lead the men in a closed-door session he made it a point to explain that this was a place of honesty where raw emotions could be vented with no judgment of any kind. It was important for him, as leader of the exercise, to make it clear men can cry, show their emotions, and lean on one another for comfort and understanding. But it didn't work.

"To say it was an uphill battle is an understatement," David said. "I realized as I was trying to get guys to talk about their feelings it just wasn't happening. Not only that, I felt with my insistence on having everyone talk it out I was just making it worse. My only hope is that at least they were getting something out of simply realizing other people are going through the same thing. For me, that was half of my recovery and unburdening of emotional weight. This let me know I could devote time to going through my emotions because, prior to that, it wasn't something I felt I was allowed to do."

The other thing David did was start a blog when his kids were born. Shortly before his twins' first birthday, David began chronicling his thoughts on fatherhood via Tumblr. At first it was more of an online diary of sorts and a glimpse inside the head of a new father. But then David started to gather a niche following and met more parents online who wondered why no one was giving an honest accounting of miscarriage and infertility in the online space. Suddenly a light bulb went off and he found a renewed sense of purpose along with an eager audience.

"It really helped me to help others realize that they're not alone in experiencing something really painful and to see how they could get help. Before it was just some dumb shit in my head but when I started writing about the miscarriages and our struggle to get pregnant, it was truly a leveling up for me because now I was helping people."

David is far from alone. Vernon wrote a *Washington Post* article about losing his twins to let men everywhere know it was acceptable for them to grieve, too. Daniel spoke out about miscarriage on Twitter where he discusses parenting issues. Benjamin detailed his thoughts on pregnancy loss for several online outlets including his own website and *Still Standing* magazine in order to let men know they are absolutely part of the conversation. And Jeremy said he is planning on capturing his experiences in writing and turning it into an article or even a book.

I also found it helpful to focus on others to help myself. From my unwitting foray into the therapist's office under the guise of helping my wife with her mental health to confronting the abortion protesters who verbally accosted MJ and me to eventually penning articles in high profile media outlets like *NBC*[1] and *TIME*[2], the only thing that spurred real progress for me in terms of getting any kind of help I needed was to share my experiences with others.

For me, writing about it almost felt like a loophole. Sure, the "Man Code" didn't let me outwardly express my feelings to friends or even my wife and I certainly knew I couldn't break down and let everyone see me in tears under the crushing emotional gravity of my situation, but there seemed to be no defined rules when it came to the written word. And while other guys would surely laugh and call me feminine or even—*gasp*—"gay" if I sat around in a drum circle weeping and singing kumbaya (yes, this really is how a ton of men think about what it's like getting help) while sharing my innermost feelings, talking to other guys in an online group or more private setting felt less risky.

---

1 Gouveia, Aaron. "My Wife's Miscarriage: What You Should Know About It." *TODAY.com*, August 22, 2013, https://www.today.com/parents/my-wifes-miscarriage-I544002

2 Gouveia, Aaron. "More men need to talk about miscarriage." *TIME*, July 31, 2015, https://time.com /3980990/men-fathers-discuss-miscarriage/

The most meaningful compliment I receive is when someone reads something I've written and says, "Thank you for putting into words exactly what I was feeling when I couldn't find a way to say it." Making other people feel less alone or inspiring them to get help is what helped me help myself, and by publishing my thoughts on miscarriage and pregnancy loss, I've had the privilege of connecting with dozens of people one-on-one who reached out either to ask for help or to offer it—both of which I value exponentially.

Is it a bit of a copout for men to focus on others when they need to be fixing their own problems? That argument can definitely be made. But for those who aren't ready to dive right in and face down their demons directly for whatever the reason, honing in on your experiences as a way to help others definitely can have a cornucopia of benefits. Whatever gets men closer to helping themselves is a good thing.

\* \* \*

*Being naive in the ways of social media, I thought giving Aaron permission to share our story meant he'd be the one doing the sharing and the heavy lifting while I sat on the sidelines. I shared my perspective exactly one time on his website, after my abortion, but other than that I expected him to be the point of contact for people who wanted to talk.*

*But that's not how it works. While a lot of people did reach out to Aaron because they had walked a similar path, a whole bunch of people related to my story and wanted to talk to me.*

*At first I rejected every form of outreach because of how private I am, but as I saw Aaron soften up around the edges after sharing his feelings, I wondered if I'd see the same benefit. So I* answered an online comment here and there. And then some more. Then those comments turned to more in-depth emails and before I knew it I was sharing with and listening to people from all walks of life who had been in my shoes.

It wasn't until I was done having children that I fully realized what impact my story had on people, both strangers and people already in my life. I would get calls from friends who needed a kind ear for listening after they suffered a miscarriage, infertility, or an abortion. It was a double-edged sword because while listening to them brought up painful memories, the process also helped me heal. As someone who routinely gives to charity and has volunteered at my local senior center, I got back to trying to make the world a better place. I know that sounds corny, but it's true. I was giving people a safe place to talk and listen, but also a place where they can get advice (if they want it and asked for it).

As time went on, I became the go-to person for advice about miscarriages and abortion. My hand was forced a bit because Aaron was so outspoken online about everything, and inevitably people would contact him trying to get in touch with me. But seeing how many other people were in the same boat, I eventually opened up about these things to other people. Sometimes they wanted to pass on kind words. Other folks wanted to get advice for friends or even how to deal with their husbands. But most people seemed to simply be put at ease knowing they were not alone.

Another reason I eventually started sharing was to pay it forward for the people who tried to reach out to me after my abortion. I had an old friend find me afterward to let me know she was thinking of me and offered to help. She understood what I was going through and wanted to offer a kind ear because she had been in a similar position years before. I regret not taking her up on it but, at the time, I just wasn't in a place where I could rationally discuss what was happening. She was trying to help and help me get through the situation and while I wish I had been able to lean on her, I always appreciated the offer and felt it was my responsibility to be that person for others.

The other common thing people contacted me about was infertility. How to get through it, what to expect, what it does to relationships, and how people can be so cruel with the words they use. When going through infertility I never thought to reach out to anyone who had gone through it because I thought it was shameful, and something I had to do by myself. Now when I hear of friends and family planning on fertility treatments I proactively offer to listen and, if invited, share what I have learned. While it's good to help others, I readily admit this also helps me process what we went through years ago while trying to conceive our second baby. All the heartbreak, shots, and doctors' egos that still irk me to this day.

To the people who reached out to me when I had my abortion, miscarriages, and infertility, I appreciate you beyond words. I couldn't fully accept your help at the time, but the selflessness of your offers and the kindness you showed helped me heal. Each of you made me feel less alone and inspired me to make sure no one else had to endure this in isolation.

# Chapter 15

## *How to Handle the Kids You Have During Pregnancy Loss*

Another added wrinkle very few people consider when starting out on this journey is how existing children will be impacted by repeated pregnancy loss. For some couples this isn't an issue because they don't yet have kids. Also, if couples have a newborn or very young toddler at home, it's likely they don't have the wherewithal to comprehend what's going on. But for folks like me and MJ, with nearly six years between children thanks to multiple losses, trying to explain to a small child that the brother or sister they're expecting isn't going to be arriving after all can be a tremendously difficult and unpleasant experience.

Will wasn't old enough to register the first few miscarriages but he was six years old for the most recent one in 2014. And as all parents know, he had questions. Lots of questions. A never-ending onslaught of questions only children are capable of pumping out with machine gun efficiency. "Where did the baby go?" "Did the baby die?" "Did you do something to hurt the baby?" "Did I do something to hurt the baby?" "Are we going to bury the baby?" "Did the baby have a name?" "Will I get another brother or sister?" "Are you sad?" "Is it okay if I cry?" "Where did the baby come out of if it's gone?" "Can I say goodbye to the baby?"

Some of the questions were cute, some were surprising, and most of them were absolutely heartbreaking. We tried to keep it pretty basic and age-appropriate for him, hitting on the fact that a lot of pregnancies end because something goes wrong early on and that isn't anyone's fault. We told him whatever he was feeling was okay and we gave him a chance to say goodbye to the baby by drawing a picture and verbally giving the baby a sendoff. I'd be lying, though, if I told you watching your six-year-old kiss your wife's belly and tearfully say farewell to his would-be brother or sister wasn't traumatic. Also, he'd randomly blurt out "Mommy had a baby in her belly but it died" to relatives and even strangers after that, which is normal but still deeply uncomfortable.

Daniel and Laura had experienced several losses, including one in 2012 that occurred after they already had five children. Opting to forego hospital visits (Daniel said, "If nothing is wrong, why go to the hospital?") in favor of a registered nurse midwife, meant not only did childbirth happen at home but miscarriages occurred there as well. When you have five kids in a house and something goes haywire, there are going to be questions and tough conversations.

As Laura was examined by her midwife in the comfort of her home, things took a very dangerous turn. She had already been spotting but suddenly the blood loss and severe ectopic pain became alarming and Laura's midwife was not taking any chances, advising her to go to the hospital emergency room immediately. The problem, Daniel said, was that he and Laura had no family or friends to help watch the kids and so he had to send his wife off to the hospital alone while he stayed home to take care of the children.

"I was scared I was going to lose my wife but I felt like I couldn't be scared because I had little kids. We try to be open and honest with them about things in general, but this was something they weren't ready for so I had to keep it limited to high level concepts because I didn't want to scare them. It's a tough tightrope to walk."

Charlie and his wife, after their two miscarriages, first told friends and extended family about what happened. But when those family members all started to come by offering hugs and bringing meals, the couple's three young boys knew something was up. So they made a plan to make a special night to tell their kids what was going on.

"They didn't need to know everything, but eventually we decided they did need to know some things. So we told them as openly and honestly as we could. It was tough but we cried together and consoled one another and then we had a movie night planned for some family time."

Having a young child and then unexpectedly losing a baby at 37 weeks complicates matters even further, said Jennifer. Because everything moved so quickly from a precautionary ultrasound to the emergency room for surgery, she said she had to make a decision about whether to tell their three-year-old, Miles, in the middle of a whirlwind. She and her husband, Matthew, ultimately decided to tell Miles because Jennifer was worried she could go into surgery and not wake up, so she felt it was important to explain it to her son personally.

"I decided I had to because what if something happened to me and I didn't tell him or wasn't able to say goodbye to him?

It was such a brutal reality setting in. So I told him his baby sister couldn't stay with us and was going to heaven right away to be our angel above us. His sweet little three-year-old self didn't know what to make of that and they had to pull him away from me to get me to the hospital as we all cried."

However, after things had calmed down, Jennifer said taking care of Miles represented a return to at least a tiny bit of normalcy for her and her husband, for which she was eternally grateful. She called it a "saving grace," and said the caretaking responsibilities for their son kept them busy and moving, and helped avoid immediately giving in and sinking like quicksand into the grief following their loss.

Sometimes it's not enough for people to stay strong for themselves, but when there is a tiny human who depends on them for everything, that becomes the reason to keep going and not throw in the towel. That was certainly the case for me with Will at home, as I was his primary caregiver at the time and I just didn't have the option of falling to pieces. However, everyone is different and sometimes that trauma of a loss combined with the responsibility of caring for a child—especially if things like postpartum depression are part of the equation—can actually make things worse.

The bottom line is every person is different and there are a lot of variables in play that determine when, if, and how young children should be told about what's happening. Some people will talk about unborn babies going to heaven to watch over us while others will take a more fact-based approach. For me and MJ, it was about realizing that these kinds of losses impact the whole family and feeling like we had a responsibility to address it as best we could.

In a 2019 article[1], Dr. Tamar Gur, a maternal-fetal psychiatrist specializing in pre-conception, pregnancy, and the postpartum period at the Ohio State University Wexner Medical Center, said failure to address pregnancy loss with children sends a potentially harmful message. Gur said parents who are transparent with their grief send the message that it's perfectly acceptable to be sad and cry, and urged parents to have age-appropriate conversations and meet kids wherever they are.

"Pretending everything is fine teaches kids there are things that are so scary and upsetting, we shouldn't even talk about them. Instead, parents should give children more credit. Kids are incredibly resilient. Kids also see that it's okay to reach out and ask for help when your feelings are too big, and that grief is survivable."

The other thing to be aware of is that kids will react differently to the conversation.

Shortly after we told him about the loss, Will became borderline obsessed with death. He wanted to know how long humans live, what the life expectancy of different animals are, and whether he was going to suddenly die. As a parent, those conversations were not fun, but they were important. And even though it was unbelievably tough to have to tell him that we all die at some point but he had a long, long life ahead of him, I do believe it helped. Much more so than if we had simply told him the baby in mom's stomach went to sleep, because as any parent can tell you, the magical thinking children engage in can lead to some problematic assumptions and connection of dots. We didn't want Will to worry about dying every time he closed his eyes at

1   Willets, Melissa. "It Isn't Just Moms Who Grieve Pregnancy Loss—Kids And Partners Do Too." *POPSUGAR*. October 8, 2019, https://www.popsugar.com/family/how-to-talk-to-kids-about-miscarriage-46656008

night, so we chose to have a tougher, more honest conversation with him that I hope benefited him in the long run.

There are no easy answers and parents have to decide for themselves what the best approach is. But as tough as these moments are, they can also be opportunities for growth.

\* \* \*

*With each pregnancy lost, Will was a constant joy in our lives. He was there asking questions, sharing the excitement, and grieving the losses. There is no one-size-fits-all for parents when they have a loss and a child to take care of at home. Even when it comes time to tell them you are pregnant, there is no right answer. The first few times we were pregnant we chose to share with Will, but each time it ended in heartbreak, at which point he began to internalize it and ask questions. Since we always encourage curiosity because it's natural for kids to ask questions, especially around death, we were very open and honest with him.*

*We thought it would be best to tell Will about the pregnancy just in case we did lose the baby. Many parents think kids don't know what's going on because they're too young, but I don't believe that at all. When we were nervous and scared and anxious, he could feel that. All kids can. And because he was being impacted by it, we felt he needed to understand why we were so upset.*

*I remember Will being two years old when we had our abortion. We didn't go into details about the abortion but told him there was something wrong with the baby and the baby had died. When we first told him he was going to be a big brother and there was a baby in mom's belly, he was so excited. He proudly wore his "Big Brother" shirt and showed it off to anyone who wanted to see it. He would tell everyone we would meet he was going to* be a big brother. When it ended, he was incredibly sad with the situation and showed pain on his face when we told him about the loss of the baby. I wish we could have spared him the pain but we had already told him about the baby, so there was no going back. Otherwise we'd have a two-year-old constantly asking where the baby in mommy's belly was and that's actually more painful than anything.

As all kids do, he had a million questions about why the baby died. We tried to answer them as best as possible, but really, we didn't have the answers. After all, we felt completely baffled as full-grown adults so it's pretty difficult to get a two-year-old to comprehend it all. To express himself he drew pictures and we allowed him to talk freely about how he was feeling. However, the more he talked the harder it became for me.

Like many kids, Will was living in the moment and seemed not to dwell on the loss. I would not do anything different if we were to get pregnant again. We would celebrate with our kids and share the joy of the news, even if it meant taking it back with the news of a miscarriage. That's the push-pull symmetry of life and it's difficult for kids to fully appreciate the good if you constantly shield them from the bad.

Some people may think we are cruel to make our children go through our losses and death, but I think it's important for them to know it is okay to express all of their feelings, including joy and sadness.

# Chapter 16

# *The Best Advice from Folks Who Have Been There*

I N ALL, FIFTY-SEVEN PEOPLE TOOK OUR SURVEY AND NINE PEOple conducted in-depth interviews with me and MJ for this book. I wish I had gotten more men to agree to speak on the record regarding miscarriage, infertility, and pregnancy loss, and despite actively seeking them out, I wish I could've included more diversity as only 11 percent of the folks we interviewed were underrepresented minorities. But we are immeasurably grateful for the data we did collect and the intimate stories people shared with us, as the topic of men and pregnancy loss is virtually unexplored among researchers and in popular culture.

While it's very much impossible for a book like this to give blanket, one-size-fits-all advice to people going through tough times that truly do differ depending on the individuals and individual circumstances involved, it is our sincere hope that presenting the lived experiences of a variety of people will be helpful to readers. Whether it's men who are wondering if they're allowed the space to grieve or the partners of men who wonder what might be going through the head of the person they love following infertility or loss, the goal is to offer a look at how men fit into the conversation surrounding these very difficult and emotional topics.

To that end, we asked each of the people we interviewed for their most important piece of advice for others, as well as what had to be done to get this conversation out of the shadows and into the mainstream.

Charlie believes the hesitancy on the part of men to discuss miscarriage stems from how uncomfortable it is in general for society to discuss the death of unborn babies, as well as the stigma involved with men asking for help. He recommends advertising on local television and radio with anonymous helplines set up to provide an instantaneous one-on-one outlet for men. He also recommends men not be ashamed to get the help they need, and then be prepared to pay it forward.

"Don't be afraid to reach out for support. I feel it helped me to not get too upset and also talk openly about my thoughts. Had that not happened, I might have let it stay inside for too long and possibly ignored the realities which could've really hurt me later in life. Now I can be prepared if a friend, or perhaps my own child someday, were to ever experience a miscarriage."

Zachary is another person who feels a public advertising or awareness campaign is a necessity, but because of his circumstances in Brazil when he feels he and his wife were shamed by the anti-choice culture, he believes it should focus more on a pro-choice sentiment.

"In Brazil, we first need a proper conversation about legalizing abortion, first and foremost. After that, we need some sort of campaign saying it is okay for men to go through this kind of stuff. Something specialized that constantly puts out adverts on social media, offering men advice and answers to frequently asked questions."

Reaching out for help was a common theme for many of the men interviewed.

Vernon admits he might be biased because his wife is a psychiatrist, but he wants other men to know no one should be so afraid to reach out for help that they crumble under the weight of it all.

"Men going through this need to realize they're not alone and it's not only happening to them. Sometimes you have to let people know what you're going through because, if you don't, how can they help? You don't have to rely on Facebook's fake perfection or plaster it all over social media, because we're all flawed and we're all a mess. Just reach out."

Jeremy agreed with Vernon and said while women absolutely have a tougher time because they deal with the physical as well as the emotional aspects of loss, men hurt too. "Find somebody who you can talk to and open up about it. Just get out everything that you are feeling in a healthy way because it's okay for guys to grieve. Men will always be a bit marginalized in this regard, which is reasonable, but that doesn't mean we should be completely overlooked."

But acknowledgment was what most people we interviewed felt was most important to discuss.

Daniel said, "Acknowledging and sitting with it [the pain of miscarriage] is hard but probably the most important thing anyone can do." His wife, Laura, agreed and said, "I think we have to talk about miscarriage more often and make it more a part of us instead of something that happened to us."

Daniel seconded that sentiment, saying, "You have to let yourself feel it all. The sadness, the rage, the loneliness, the darkness. They will live side by side in your heart forever so keep your face to the sun and get your feet and hands in the dirt to feel grounded. Make yourself get outside each day—even if you're still in your pajamas. Water plants or start gardening as a healing ritual and spend time at the beach or in the woods to heal."

David said the issue of men and miscarriage definitely needs to be talked about more, but said the manner in which we discuss it is equally important.

"The challenge is this is something we should all be talking about, except for when the people going through it don't want to talk about it. Basically, we need to make people more aware that this happens to a shitload of people, and when this happens to you, you find out everyone in your life has experienced this and wonder why the hell we haven't talked about it before?"

Benjamin said acknowledgment is important, and that it must include acceptance of people who don't feel the losses as deeply as he did. But most important is opening the door for men in general.

"There needs to be open discussion and acceptance of a father's role. There is so much capacity for a woman's perspective in loss, but when all of the graphics, articles, and conversation centers around the mother, men get left in the wind. The more we talk about it and normalize it, the more these discussions will involve men moving forward."

My take is that the most important thing for men is to convince them they actually belong in the conversation. Before we can have a public campaign to raise awareness or get professional counseling when we're hurting, men have to know that it's okay to hurt. They have to know they're allowed to be in pain. There needs to be a realization among men that they are more than a rock and a leaning post for emotional support. They should know they matter and they count. If guys don't confront and move past the stranglehold toxic masculinity has on them, then it's virtually impossible to take any of the next and necessary steps following infertility or miscarriage.

So men, if you take anything away from this book I hope it's that your emotional pain is valid, there's nothing shameful about experiencing the emotions of a crushing loss, and asking for help is not a sign of weakness, but strength. Subsequently, I hope women and partners of men in need understand that just because it seems like he's not upset about losing pregnancies doesn't mean that's the reality of the situation. It's tough because women going through miscarriage have so much on their plate and are going through their own emotional turmoil, but try to push for those hard conversations and move them along. Even when you think you're talking to a brick wall, some of it is getting through. Appeal to the part of men that wants to be strong and protect their families by letting men know there is strength in getting the help they need to be a better husband and father.

But most of all, please know no one going through these losses is alone. This book, although a tiny sample size, proves that. If you or someone you know needs help there are in-person resources and online groups filled with people who have been in the trenches and understand the battle, because no one needs to fight this fight alone.

\* \* \*

*When I was at my lowest point, all I was looking for was advice on how to survive. I felt like I was drowning in a whirlpool of my own emotions with no way to keep my head above water. When I looked to the main support in my life, my husband, I realized with horror that he was drowning, too. Friends and doctors tried to help but they were just saying all the wrong things.*

*I wish I had known then what I know now, which is that each instance of loss came with its own challenges and solutions. There was no one-size-fits-all approach that served as a silver bullet and what worked the first time might be totally ineffective the next time due to the nature of battling miscarriage versus infertility versus abortion.*

*People going through miscarriages should know it's not their fault and they didn't cause it. Also, no one should feel guilty for how they mourn and they are definitely allowed to grieve the loss of a baby at even the earliest stages of pregnancy. Those enduring infertility should not feel embarrassed or ashamed to reach out to like-minded people for support, either online or in person. I truly feel that if I had, my mental health would not have suffered nearly as much as it did. And for those people in a relationship with a man who won't get help, keep trying to find ways to get him to open up but, at the same time, know there's only so much you can do. When your partner is fighting you and you feel all alone like the world is against you, get help. If he won't go with you for couples counseling, go by yourself and then worry about him. The important thing is being heard and feeling less isolated because not connecting with those feelings can be fatal—for relationships and in the literal sense.*

*My sincere hope for each and every one of you is that you never have to experience an abortion, but if you do you need to know this is reproductive health care. It's a legal medical procedure and you don't need to feel shame for having one, no matter the reason. I wish I had the magic combination of words to make a person feel better when faced with the difficult decision of an abortion, but my best advice is to figure out what's best for you* and your situation and do what you think is right. Believe in your instincts and have confidence that you know best about your body. Do not let anyone bully you into making a different decision on either side of this debate, and if telling your story brings you peace of mind, then go for it. I guarantee you're reaching a larger and more sympathetic audience than you realize.

Bottom line: Just reach out for help and silence that voice that's trying to shame you or make you feel like a failure.

Seek out a support group if you need to talk and think the problem is bigger than you can handle. There is no shame in admitting you need help from someone outside of your family and friends. Whether it's couples counseling or going separately from your partner, there is no shame in asking or accepting help from professionals, friends, or family. And men, please examine your mindset in this area. You all keep saying you'll do anything to protect your family and be strong for them, so the simple act of talking through your emotions or admitting you need help cannot be off-limits. Watching my husband struggle solely because he didn't want to look like a "pussy" remains the dumbest and most disrespectful thing I've ever witnessed from the man I love with all my heart. Admitting weakness is strength, because none of us can do this alone. If you can't see that and you're raising boys, then they won't be able to see it either and this is a cycle that absolutely cannot continue. Please, guys. Know better, do better.

Just stay open and communicate because shutting down only hurts yourself and your partner. I have learned the hard way that this eats away at your mental health and your relationships if you let it go unchecked or think you can deal with it alone. Everyone involved is grieving a loss of something and needs to be gentle with themselves and their partners.

*Anyone who has had even one miscarriage knows that's one loss too many. But people who fail to allow themselves room to feel all of these emotions and who don't share their burdens with anyone else will likely lose so much more.*

*It's not your fault. You're not alone. You can and will get through this.*

# Acknowledgments

WHEN I ASKED MY WIFE TO COAUTHOR A BOOK WITH ME, she told me to get lost (except with laughter and more expletives). But I knew I couldn't write this book alone and so MJ humored me and went way out of her comfort zone to write it with me. We did it during a pandemic. We did it while I started a new job. We did it while coordinating remote learning. We did it while finishing the basement so I could have a workplace without going insane from the pandemic and remote learning. But most importantly, we did it together without getting divorced. I am so, so proud of you, MJ, and I love you more than words can ever express. Thank you for our three beautiful boys and thank you for putting your body and soul on the line to complete our family. It wasn't always the smoothest road, but it's one I'd travel again and again as long as you're by my side.

Will, Sam, and Tommy—the path that led to the final formation of our family was an often broken one, but the destination is the most rewarding thing I could've ever imagined. You boys are my life and while I will always wonder what might have been with the pregnancies we lost, having you three and being your dad is the gift of a lifetime. I love you boys with all my heart.

Thank you to everyone who contributed to this book, especially the nine brave souls who volunteered their innermost thoughts. That you trusted me with your stories is an honor and a responsibility I take very seriously, and I hope I've done you all justice. It takes people willing to shine a light on their journeys and vulnerabilities to begin to combat the darkness, shame, fear, and stigma that surrounds these issues and I am forever in your debt for stepping forward and helping others.

To every single person who sent an email or left a comment or wrote a letter supporting us through our infertility, miscarriages, and abortion—you are all heroes. That you not only took the time to reach out and comfort us in a time of need but also shared your stories (some of which you never told anyone else) is a truly special and utterly remarkable thing that got me through some tough times. You picked me up when I couldn't pull myself together and that's why I wanted to write this book—to pay it forward for others like you did to me. Thank you from the bottom of my heart.

My parents, Bill and Cyn, for being the best at just about everything. You helped us when we were down and then you took the boys for entire weekends at a time so we could write this book. As usual, we'd be nowhere without your love and support.

Nate, you got me started writing about parenting on my own all those years ago and none of this would be possible without the virtual home you gave me for my thoughts. I love and appreciate you so much.

Thanks to my good friends Alex Meaney, Mike Micalone, Bill Hickey, Dave Sullivan, and Victor Banks, who all propped me up or brought over a six-pack. Even though we all give each other hell, I appreciate all of you. A lot.

When Doug French and John Pacini founded the Dad 2.0 Summit, I was able to connect with a host of fathers from all different backgrounds who became friends and trusted confidantes. Several of them are included in this book and the rest helped me find other participants and took our survey. The dad community is an amazing one that has forever impacted my life in a wonderful way, so thank you all.

To (most of) the doctors and nurses we encountered along our journey, thank you. You made a horrible journey slightly less so with your kindness and care, and you're a big part of the reason we were able to finally complete our family.

To my 11th grade English teacher who tried to keep me out of her AP English class because she said I didn't have the necessary writing chops, thank you for the chip on my shoulder that's helped me become a professional writer with two books under my belt.

To the two horrible husks of humanity who screamed at me and MJ outside that Brookline abortion clinic in 2010, somehow your callousness and disregard for basic empathy and compassion managed to spark life and a sense of purpose in me when I needed it the most. But seriously, to hell with you and to every single other monster who thinks it's acceptable to shame strangers by shouting horrible things at them about a decision that has nothing to do with them. You're all absolutely terrible.

Leah Zarra and Skyhorse Publishing, thanks for believing in me for a second time and helping to turn the scattered thoughts in my head into an actual book.

\* \* \*

*I want to thank Aaron for trusting me to write a book about our stories and the stories of the people we interviewed. Also, for always believing I was making the right choices for our family and for myself. Even though you worried every step of the way.*

*To my three boys—Will, Sam, and Tommy—thank you for giving me the strength to write this book. I love you all.*

*I want to also thank all the brave souls who told me their stories but didn't want to be interviewed for the book. We hear you and understand why you couldn't. May you find all the peace possible.*

*Thank you to my parents, Martha Buler, Thomas Howell III, and Donna Merrick. These past twelve years would have been terrible to bear if it were not for your love and support.*

*George, I love you and miss you terribly. Your hugs, your smile, and your homecooked meals. I wish you could've met Sam and Tommy but we tell them stories and they love their Grandpa B.*

*Thank you to Aimee McCormack for making sure my shifts at work were covered when I had to take time off and for letting me cry in my office. You always wiped my tears away and had my back no matter what life threw at me.*

*Thank you to Alicia Banks for making sure I always had the best medical advice and for helping me decide where I should go to have medical procedures done. I will forever be in your debt for all the things you have done for me over the decades we have been friends. There are no words to describe the amount of support you have given me through the years. Thank you from the bottom of my heart.*

*Mariana Barry, thank you for making me understand how important it is to be a good friend in a time of need. You never turned me away, no matter what I did. Thank you for making me a better and more understanding person.*

# About the Authors

Laura Fielding Fiorillo

AARON GOUVEIA IS THE AUTHOR OF *RAISING BOYS TO BE Good Men: A Parent's Guide to Bringing Up Happy Sons in a World Filled with Toxic Masculinity.* He is a former award-winning journalist whose byline has appeared in *TIME, Washington Post, Parents Magazine, American Baby,* and the *Huffington Post* and has also been featured on the *TODAY Show, CNN, Good Morning America, People, Mashable,* and *USA Today* to discuss parenting and politics. He started the website The Daddy Files in 2008 to promote involved fatherhood, has contributed to a host of online and print publications on the topic, is a regular speaker at parenting conferences, and his content on topics like gun control and abortion has been seen by millions around the world. When he's not going to Gillette Stadium as a season ticket holder to fanatically cheer on his beloved New England Patriots, he's kayaking and bass fishing in various lakes, ponds, and rivers across New England. Aaron works as Public Relations Director for a land conservation nonprofit and resides in Franklin, Massachusetts, with his wife and three sons.

M ARTHA (MJ) GOUVEIA IS A MOTHER OF THREE BOYS, former bank manager, Norton, Massachusetts native, and current pharmacy technician who inexplicably decided to start a new career during a global pandemic. After stints as a top-performing bank manager at Bank of America and Citizens Bank, she spent a decade as a stay-at-home mom and discovered going to the office every day is nothing compared to caring for multiple human beings who depend on you for survival. MJ has been featured in *TIME*, *The Today Show*, *CBS*, and *NBC* regarding topics ranging from childhood bullying to buffer zones at abortion clinics. Despite being an intensely private person, she married someone who lives his life on social media and now is a reluctant co-author of this book who just hopes it helps at least one person cope. She now lives in Franklin, Massachusetts, with three kids, two cats, and a dog.